Under A Gravid Sky

The Strathavon Saga

ANGELA MACRAE SHANKS

Braeatha ◆ Books

Cover Design by Morven MacEwan

For my father, James Shanks, who helped nurture my love of the Scots tongue, and for whose constant, unchanging love I am forever grateful. Thank you for always being there.

ALSO BY ANGELA MACRAE SHANKS

The Blood And The Barley (The Strathavon Saga)

CHAPTER ONE

Strathavon, a glen in the
north-eastern Highlands,
February 1747

SHE WOULD ONE day believe what happened was predetermined, and a greater force guided the events of that day, the day God took her mother away, altering the course of her life forever. But on that morning, a bitter, frozen one, the morning of her fifth birthday, Rowena Innes knew only fear and confusion.

Three days and nights she'd waited for news of her new brother or sister—endless hours of frightening sounds and strange faces, frayed nerves and short tempers. Da sat hunched at the fire downing whisky, dark-eyed and sullen, James and Grace silent in the shadows. Womenfolk came and went, older women from the glen who sighed and shook their heads, rubbing their brows with trembling fingers. They spoke of something called an 'afterbirth', muttered 'twas placed wrong in the womb. It blocked the bairn's passage into the world.

Rowena followed them about the cot-house, hoping to slip unnoticed to her mother's side to witness the coming of the new baby. Yet always, she was prevented with a sharp prod or grim shake of the head. None of her pleas bore fruit. Her questions went unanswered. The only comfort she received came from Grace, who knew no more than she did but was always prepared to share her theories with a quick smile and ready embrace.

Finally, to escape the sounds coming from behind the closed door, she

1

blundered down to the Avon to watch for the secretive otter that played in the pool beneath the alders. But the pool was silvery and still, half-frozen, its banks ledged with snow and ice. The otter did not come.

When she was finally allowed into the bedchamber, her mother was so weak from pain and toil, her eyes rolled in her head. Rowena struggled to understand.

'Mam.' Standing on a stool at the side of the bed, she peered through the gloom, a frightened whimper caught in her throat. Mam looked funny. Like she'd done thon hot day near the end of summer when she'd been out too long cutting oats. The sun had blazed from a sky bluer than a harebell. It reddened Mam's face and the back of her neck, making sweat run from under her kertch. Da had scolded her. He said she'd feel the back of God's hand for her foolishness.

He was right.

As darkness fell, Mam did, too, jerking and thrashing among the stubble, foam oozing from her lips. She'd whimpered then, too, for Da said Mam was possessed by a devil's imp. Her memory of that day remained vivid. What a devil's imp was, Rowena had no notion, but the very name curled her toes.

Fearn Innes tried to moisten her lips with her tongue now and reached for her child's hand but had not the strength to take it.

'Be brave,' she whispered. Her eyes watered. 'I'd nae leave ye had I a choice. Remember that. Aye mind it.'

'Dinna leave me!' Her heart fluttered, and she clutched at her mother's shift, staring at the mound her belly made beneath it. Clambering onto the bed, she buried her face in Mam's damp hair, smelling the strange sourness on her.

'Away,' Da grunted. He disentangled her, holding her awkwardly against his hip.

She stared up at him. He looked funny too—grey, his face puckered like an old mushroom. She looked over his shoulder at her brother and sister, ten-year-old James and Grace, who was seven. They looked queer, too. Grace's neck was mottled, and she hid her face in her hands. She flicked her gaze to James. His face was even stranger—all twisted and fierce.

'Where's Mam going?' she whimpered. 'Where's the babby?'

A rattling sound came from the bed; she twisted in Da's arms. Mam's eyes were heavy now, dull as they'd never been. She twitched and ground her teeth, then finally lay still. So still, Rowena could hear the creak of snow shifting on the thatch above.

2

Clinging to her father's side, she watched him reach down and close Mam's eyes.

'She's dead, child,' he said. 'Ye ken what dead is. Ye've seen it afore. Seen beasts die of cold or hunger, or disease atimes. 'Tis the same, only 'twas the infant killed her. 'Twas trapped inside, and no amount o' pushing nor praying would bring it forth.'

She stared at him in horror, then struggled to get down. From the stool, she searched her mother's face, waiting for her eyes to open and her familiar smile to light the room, keeping her own smile ready in return. But Mam's face was lifeless. Her eyes stayed closed.

A great thumping began in her chest, hurting her throat. She touched Mam's belly. It was warm still. Damp.

'The babby's still in here? Is it ... alive?'

'No, child.'

Despair cut her to the core. It lanced so deep, the pain so alien, she was momentarily transfixed, envisioning the landscape of her life stretched out vast and empty before her. Everything in her existence that was ever tender had gone. She could only stare at Mam's dear face. She knew every freckle; every line Mam's smile made was beloved by her. She'd never see that smile again, never feel the giddy swoop in her belly when Mam's soft grey eyes lighted solely upon her. Her vision blurred, the face smudging.

There was talk in the room now, low murmuring, but she made no attempt to follow it. It flowed around the walls, swirled past her as deep and fathomless as the ocean. From outside came the plaintive cry of curlew and grouse.

She began to wail, long, agonised cries that caught in her throat, and crawled back onto the bed, worming her arms around her mother's neck, burrowing in. 'Twas warm there, and there her tears came in a slippery spate. Sobbing, she nuzzled vainly for comfort until James pulled her away.

'J ... James.'

'I'll look after ye now,' he choked. 'I swear.'

He wrapped his arms around her, drawing Grace in, too, her face a mask of tears, and they clung to each other, too numb for words, the ache in their hearts a shared suffering holding them fast. Rowena continued to wail.

Looking on the scene, Lachlan Innes turned away, his throat convulsing. There was the priest to see.

* * *

3

Despite efforts to remove her, over the next few days, Rowena remained steadfastly by her mother's side. Women came to wash Fearn's body and prepare her for burial, muttering superstitiously at her presence. Yet, on seeing her wretchedness, they allowed her to stay, and from the shadows behind the door, she watched the final intimate tasks they performed for her mother.

With gentle hands, they washed Fearn's body, lifting limbs, sponging into crevices, and dressed her in a clean gown. They brushed her hair and coiled it upon her head as she'd worn it on her wedding day. When they crossed her hands over her swollen belly, they wept unashamedly, and in her dark corner, Rowena wept, too. Then, drying their eyes, they wrapped Fearn in a winding-sheet and lifted her into a wooden box.

Finally, they fetched her da and James, who helped them carry the box from the bedchamber to the other room where they laid it upon the table. It would remain there for the wake—several days, depending on the weather. Travel in the glens was always perilous in February.

Rowena loitered by the door, waiting for them to go so she could be alone with her mother again.

* * *

From throughout Strathavon and neighbouring Glenlivet, folk travelled to Tomachcraggen, the holding held by Lachlan Innes, to extend their sympathy to him and his family and pay respect to the dead woman. Fearn had been liked by all, and the sorrow was genuine, despite the lure of whisky that accompanied all Highland funerals. Father Ranald Stewart oversaw the proceedings.

Despite the rigours of the past year, the father stood staunchly at Lachlan's side, meeting each new traveller as they arrived, helping dispense whisky from the cache hidden beneath the cot-house. Lachlan was a smuggler, like most in the glen, his illicit whisky rumoured to be among the finest in the Highlands. A fact the man was proud of.

The father glanced sidelong at him, noting the unhealthy sheen to his face, the tremor in his fingers as he shook the hand of each new mourner and bid them welcome. The customs of Highland hospitality demanded he take a dram with each new caller, and there'd been many.

The priest sighed, perhaps 'twas as well. A drop or two of *uisge-beatha*, the water of life, might help Lachlan through the trials of the lyke-wake. The man had expected to be celebrating the birth of another bairn, not mourning the loss of a wife, and Fearn had been precious to him,

4

incapable though Lachlan had seemed of showing it.

As mourners passed the coffin, it was customary to briefly touch the deceased or risk being haunted by fearful dreams before the soul of the departed reached heaven or hell, whichever case applied. Most touched Fearn lightly on the shoulder, one or two, womenfolk mostly, brushed her cheek, but all avoided the mound of her belly with its ill-fated occupant. He noted the bowl of salt placed upon her chest, a necessary precaution to deter the devil from stealing her soul.

The youngest of Lachlan's offspring, a wee lass with tousled hair and swollen eyes, sat trembling at the table. She looked up at each new arrival as they filed past, searching their faces, perhaps hoping to find a face that resembled her mother. Father Ranald couldn't think when he'd seen a sight more forlorn.

Leaving Lachlan with the McHardy clan bearing sods of peat for the fire, he squatted to her level. 'What's yer name, child?'

She eyed him warily. 'Rowena Innes.'

'Have ye had something to eat, Rowena? A drink of something?' He was at a loss over how to console her but sensed he possessed more delicacy in such matters than her father.

'My throat hurts.'

'Has someone been caring for you? Your da, or someone else?'

'James.' Her voice was leaden. 'And Grace.' She turned her head to the hearth where a white-faced girl ladled broth into bowls for the mourners. He recognised her brother there. James was lifting bannocks from the hot bannock stone, cutting them into wedges.

'Your siblings.'

She looked blankly at him.

He knelt on the earthen floor and took one of her hands—'twas icy cold. Tradition dictated a window be left open, despite the rawness of the winter air, to allow the souls of the deceased to depart in peace. The child was sitting in a frigid draught. He wondered how long she'd been there. A watch was traditionally kept to protect the souls of the dead from wily faeryfolk; perhaps she'd been there all night.

He rubbed her hand and looked into her face. Her nose was running and was none too clean around the nostrils. Spitting into his kerchief, he cleaned her face. At the touch, and perhaps the tenderness in his expression, she began to cry.

'Here, now.' He took her into his embrace, feeling her chest convulse as she tried to stifle her sobs. 'Let it out, dear heart. Ye'll miss her terribly, but the pain will fade in time. I hope it eases your heart to know she's in a better place now. Or will be soon. Is loved there as much as she was here.'

'Where is she?' she gasped, pushing him away in her eagerness to know.

'Well, likely purgatory.' Aware that was not what she wished to hear, he added, 'But she'll soon be in heaven with Our Lord. Fearn was a goodly soul, so I see no reason to doubt it.'

'Where's purtagory?' She frowned, fixing him with a hopeless look.

Folk were still crowding around the coffin, clutching their whisky; he tightened his grip on her hand. 'I'd need to explain it, but in a more private place, dear heart.'

Father Ranald could remember baptising all of Fearn's children, even the foundling infant, Grace, they'd named her, as Fearn had viewed her coming as a blessing. But he couldn't recall seeing any but the boy James in chapel, or at any Mass he'd conducted more recently, of necessity by moonlight under the gaze of moor and mountain. He would need to employ patience and tact to avoid distressing her further.

'I want to stay here.'

'I understand.' He frowned, imagining what it must be like for her—the confusion and loss. Rubbing his forehead, he smoothed his fingers over his brows. What would entice her to leave her mother's side?

'A stroll in the fresh air, perhaps?' he ventured. 'Then we'll return for bannocks and broth. Agreed?'

She gauged him with dark eyes, then got to her feet.

'Splendid.'

Taking her hand, he led her out into a winter-blasted land. The bones of a tree, a birch most likely, lay on its side where it had succumbed to the rage of a winter's storm. It made a tolerable seat for them both.

She sat beside him, head tilted up expectantly. Her face was perfectly symmetrical, he noted, her rounded cheeks retaining a hint of her baby self, but the set of her cheekbones and luminosity of her skin spoke of the striking woman she would become. Her eyes were the darkest brown and seemed to fill her face, framed by exquisitely drawn brows that arched from the centre of her forehead to become lost in the sweep of her hair. Extraordinary eyes. She would be a beauty one day.

There was a biting chill in the air, the snow crusted with frost. She was hardly dressed for the cold and shivered stoically beside him, waiting for word of her mother. As he drew her close, she leaned into him, resting her head against his side. His heart fluttered. Unbidden, his thoughts turned to Duncan, the boy he'd given shelter and protection to over the last few months. Shelter of a kind, and his chest tightened.

For the past ten months, as a wave of atrocities swept across the Highlands following the disaster of Culloden, he'd been forced to seek shelter wherever he could, taking the boy with him. They'd hidden in cothouse and byre, bothy and shieling hut, staying no more than a night in any one place. The glens of Strathavon and Glenlivet were garrisoned with government troops bent on retribution. Soldiers were hunting down those from the area, Catholics principally, who'd followed the Royal Standard. There were many, himself included. His home and the chapel at Findron had been razed to the ground.

Duncan, at seven years old, had crouched under the bank of the Crombie Water where he was filling pails and had witnessed his home ransacked and set alight with his mother, infant sister, and bedridden grandmother inside. The lad had listened to their screams with fists pressed to his ears. He was now an orphan since his father, recruited into Gordon of Glenbuchat's regiment, was wounded in the first charge at Culloden, then bayoneted as he lay bleeding in the heather. Active at Culloden, too, he'd been powerless to aid the man and had only just escaped the bloodbath. Many others on the Jacobite side had been less fortunate. They were of a kind now, he and the boy, connected in some way, and he knew he'd protect him with his life.

'Where is it Mam's gone?' Rowena pressed him. 'Ye said ye'd tell me. I want to see her.'

'I know, dear heart, only that's not possible, though 'tis my belief ye'll meet again one day when 'tis yer time.'

'Now, though.'

He swallowed. 'Your mother's body will be buried in a day or two when the ground thaws enough. But her soul's destined for heaven, I believe, and the child, only there's a kind of halfway house they must go to first where their souls will be made ready to enter heaven. D'ye understand?'

She appeared to consider this, her brows drawn forlornly. 'I want her to be going to hevin and all. Only, I dinna want her to be gone. I need her.' Tears slid over her cheeks.

'I know, dear heart, but heaven's such a splendid place. 'Tis where Our Lord lives, and He'll make her welcome. She'll be happy there. They both will.'

She pushed herself away from him, searching his face. 'James says we must pray fer her soul afore we go to sleep each night, and I do. I pray and pray. I pray she'll come and tuck me under the blankets aside Grace and kiss me here.' She pointed to the centre of her forehead with a grubby finger. 'Like always. Anyhow,' she slanted her eyes, 'Mam was happy here, and hevin's nae where ye said she was going.'

'No, not yet, her soul will likely be waiting in purgatory.'

She continued to gauge him, her eyes moving over his borrowed clothing, returning to his face. He sighed. 'Twas hard to explain to one so young, but Catholic doctrine was steadfast on this subject. All baptised souls, no matter how saintly, except for Catholic martyrs, went to purgatory to be purged of their sins: cleansed by pain and fire before going on to heaven to be with the Lord. How to tell her that? He drew a deep breath. 'You remember I said there was a halfway house?'

She nodded.

'Her soul's the part of her that never dies. 'Tis the essence of her— what made her sweet and kind and funny. That's her soul, but it cannot go straight to heaven, for 'tis not yet pure enough. You see, naught that's flawed or imperfect can enter God's presence. Not without first being purified.'

She'd gone very still, her gaze fixed upon his face.

'Cleansed, in a way.'

'Like haeing a bath?'

'Well, in a way, but not with water. Generally with fire.'

Her eyes widened and filled with tears. ''Twould hurt her. I dinna want Mam hurt. I want her here wi' Da and us, and the new babby. I dinna like God!'

'You mustn't say that.' He rubbed his mouth, trying to wipe away her blasphemy. 'God loves you. You must love Him back.'

'But I di ... di ... dinna.'

'You do, dear heart. You're just lost and sad, and yer world has fallen about ye. But that world will heal in time, you'll see. And I say fire, but I don't mean the kind that burns on the hearthstone. I mean a kind of cleansing fire, the kind that burns away the stubble and chaff, leaving the precious grain behind. Or the kind that takes away the silt leaving only the gleam of a pearl. That pearl can then shine in heaven. Your mother is a pearl, dear heart. As is any child of hers, I'm certain. Ye'd wish her to shine, wouldn't you?'

She sniffed and swiped at her tears, and an anguished expression twisted her mouth, but, eventually, she nodded. He let his breath out. She would accept her mother's loss in time, but for now, the pain was fierce. He wished as fiercely he could take it from her.

Rummaging for the kerchief again, now a mite grubby, he pressed it into her hand. She cleaned her face and pressed her lips together, then handed it back. Her eyes were dry now. She looked up tightly at him. There was something about her face, a wisdom in her eyes, almost as if he could see the thoughts processing in the dark background of iris and pupil. He felt strangely affected.

'It willna hurt her? Purtagory?'

'A little, I believe.' He must be truthful, yet distressing her was the last thing he wanted.

She blinked and glanced away, perhaps seeing a blazing pyre with her mother on top. He sighed, passing a hand over the growth of whiskers on his chin.

'I never want to go to purtagory,' she said with quiet certainty. 'Nor hevin, nor any place God lives.'

He sat back, letting his gaze sweep out over the ageless grandeur of the strath. 'Twas to be expected. She was too young to understand. Yet, he hoped one day to bring her back to the Lord with a gentle, guiding hand. Rubbing the back of his neck, he canted his head, bringing the eastern slopes of the Cromdale hills into view lit by a wintery sun. Even grizzled with snow, they took his breath away. He shifted his gaze to Ben Avon and the hazy, cloud-wreathed summits of the Cairngorms, inhaling deeply, instinctively drawing strength from the wonder of it all. The Lord's creation.

To his left, the shoulder of *Tom na Bat* was just visible, sheltering the blackened remains of his chapel. Naught but a roofless shell. An insult to God, one that shamed him, although he and the faithful of the glen nurtured secret plans to rebuild it. Theirs was an outlawed faith. They'd need to make the chapel look indistinguishable from the stone-and-turf homes scattered throughout the glen. In these dark, suspicious days, he was in constant danger of arrest and execution, rumoured, correctly, to have been the chaplain in Glenbuchat's regiment. He hoped someday to rebuild his home and old life, but, for now, the chapel was more important.

'Ye must be strong, dear heart,' he whispered to the girl. 'A brave lass. Ye'll come to understand one day. But for now, I pray ye keep faith and never lose your tender heart. 'Tis a flicker of the Almighty living within ye.'

Despite his words, he sometimes wondered at the workings of the Lord, especially these last few months. So much suffering. Such fear and loss. What was the purpose of it? But it wasn't his place to question or judge, only to keep faith and ease suffering wherever he found it. Yet he sometimes wondered what stretch he would serve in purgatory himself, how long his own sentence might be. An aeon, perhaps. For although he loved God, he was likely guilty of loving his fellow man more.

'Should you ever need me, dear heart, wish to speak with me about yer mother and why God chose to take her, or about anything, I'm at yer service. Remember that. I've been evading government soldiers and zealous Kirk Elders most of my days, but I'm not so hard to find. Your father will manage to find me.'

He tightened his grip on her hand, the child allowing it with no more than a deepening of the furrow between her brows. Looking down at her, he saw what he took for a flicker of gratitude cross her features and experienced a warm expansion in his chest. His thoughts turned to her older brother and sister. He must minister to their needs, too.

'Shall we see if there's any broth left, dear heart?'

CHAPTER TWO

SHE'D NOT BEEN there before, he was certain, but she drew his gaze at once. A woman, how old? Father Ranald could not tell. She could be as old as the lichen-freckled standing stones atop Seely's hillock, where he'd heard aborted babes were buried, or only middle-aged, younger even. Her age was hard to determine on a face weathered to the texture of leather and stained with earth, or peat, or whatever it was she laid her head upon, for it was not a bed as most folk knew it. Her home was the woods, he sensed.

She had covered her head with the remnants of a tattered arisaid, snagged with twigs and shards of pinecone, and likely housing creeping insects—forky golachs, perhaps. He shuddered, hating the scuttling creatures with their wicked pincher tails. She kept her head bowed to avoid the drawing of curious eyes, yet he'd seen her before—at the bedside of a young woman who died in childbirth. A fallen woman 'twas rumoured, unwed, though he'd made no judgment of her himself.

She had muttered the shame was not the girl's but belonged to those who used and discarded her like the dregs at the base of a draught of ale. Human dregs. He'd seen such things and pitied them as much as this strange woman. MacNeil, aye, he believed that was her name.

She moved away from the shadow behind the door and approached the coffin, standing in line. Folk fell back from her with a mutter, menfolk chiefly, burying their noses in their whisky. 'Hag,' someone muttered, and worse, but she waited patiently, the tightening of her jaw the only indication she was aware of the mistrust and aversion around her.

11

She had with her an unusual gift. Most folk brought food or peats for the fire or whatever they could spare, and he encouraged this. Providing for so many was always a burden on the bereaved family. But she brought naught but a handful of greenery. He wondered where she'd found such tender shoots at this time of year, but they had some compassionate purpose. Or so he hoped.

On reaching the head of the line, she stretched out a grimy hand. Folk paused and held their breath, suspicious of her motives, but she was as gentle as a hind to its fawn. She ran her hand over the mound of Fearn's belly, cupping and caressing, then drew a long breath, trailing her fingers to Fearn's heart, letting them linger there. Whispering a few words, she tucked the greenery inside the winding-sheet.

Folk muttered a deal more. 'Twas hardly seemly to be so familiar with a corpse, but Father Ranald was struck by how almost religious her gesture seemed, though she was, of course, as heathen as 'twas possible to be. Not one Mass had he seen her attend, nor any other Christian service that he knew of. She was rumoured to be a witch, albeit likely a benign one.

Curiously, many of the womenfolk treated her kindly. They looked her in the eye, nodding with a smile that signified something. Their exchanges spoke of a deep connection of old. Perhaps she'd aided these women in some way or those they loved. He'd heard she was a healer. She used plants and herbs as most healers did, but also other methods he could hardly sanction. Charms and spells and witch-like things. 'Twas said she left offerings at devil's stones, even prayed there.

Highland superstitions made him uneasy. They should have been forsaken long ago; Scotland was an enlightened nation now. Not here in the Highlands, though. Here the auld ways still lingered. 'Twas his duty to shepherd his flock into the full light of Christ, but he must do so with tact and understanding.

With a sigh, he shifted his gaze from the witch to the young girl, Rowena. 'Twas hard not to look at her, and she was a joy to the eyes after the MacNeil woman.

Rowena had moved to the firestone as he'd hoped and was sipping from a bowl of broth, her face half hidden by a drape of dark hair. Duncan was sitting by the fire, too, his Duncan, quietly watching the mourners descend into a kind of reverent drunkenness. The lad looked at the girl seated beside him and offered her a shy smile.

He would do that. Duncan would always give small kindnesses wherever he could, 'twas his way, though he'd likely not speak. Duncan was not one for words. He used his face, his eyes, especially, to talk for him. Those eyes, what had they seen? And at such a tender age.

He often wondered if Duncan had been a boy of words before. Perhaps he'd once been full of words, his face said so, for always he appeared eager to express himself, though rarely did. Yet, his eyes spoke, and the anxious crease between them. They said more of what he'd seen and heard and likely smelled than could a thousand words.

* * *

The broth was good, better than Rowena imagined considering Grace had made it and 'twas only the first time she'd done so on her own. Yet, enjoying food not cooked by her mother's hand felt disloyal. She sipped wretchedly, hunger gnawing, thinking on what the father had said. He was wrong. God hadna loved Mam. How could he when he'd taken her and her babby away only to burn them both? 'Twasna love, that.

A kindly God wouldn't hurt Mam. Mam never harmed a soul in her life. She lifted baby birds back into their nest beneath the eaves whenever she found them floundering on the ground. She cried when a calf was born all limp and blue and never knew its mother licking its eyelids, for 'twas never able to know anything, and she sat up all night in the freezing byre when Bracken was born.

Bracken was their newest pony, her favourite, though he was still only a frolicking foal. Mam had stroked the mare's swollen belly, whispering encouragement, thanking her for every barrel of whisky she'd carried through the hills. Mam loved all creatures; she didna hold with suffering. If God wanted Mam to suffer, He must be cruel, and Rowena wanted naught to do with Him.

She shivered. Father Ranald said God loved her, and she must love Him back, but He'd taken away the person she loved most in the world. He was hurting that person now, as she supped her broth. She put her bowl down and pushed it away. Inside she felt empty, full of a kind of nothingness, but it wasn't the kind of empty she could fill with food.

A strange boy was looking at her, a lad she'd not seen before, with a long face and close-set eyes. He nodded, and half smiled. She tried to smile back, but her face felt too numb to tell if she'd managed. He was wearing a woollen coat plainly too big, his hands cradling the front. Something moved beneath the fabric. As she stared, it wriggled more.

Puzzled, she studied the boy's face. He blushed, drawing back into the shadows.

'What have ye in there?'

He glanced around a mite fearfully. 'I was to leave her in the byre, only I dinna like thinking on her all alone. She hates to be alone.'

Her curiosity piqued, she inched closer, trying to shield the boy from the crush of folk with their brash voices and whisky-sour breath. 'She? Is it a creature?'

'A puppy,' he whispered. 'A Gordon Setter nae weeks old. She's mine to keep; Donald Gordon gave her me. She's a runtling, nae worth the meat once she's weaned. She was fer the drowning sack, but he said I could have her if Father Ranald agreed.'

'And he did?' Her eyes widened. 'Is he yer da, then?'

He shook his head, avoiding her eyes. 'My da's dead. Father Ranald's a priest; he canna be having bairns, nor a wife, nor any common life. God willna allow it. He's in hiding anyhow, though I'm nae supposed to speak o' that. Ye'll nae say I did, will ye?' He looked anxiously at her.

Who would she speak of it to? But she shook her head, more interested in the puppy squirming ever more frantically beneath his clothing and now making snuffling sounds. Other eyes would soon be drawn there.

'Ye should take her back to the byre,' she said. 'Folk might hear her. Mam willna mind, but Da ....'

She swallowed. She kept doing that: forgetting Mam was gone. 'I could come wi' ye,' she croaked. 'I like puppies. I think I like them better than folk.'

He nodded, looking curiously at her, and she saw his eyes clearly for the first time. They were the palest green-blue. The colour Loch Avon had been the day Mam took them there to gather blaeberry and sloe. The water had shone like metal, so cold it glinted green. Drinking it had hurt her teeth. When she knelt to peer beneath the surface, her heart had fluttered, for the whole sky shone back at her. The heavens had slipped beneath the water, reflecting the colour of this boy's eyes.

It was cold in the byre and smelled of damp cow and dung, but without the clamour of folk, 'twas easier to think. The boy unfastened his coat, and a tender face peeked out, then the puppy came tumbling into the straw. She was tiny and velvety, all head and trembling legs, but her tail had a life of its own. It wagged excitedly, her whole body quivering as she tilted her head to look at Rowena, then tried to climb onto her lap.

'She's brave,' she chuckled. 'What's her name?' But she didn't know the boy's name either.

'Jem. I'm Duncan.'

'Where is it ye belong? Which holding?'

He hesitated, avoiding her eyes. She had the feeling she shouldn't have asked.

'I dinna belong anywhere,' he said at last. 'I was born in Glenlivet. Wester Auchavaich, but that place is no more. The redcoats burned it on their way from Culloden. They burned and butchered as they pleased, heading fer Scalan, laying waste to everything in their path.' He frowned. 'I have nae hame. Nor kinfolk. I've naught but this puppy.'

Her mouth fell open. 'No kin?'

'I stay wi' Father Ranald. We're on the run from the redcoats, or the father is. I'm nae sure why.'

She stared at him, wanting to ask more but deterred by his expression. He turned away, hiding his discomfort, and she looked down at little Jem. She was all Duncan had in the world.

She knew of redcoats; they were hard to miss with their crimson jackets and strange tongue, and they were everywhere, billeted throughout the glen. Folk were afraid of them. Mam had crossed herself whenever she saw them, pulling her arisaid over her head, urging her to do the same. She didn't understand it all, why they were here or what they wanted. She knew only what James had told her. Highlanders had risen in arms against the king; the king wasna the true and rightful one. Glensmen had joined an army and marched away, and most never came back. Da had wanted to go, but Mam had spoken of the whisky and the rental due at Lammas. How would she manage? He'd gone quiet and stayed by her side.

She looked down at Jem, stroking her velvety ears.

'She likes ye,' Duncan said. 'She's scared o' most folk, but she likes you.'

'I like all creatures. Mam did too.'

She hadn't thought of her mother for the last few minutes. She'd been thinking of puppies and this sad boy. Now she remembered why he was here—him and the father. They'd come because Mam and the babby were dead and gone and needed to go in the ground. She remembered she was no longer the centre of someone's world, and no one was the centre of hers. She was alone, or so it felt. The knowledge made her drag her feet, think slower, and everything mattered less, but this boy was even more alone. He had naught but a puppy while she had James and Grace, and they still had their da and a place to live.

She picked up the puppy, kissing her dark head, and laid her in Duncan's lap. 'She needs you. Ye're her family, and I need to get back to Mam.'

There were only a few days left now for looking at Mam's face, then she'd be gone forever. There'd only be memories of her, and they might fade and become hard to catch. Thinking of those memories dwindling made tears come. Already she'd cried so hard Da had scolded her. She must toughen herself; he couldn't be bringing Mam back no matter how hard he wished to. So, now, she kept her tears inside till nightfall, spilling them into the feathers of her pillow, choking on them not to waken Grace. She wondered if Duncan did the same.

He opened his mouth to say something, but the creak of the door stopped him mid-breath.

'There you are.' Father Ranald stood in the doorway. 'I might've known.' His brows rose. 'And young Rowena. You like puppies, too? Of course. No need to hurry back. You've found a friend, Duncan, someone who shares your love of puppies. Splendid, splendid.' He beamed at them both.

Strangely, he seemed pleased they'd sneaked away from the wake. Maybe he hated tending bairns as much as her da. Yet, for all his clumsy words, she felt the father meant well.

'I need to get back,' she muttered. ''Tis a good thing ye did, though, Father, saving Jem. I like her. I like Duncan, too.'

Duncan blinked, turning his strange eyes upon her. They widened and seemed to shine, the crease between his brows melting away, and she knew she'd just done a good thing too.

'My dear, you hardly know how that gladdens my heart,' the father replied.

* * *

Duncan and Father Ranald were to stay at Tomachcraggen until the burial. Those from the farthest reaches of the glen would also stay. The hill passes were choked with snow; they all waited for a thaw.

That night, sitting at her mother's side, Rowena struggled to keep her eyes open.

'To bed,' her da ordered.

She shook her head. 'I'm wanting to stay here.'

He sighed and turned to James, and James also tried to convince her, but there was pity in her brother's eyes. She knew she'd stay put.

Duncan shared her vigil for a while, sitting quietly with Jem in his lap. Occasionally, he asked about Mam, seeming to know speaking about her kept her alive. But when it grew late, he rose and murmured, 'I'll leave ye now and bed mysel' down in a corner.'

16

She sat on, pinching herself to keep awake, but must have finally succumbed, for she woke to the sensation of being carried, cradled against a warm body. She relaxed; Mam did that, lifting her half-asleep to bed, tucking her in beside Grace. But then she remembered it couldn't be Mam.

She wanted to protest, to fight whoever was taking her from her mother's side, but even prising her eyes open was beyond her doing. 'Twould be Da, though he smelled funny, not all malty with a whiff of whisky, but of something more subtle. He settled himself by the fire, cradling her close.

'Ye'll spoil her, Father,' her da said, and she realised 'twas Father Ranald that held her.

'The child's bereft, Lachlan. D'ye not think you should've warned them their mother was dying? At least let them in to see her. Explained the child couldn't be born; that there could be no end to it but a final one.'

Her da made a choked sound. 'I see that now, Father. James, I told, but I asked him nae to tell the wee one. Nae to upset her. It didna seem right letting her watch her mam suffer. Watching it myself was torture enough. I'd no comfort to offer, anyhow.'

'No comfort to offer?'

Her da cleared a gruffness from his throat. 'Ye ken yerself; I'm little use at soothing bairns. I'm a man o' the land, a rough man. I'm at home wi' cattle and whisky and other menfolk, nae wi' littlins. Nae wi' ....' He made a snuffling sound, and she pictured him rubbing his face.

'Tenderness?'

'Aye, I'm nae use wi' soft-herted things like bairns, specially crying ones. I've nae the knack o' making them stop. 'Twas Fearn was good at that.'

She was wide awake now. They were talking about her and what happened to Mam. No one had done that. No one had sat her down and explained it.

The father stroked her hair. She kept still, deepening her breathing.

'Fearn was a rare woman, but the future without her needs to be considered. Lacking a mother, these youngsters need a father more than ever. A loving, providing one. I'm not saying ye're not a good provider. Lord knows ye've skills enough when it comes to the barley and oats, the cattle and whisky. But wi' bairns ....'

'I'll do my best by them, I swear.'

'You'll do well enough with the lad, I'm thinking. Will make him into a fine smuggler. But dealings with the fairer gender, particularly delicate,

17

grieving ones, is hardly your strength, Lachlan.'

'Likely yer right, Father. Lassies are different. They're hard to understand, slippery to handle, and althegither a mystery to me. But I love them,
Father. *Both* o' them.'

Father Ranald drew an expansive breath. "Tis what I thought. I may
have a solution, then, one for us both.'

'What would that be?'

'As you know, I have a boy with me. Duncan. The lad needs a home, a
family, and to be with youngsters his age. He needs a decent chance at life.
Something that I, sadly, am not able to give him. Troops are still hunting
down rebels in these glens. I'm a wanted man—a prized trophy. If
captured, they'll execute me for my loyalty. For my deeds, God forgive me.
I feel my enemies drawing close. What can I give Duncan but more
danger? More misery. Yet, I love the lad as if he were my own.' He faltered.
"Tis a strange admission from a priest, but I believe I love him as fiercely
as would any father.'

'Likely more. Kenning ye the way I do.'

The father sighed. 'The lad was born at Wester Auchavaich and has
suffered unimaginably.'

'He's an orphan, then?'

'His father was recruited by old Glenbuchat on the promise of
freedom from the Malt Tax, as were many. I saw him struck on Culloden
field.' He shuddered. 'As ye know, few escaped the execution squads sent
in after the battle with bayonet and sword.'

'And his mother? His kinfolk?'

'All dead at the hands of the British Army.'

'Wester Auchavaich?' Her da made a rasping sound as realisation
dawned. 'One o' the holdings fired by dragoons on their rampage to
Scalan?'

The father's breathing grew ragged. 'Before they burned the seminary,
and that burning was not so bad in that the boys and their master knew
the redcoats would come for them and spirited themselves away. But
those in the army's way, whole families, were shown no mercy. I've not
spoken of it with Duncan; the lad's not ready. But he witnessed the entire
atrocity, was filling pails at the Crombie when dragoons ringed his home.
He hid there while they set the cottage alight, his mother and infant sister
inside, along with his bedridden grandmother.'

'We heard tales, Father, but they were ower-gruesome and hard to
believe.'

'Believe them, you must. Duncan doesn't speak o' it. The lad has few words at the best of times, but in his sleep, he rambles and weeps. He speaks of their screams, tells them he's coming to help them, then cries piteously. There's naught a grown man could've done, and he was a boy of seven.'

'Christ in heaven! The bastards.'

'I fear his mother was too afraid to leave the house.' The father ignored Lachlan's blasphemous outburst. 'Afraid of the wrathful soldiers with their bayonets and swords. She could hardly have carried her mother anyway and would not leave her to the flames. The thatch likely went up quick, and the timber frame, once weakened, would've crashed upon their heads, bringing the flaming thatch with it. That's if the smoke didna choke them first.'

There was silence as they considered this, perhaps seeing the dreadful image in their minds, as Rowena now did. Her heart began to pound, making it hard to breathe.

'Yer certain she's sleeping? She shouldna be hearing this.'

The priest shifted position. She felt his breath on her cheek as he peered at her and kept her eyes tightly closed, hoping to fool him.

'Dead to the world, poor mite.'

'Best be putting her to bed, then. 'Tis what I do when I doubt she'll waken again. She's spent ower-long staring at a dead woman in a wooden box fer my liking. Fer a child o' five. Canna be right, that.'

'She's not yet accepted her mother's passing,' the father murmured. 'A moment longer will do us both good.' He began to rock her gently back and fore, cooing like a pigeon. ''Tis rare I'm able to comfort one so tender. And with such a fiercely loyal heart. I confess, I'm loath to put the dear heart away.'

'Hmm.' She heard her father's disapproval. 'And the lad? Ye said ye had a solution.'

'I do.' He sat forward. 'I believe the boy would make a fine apprentice. On the land and in ... other matters.'

'An apprentice?'

'Come, you know well what I mean. The lad needs a home, a family, and to be with youngsters like himself. He's made friends here. With young Rowena, and with your son.' He drew a long breath. 'What d'you say, Lachlan? Will ye take the lad in?'

Her da exhaled forcibly through his nose. 'Have I nae enough wi' three o' my own, Father? And nae wife to feed and mother them. Ye'd saddle me wi' another? I'm nae saying I've no sympathy fer the lad. But to take him in ... and especially now.'

19

'He would work for his keep, of course, and I'd contribute what I can. He's a willing worker, a quiet boy, but decent and loyal. I believe he'd help Rowena and the others adjust to their mother's death.' The priest held his breath, waiting for her da's decision. She felt the tension in his lungs and found herself waiting with bated breath, too.

'How would he do that?'

'Shared loss, Lachlan. Shared suffering. The knowledge that another has suffered even more than oneself. It helps bring things into an orderly perspective. I believe, in many ways, his presence here would make your life easier too. He and the pup,' he added.

'Jesus God. I'm to take the runtling as well. God's blood!' There was a pause, then her da muttered, 'Forgive me, I do speak roughly a' times.'

'You'll take him, then?'

Silence stretched. Eventually, her da muttered, 'It do look that wey.'

'Splendid, splendid! I'm confident you'll not regret your decision.'

'Humph.'

She was lifted then and carried to bed, her mind turning.

Since God took Mam away, the colour had faded from her life. She'd imagined no one could feel as lost, but that wasn't so. Duncan had suffered as much—more, for he'd seen terrible things and had no one to speak of them to but a priest. He spent his nights sleeping on strange floors, half-forgotten, eating with folk who barely knew him and likely cared as little.

No one knew if he liked his porridge stiff with salt or only a little briny; if he preferred a drop o' honey in his buttermilk. Mam had known these things. Likely his had, too. Yet, she doubted the father understood since he hoped to rid himself of the boy to the first glensman who'd take him.

An indignant rage grew. She didn't want another brother, and she'd never accept Mam's death, no matter who came to live here. Yet, despite that, she wanted Duncan to have a better life. A safe one with some joy in it. Since Mam died, all she'd wanted was to have her back, but she wanted something else now, too—to show Duncan the same kindness Mam would've shown.

CHAPTER THREE

SHE'D MEANT TO sneak back to her mother's side as soon as the priest finished tucking her into the box-bed beside Grace, only, peeping around the heavy woollen curtain, two figures were now sitting at her mother's coffin. The room was dim, lit by the embers of the fire and a lone fir-candle, but she could see enough to recognise the lean outline of the priest and the bulkier one of her father. With a sigh, she let the curtain fall back into place.

She lay down on her back and listened for their voices, but they talked on until her eyes grew heavy, and although she could hear their low murmuring and the soft thump of whisky cup on heavy pine plank, their words she could not catch. Tears welled; she let them slither down her cheeks.

She missed Mam till the emptiness made her sore. She missed her voice and the stories she told—tales of the life of a glen. She especially missed the way she spoke of the changing seasons. Mam could conjure the sweet scent of a summer hill pasture with naught but her words. Each night, as she and Grace drifted off to sleep, they'd breathe the heady perfume of a thousand clover blossoms nodding on the breeze. The scent, so subtle on one tiny bloom, rose in a rich cloud as in their dreams, they crossed the pastures together.

She looked over at Grace's shadowy form, recognising the familiar rhythm of her breathing. The sound eased her heart a little. Slowly, sleep began to lull her under its spell.

'Twas an eerie sound that jolted her awake. She blinked, rubbing the

21

sleep from her eyes, thinking she'd dreamed it. She held her breath, straining her senses in the darkness, then sat bolt upright, knowing she had not. Parting the curtain, she peeked out. The sound came again, a keening howl. She snatched her head back, gasping with fright.

'Twas an animal sound, like a wolf, yet wolves were no more. So Da said. They were only tales now to frighten bairns and keep them close to home. A *cu-sìth*, then? The thought made her quake. A *cu-sìth* was a demon dog that roamed Highland moors making its lair in rocky clefts. Big as a calf, its blood-curdling cry signified death. Or the stealing of a soul. She thought of her mother, and her breath caught in her throat.

The sound came again, this time choked off, followed by a whimpering cry, and she knew 'twas not the baying of a faery-hound, but a human sound. The cry of a child gripped in a nightmare.

Her father's snores reverberated from the table where he was slumped, another snort coming from a more distant part of the room. How could they sleep through such a thing? But even at five years, she knew 'twas what whisky did.

Swinging her legs over the side of the bed, she dropped to the floor, listening. The wailing came from a dark corner where an ill-defined form lay on the floor. She took a quivering breath, her heart pounding, and crept closer, pity finally overcoming fear.

He had no blanket, no warm covering, not even a sack to keep him warm. Naught but his coat with the puppy likely cooried inside. He was weeping now, twitching and rambling.

'Duncan.' She touched him on the shoulder, and he jerked violently away. ''Tis only a dream. Ye're safe; ye're at Tomachcraggen.' She was about to say he'd be staying here from now on but stopped herself. 'Twas for the father to tell him that.

He quietened to a muffled sobbing, and she lay down beside him, feeling for his hand in the darkness, working her fingers into his damp palm. 'Twas cold on the floor, and mighty hard, but knowing she was, perhaps, a comfort to him was a good thought. She began to hum an old lullaby her mother used to sing, a soothing cradle song, and he whispered, 'Is that you, Rowena?'

'Aye. Can I lie here aside ye a while?'

He sniffed. 'If ye like. But I'm nae the best company.'

'Ye're fine company.'

He took a hiccupping breath and pressed her hand, and she realised he was warm, despite his cold sleeping place. He was accustomed to such sleeping places, she supposed, but she knew not to ask what he'd dreamed of. She could imagine that well enough. 'Twould be a fearful, fiery dream, like Father Ranald had described. She shuddered.

In her short life, Rowena had learned to fear one thing above all else—being alone in the world. A lost child. Now, without her mother, that fear consumed her.

She slipped her arm around Duncan, stroking his back, trying to show him affection as she imagined Mam would've done. His chest spasmed as he struggled to bring his sobbing under control. ''Tis alright,' she whispered. 'Ye were dreaming.' But she knew it was not all right. Nae yet.

She hummed again, softly, so no one but Duncan would hear, for she supposed 'twas a curious thing to do, seeing she'd only just met him. But there and then, she decided something. 'Twas the first decision she'd made without her mother's prompting or approval, although she knew Mam would certainly have given it. She would mend Duncan's brokenness.

She tightened her hold, exploring the notion, and a tender feeling stole over her. To be healed, she imagined he'd need to feel safe and valued like he belonged. Nae so easy when her da had made his resistance plain, but it would be her mission to help him feel so. No mention would she make of this to anyone, for it might seem like meddling. 'Twould be her secret. After all, she supposed they were alike, Duncan and her, in their hearts, they must harbour the same fear.

So, as far as she was concerned, Duncan was now kin. Not in blood or name, but in every other way that mattered. She'd treat him like a brother, much as the new babby would've been had it lived and been a boy. The notion was a comforting one but a sad one, too. The tragedy was not lost upon her, and she had a sudden desire to cry. Her nose nipped, and her eyes filled with tears. Only she shouldn't cry, not when she was trying to comfort Duncan, and there was no room in her heart for more sadness.

She'd wanted the new babby as much as Mam had. Poor Mam, all stiff and cold, waiting to go in the ground where no one would see her or know how blithe she'd been. She'd rot away. Be eaten by worms. She tried to smile through her tears, to chase the dark thoughts away, only her face felt stiff, and it seemed a long time since she'd smiled.

Duncan's breathing finally slowed and seemed easier. He shuddered and buried his face in her hair, then cautiously brought an arm around her.

''Tis alright,' she whispered, stroking his shoulder. She felt warm now and safe. Sleep would come quick.

'Bless ye,' he whispered.

* * *

She woke a little before dawn, cold, a stiffness in her limbs, and gently eased herself upright. Duncan was still sleeping. When she looked down at him, an odd tingling grew around her heart. She'd expected to find her da and the priest still sitting with her mother, likely asleep, but 'twas a strange woman she discovered there, her head swaddled in a tattered old arisaid.

At first, she thought her a *cailleach*, an old woman, but when the woman turned, she saw that her eyes danced with life, and there was a warmth about her face, her smile, that stripped the years away and made her smile shyly back, despite her troubles.

'Welcome,' the woman said, though 'twas hardly her business welcoming her to her own home, but still, it somehow seemed a fitting thing to say.

She slipped onto the seat beside the woman, scrambling onto her knees to better see Mam's face. 'Twas a comfort seeing her. Canting her head, she eyed the woman a mite curiously. She looked funny, smelled funny, too; a grassy smell with a hint of animal, though agreeable enough. Like warm pony or cattle fur on a summer's day.

'I'm thinking ye must be Fearn's youngest.'

She nodded, aware the woman was assessing her, though not in an uncomfortable way. Not judging as some folk seemed to do. The woman didn't appear to find it odd she'd wish to sit beside a coffin, desperate to treasure every last moment with the person most precious to her.

'Rowena, then?'

She nodded.

'Fearn spoke o' ye. She said ye were special.'

'Ye knew her?'

'I knew her soul.'

Rowena blinked. The woman now had her full attention.

'Folk call me a *draoidh*, fer I've the gift o' healing and second-sight, though some have other names fer me. I see folk's souls, the essence o' them if ye like. The colours that pulse from folk and reveal their true nature.' She laughed. 'I can see straight into the blackest heart, whether I wish to or not. Fearn's heart was full o' kindness, and she did only good wherever she went.'

'Ye did know her.'

'I do still.'

'But ....' She stared, searching for signs the woman teased, but the face that gazed back was open, uncomplicated, her eyes immeasurably wise.

'But she's dead and gone. How can ye still know her?'

''Tis only her body that died. Her soul still lives. The force that powers a life can never die. She watches ower ye.' The woman's mouth relaxed into a smile. 'I feel her presence now.'

'Who are ye?' The woman no longer appeared as shabby and draggle-tailed but vividly alive. Despite her natural suspicion, a wild longing tore at Rowena's heart.

'I helped bring ye into the world, though ye'll nae mind that.' The woman chuckled. 'Yours was an easy birth, but this poor child,' she brushed her fingers over Fearn's belly, her expression infinitely sad, 'was never meant to be born.'

'I dinna understand. Why was the babby nae meant to be born?'

'A placement went wrong in the womb. I might've changed that had I been permitted, but it wasna to be. My ministrations were deemed unwise.' She glanced over her shoulder. 'There's a priest here, I think.'

'Father Ranald? He wouldna allow it?'

'Perhaps. Or perhaps a judgment was made against me by some in the glen.' She sighed. 'May I take yer hand, Rowena? I wish to sense a little o' yer inner self. Yer possibilities.'

Mystified, yet filled with a strange excitement, she held out her hand.

'My name is Morna MacNeil.' The woman pushed back the woollen plaid covering her head, revealing a finely-boned face and dark hair plaited in places and flecked with silver. She took Rowena's hand, turning it with her grimy fingers, then looked up sharply.

'Why, the blood o' the *draoidh* sings in yer veins.' She looked intently at her. 'As it does in mine. I was right to come. To let my instincts guide me. Only, ye're ower-young yet, still a mite unmade.'

'What d'ye mean? Why can I nae see Mam? If she's still here, why can only you see her?'

Morna smiled. 'In truth, Fearn's just as out o' sight to me as she is to you. I dinna see her like I see you, but 'tis as if she's slipped from the room for a moment. Or is waiting behind a half-closed door. I sense her soul, the essence of her, as if she's sitting here aside me, though I ken she's passed to the next realm.'

Rowena frowned in confusion, her gaze furtively roaming the room, hoping to catch a glimpse of this shadowy realm. Most folk would be afraid now, judging this devil's talk, but she felt no fear, only a great longing to know more.

'How do ye sense her? I mean, can I?'

25

''Tis a gift I was born wi'. A curse, some call it, though that has never been my word. But aye, the skill can be nurtured in those who're ripe fer such things.'

'Am I ripe, d'ye think?'

Morna laughed, squeezing her hand. 'Ye're a rare find. A young bud just waiting to bloom. 'Tis long I've waited fer ye.'

Rowena shivered with a strange thrill.

A wariness crept into Morna's voice. 'Only, these skills can bring dangers. Many a fearful name's been flung my way. Names that could put me in gaol or worse. I've been called gallows-born; fit only fer the scaffold. This from menfolk. Kirk elders and men who know naught of me. Women are kinder, they know they deny me at their cost, fer I've skills aplenty when it comes to bringing bairns safe into the world and keeping them here. Healing's my special gift, as 'twill be yours. Only that gift can be a curse. 'Tis likely what befell my mother. Never would she willingly leave her child. But she watches ower me now as Fearn watches you.'

Rowena's breathing grew ragged as she struggled to take this in. Morna spoke of things both wondrous and fearful. Things she'd never heard before. A scaffold? She knew not what that could be, nor did she know what gallows-born meant, though she didn't much like the sound of it. But she knew all about gaol. 'Twas a miserable, cruel place where smugglers landed if the gaugers caught them. Anyone but John Meldrum, the local exciseman.

But it was the revelation that Mam wasn't truly gone that made her stomach swoop. Mam was someplace close, waiting behind a door, and could be sensed, somehow. She couldn't sense her herself but hoped Morna would show her how. And there was something else. Morna had lost her mother, too.

'Were ye a bairn when yer mam died?' she asked. 'Had ye kin to care fer ye?'

'I had the skills shown me since ever as I could walk. I hid in woods and wild places. I do still, giving thanks to nature for her gifts and lessons. I depend upon no one, nor have I since my mother disappeared.'

Seeing Rowena's incredulous expression, Morna smiled. ''Tisna so hard, fer hasn't the creator provided all o' nature fer our needs? Ye didna think all this ...' she turned her head, looking out of the window at a tiny square of world: a few coppiced trees and beyond, the snowy Cairngorms lit by a fiery dawn. 'Just is, wi' no hand to guide it?'

'No, but—'

'In nature, everything works in harmony, and we must do the same.

When we do, all is well.'

Rowena shivered, liking this kind of talk. 'So,' she ventured, 'ye were left alone. Still a bairn?'

'I couldna say how old I was, but I'd nae yet started my courses so wasna yet a woman.'

She frowned.

'Ye'll understand when ye're older. I promise.'

Never had she heard of such a thing. A girl living on her own? 'Twas unimaginable. Glenfolk lived together, their kinfolk around them, tending the beasts and working the land. There were always neighbours to turn to, the whole community of the glen.

'I didna know 'twas possible to live alone,' she said. 'That 'tis allowed.'

'Who's to prevent it?'

She shook her head, thinking the factor or Father Ranald or someone in authority would likely do so. Maybe the redcoats or the king that wasna the right one. Or even their laird, his grace, the Duke of Gordon.

'I dinna ken,' she mumbled, trying to grasp how this could be. Yet she sensed Morna told her no lie. 'And what's a *draoidh*?'

Morna's smile brought her face vividly to life. Rowena was struck again by how unusual-looking Morna was. Beautiful, yet she managed to conceal that fact beneath a semblance of raggedness as if she were a beggar. She was far from that.

'Druids are healers and lore-keepers, Rowena. They keep the auld wisdom, fer no books hold knowledge like druids hold. We keep the traditions folk long followed, the ways that helped us survive through the ages. Wisdom of plant magic, and of the beings we share our glen with.' She laughed. 'Or, at least, how nae to rile them ower-much. Tales of our glen and the folk who once lived here. To forget them is to dishonour them, and that we must never do. The story of *Stratha'an*.'

She spoke the local name for the river so softly, *A'an*, that Rowena was instantly standing upon the riverbank. A peaceful stretch, amber where the sun warmed it, watching strings of bubbles lap like glistening jewels on a shingle beach. A dragonfly swooped over her shoulder in a purr of wings, and she flinched, so real was it. She stared at Morna, and the woman laughed.

'The *A'an* is an ancient river, full of magic as all rivers are. It's flowed fer longer than you or I can fathom, rising among the ancient wind-worn summits o' the Cairngorms. Our glen's an enchanted place, and we must keep it so. I feel the weight o' that duty heavier than most, fer I feel all things more than most. D'ye understand?'

She nodded, though, of course, she did not. Nae yet. But she sensed Morna would teach her, and she longed to learn. Perhaps she felt things more than most, too.

'When ye're ready, I'll teach ye all this. Would ye like that?'

'I think so.' She agreed to it without thought; it seemed to require none. 'But first,' she pleaded, 'will ye teach me how to sense Mam's presence the way you can do?'

Morna smiled sadly. ''Tisna something ye can teach, fer it must come from within. Ye must attune yerself to her spirit, but there are ways to make that easier.'

'Will ye show me how? Oh, please, Morna.' She clutched at the woman's arm, willing her to agree.

Morna glanced around uneasily. 'We must be heedful,' she muttered. 'I'm nae altogether welcome here. Folk disapprove o' me. They think me wicked, though there's nae an evil bone in my body. Such is ignorance; much has been done in its name.'

Rowena swallowed, her gaze skimming the many dark mounds strewn across the cot-house floor. Most were well ruined after the brimming cups of whisky her da had doled out as a welcome to his guests. And as a deadening agent for his heartbreak. Drunken though they'd been, they'd soon be stirring. A broad band of light now slanted down the chimney, a narrower one showing under the door, while, through the tiny window, dawn flamed pearly pink.

She understood. Even at her tender age, she knew Morna was like no one she'd ever met. No glen women spoke as she did—folk would disapprove.

'I fear ye're nae yet old enough to learn my ways, Rowena. But when ye're ready, I'll come back and teach ye all ye need to know. Fer now, though, this must be our secret. Ye see why I think?'

She nodded, then suddenly realised what Morna meant. 'Ye're nae leaving?' The wild hope sown in her heart began to wither. 'Dinna go. Please. I'll learn now. I swear. Please, teach me now.'

Morna sighed and took her hand, examining it for what seemed an age while she silently pleaded with her eyes. But the answer was plain on Morna's face.

'I must, fer 'tis no place fer me, this. I came fer Fearn. Fer the love o' her, and, aye, fer you, fer I was curious. But I did forget how young ye'd be.'

'But ....' She struggled to put her longing into words.

Morna squeezed her hand. 'Ye can still ready yerself, even now. Spend time in nature; let her be yer guide. Visit the places Fearn loved to go, the special places where something of her still lingers. Still yer mind and leave yer earthly cares behind, but do so on yer own. Dinna let others deflect ye, fer they will. Can ye think o' such places?'

She nodded, remembering the times Mam had taken her to gather wild garlic and silverweed. The forest glades, the hill with the queer stone rooted into its slope Mam liked to touch; the pignuts and sow thistle they'd found on the way there.

'Those are the places ye need to go, and ye'll soon find ye like being there, for there's great peace to be had in wild places. Ye'll find that peace, and soon ye'll feel different. The difference will be Fearn.'

Her desperation subsided, replaced with a growing fascination. She knew 'twas anyhow useless to argue, and she longed to get started. 'Where do ye bide, then?' she asked a mite boldly. 'Should ever I need to find ye.'

'In nature,' Morna said simply. 'The trees are my kin, the hills my neighbours, the forest my holding, fer she provides all my needs, simple as they are.' She laughed, a tinkling sound, ruffling Rowena's hair. 'No need to look so worried, I have all I need. And ye'll know when it's time, fer one day ye'll turn, and there I'll be, waiting to show ye all ye need to know.' Morna smiled softly. 'Ye're young. Ye've a tender heart, a flicker o' the creator living within ye, and that means a good life. Time'll pass quick, ye'll see, and I'll be back fer ye sooner than ye know.'

Hadn't Father Ranald said something similar when he spoke of the flames? 'Is Mam in purtagory?' she asked, suddenly suspicious.

'No, child, she's with you. She's in the quiet places, the still moments in yer day.' Morna stiffened, fixing her gaze on something beyond her shoulder. Rowena turned to find Father Ranald watching from the shadows.

'What is it ye want with this child?' he demanded.

'Naught, I came fer Fearn. To pay my respects. Now I've done so, I'll take my leave.' Morna rose and hooded her arisaid, moving to the door. As she passed, she brushed Rowena's arm. 'Be brave,' she whispered. 'I'd nae leave ye had I a choice.'

She shivered; those had been Mam's dying words. She tried to follow her to the door, but the father clamped a hand on her shoulder.

'Let her go.'

She squinted up at him, and he nodded sternly to her.

CHAPTER FOUR

IT NOW SEEMED almost commonplace to Duncan to be standing at a graveside with his head bowed and heart heavy. He fidgeted in the heavy plaid lent to him for the occasion, the damp wool chafing the back of his calves. It was made for a full-grown man, Lachlan, most likely, and he was hardly that. At eight, he was small and finely made. He rubbed his frost-numbed hands together and stamped his feet to stimulate some blood flow, then glanced up at Father Ranald. He'd meant no disrespect, hadn't meant to imply his impatience for the service to be over.

'Hush, lad.' The father patted him on the head.

He swallowed, glancing at James, his newfound friend waiting by the wooden box containing his dead mother. James nodded back, wretchedly.

Lifting his gaze to the ranks of grim-faced glenfolk gathered around their priest, he recognised sorrow upon every face. 'Twas likely on his own, too, though he'd not known the dead woman. The simple act of standing small among the mourners brought back an aching memory of his family and their loss. His heart might still beat, yet 'twas empty now where once it had brimmed, back when he'd had a family of his own.

The father's voice droned in Latin, soft and edged with the lilting cadence of the Gael. He was Highland-born, as were they all. As he spoke, in Gaelic now, of the dead woman's life, he paced the ground at the head of the grave, his face betraying his despair. This woman's death was yet another tragedy to befall the humble folk of Strathavon in the past year.

A bitter wind swirled, catching the father's cassock, and it flapped about his meagre frame. He seemed not to notice, and Duncan marvelled at the man's capacity to withstand so much suffering and make no unseemly show of it. He doubted he possessed such fortitude himself. He'd never confessed the miserable truth, but in his heart, he knew it only too well. He was spineless. Whey-faced, his da might've called him, for his da had been brave. He'd fought to restore the rightful king and had died in that struggle. 'Twas true courage, that. While he, feeble in fibre and character, hadn't lifted a finger to save the mother he adored, his grandmother, or his sweet wee sister Eilish when the soldiers came.

Thinking of that day still brought a clamminess to his palms, a sickness to his heart. He'd crouched under the bank of the Crombie Water, his feet in the icy flow, listening to the roar of flaming heather, the crack of wood splitting, knowing 'twas his home that burned with his family inside. He'd heard the shouts of dragoons, his mother's screams, his baby sister crying, but fear crippled him. He trembled there till it was over, blubbing like a babby, saving his own miserable skin instead of rising and showing himself—rushing upon the soldiers with a flicker of the courage that blazed in his father's heart. He'd even wet himself. He remembered that, too, the pungent, hot stream, the shameful stain on his breeks.

Choking back a sob, he looked up into Father Ranald's face, and his heart gave a fiercely loyal thump. One day, he hoped to emulate the father, to be graced with the courage and compassion the warrior priest possessed. When he had naught and no one in the world, the priest had placed himself at further risk by taking him under his wing. He'd cherished and protected him as if he were his own, and for that, he'd be forever grateful. Supposing it took the remainder of his days, he intended to repay that kindness. 'Twas his hope by becoming a priest himself.

Shifting his gaze from the father's face, he peered into the grave. It was shallow, no more than four inches deeper than the wooden box it would contain, and even that scant hollow had been hard-won from the frozen ground. He'd not been obliged to help dig the grave and was thankful for that mercy, though the admission stirred a niggle of guilt. Fearn Innes had been kind he'd heard; gentle, like his own mother. Thoughts of his mother brought tears nipping.

As glensmen lowered the coffin into the grave, a fresh flurry of hail hammered upon the lid. Folk hunched themselves, gritting their teeth against the cold, wrapping their plaids tighter.

'Earth to earth, ashes to ashes,' the father murmured, 'dust to dust.'

At that cue, members of the bereaved family leaned forward, dropping fistfuls of frozen earth into the grave to thud like leaden snowballs on the coffin, showering earth over the letters of the woman's name and the delicate likeness of a leaf carved into the wood. The smallest of the mourners squeezed through the crush of bodies and squatted to whisper something before dropping her own handful of earth into the grave.

Rowena Innes rose to her feet and looked out over the wintery glen. He could see no tears in her eyes, although her lips had trembled as she whispered her prayer. He wondered at that. She'd cried every night since he came here. He'd heard the racking sobs she tried to smother in her pillow when she thought no one could hear. She'd done that every night, barring the one she spent on the floor beside him.

Her father nodded to her, his face set in a grim expression, and he imagined the man would take her hand, squeeze her shoulder or extend some gesture to her and her sister to show his affection for them. He did not. The nod was all she received, and she seemed to accept it.

Duncan tried to look away. He'd long been taught 'twas rude to stare, but he found his gaze drawn back to her. The poignant gravity of her expression drew his sympathy and respect. Such a pitiful sight she made, a lump began to clog his throat. Yet, there was dignity in the carriage of her head, nobility in the courage she displayed in keeping her grief so rigidly under control.

Was such hardiness nae unusual in a child her age? He imagined so, and it fascinated him—as did she. His heart gave a queer little flutter knowing 'twas only three nights ago she'd lain her wee self down beside him, and despite her heartache, had managed to soothe his worthless skin.

Looking around, he spied a clump of white flowers poking through the snow, a herald of spring and, God willing, a sign of better times to come. He bent to pick them. Snowdrops, he remembered his mother calling them, dangling little blooms with an innocent, childlike appeal. As the crowd of mourners waited in line to drop more clods of earth onto the wooden box, he held the flowers behind his back, waiting for an opportunity to press them into Rowena's hand.

Menfolk took up shovels and spades and began filling in the grave. As the timber disappeared beneath a growing pile of earth, a piper began a pibroch, and the women of the glen raised their voices in a keening lament—an undulating and sorrowful sound that again brought tears to his eyes.

He glanced at James, seeing him swallow and tighten his jaw, then flicked his gaze to Rowena. She closed her eyes, her face set in a poignant but stoic expression, and raised her voice with the other women to sing what seemed a personal coronach to the memory of her mother. It was, he thought, the bravest thing he'd ever seen.

A stab of guilt caught him, knowing he was not made the same way. He had not her strength of character, for he was, without doubt, the most craven creature that walked God's earth. Next to her, he barely deserved to draw breath. He'd howled like a dog at his own family's burial, knowing there were no recognisable bodies in the wooden boxes, only ashes and shards of blackened bone.

Father Ranald had given a shortened Mass in the heather moor by the remains of his chapel. This not only for his sake, for he'd needed bolstering under the arms by two stout cottars lest his trembling legs gave way. But owing to it being too dangerous for the faithful to gather around their priest for any reason. 'Twas an offence to keep a popish altar cloth in the home, never mind consort with a wanted Jacobite priest. Yet, there wasn't a Glenlivet cottar who wouldn't risk his life to attend the burial of his kinswomen—the family of a fallen Jacobite and one of their own.

The grave was now heaped with earth; folk flocked forward to press it down with their feet while the piper began his final touching lament. Grace fumbled for her sister's hand, her face streaked with tears, while James took her other hand, and together they raised their voices in a final moving tribute to the memory of their mother.

He was struck by how handsome the three of them were. James and Rowena, both dark-eyed and dark-haired, displayed a quality he had no name for but wished he possessed. A dignified air that spoke of natural grace, of Highland-born self-reliance. Tall and athletic in build, even though he'd barely reached ten years, James had the dark arched brows of his sister and the same intense eyes, but with a stronger, more sharply defined jaw, and his hair had a slight wave to it.

Long and silky-dark, Rowena's hair billowed in a mesmerising fashion about her shoulders. Grace was different: fairer, less exotically coloured and featured, but possessed a warm and loving nature that was difficult not to like.

Rowena reached back and caught her hair, effortlessly twisting it inside the neck of her shawl, revealing an exquisitely featured face. The sweep of her hair typically hid her face; a tragedy. Her face should never be hidden. She was beautiful with a face 'twas difficult not to look at, that perfect was it. She opened her eyes, her brows drawn in a look so earnest and sincere, he sensed she was trying her hardest to send whatever message her song conveyed up to her mother in heaven, and he should avert his gaze from such an intimate thing. Only he found he could not. He stared in open fascination at her.

'Duncan.' The father nudged his elbow and gestured with his eyes, indicating he should respectfully divert his attention elsewhere and leave the family to their private grief.

'Forgive me.' He stumbled to the side, fearing he'd behaved improperly, that his fascination with the girl had been misconstrued. The father nodded and blessed him with the sign of the cross.

With the service over, the piper led the way back to Tomachcraggen, folk falling in behind in a train of sorrow. The wailing of the women continued, albeit at a more muted level. The bereaved family took up the rear, Lachlan walking with Father Ranald and another man dressed in the garb of an exciseman. Duncan stood back to let them pass, keen to hand Rowena his gift.

As she drew level, her head bowed, he stepped forward and thrust the flowers into her clasped hands. A look of surprised confusion crossed her face, and instinctively she took the flowers and glanced up at him. He experienced a moment of doubt as she walked on, imagining he'd made some grievous error of judgement, but she turned and looked back at him, her face relaxing into something approaching a smile. It brought life to her sad eyes, and he knew he had not.

Still looking back at him, she broke from the procession, retracing her steps to where he stood at the side of the track, feeling foolish in her father's plaid. Clutching the flowers, she stretched on her toes and brushed a kiss upon his cheek, then offered him her hand. He took it, feeling the coldness even against his frost-numbed fingers. She tugged him into the train, and they took up the rear behind her father, their hands now at their sides.

As they walked together, a strange feeling swelled inside him, one he'd felt before but so long ago it took him a moment to identify. *Joy.* Though, of course, he should not, nae at a funeral. He glanced sidelong at her to find she was also looking curiously at him. He supposed he should say something, should explain himself, when she offered him a shy smile.

He'd never seen her smile, not this charming, dimpling of the cheeks. What had she to smile about? But he wished she'd do it more; her smile was a magical thing. It struck him then, when it came to this girl, no words were needed. She had no more need of words than he had a want for them, and strangely, that thought also brought him joy.

* * *

After the bone-numbing cold of trudging then standing in the frozen

34

snow at her mother's grave, the warmth of the cot-house made Rowena's nose run and her face and fingers tingle with blood. She sniffed forlornly; Mam was truly gone now. She'd tried to burn an image of her face into her memory as the coffin lid was nailed down. The last glimpse of her vanishing into the darkness.

Thinking on what Morna had told her, she knew she'd been brave. Not one tear had she shed, although holding back thon quivering spate was the hardest thing she'd ever done. Mam would be proud of her, *was* proud, she reminded herself, for she was watching over her.

The mourners had returned to the cot-house; Grace was tending to them, handing out bowls of broth while her da doled out whisky. He gave each of his offspring a measure, too. The smell of it brought tears to her eyes, and she left hers on the window ledge next to the bowl she'd found for Duncan's flowers. She needed to harden herself and sensed whisky wouldn't be her friend in that.

Remembering the puppy, she weaved through a forest of legs in search of her. She'd be fearful of all these strangers and likely hungry. Duncan said Jem needed feeding often. Crawling under the table to the hearth, she spied the puppy in Duncan's lap, wrapped in a fold of his plaid. He was feeding her the warm mixture of sheep's milk and hen's yolk Grace had concocted for her. She seemed to like it.

James motioned with his head, indicating she should find a space on the hearthstone next to Duncan. She sat down to watch him nurse the puppy. He was gentle, feeding her from a hide flask. Unsure at first, Jem seemed taken with it now. She fed greedily, eyes closed, pawing Duncan's plaid with her forefeet, the creamy liquid oozing from her mouth.

Suddenly tearful, she longed to nurse Jem too, the swelling tide of sorrow she'd struggled to hold back all day lumping in her throat. The puppy was too small to be away from her mother, was a petted runt her da said, no use to man nor beast and better drowned. Yet, hearing that only made her love Jem even more. She was Duncan's, though, and her da knew it. Anyhow, being deemed a petted runt seemed a small price to pay for escaping the drowning sack.

'Would ye like to nurse her, Rowena?' Duncan was watching her.

He said her name funny, seemed to take an age over saying it, drawing the sounds out, but he made it seem such a lovely name, she looked hopefully at him. 'Ye'd let me?'

He nodded and handed the puppy over. Their eyes met briefly, hers full of tears. When he sat back down, he continued to glance anxiously at her, and she had the feeling he wished to say something. Perhaps how sorry he was. He didn't, though, and she was glad. She needed to be brave; pity made it harder.

She wondered why he'd given her the flowers. They were to cheer her, she supposed, a brotherly gift. His thoughtfulness touched her.

Grace sat down beside her, laying her head on her shoulder. She was crying; she could feel Grace's chest convulsing and daren't look at her. They sat in silence, each sunk in their private misery.

Once fortified with whisky and broth, the mourners began to leave. Father Ranald urged them all to take care, darkness wasn't far away, the ways slippery, snow deep in places and hard with frost. But they seemed to judge they'd stayed away from their holdings long enough and needed to get home.

'Will ye stay another night, Duncan,' James asked, 'or does Father Ranald need to get away?'

Rowena looked curiously at him, wondering what he'd say.

He thought a moment. 'The father's never keen to bide anywhere fer long, but I'm hoping we'll stay another night. To make sure all's well wi' yer da,' he added by way of explanation.

James nodded, looking downcast.

As their neighbours took their leave, folk patted her on the shoulder, muttering how sorry they were, and a great many hands needed shaking. James, ever conscious of his responsibilities, went out to see folk off, fetching garrons from the byre and pressing yet more hands as Da sat bleakly at the table drinking whisky with Mister Meldrum.

John Meldrum was often at Tomachcraggen; Da trusted him. Mam had liked him, too. She'd said they were fortunate to have such a fair-minded gauger working their glen, for hadn't they all heard tales of battles between smugglers and excisemen? Of cracked heads and bloody noses, muskets and sabres, and glenfolk rotting in gaol ower unpaid duty, whole families evicted without the coin needed to pay rents. Da called Mister Meldrum his business partner, though what he meant by that, she had no notion.

When the last of their neighbours had gone, Father Ranald ushered her da and Mister Meldrum to the fire. While they fed the flames, he paced between them, fingering his crucifix, finally squatting on a stool, his robes folded under him.

'Fine though I'm certain your whisky is, Lachlan,' he said a mite curtly, 'I'm thinking ye've consumed enough. You'll not find comfort at the bottom of a glass. 'Tis the Lord ye must look to fer that.'

Her da continued to stare into his cup, and she wondered if he'd heard.

'Aye, Tomachcraggen,' John Meldrum placed his empty quaich on the floor. 'Likely, we've both had enough.' He chuckled, a genial rumbling sound. 'Though yer *uisge-beatha* does light a welcome fire in the belly.'

'Thank you, John.' The father inclined his head to the exciseman, then turned back to her da. 'We've something pressing to discuss with Duncan, have we not, Lachlan? Indeed, the rest o' the family needs to hear it.' At her da's blank expression, he added, 'Ye'll be remembering what we spoke of, Lachlan?'

She certainly remembered, even if her da did not, and sat up, Jem now dozing in her lap.

'Lachlan?'

'Aye, Father, I mind.'

'Splendid.' He turned to Duncan. 'No need to look so worried, lad. Far from it.' He hesitated, slipping on a brave face. 'I've wonderful news, especially after all today's sadness.'

Puzzled, Duncan shifted his gaze from the priest's overly beaming face to her da, staring morosely into his whisky.

'I've spoken with Lachlan here, and the man has generously agreed to give ye a home. A family, lad. Nae your own, of course, but the next best thing. You've made friends here; I've seen it myself, and it's done my heart good.'

Duncan stared at him.

'Now, dinna go looking like that; I'm not forsaking you. But ye must see life with me is no life at all. Nae fer a boy. I can give ye naught but danger, uncertainty. I know not what my future holds. Or even if I have one.'

'Ye mean,' James interrupted, 'Duncan's to live here wi' us?'

'Exactly that.'

James blinked, flicking his gaze to Duncan. His eyes widened in delight. 'But that's grand!' His mouth twitched as he tried to control his excitement, aware it was unseemly to show glee at such a time.

'Aye,' the father agreed. ''Tis grand tidings.'

'Is this right, Tomachcraggen?' John Meldrum leaned forward, staring at her da. 'Ye're taking this lad in?'

'I've agreed to it, aye.'

'And what'll the lad be doing whilst he's here?'

'He'll be helping Lachlan work the land,' Father Ranald replied. 'What else would he be doing? The same as Lachlan's son. Tending the beasts and crops. Is that not right, Lachlan?'

'And what o' the ....' The exciseman frowned, his mouth working as though his teeth had come loose.

'The what?' Father Ranald fixed him with a stern look.

'*Uisge-beatha*,' he muttered, giving the whisky its Gaelic name. 'What o' that?'

'I'd rather the lad wasn't mixed up in that.' The father frowned. 'I see no need for him to be smuggling illicit whisky, though, of course, I understand the general need for it. The government's taxes are unchristian, bent on pauperising the Highlands and her people.' He frowned, appearing to reconsider. 'Though, 'tis not fer me to say how the lad's to be raised. I'll not interfere in Lachlan's business. He's the lad's father now, at least in the day-to-day matters, and must make his own judgments. Bearing the lad's welfare in mind.'

He turned to her da. 'Ye've little to say on the matter, Lachlan? Ye've not had second thoughts, I hope?' His voice hardened, his face, too, and he rose to his feet.

'Did I say I had?'

'You've said naught, so I've little to measure your thoughts by.'

Her da looked up at the priest. 'If the lad's to bide here, he'll be needing to pay his way. In labour, in learning how things are done. Those are my conditions. And by that, I mean learning the whisky as soon as he's trusted enough and, just as important, learning to keep quiet about it. I canna hae a blabbering bairn risk my livelihood, my life forsooth, just to please you, Father. I've other bairns and other responsibilities. I've rent to pay to his grace, a roof to keep ower our heads.' He frowned into his whisky, appearing to weigh what he'd said, then rubbed at his beard. 'Beggin' yer pardon, but I mun speak plain.'

'Weel said, Tomachcraggen.' Mister Meldrum sat back.

'No, Lachlan, you're right. I see that. And I'm grateful. If a bit of smuggling's the price of a safe and loving home, then so be it.' The priest glanced over at Duncan, struggling to meet the boy's gaze, and squinted almost shame-faced at him.

'Is no one going to ask the lad what he thinks?' John Meldrum said.

All eyes turned to Duncan.

He'd paled, staring at Father Ranald, his alarm evident. He seemed to be willing the priest to guide him.

'I'd have your thoughts, lad,' said the father. 'And I wish ye to know, I'd not give ye up but that I believed 'twas for the best. For your safety and a better future.'

Duncan swallowed, looking wretched. After what seemed an age, he found his tongue.

'But I thought to stay by yer side, Father. To one day even follow ye into the priesthood.'

The father's face registered surprise. He frowned while he digested this. 'Did ye, lad?' He stared at the boy as if seeing him for the first time. 'But Scalan's reduced to ashes. My chapel, too. Where did ye imagine ye'd go fer training?'

'I hadna thought,' Duncan said vaguely. 'Other than to receive it from you.'

The priest's face crumpled before he regained mastery over it. He paced back and fore. 'I'm hardly equipped fer that. In another time, another place, who's to say, but as things now stand, wi' the Hanoverian army searching fer me ....'

'I understand. And I'm grateful fer everything ye've done fer me.' Duncan's voice trembled. 'Then afore ye leave me, might we pray thegither one last time?'

'We'll do that, lad. We'll do it now, in private. Then, afore I go, we might all pray together for a safe and decent future. One where we can each find freedom and joy in our path to the Lord.'

He put out his hand to the boy, and Duncan scrambled to his feet and followed him outside. As he passed, Rowena recognised something in his expression she was now familiar with. Signs of someone hurting but trying to be brave.

CHAPTER FIVE

WHEN FATHER RANALD had gone, Rowena helped Grace put together a makeshift bed of heather for Duncan. They placed it near the fire, heaping it with blankets. She even fashioned a nest for Jem out of a clump of wool while her da promised to build Duncan a proper bed in the morning. A box-bed with a curtain like she and Grace had, so he might pray in private or do priest-like things there if he wished. Satisfied with their efforts, she stood back, hoping he'd be pleased.

Duncan blinked, staring at his warm sleeping place as if he couldn't quite believe such luxury was solely for him. He uttered no words of thanks but hardly needed to; his eyes thanked them. He nodded tightly, his gaze moving over their faces, pitiful in his gratitude. Likely he remembered all the draughty, forgotten places he'd slept in the last few months and was mighty glad to leave all that behind. She fancied he'd be the snuggest he'd been in months and might sleep soundly now 'twas unlikely dragoons would come bursting in and seize him during the night.

She was wrong.

Through the tiny gap in the drape around her box-bed, she watched him lace his fingers together and kneel to whisper his prayers. Stroking Jem, he lay down, his face thrown into shadow by the glow of the fire. He lay on his back, staring up at the cruck frame of the roof.

'Go to sleep,' Grace whispered. ''Tis unchristian to spy upon him.'

'I'm nae spying. I want to be sure he's as comfortable as Mam would make him.'

Grace sighed. 'I know. I miss her, too. I didna mean to chide ye. Are ye ... still as sad?'

She twisted to face her sister, finding only kindness in her expression. They'd not spoken of their grief. Each had their own pain, she supposed, and no amount of talking could take it away. She nodded and lay down, turning her face away lest she should be weak and cry again.

But even lying flat, she could still see a strip of Duncan's face, the occasional flicker of his lashes as he stared at the timbers of the roof. She wondered what thoughts were turning in his head. As always, her own thoughts were with her mother.

Although she couldn't see her, she liked to think of Mam close by, perhaps aware of what was in her heart and mind. Maybe even hearing the same sounds she could hear. The ripple of the peats, the eerie shriek of a dog fox from distant Sìthean Wood. Such thoughts were a comfort. If Mam were here, she'd be fretting over Duncan, wondering if he missed the priest and the family he'd lost.

She'd hoped to watch him fall into a peaceful sleep, to feel right about at least one thing the day had brought, but her eyes grew heavy and hard to hold open, her nights of wakeful vigilance taking their toll. Only Duncan's eyes were still wide open. That his body was comfortable didn't mean his thoughts were, she supposed. 'Twould take more than a warm bed to make him feel he belonged.

* * *

When it came to constructing his bed come morning, it soon became clear Duncan was as able as her da and was used to working with wood.

'Wester Auchavaich?' Her da frowned. 'Was yer da a cottar, Duncan? A craftsman more than a herdsman or fermer?'

'A woodworker, sir, skilled in woodturning. He made bowls and chair legs, spindles, dirk-handles, but as fer land, we had little o' that. A strip fer growing food and grazing rights fer a single cow. We lived in a but-and-ben,' he added, 'though my da had a barn where he worked his lathe and kept his tools.'

'Ye'll ken naught o' malting barley, then?' Her da fixed him with a searching look. 'How whisky's made, ye ken naught o' that?'

He swallowed and shook his head. 'I've a mighty yearning to learn, though, sir. To repay.'

'Do ye?' Her da snorted. 'We'll see.'

But it soon became clear Duncan meant what he said. He was an able and willing worker, applying himself diligently to every task. One of the first chores her da gave him was gathering muck from the byre.

This was an unpopular task owing to the pungent odours released by the steaming dung. The smell made Rowena's eyes water and caught the back of her throat, but muck was precious stuff, for when spread upon the land, magical things happened. Strips of weedy ground or stubble the beasts had gnawed to the quick could become lush and green again with naught but a drop or two of rain and a layer of cattle muck.

'Twas nature's magic, Mam said. Grass grew, and cattle ate it, and, through their dung, that eaten grass became fresh grass again. Or oats, or barley, and could then become ale or whisky. 'Twas how nature worked. So, gathering muck was mighty important work. 'Twas what Mam told her whenever 'twas her turn to toss the nasty stuff on the dung heap, and it was what she told Duncan now lest he imagined her da was being unkind.

'I dinna mind,' he said. 'Someone must do it. May as well be me.'

She nodded, pleased he saw it that way. 'I could help, if ye like.'

'Have ye nae work o' yer own?'

She should be helping Grace make the blood pudding but didn't much like that job either. Grace wouldn't mind; playing at being Mam was what she liked best. She'd only get under her feet.

'I've the beasts to feed, but I could help ye first.'

He smiled shyly. 'If ye're sure.'

Taking a fork each, they began gathering the muck into one big pile.

The byre was a cold place in winter, even with the beasts there. Their steaming breath and body fluids made it damp, too, but the work soon chased the chills away. Grown warm, she pulled her hair back and secured it at her nape. Mam had known how to make it look nice; now it just did as it pleased.

She emerged from a dark tousle to find Duncan watching her. They measured each other, and she was struck again by the unusual colour of his eyes. Not green, not blue, but some pale fusion of the two. The colour of witch's hair lichen as she'd seen it hanging from old pine trees in Meilich Wood. His hair was striking too, tawny-fair with flecks of gold glinting in it. Like bracken come the end of summer.

By the time they'd finished tossing muck, the beasts were noisy in their objection to waiting so long for their feed. She murmured to them, apologising to each cow in turn. She had names for them all.

'This one's Isla.' A shaggy fringe flopped onto the cow's face, hiding her eyes and making her look comical with her horns poking out. She parted the cow's fringe so they could look each other in the eye, and the beast could see how much she loved her.

Duncan chuckled to see her so familiar with the beasts. 'Can I help wi' your chores now?' He stroked Isla's neck. 'Seems only fair.'

She nodded, pleased he'd want to.

When no grazing could be had during the long winter months, they fed the cattle on draff: the spent husks and grains left from the whisky-making. Her da spirited sacks of this valuable stuff to the cot-house from his hidden bothy, stashing them in a cave beneath the house. He said draff was evidence of whisky-smuggling. If a gauger or revenue man, a redcoat or even the factor found it, he'd be arrested and thrown in gaol. They'd serve him a fine so steep he'd never be able to pay. They'd lose their home and land, for missed rent meant an eviction notice.

Young as she was, Rowena knew all about eviction. Every glensman was afraid of it. Before she was born, her da had chiselled into the granite bedrock under the cot-house, carving out a cave for hiding malt and draff, sometimes whisky, until it was safe to smuggle it away.

She led the way back into the house.

Inside, she dragged her father's chair aside, peeling back the covering rug, then bent to lift the trapdoor beneath. Duncan raised the heavy door for her and peered into the darkness.

Working at the hearth, Grace paused and looked fearfully at them. The reason for her alarm escaped Rowena; she lit a fir-candle and made her way down the ladder, Duncan following behind.

Draff was light as feathers; she could easily climb the ladder with a sack of it over her shoulder, but she'd let Duncan do the carrying since he wished to help. At the foot of the ladder, she paused and held the candle high.

Duncan exhaled, his eyes widening, drinking in the sight that met him. Whisky barrels filled every corner, stacked to the ceiling, while a rich, bread-like aroma infused the air. An aroma Rowena was intimately familiar with; it had permeated her life since ever she could remember. In the room above, the scent was barely discernible over the smell of cooking and the smoky reek of burning peat, but down here, it was pungent and wonderful. Duncan stared at her.

'Is this all whisky? All these barrels?'

'Ankers, they're called. There's nae usually so many. Da's nae smuggled any out fer a while. He was waiting fer the babby to come.'

Her eyes pricked. The babby would never come. The wee soul had known naught but darkness, and now, still inside Mam and buried in the ground, he'd never know light. He'd never feel the wind in his face or see the glen all sap-fresh in spring, and he'd never know there'd been a family waiting to welcome him. She swallowed, praying she'd not be a weakling and cry in front of Duncan.

'Mam worried when Da was away on whisky business,' she croaked. 'He thought it best to wait till the babby came, and it's all piled up.'

He looked tenderly at her. 'I didna mean to remind ye.'

'No, I like speaking o' them. I'm aye thinking of Mam.' Glancing away, she lowered her voice. 'I sometimes imagine I see her crossing the infield, and my heart rushes, but when I look again, there's naught but an empty field. And then I fancy I hear her humming all blithesome-like, and afore I know it, I'm humming the same tune.'

In the murk of the cave, surrounded womb-like by barrels of whisky, she felt a strange closeness with her new brother. Something she'd not felt so keenly in the cold light of day. Conscious his face was now turned intently toward her, she confided, 'A'times, I'm nae so sure she is truly gone.' She drew a quick breath. Would he laugh, or did he sometimes imagine the same? 'But I didna think on the whisky. It must seem a strange sight.'

'It does. So many barrels hidden here.'

She lifted the candle a little higher. The crease was there between his brows, his eyes soft upon her face.

'God moves in mysterious ways,' he said. ''Tis what Father Ranald says. Believing ye see yer mam must be a comfort. A blessing from God. One ye should give thanks to Him fer, I'm thinking.'

She brought the candle down sharply. This had naught to do with God. But aye, he might think that. Spending so much time with Father Ranald had likely turned him half priest. She frowned and passed him a sack of draff, watching him negotiate the ladder with it on his back. He returned for more. As he retreated up the ladder, she held the candle high and clambered after him.

With the sacks laid to one side, they were lowering the trapdoor when the sound of boots being stamped of snow at the door alerted them to someone's imminent arrival. Grace drew a sharp breath, and Rowena reached for the concealing rug. Before she could drag it into place, the door burst open, admitting her father.

Flakes of snow sparkled in his beard, his cheeks and nose red with cold. Seeing them crouched before the trapdoor, he pulled up sharply, his eyes narrowing on Duncan.

'What're ye doing, lad?' His tone was cold.

'I offered to help Rowena wi' her chores,' he said in hasty explanation.

'She helped me, so I thought—'

'What?'

He swallowed, lowering his head.

'I dinna recall giving ye leave to go ferreting in my business. What's down there's nae fer you to be kenning about. 'Tis secret business I do risk my neck ower. Understood?'

He nodded.

''Tis what keeps a roof ower our heads. *Yours* too, fer ye've none other, I'm told.'

Duncan's face tightened as he met her da's wrathful glare. The door was still half-open; James was now visible, shaking the snow from his head. He stamped his feet and entered, pausing as he caught the tension in the air. Seeing them kneeling by the trapdoor, he flicked his gaze to his father, noting the glacial stare he levelled at Duncan. He chuckled.

'Rowena's nae roped ye into her chores, Duncan? Feeding the beasts is *your* job, littlin.' He grinned at her. 'Crafty mite.'

'He wanted to help.'

'And ye didna think on what's down there?' her da growled.

She swallowed, looking up at his livid face. 'I did forget.'

'Christ! Am I the only one who remembers?'

'I'm that used to seeing the whisky,' she stammered, 'I hardly notice it.' Her head throbbed as she tried to fathom why he was so angry. What did he imagine Duncan would do now he'd seen the whisky?

'He wanted to help,' she said again. 'He didna ken the whisky was there. It took him by surprise.'

'I'll wager,' chuckled James.

'God's teeth!'

Getting to her feet, she stumbled back from the trapdoor, wishing Mam were here. She'd sort this out, and with no need for a raised voice. Tearful, she looked at James. He flashed her a reassuring smile, roving with his eyes to indicate their da was making much out of nothing, then turned to face him with an amiable grin.

'She's just a bairn, Da. Duncan, too. They meant nae harm. Ye must see that?'

'Do I need my ane son telling me what I must see? I've eyes o' my own, and you're still a bairn, too.'

'I meant—'

'I ken what ye meant.'

Her father flicked his wrathful gaze over each of them in turn. 'Now see, Duncan's new here. I ken little o' him to be trusting him wi' my livelihood. Wi' my life, forsooth. It hardly matters that they meant nae harm; harm can be done whether it's meant or not. What's down there pays the rent on Tomachcraggen. Land that feeds us all, and that I, well, I love as though it were my own. Only, the land's nae mine, more's the pity.'

He removed his bonnet and hung it on the back of his chair. His agitation seemed to have eased, although his face was still rigid. He ran his fingers through his hair. 'I've worked this land all my days, but that counts fer naught. The duke owns the land, and he can put us out on a whim. Unpaid rent's a powerful whim fer any man, yet, unpaid my rent will go, if ever I'm caught and fined. Or gaoled, or shot,' he added bitterly, 'running illicit whisky. Ye see that?'

'Of course,' said James.

'Rowena?'

'I think so.'

'And you, lad?'

Duncan nodded.

'Good. You see it too, Grace?'

'Lord, aye.'

'So what's down there must never be spoken about. Specially by blabbering bairns. Could mean the end fer me.' He took a weary breath. 'Ye've lost yer mam.' He nodded, visibly deflating. ''Tis hard wi'out her, I ken, fer 'tis just as hard fer me. But if ye were to lose yer da, too, now where would ye be?' He looked at each of them in turn. 'Ye see how important it is to keep what's down there secret? 'Tisna just my life depends on yer tight lips.'

There was a shuffling of feet, a collective clearing of throats. They all nodded.

'Good. So, lad,' he urged Duncan to stand with a flick of his hand. 'The whisky must be treated wi' respect. But other than what the father's told me, I ken little o' ye. Too little to be trusting ye. Trust must be earned, and that's nae so easy to do. But should ye manage it, upon my oath, I'll show ye all there is to know o' mountain dew. *Uisge-beatha*,' he murmured. 'Mebbe I'll mak' ye a smuggler.' He gave a mirthless laugh. 'Smuggling's decent work. Dinna go thinking it's nae. Mebbe ye think we're all skulking rogues stealing from the treasury? The treasury.' He snorted. 'There's naught more treacherous than the British government and its treasury.'

He drew a long breath. 'Nay, smuggling has an honour o' its own. I've learned that. It raises me above lowly heather-lowper.' He grimaced at the offensive name given to Highlanders. 'I find that pleases me. After all, I do risk my life fer it.'

His face darkened. 'But should ye breathe a word o' this to another soul, God help me, I'll flay yer hide and fling ye oot on yer ear. I swear, there's nae a glensman the length o' Stratha'an would dare tak' ye in.'

'I promise,' Duncan stammered. 'I'll nae breathe a word. Never would I.'

'Never's a long time.'

'I swear, sir. I'll not betray yer trust.'

'Mebbe nae knowingly, but bairns can be blabbermouths.'

'I wish to learn,' he said earnestly. 'Especially the ... the honour o' it, sir.'

'Well, that's fine and dandy. 'Tis what I like to hear.' He took a step toward the trembling boy, narrowing his eyes as he measured him. Duncan inched back. Bending, he tugged the rug back over the trapdoor and dragged the chair into place.

'I could've been the factor at the door. Did any o' ye think o' that? Or some bastard redcoats come to provision themselves on our grain. Our beasts, our peat.' He threw himself into his chair. 'Times are perilous.' He indicated Duncan should sit in the chair opposite.

'Since Culloden, we've had naught but crippling taxes and rent rises.' He nodded as Duncan lowered himself gingerly into the chair. 'Designed to bring us Heiland vermin to heel. Aye, that's what they call us. But dodging those taxes is an honourable game, as well as a necessary one. Nae as noble as joining the Prince's army, I'll give ye that. I ken 'tis what yer da did.'

Duncan's face tightened.

He sighed. 'Lord knows, I'd have it otherwise, but that cause is dead. Smuggling's all that's left—something we've long done here in Stratha'an. To my mind, 'tis the most loyal, nay, the most patriotic act left to us. Efter all, illicit whisky helped fund the rising in the first place.'

Duncan's brows rose in surprise.

'Aye, 'tis why smuggling's deemed a traitorous crime, and smugglers can be shot on sight. On a whim, if the redcoats have a fancy. Murdering scum!' He spat into the fire. 'Running illicit whisky's the best way to defy those who think to rule us.'

Duncan blinked, his eyes widening. 'Ye mean, this is how ye carry on the struggle? Defy the usurper king and his barbarous army?'

Her da hooted. 'Spoken like a true Jacobite. There's nae doubting in whose company ye've spent the last few months. But aye, ye could put it that way.'

'Smuggling's an honourable crime, then? One that helps counter injustice?'

'Mebbe so, lad.' Her da laughed. 'Mebbe so. But now, to the matter in hand. Ye'll need to be punished, Rowena.'

'Fer what?' demanded James.

'Fer nae thinking. Fer showing off in front o' the lad. Fer revealing what wasna her place to reveal.'

'But, sir!' Duncan burst from his chair. 'She meant only to be kind. If someone must be punished, let it be me. 'Twas as much my fault as hers, and ....' He swallowed, conscious of the rudeness of his outburst, of her da's hardening expression. He slumped back down. 'I dinna mind a thrashing.'

Lachlan snorted. 'Fine. Ye can both go wi'out supper.' He pushed himself out of his chair and stalked to the window, stooping to peer out at the flurries of swirling snow. Following his gaze, Rowena could see a rider crossing Tomachcraggen land.

'Away and find yerselves something useful to do. I've business wi' gauger Meldrum. Ye'll see to his horse, James?'

James wrapped his plaid tighter and headed back outside.

'Off wi' ye, then. I've matters to discuss.' He shooed Duncan out of the chair. 'Give us peace.'

CHAPTER SIX

DEEMING IT WISE to leave Da and Mister Meldrum to their business, Rowena joined James outside with the others. They hooded their plaids against the cold. Duncan looked pale and shaken.

'What'll we do now?' said Grace.

Duncan glanced anxiously at Rowena. 'I'm sorry fer bringing trouble.' He frowned. 'I could try my hand at tickling trout.'

That sounded a mighty strange thing to do, but James merely raised his brows and nodded. They set off across the infield.

'Did ye think Da would thrash me?' she glanced sidelong at Duncan.

'I imagined so. He seemed that riled, but the blame was mine. I should've been content wi' my ane work. Can ye forgive me?'

'I was to blame,' she said sadly. 'I should've kent better.'

'Yer only crime was to be kind.' He smiled shyly at her. ''Tis no crime, that. Father Ranald would say 'tis a virtue.'

She blinked back, stumbling through the snow to keep up, pleased he acted like a real brother, trying to shield her from harm. If only she'd paid more heed to Grace's warning look. But without Mam, life was more confusing.

'Her crime was to nae think on the hidden whisky,' said James. 'As ye've yet to earn Da's trust, she'd nae business showing ye where 'tis hid. That was her crime. And that's why her punishment is only to go wi' out supper.' He grinned. 'Da's naught but fair.'

She nodded. As usual, James was wise and understood Da far better than her. Da was oft-times a mystery to her.

'He'll be pleased if we bring home a fat trout or salmon,' said Grace, looking dubiously ahead at the snow-choked river. 'Mister Meldrum, too.'

'Aye.' James glanced at Duncan. 'Ye've done this afore, then?'

'Och, many times.' Standing on the riverbank, he unlaced his deerskin shoes and handed them to Rowena for safekeeping, then rolled his trews to the knees.

'Fish aye face upstream so water can flow through their gills. 'Tis how they breathe. They like to lie under overhanging banks where they feel safe. 'Tis wise to sit and watch fer a while. Look fer flashes o' silver or dark shapes moving in the water and watch where they go. Ye must be patient and find their secret places afore ye go sploshing through the water like a great river-troll.'

Crossing his legs, he sat on the frozen bank, arms folded over his knees and cast his gaze across the Avon. Rowena copied him, a chill seeping into her bones. She wrapped her shawl around her legs, puzzled how Duncan never seemed to feel the cold. James and Grace sat down beside her.

The Avon was dark brown at its centre, fading to amber in the shallows and silver where it broke over rocks. She wondered at that. She'd seen it flow from Loch Avon high in the Cairngorms clear as the loch itself, brilliant like a shining sheet of metal. Mam said 'twas only after it left the rocky, treeless lands that it gained its darkness, flowing through heather bogs. 'Twas then it took its peaty colour.

Duncan had chosen a quiet stretch, the bank frost-spangled, fringed with bare alder and birch. The last spate had left an island of driftwood just feet from the bank, frozen over now. It disrupted the river's flow. She watched with growing fascination the battle between running water and the paralysing grip of ice, the frosty forms spreading from the island entrancing her with their crimpling shapes and changing hues. The steady drip from hanging ice lulled her senses.

'Ye're nae sleeping?' James quirked a brow at her. 'Ye're meant to be watching fer fish.'

'I was feeling .... ' She was going to say blessed, but how could she be? Mam was gone, and Da had just rowed with her, yet the sound of flowing water soothed, instilling a calm. 'I dinna ken,' she mumbled.

'I know what ye mean,' said Grace. ''Tis peaceful.'

'I feel it too,' said Duncan, 'whenever I'm sat by a river. Flowing water has the power to bewitch. 'Tis how a kelpie can beguile ye, fer the river's already bound ye under its spell.' He glanced at her, perhaps conscious of what he'd said and fearful he'd frightened her, but she felt no danger with her brothers by her side.

He shifted his gaze to James.

'Can I ask ye something, James?'

'Of course.'

He frowned. 'If yer da wishes to defy the authorities, and he's such a successful smuggler, why does he hold Mister Meldrum in such high regard? The man's an exciseman, paid to do the government's bidding— arresting smugglers, seizing whisky. Yet yer da shares a dram wi' him and welcomes him into his home, even be it the whisky's hid there. Is he nae taking a risk? I mean, the gauger must surely know the whisky's illegal. Made under his verra nose.'

James nodded. 'I used to wonder at that, too. All I know, and I'm nae fully trusted yet either, is John's different somehow. They have an understanding, my da and John. I dinna ken the details, only that he's involved somehow. Da trusts him. Mam did, too. She called John a gentleman thief.' He frowned. 'I suppose that still makes him a thief, but I think he warns of raids, mebbe even carries orders fer whisky to my da and the others.'

Duncan was silent while he digested this. 'He's a smuggler as well, then? In a way.'

'I once heard Mam say John's been paid ower a hundred times fer seizing the same still.' James shrugged. 'Only each time the still had been moved to a new site far from the real bothy. That way, it looked like a new find, and he could claim another seizure.'

Duncan hooted. 'He's a canny man, John Meldrum. I like his style. D'ye think yer da will teach me the whisky smuggling?'

'If he trusts ye and 'tis what ye want, I expect so. There's little coin to be made from it, mind, else we'd all be living in a palace now likes lords and ladies.' He turned to Grace and took her hand, affecting as flamboyant a bow as he could manage whilst sitting on the ground. She giggled. 'And Da wouldna be fretting every quarter-day ower where he's to find the rent coin.'

'Is it nae what *you* want, then? Striking back at our oppressors? The redcoats and their false king. A government that despises us?'

James looked uncomfortable. 'I'd rather live quiet-like, in peace and wi'out breaking the law.'

'Even knowing the laws are unjust? Designed to pauper the Highlands. To bring us to heel?'

'Mebbe, fer we canna go on fighting forever.'

'But if yer kinfolk had been ...' Duncan swallowed, lowering his voice, 'butchered by them. D'ye nae think ye might feel different? Might wish to see them pay? Even be it just by denying them their tax. Making fools o' them?' He spoke softly, but there was a vein of steel in his voice.

James regarded him soberly. 'I expect I would, aye. Ye speak well o' such things, Duncan. Did Father Ranald put these notions in yer head? Rebellious words in yer mouth?'

Duncan sat back, his face twitching. Rowena was reminded of a young fox: faithful and clever but wary of trusting.

'Father Ranald's been my guide these last few months. He's taught me …' he shook his head, the enormity perhaps hard to put into words, 'so much. I've witnessed his kindness and wished to be as kind. But mostly, 'tis his courage I admire. I would wish to be as fearless.' A muscle tightened in his cheek. 'Alas, I'm far from that.'

There was silence while they all considered this.

'A fish!' Rowena pointed. 'A big one, wi' speckled skin. It swam under the bank there. I saw it!'

'Shhh,' whispered Grace. 'Ye'll be scaring it off.'

Duncan peered over the bank, then grinned back to her. 'Well spied. A brown trout. Biggest I've seen in a long while.'

Pleased with herself, she craned forward to peek at it. Barely visible against the stony riverbed, the fish lay motionless but for a lazy movement of its tail and the fluid rise and fall of its body in the current.

Duncan moved farther down the bank and slipped his toes into the water, grimacing at the iciness. Gritting his teeth, he lowered his foot to the stony riverbed. Satisfied he'd gained a stable footing, he sank his other foot in until he was standing knee-deep in the flowing river.

'Have a care,' warned Grace. 'The current can take ye unawares.'

''Tis a perilous thing to do,' said James. 'Should ye lose yer footing ….'

An image of Duncan's stricken face flashed into Rowena's head as he lost his balance and plunged into the rushing water, arms and legs flailing. Her heart lurched.

Duncan merely nodded, slipping a hand into the water near the trout's tail.

'Is it nae freezing?' Just watching him made Rowena's fingers and toes ache.

'Numbing, but ye canna be rushing this. If I stroke her nice and gentle under the tail, she'll think my hand's just weed. Then I can work my fingers up to her belly, stroking gentle-like, and she'll go into a wee daydream.' He reached his hand down a little farther.

Peering over the bank, she tried to imagine what was happening under the fish.

'There now,' he soothed, 'let my fingers sing ye a wee lullaby. Ye're a beauty. Feeling sleepy, aye?' His voice took on a tranquil rhythm as if calming a fretful child. 'Have ye a wee itch needs a-scratching?'

She giggled. 'Why does it nae just swim away?'

'I'm making her drowsy, numbing her wi' my fingers. She's nae thinking fearful fishy thoughts o' poachers and pike; she's dozing all dream-like. She's forgotten about fleeing.'

'Ye're a spell-weaver,' murmured Grace, and he smiled up shyly at her.

Nodding to Rowena, he reached out with his other arm, indicating she should push his sleeve up. He slipped that hand under the water, too. Still stroking the trout's belly, he inched his fingers toward its gills. 'Bonny lass,' he murmured. 'Such a bonny lass. Ye'll make us a fine supper.'

'Nae you and Rowena,' Grace pointed out. 'Ye've to go wi' out.'

He acknowledged this with a grim nod, gritting his teeth as a fresh assault of icy water stung this arm too.

'Yer hands must be numb,' observed James. 'Thundering hell!' He leapt to his feet as a shower of icy water splattered him. An enormous fish landed on the bank beside him, thrashing frantically amongst the frozen undergrowth.

Rowena shrieked, dodging out of its way as it writhed toward her.

'Rowena!' shouted Duncan. 'Dinna let it get away!'

She ran back, crouching, arms wide, trying to stop the flailing fish from plunging back into the river.

'Faith!' squealed Grace, leaping out of its way.

Only James had his wits about him. Grabbing a length of driftwood, he ran at the fish, delivering a bone-crushing whack to its head. It lay motionless in the deergrass, one glazed eye staring up.

Rowena bent over it, feeling guilty the creature's life had ended so abruptly. 'I'm sorry,' she whispered. She stroked its cold underbelly as Duncan had done only seconds before. Da would think her soft, but not Mam. Mam always said,'twasna a weakness, pity, but a blessed gift; she'd have understood. A lump filled her throat. Why did God have to take her? Then she remembered Mam wasn't gone. Souls can never die. She was close by, watching over her from behind some half-open door.

She dried her tears. If feeling sad about the ending of a life was a gift, she was glad she had that gift. Her heart beat a little lighter.

Soaked and shivering, Duncan grinned at her from the river.

'Well done!' James reached down to help him onto the bank. 'Ye made that look mighty easy.'

Duncan beamed, grasping James' hand, and was scrambling up the banking when a piercing whistle from the far side made him stumble.

Looking up, Rowena froze in alarm. Motionless among the alder of the far bank, mounted and armed, a detachment of dragoons stared across at them.

'What have you there?' one of them shouted. He drew his sword. Gesturing for the others to follow, he urged his mount into the river.

She gasped and scrambled to her feet, backing away from the fish. More mounted men followed the first into the water. They surged toward them, churning the water to a muddy froth.

'Saints preserve us!' Grace glanced around for somewhere to hide.

'Dinna run,' James warned her. 'Dinna give them an excuse to ride ye down.'

Ashen-faced, she stumbled toward Rowena, and they huddled together. 'Lord, save us,' she whispered.

''Twill be all right,' Rowena soothed. 'We've done naught wrong, have we?'

Duncan hauled himself out of the river, shivering but looking for all the world as if he intended to defend his fish. He made a bedraggled sight: bony arms poking from dripping sleeves, sodden trews rolled to reveal blue-tinged legs. Keeping his gaze firmly on the approaching horsemen, he stood his ground, his fists bunched at his side.

The soldiers circled him, flattening the grass in a thunder of hooves, whistling to each other as they caught sight of the enormous fish. Still brandishing his sword, the leader brought his horse to a halt.

'What's this, boy?' He prodded the dead fish with the point of his sword. 'A spot of poaching, eh? To whom does this beauty belong?'

Rowena looked blankly at James; the man's clipped English words were beyond her understanding.

Duncan shrugged. 'It's mine. I caught it.'

'Did you, now? Well, I didn't ask who caught it, I asked who it belonged to. Hardly the same thing. Entire worlds apart, I imagine.' He glanced at his men and laughed bullishly. 'I very much doubt this magnificent creature belongs to you. So, I ask again, to whom does it belong?'

Thrown by this, Duncan glanced at James, who shook his head, just as mystified.

'I'll have an answer.'

Swallowing, Duncan lowered his head.

'I'll have it now.'

Duncan's jaw tightened.

'Damn it, you understand English perfectly well. You just spoke it, you little savage! Private Ross.' He turned to his men, singling out a younger man. 'Translate for the wretch.'

'Sir.' The private leant forward in the saddle. 'Now, see here.' Frowning, he lapsed into Gaelic. 'The fish isna yours, lad, so who would it be belonging to? Better answer sharpish, Lieutenant Hardwick's nae accustomed to being kept waiting.'

Understanding, at last, Rowena threw the man a puzzled look. Fish didn't *belong* to anyone; everyone knew that. They were just there, free creatures, same as the deer on the hill and the birds in the sky. They were there for the taking if you could catch one. 'Twas well understood, that. So why did this dragoon nae understand? Wishing to spare Duncan further humiliation and thinking the man a mite dim, she stepped forward.

'The fish just belongs to the river,' she blurted. 'The A'an. 'Twas just now swimming aboot in the A'an.'

The young dragoon laughed explosively, then translated for the others. They sniggered too, glancing uneasily at Hardwick.

Lieutenant Hardwick's face darkened with rage. He swung down from his mount; three strides took him to her side. 'Insolent little heather-rat!' He slapped her face so hard the blow sent her reeling into the long grass.

Grace gasped, and James ran to help her up. 'Best say naught,' he whispered. ''Tis mighty easy to rile these devils.'

She staggered to her feet, her cheek smarting. Tears welled; she choked them back, half hiding behind James. What had she said to anger the devil?

A strange growling had started. Peeking around James, she realised it was coming from Duncan. Flushed and trembling, he glared at the lieutenant. 'She's a child,' he choked. 'She knows not your meaning. Look at her; she's five years old. Folk hereabouts take what they can catch. 'Tis how it's always been.'

'Is it?' Hardwick rounded on him. 'Then little wonder the inhabitants of these lawless glens are such rebellious savages. This land, this river,' he pointed with his sword, 'belong to someone. Your laird. And so, therefore, does all that comes from it.'

His meaning at last apparent, Duncan frowned. 'The land belongs to the Duke of Gordon. But as for the fish in the river, they just belong to whoever can catch them.'

'That's where you're wrong,' Hardwick snapped. 'I think you'll find if the land belongs to his grace, then so does the river and all that swims in it. That,' he again thrust his sword at the dead fish, 'is stolen property. I daresay the penalty for poaching hereabouts is a capital one.'

Duncan paled. 'I can hardly put it back.'

Rowena stared open-mouthed at Duncan. Never had she heard him speak so much. And in a foreign tongue to the brute who hit her. He was glaring at his feet now, a vein throbbing in his neck. Her chest swelled. He must be brave. Were these nae dragoons like the ones who'd killed his family?

But Hardwick seemed to have forgotten Duncan. 'So, this is Gordon land,' he mused. 'The Cock o' the North. As I recall, the duke's loyalty has been much debated. He fought for the Pretender at Sherriffmuir, then declared for the king. His brother's a notorious Jacobite. In hiding in France, they say. He raised two regiments from these very lands, so how loyal can that make the duke?' He turned back to his men. 'Corporal Langton.'

'Sir.'

'Take the fish. We'll call it a gesture of loyalty from his grace to His Majesty's forces garrisoned in his rebellious lands. It'll make a fine centre-piece for tonight's dinner.' He chuckled. 'Have the young poacher string it through the gills and tie it to the back of your saddle. If I'm expected to civilise these primitives, I might at least do it on decent fare.' He sheathed his sword and remounted, turning his back on Duncan, evidently done with him.

The corporal got down and shoved Duncan toward a clump of deer-grass. 'Get to it.'

He stumbled and almost fell, but righted himself and stood his ground.

'Duncan,' James hissed.

Private Ross leant down from the saddle. ''Twill go better fer ye, lad,' he said in Gaelic. 'If ye do as yer bid.'

Duncan glanced at James for direction. He was trembling, resentment etched upon his face. Handing his hard-won fish over was clearly the last thing he wished to do.

'*Duncan.*' James lowered his voice. 'Ye must. We need no trouble from the redcoats. Nor will Da thank ye fer bringing it. Ye see that, aye?'

He nodded bitterly, then bent to gather strips of deergrass for trussing the fish, managing to secure it to the back of the corporal's saddle without ever making eye contact with him. He stood back.

'Good decision,' muttered Langton.

Hardwick swept Duncan a mocking bow, and the company rode off through the trees.

No one spoke as they watched them go. When they'd vanished from sight, Duncan turned to Rowena. 'Are ye all right?'

She nodded, exploring her hot cheek with her fingers.

He continued to study her, appearing to satisfy himself she was unharmed, then cast his gaze back over the now muddy river. 'We'll need to find another stretch.'

'Ye dinna mean to get back in the freezing water?' James looked incredulously at him.

'I do, and I'll nae be coming out till I have us another fish.'

'But ....' James shook his head. 'Ye heard what thon redcoat said.'

Duncan shrugged, moving off upriver. Exchanging uneasy looks, they followed.

'Where did ye learn the redcoat's tongue, Duncan? The Inglis?' asked James. 'Was that Father Ranald, too?'

'Aye, he taught me to read from the bible. He was fond o' saying 'tis good to know what yer enemies are saying since ye might need to defend yerself one day. Wi' words, he meant. He taught me more than I imagined, fer I kent what those divils were saying.' He exhaled. 'Father Ranald's a thousand times more a man than thon strutting scoundrel. Striking a lass,' he shook his head. 'What kind o' man does that?'

They found another stretch of river, and Duncan again removed his shoes and settled down to watch for fish. Rowena glanced sidelong at him, seeing the determination in his face. She couldn't help wondering what kind of man he'd become. A priest like Father Ranald? Would he go to war? Talk of purifying flames? She hoped not. He yearned to one day be as fearless as the father, yet already he was braver than anyone she knew.

* * *

Good to his word, Duncan managed to guddle another trout, smaller than the first but big enough to make a decent supper. Grace later cooked it to perfection, or so Rowena judged by the aroma that wafted from the hearth. She and Duncan were made to sit at the table and watch it being eaten, their mouths watering.

Sitting next to her, his belly rumbling, Duncan said grace when her da, forgetful with whisky, neglected to say it and would've begun eating without first thanking God for their bounty.

Her da made no great fuss over the unexpected feast other than to grunt his approval whilst spooning great chunks of succulent trout flesh into his mouth. On hearing of their encounter with the British soldiers, he took a moment to examine her face, swearing under his breath at the bruises forming. He traded looks with John Meldrum, then glanced a mite curiously at Duncan.

'A grand feast ye've given us, Duncan.' Mister Meldrum raised his whisky in salute. 'Pity ye canna be sharing it.'

Later that night, hidden by the curtain around their box-bed, Grace managed to smuggle a dry bannock to Rowena.

'Did ye save some fer Duncan?' she whispered as she devoured it.

'Aye, but he wouldna take it. Said he'd been given a punishment and likely deserved it. He'd try to learn from it.'

'Oh.' She choked on what was left of hers, only her empty belly told her she shouldn't be too hasty in handing it back.

'I disturbed him praying,' Grace added. 'Fer guidance from the Lord fer harbouring murderous thoughts about thon red-backed divils.'

CHAPTER SEVEN

AS THE WEEKS passed, Strathavon moved slowly into *earrach,* spring. The days lengthened, snow and frost loosened their grip, and every day Rowena noticed something new. Fresh green growth on the birch trees, tiny clover shoots unfurling amongst the rough pastures, and yellow buds on the whin bushes. Daily, geese flew overhead, leaving the Highlands for their summer homes in far-flung northern lands. Lands Rowena knew only by fabled names like *Innis Tile* and *A' Ghraonlainn*, and she knew not if these were real places or faery lands.

The geese were hard to miss as they flew over. They alerted even the most inattentive with their bleating cries, creating a shimmering tide of sound as they flew in merging thread-like skeins. Mam had loved the sound; it meant summer was nearly here, and everywhere there were catkins. They budded on the goat willow, downy and silver-soft, and on the alder groves by the river in tiny cones and dangling yellow baubles.

Perhaps best of all, Da was mighty busy and had little time to be noticing where she wandered. He spent almost every daylight hour breaking ground, spreading muck and sowing oats and barley. And almost every evening planning his next smuggling trip.

After dark, menfolk came, and there was much talking. At first, her da took them down to the cave to do their planning, but more and more, he entertained them at the hearth as was his way before Duncan came. He was trusting him more, she supposed. The tracks and drover's routes were free of snow now. 'Twas possible to lead a laden train of garrons out of the glen to buyers in the south, though 'twas mighty dangerous to do so.

Since the rising, soldiers were everywhere, lurking behind every tree, according to her da.

Now the snow had retreated, and the land was renewing itself, she longed to be in wild places searching for signs of her mother. During the dark winter days, it had been impossible to get away. They all lived atop each other, or so it felt. 'Twas hard to find a place to feel sad or angry, two feelings that jostled inside her, never mind find a place where she might sense her mother's presence.

As she'd grieved, she'd withdrawn into herself, searching for a reason why her mother had been taken. But always it came down to God's will, and however hard she searched for someone to blame, she could only ever find God. Duncan told her God loved her, and he seemed to believe it, for his eyes shone, and he spoke that earnestly, 'twas as if he professed that love to her himself. Yet, more and more, she hated God.

Now spring was finally here, she longed to lie in the heather gazing up at the scudding clouds, watching for the beating wings of an osprey flying over with a fish as big as Duncan's tickled trout in its talons. Wondrous things Mam had shown her every spring but that she'd need to discover for herself now.

Most of all, she longed for a secret place of her own. A place to conjure her mother's face and scent, the touch of her hand. Where she might howl and kick rocks, tear up bracken, or just curl down small and let her sorrow choke her with its tears.

Da still muttered whenever he found her tearful, and she'd learned to hide her tears. She was ower-sensitive, he said, and the others seemed to agree, but 'twas fear ate away at her. Losing those she loved and needed, being abandoned; that fear consumed her. Her chest would tighten, and she'd struggled to breathe. Only, who could she tell? They'd just say she must be brave, must grow up quick.

She tried that hard to be brave, she supposed she must outwardly appear so. Yet fear tightened its cords. 'Twas a failing she must overcome. Only, how? The how of it was not yet clear.

Her da toiled hard from dawn to dusk, working James and Duncan just as hard. Duncan, he tasked with cutting peat from the peat bank at Fèith Musach. Here they cut the fuel that kept their hearth fire burning. That fire was never allowed to go out. Letting it die meant dire things would happen.

Cutting peat was back-breaking work for a grown man, never heed a boy, but her da and James were busy elsewhere, Grace, too. So, every morning, she rose early and headed to Fèith Musach with Duncan, Jem bounding at their heels. Duncan did the heavy work, carving long cubes of wet peat from the living bank with a peat-iron while she lifted them onto the top and laid them out to dry.

If the rain stayed away, she'd build them into *cas bhic*, little feet, in a week or two; three peats propped against each other with a fourth balanced on the top. Stacking them that way helped them dry quicker. Wet peat never burned well. Same as peat cut when the moon was waxing; that never burned right either.

'Twas glorious to be outside after the long winter trapped inside the cot-house, and even better to see Jem gambling and frolicking alongside them. Jem had grown so much, 'twas hard to believe she was the same wobbly wee pup who only a few months ago could barely climb onto Duncan's lap. Now she could run and run.

She especially loved to run through heather where she'd bound then halt, body quivering, pointing with her nose to some imaginary creature hidden in the heather. Then off she'd sprint, ears flapping and tongue lolling, wearing the funniest expression. But she was still a baby and tired quick. Then she'd sit beside Duncan, tilting her head at him with such a wistful look, 'twas plain who she loved most in the world. Rowena didn't mind; who else did Duncan have?

Duncan toiled hard, cutting close to a thousand peats a day, almost as many as James could cut. Most days, he was too weary to talk, but he spoke little anyway, and she didn't mind. He wanted to prove his worth. She understood.

Others were working the peat bank, too; every tenant was allocated a share of the moss and 'twas the time of year for cutting peat. She recognised the McHardys, wiry, bearded men who argued a lot, but they were working the far side of the moss. Closer, the Gordons of Craigduthel and the MacRaes toiled, neighbours and fellow whisky smugglers. They seemed to spend a deal of time observing Duncan, judging his performance, and she wondered what they made of him. He might be small, but he laboured just as hard.

Perhaps conscious of her gaze upon him, he laid his peat-iron down and rubbed his back. 'We'll stop a while, will we?' He smiled shyly. 'Have some fare?'

She nodded and helped him onto the bank, and they sat together, sharing the parcel of food Grace had packed for them. 'Twas only buttered bannocks and cheese and a flask of watery ale, but they were glad of it. She lay back in the heather and let the peace of the place settle upon her. It smelled woody and fresh with a hint of earthiness, and she watched the clouds for a while, enjoying the feel of weak sunshine on her face.

Duncan lay back, too, Jem flopping down beside him, resting her head on his stomach so he could ruffle her ears. Within moments, the young setter was snoring. 'Twas easy being in Duncan's company, it felt more and more natural to be so. Though she'd not known him long, she felt comfortable with him. She thought to sit up and tell him so but felt that languorous, she half dreamed she'd done so, and within a few moments, 'twas too late. From his breathing, she could tell Duncan was sleeping, too.

Turning on her side, she propped her head in her hand to watch him. He intrigued her, yet rarely could she observe him so closely without appearing rude. When he slept, there was no crease between his brows, and he seemed even younger, his face sensitive, vulnerable. How old might he be? Eight, she supposed, though he seemed older, but that was because he was wise. From where did his wisdom come? From the tragedy that took his family? Or from Father Ranald? That thought disturbed her. 'Twas just part of him, she decided; as essential to him as his faith.

She lifted her gaze to the hills in the distance, waiting for her focus to settle. They were hazy and dark, but something on the side of the nearest hill caught her eye. She squinted to see it better. A stone. One that stood upright and looked oddly familiar.

A queer feeling came over her, a quivering excitement, for she knew that stone. Or rather, Mam had known it. Mam had taken her there, and they'd whispered to the ancient slab, pressing their fingers into the grooves cut into its surface, tracing the knotted shapes they made. Mam had asked the spirits of the stone to protect Da and the whisky, for since the battle to end all at Culloden, the rents had been sore.

She blinked, her eyes watering, reliving the wonder of that day, and a strong sense of her mother came upon her. She shivered with longing. Shielding her eyes with her hands, she got to her feet to better see the hill and its stone. How best to reach it?

Duncan didn't even stir as she crept away, and although Jem lifted her head and looked at her, when Duncan failed to move, she flopped back down with a little sigh. Before she knew it, she'd skirted the peat moss in search of a trail to follow, a winding deer track, for the red deer lived up in the hills. They only came down to lower, more dangerous ground when snow and storms forced them. If she could find one of their trails, she might reach the stone and spend time there, feeling for Mam's lingering spirit. She could be back before Duncan even missed her.

Quickening her pace, she almost tripped over the heather in her eagerness and left the moor behind, entering an area of scattered trees. They were pines mainly, mingled with birch and rowan and thick with bracken. Pressing through the unfurling fronds, she began to climb, searching for one of the many tracks left by deer.

Finding one, she left the trees behind as the soil thinned and great spurs of weathered schist broke through the hillside. She grew hot and breathless, shifting her shawl from her shoulders to her waist where it hampered her less. Gradually, the going became easier as the heather thinned and smaller creeping plants took their place. Lush green mosses, fragrant thyme and cowberry were tenacious plants that sat tight to the ground and hardly minded if she crushed them; they'd weathered far worse.

She stopped to check her position to the stone, thinking she'd lost it, but no, 'twas still there, above her to the right. She left the track and scrambled over rocks, feeling like a mountain goat, then halted with a gasp as the stone reared up in front of her. She stepped back, almost losing her balance as the wonder of it struck her.

It rose straight from the ground, as tall as her but unlike any stone she'd seen before. Although chiselled from a natural crag, there was naught natural about this stone. People had set it here, not nature—long ago, mysterious folk with some intention in mind. 'Twas no simple task to mount such a tablet on the side of a hill. They'd skilfully carved the stone, using it to convey some message or meaning, one that escaped her and was perhaps lost now to the world. But the beauty of their work, the mystery and wonder, that she understood.

Creatures were depicted, a boar and an eagle, and another beast, one that made her shiver, for she'd never seen a real one and hoped never to. But she knew 'twas a kelpie. There were images of mounted horsemen, all entwined with intricate knotted designs that were a joy to look upon.

She sank to her knees, remembering Mam's eyes that day—dark with wonder—and the hushed voice she'd used. She'd been respectful of this weathered stone that centuries of mountain gales had barely troubled, regardful of those who'd carved and set it here, the import they'd placed upon it, whatever its meaning.

She remembered it had been a day of soft breezes, the scent of gorse flowers coming to them, as it did now. She breathed in deeply. The heady perfume permeated the mountain air, though strangely, she'd not noticed it before.

Reaching out, she touched the stone, letting her fingers follow the markings, a mounting joy growing inside her. She closed her eyes, and a sense of her mother came powerfully upon her. The air seemed to pulse with her presence, her gentleness. She trembled with longing.

Remembering Morna's advice, she tried to still her mind, to reach for a sense of peace and found she could do so easily. The wonder of the place seemed to chase all cares from her heart. Morna had urged her to visit wild places, and this was such a place. Perhaps the *draoidh* she'd spoken of, the lore-keepers, maybe they had even carved this stone. Tingling with kindred feeling, a strong sense of connection with the stone, and, through it, with her mother filled her heart.

Morna said 'twas as if Mam were behind a door that was only half shut. She sensed that door stood open here, on this hill, on this day, and that it had somehow drawn her here. Now it swung open even wider. She sat back on her heels and clasped her hands together.

'Mam,' she whispered. 'Please, dinna be gone. Stay aside me. I need ye. I'm afraid wi'out ye, and I dinna ken how to harden myself. I miss ye.'

She'd not even said goodbye to her mother, for she'd not known Mam was dying. Even at the last moment, she'd not understood. No one had explained. Sadness at that brought tears, and her insides twisted. Yet Mam wasn't gone. She was in wild places, as Morna said.

Shivering with joy, she settled down among the thyme and the cowberry.

* * *

It was an oystercatcher's pip-pip cry that woke Jem. With a bark, she was after it, giving chase until the bird took to the air, piping its alarm with shrill, piercing cries. Duncan sat up and blinked, experiencing a moment of guilt as he realised he'd been sleeping. He turned to apologise to Rowena, but she was no longer lying beside him. Glancing around, he got to his feet. There was naught where she'd been but an empty square of linen and a few crumbs.

He scanned the peat moss, noting the McHardy men at the far side, no longer feuding but sitting companionably, drinking what he took for ale from a shared flask. The others were still there, too, MacRaes he thought, cutting and laying out peats, but there was no young lass with them.

He span around, alarm pricking. She'd vanished into thin air. He tried to conceive a sequence of events that might prompt her to leave his side without telling him, without even waking him, but could think of naught. Had something befallen her whilst he, work-shy sluggard, slumbered the day away?

Trawling the moor for clues, he called Jem to heel and approached the MacRaes. What if soldiers had taken her? A sickening image of the red-backed devils dragging her away flashed into his head, and he heard again the shouts of dragoons ringing his home. His mouth dried. Without meaning to, he summoned one of the images that so tormented his dreams: Father Ranald's face awash with tears, telling him what he already knew—his family were dead. His mother, even wee Eilish, who'd spent her short life toddling after him. He choked back a sob.

The MacRae men squinted suspiciously at him, exchanging baffled looks.

'Aye, lad?' A grizzled old man in threadbare plaid addressed him.

He rubbed his forehead. 'The young lass who was here.' He gave a rough approximation of her height with his hand. 'Beggin' yer pardon, but d'ye ken where she might be?' He glanced from one blank face to another. 'She was here, and then ....' He swallowed.

They frowned, looked him up and down, likely thinking him deranged, not to mention rude. He'd not even introduced himself.

'And ye might be?'

'Forgive me. Duncan Forbes. I bide at Tomachcraggen. At least, I do now. Wi' Lachlan Innes and his family. He took me in after—'

'I ken who he is.' This was from one of the younger men. 'He's the orphan lad Father Ranald took under his wing.'

He nodded wretchedly.

They eyed him darkly, muttering amongst themselves, then one by one fell silent as each man appeared to find his own feet inordinately interesting. The old man cleared his throat. He seemed to be the acknowledged spokesman.

'Are ye now?' He moved in closer, peering into his face, a spark of some emotion softening his rheumy eyes. 'Then I'm michty glad to be makin' yer acquaintance.' He extended a wizened hand. 'Alexander MacRae, at yer service.'

He took the proffered hand and let his own be powerfully squeezed. There were more hands to be shaken and a deal of pressing upon his shoulders accompanied by much muttering and head shaking. They recited their names: Alexander and Dougal, Iain and Andrew, all of them MacRaes, so many he hadn't a hope of remembering them all. Finally, it dawned upon him they were attempting to express pity and shared feeling. Although he was only a boy, he belonged to the strath, was a fellow worker of the soil, son of a fallen Jacobite. His suffering and loss humbled them. Perhaps they even shared it, for his was not the only home burned during the Hanoverian army's rampage through these lands. Nor was his da the only man of the glen to die in support of their true king.

Knowing himself to be wholly unworthy of their pity, he swallowed, wanting to direct their attention away from his wretchedness and back to Rowena but not wishing to appear rude or diminish their kindness.

'I'm pleased to be making yours.' He cleared his throat. 'The thing is, I dinna ken what's become o' Rowena. I fell asleep, I confess, and when I woke ....' He glanced around in the forlorn hope she might have mysteriously reappeared. 'She was gone. I'm wondering if ye saw her leave? Any o' ye?'

Alexander MacRae shook his head. 'Nay, lad, but—'

'I did,' blurted the youngest of them, a red-haired lad, a similar age to himself although taller and more solidly made. 'She went thon wey.' He pointed in the rough direction of the nearest range of hills.

'Ye're sure?' A wave of relief swept over him.

'Toward Carn Liath.'

One of the others turned on the lad. 'And how d'ye nae say afore, Malcolm? Ye great neep.'

Malcolm bristled, less than overjoyed at being likened to a turnip. 'I didna ken 'twas so important, Uncle Iain.'

Iain MacRae exhaled irritably. 'So, ye imagined the lass auld enough to be wandering off on her own?'

Malcolm shrugged with an aggrieved expression. 'I niver gave it much thocht. And I only heeded her in the first place,' he muttered in an injured tone, 'on account o' she was bonny and did catch my eye.'

'Ach, Malcolm!'

'Only, she didna *wander*,' he piped indignantly. 'She seemed to ken where she was going.'

'Ye feather-heided gowk. What've I telt ye aboot paying heed to what's going on aboot ye whilst we're all grafting doon there?' Iain nodded at the lower bank. 'What if redcoats had come upon us? Would ye've even noticed?'

'Course I would,' he muttered. 'But I'm nae thon lassie's keeper.'

'So,' Duncan interjected. He caught the boy by the sleeve, wishing to press a degree of urgency upon him. 'She went toward that hill?' He pointed in the direction the boy had indicated.

'Aye, in a fair haste.'

He stared at the hill. Why would she do that? But he could think of no logical reason. Jem whined at his feet, catching a sense of his disquiet, and he squatted down to her. 'Where is she, Jem? Where's Rowena?'

She barked and hared off, halting to look back expectantly at him, tongue lolling. Whining, she lolloped back.

'Mebbe the young setter kens,' observed old Alexander MacRae.

He blinked; maybe she did. 'Come on, Jem. Let's find her!'

'Wait!' cried Iain. 'Afore ye go takin' off, d'ye ken what thon hill is? The closest one? And mair important, d'ye ken what day the morrow is?'

He frowned and shook his head.

Men from the next section of peat moss were now making their way over, wearing inquisitive expressions. They'd likely observed his puzzling behaviour and the MacRaes making a fuss of him and wished to satisfy their curiosity. He groaned inwardly. Gordons from Craigduthel, he remembered Rowena calling them.

'Alec?' A gaunt, sandy-haired man in his middle years addressed Alexander MacRae. 'Is sumhin wrong?'

'Thon lad means to climb Carn Liath.' Malcolm MacRae pointed an accusing finger at him. 'On the eve o' Beltane, and wi' naught but a puppy to protect him from witches and faeryfolk!' His mouth gaped open, so clearly unthinkable was the notion.

The man turned to Duncan with raised brows. It was Donald Gordon, the herdsman who'd given him Jem. He smiled back feebly.

While Iain explained the situation to the Gordon men, the McHardies also made their way over, reluctant to be left out of whatever was afoot. He fidgeted, anxious to be searching for Rowena. If dragoons found her, what might they do? His imagination was more than willing to supply lurid answers. He struggled to thrust the images away, his stomach churning.

'Nay, lad.' Donald Gordon gave him a pitying look. 'Ye canna be doing that. 'Tis no common hill, Carn Liath, but a faeryhill. Dangerous fer the unwary at any time o' year, but on the eve o' Beltane, and wi' the rite due to go ahead later the night.' He sucked his breath in through his teeth, making a hissing sound that conveyed the foolhardiness of such a venture. 'The brushwood's already in place around the great stone on the crown o' the hill, and all's ready. 'Tis no time to be going there alone. Ye mustna be doing that.'

'But I need to find Rowena.'

'I'll wager she's nae gone far. I'd come wi' ye and look fer her, only,' he shuddered, glancing up at the hill, grey and part-hidden in cloud. ''Tis wise to leave the place till later when we'll all be there fer the ritual. On the eve o' Beltane, the veil atween realms is thin. Witches are flying; all manner o' unchancy beings are abroad.'

He'd heard of such things, he knew of Beltane, but he couldn't just leave Rowena to whatever was up there. He'd find her, no matter what hill she'd chosen to climb, and no matter her reason.

Frowning, he thought of all the nights his da had attended the Beltane rite. He'd deemed participation necessary. Those who shunned the hilltop were left unprotected. The custom was age-old, a pagan practice Father Ranald vehemently condemned. Every year upon the crown of Carn Liath, the grey mount, on the eve of the first day of May, a sinful, fornicating ritual was enacted. One deemed ever more needful now the rentals were fierce, and the word eviction lingered on every tongue.

The rite would hopefully enlist the help of the *sithiche*, the faeryfolk, safeguarding crops and beasts over the coming year. Maybe even protecting the whisky, something that now interested him greatly. Yet, how could it? 'Twas a depraved act. Having faith in the Lord, praying and living a decent life, working hard and supporting the true king, those were the righteous paths to all good fortune in life. 'Twas what Father Ranald preached, and the father knew better than most. Superstitions were for the ignorant and ungodly.

'I trust the Lord will protect me,' he muttered. 'I'll go alone.' Whistling to Jem, he turned toward the hill.

CHAPTER EIGHT

'THEN KEEP YER wits aboot ye,' Donald called after him.

He turned back.

'Trust nae one and naught, fer the *sithiche* can fool even the wariest and can take the guise o' hare or deer, even rock. And beware the green hummock; the sward that's greener than the rest. 'Tis what marks the entrance to their underground dwellings. Faeryland's nae a place ye can easily return from.'

He nodded, knowing this was well-meant. As he turned away, Malcolm MacRae broke from the group of watching men and sprinted to a nearby copse. Leaping up, he caught the lowest bough of a sapling and swung from it until it snapped off with a crack. Picking himself up, he brought the branch over and awkwardly held it out.

'Rowan. To protect against witches and evil.' Frowning, he indicated Duncan should take it. 'I didna mean to mock ye. I'm thinking ye're brave. Foolish, but brave. I hope ye find the lass, and I hope ye can forgive me.'

At a loss over what to say, he took the branch.

Malcolm nodded, appearing satisfied, then returned to his kinsmen, his red hair a beacon amongst the grey and darker heads.

Clutching the branch, Duncan again turned to go.

'We'll work yer stretch o' peat fer ye,' Donald called after him. 'Aye, lads?'

There was a rumble of agreement, then Iain MacRae shouted, ''Twill be as if ye've niver lain yer peat-iron doon, lad. Ye hae my word.'

Touched by the men's gesture, he raised a hand in salute, then broke into a run, a sob catching in his throat. He was undeserving of such gallantry. He could barely look these men in the eye, especially Malcolm, who believed him brave. *Brave*? But then, Malcolm MacRae knew little of him. If he knew the truth, he'd not waste breath upon him.

He lengthened his strides, quickly putting distance between his worthless skin and the generous spirits of the men he'd left behind, hoping to numb his guilt with the burn of muscle and fiery pump of lungs.

If Rowena had wandered up a faeryhill on the eve of Beltane, her life might be in danger. Certainly, her soul would be. He grew cold and clammy thinking of such a thing. 'Come on,' he urged Jem. 'We need to find her.'

But it quickly became apparent Alexander MacRae was right; Jem did seem to know where Rowena had gone. Following her nose, she bounded off, barking with excitement. He sprinted after her, letting her decide their course, only thinking to alter her path should she veer off in the wrong direction chasing ptarmigan or grouse. But she stayed true.

When they reached the foot of Carn Liath, he faltered, an ill feeling creeping over him. The hilltop ritual offended him, even though he was not entirely sure what it entailed. But Father Ranald had been ferocious in his condemnation. He remembered standing in a clearing in the woods on Easter Sunday, newly orphaned and under the father's care, listening to the priest's damning sermon on the subject.

The Beltane rite was pagan, from a time before Christ. It could unleash lustful thoughts and appetites, all manner of carnality that might play out in the darkness. Lit by a fiery ring of brushwood and enacted to the skirl of pipes and beat of drum, he understood a fornicating beast would come amongst the folk. And then anything might happen, but 'twould likely be something shameful.

As he started to climb, the wind rose, and he wrapped his plaid tighter. The sky had darkened, and the wind made a plaintive howling sound, something he was none too keen upon. How wolves once sounded, he imagined, although Father Ranald said wolves were no longer a threat. The last of their kind had been shot by the river Findhorn close to four years ago.

He paused to look up at the ominous sky. In the west, 'twas almost black, stained with bloody streaks, and an eerie shape was forming. Through the layered strata, the full moon appeared in a hole in the cloud, looking like a single round eye, bloodshot and all-seeing. He shuddered. The temperature had dropped, the last few stunted trees bending themselves to the wind, while below him, like some noxious miasma, a mist gathered in the corries.

'Where are ye, Rowena?' he muttered. Donald Gordon was right; the veil between realms was thinner here. Here and on this day. So flimsy, the eye of the devil could peer through and see all he needed to see.

A fear of the supernatural had been sown in him from birth, as it had in all Highland folk. It lay at the core of his being, a seed ready to flourish, finding fertile ground in the teachings of Father Ranald. He hunched his shoulders against the wind, clutching the bough before him, knowing 'twas a pagan charm, and he should be carrying a holy cross.

The trees dwindled, Jem snuffling amongst the mountain plants, her tongue lolling. He was sweating, too, but strangely, he felt cold, gooseflesh puckering his skin. Jem veered off the trail, scampering over rocks. 'Here, Jem!' But she refused to be brought to heel. He followed her, scrambling through thyme and cowberry, then a strange stone rose like a phantom before him. He gasped in fright, but Jem showed no fear. She bounded forward, whining and wagging her tail.

A small shape unfolded itself at the foot of the stone, putting a hand out to stroke Jem's head.

'Rowena! Thank the Lord.' He near fainted with relief. Tears welled, and he fought a desire to get down on his knees and clasp her to his chest.

Blinking, she rose to her feet. A screen of dark hair partly concealed her face. She pushed it back, gazing around dazed-like, then stared at him in horror.

Her gaze moved over his face, flushed and sheened with sweat, lingered at his eyes, bright with tears he supposed, then dropped to his hands, white-knuckled as they gripped the length of rowan-wood. Her hands flew to her face.

'Oh, Duncan! I didna mean to drag ye from yer work.' Her brows drew together, and she looked so pitifully contrite his chest tightened. 'Forgive me. I thought I'd be back afore ye woke. 'Tis just, I was that glad sitting here. That blithesome.'

Blithesome? He gaped at her, then stared around at the rugged hillscape. Petrified roots of some long-ago forest poked like bones through what soil the gales had left. The trees, if they could be called that, were no more than inches high, splayed against the hillside by innumerable storms. In the distance, the dark mass of the Cairngorm plateau brooded, while a hundred feet above them, on the crown of the hill, he knew another stone stood. One with perhaps an even more ungodly purpose. Ringed with brushwood, it awaited tonight's ritual. There was naught here that could possibly make him feel blithesome.

'What're ye doing here?' he stammered. 'Whatever possessed ye to climb a faeryhill alone on the eve o' Beltane?'

Acutely aware of its presence, he turned with trepidation to look at the stone that was impossible not to look at—its strangeness, the devilish markings that spoke to him of ungodly things. His scalp prickled, a shiver coursing up his spine. He hadn't known this stone existed. He knew only of the Beltane stone on the crown of the hill. Yet this stone was clearly as unholy, imposing itself brutally upon his consciousness. Only, Rowena had been sitting motionless before it, as if in prayer.

Smiling, she gazed back at the stone, a look of enthralment quickening in her face. 'Is it nae wondrous, Duncan? Does it nae make yer insides feel funny when ye look at it? It does mine.'

Incredibly, she showed no fear in the presence of the demon slab and whatever it stood for but reached out and touched it, turning to share her wonder with him. Her eyes were earnest and dark. They radiated a strange ardour making it difficult to look away. So rapt and sincere was her expression, 'twas impossible not to be affected. He had a sudden desire to smile foolishly back, to pledge her everything he had if only she'd promise to keep herself safe. But, of course, he had naught.

At a loss over what to say, he stared at her, a gradual realisation dawning. 'Twas an awareness that first took shape the night she'd lain herself down on the cold floor beside him. She was all that was pure and innocent in the world, and he desperately wished to keep her so. If harm had come to her, if she'd become lost to him ... but he couldn't think on that.

She was still looking at him, waiting for him to confirm he shared her strange enthralment with the demon slab. He cleared his throat.

'Whatever possessed ye, Rowena?' Then the horrifying truth dawned—she'd been lured here, an innocent, by the devil or his imps— enticed here for some demonic purpose.

Her eyes dulled with disappointment, and she blinked, dropping her gaze. He supposed 'twas plain he hardly shared her enamour with the demon stone. Her shoulders fell, her face adopting a crestfallen expression.

'Mam loved this place. She took me to see this stone afore. She called it a symbol stone, said there were others like it in the glen, and she'd show me them all one day. Only,' a wistful look troubled her face, 'only, now she's gone, I need to be finding them myself.'

He shook his head, bewildered by her reasoning. 'So, ye just wandered off to see what ye could find?'

She flinched at his tone. 'It called me here, I think. Or Mam did. Her spirit brought me here. Through the stone.'

He gasped at her blasphemy. The souls of those who'd departed this world went to heaven if they were worthy, as he imagined her mother had been. They didna linger around demon stones, luring the innocent.

'That's divil's talk, Rowena. And that,' he nodded at the stone, 'is a divil's stane.' He was breathing hard now. What did she mean? Could she be possessed? He'd heard of such things. Father Ranald had performed exorcisms, as he called them. Fearful procedures he'd not wish upon an innocent like Rowena.

'Come away from here. I'll tak' ye home afore the storm that's brewing catches us out in the open.' He took up her cold hands and drew her to him, feeling a swell of love for her, an urge to hold her so tight naught could ever harm her. The desire prompted a strange swoop in his belly, though he suspected such an action might be improper, and he stood awkwardly in front of her.

''Tisna a divil's stane.' She let him take her hands but led him behind the stone to look at it from the other side, the side the hill had sheltered through the ages from storms and scouring gales and whatever else the heavens had chosen to hurl at it.

'See?'

He blinked in confusion. The back of the stone had been carved, too, even more intricately than the front. Protected by the hill, its design was still sharply defined. It depicted a Celtic Cross, the Lord's cross decorated with all manner of swirling, interweaving patterns. His mouth dropped open, and he craned forward to examine it more closely.

The twisting patterns portrayed creatures with heads and tails and legs. There were serpents and maned, horse-like beasts with fish-tails. Others had swan heads with slithering tongues and elongated bodies that writhed and came together in a lewd and shameful fashion. He stepped back with a hiss. All manner of scandalous couplings had been etched into the stone.

'Dinna look at it.' He moved to draw her away, but something stopped him. They'd been Christians, the people who'd done this, of sorts at least; the cross was a powerful symbol of their faith. And this hill had been important to them, much as folk still held it today. His head spun with questions. Could tonight's ritual have a connection with this stone? Or with those who'd carved it? But he didn't want to consider that.

'Ye see!' She shook his hand as if to shake some sense into him. ''Twas set here by long-ago mysterious folk, nae the divil. Just folk. Christian folk. Mam said so. It has some meaning, though I dinna ken what. Naught bad, though. They just kent things. Things we've likely forgot.'

He frowned at her earnest face, at her eyes that urged him to see things as she saw them. A blast of wind caught her, and she stumbled, shivering. The signs of a storm were now unmistakable. Whatever all this meant, there was little time to quarrel over it.

He squeezed her hand. ''Tis the eve o' Beltane, Rowena. I dinna expect ye to understand what that means but trust me, there's danger here. Something sinful will happen at the top o' this hill tonight. At Beltane, the veil atween realms is thinner.'

'Oh, Duncan, how did ye ken that? 'Tis why I've come, I think. Been drawn here,' she corrected. 'So I might find Mam's soul, fer souls can never die. 'Tis mebbe easier at Beltane. And I did,' she said excitedly. 'I sensed her gentleness. I felt that safe and loved, I forgot about everything. Forgive me, I did forget about you and Jem, too.' She stroked Jem's neck. 'I didna mean to worry ye, but now I ken Mam's nae truly gone, I'm just that glad.' Her smile lit her face. 'That joyful. 'Tis the first joy I've felt since God took her away.'

Once more, she caught him at a loss.

'Well,' he muttered. 'That's good, I suppose.' He wanted to be happy for her, but she was rambling, and the urge to get her to safety was too strong to be distracted by her queer notions. 'Only,' he glanced at the darkening sky. 'We must be getting away.'

She nodded, looking around one last time. 'I need to explain about being in wild places.'

'Tell me once we're gone from here. I'll nae be happy till I've gotten ye to safety.'

She nodded, canting her head at him. 'Ye worry about me.'

'Twas not a question; he sensed she simply stated what she intuitively knew to be true. A wealth of words tumbled and jostled in his head, eager to burst free, but he knew not how to let them, so he merely nodded.

Once they were scrambling down the hillside, he could breathe a little easier and took her hand. 'If we make haste, we might be hame around our customary time, and yer da need never know we've been anywhere but cutting peat all day.'

She looked up at him. 'Ye'd do that? Lie to save me a thrashing? Would it nae be wrong, though? Anger God, I mean.'

He almost laughed at her innocence. Whatever they'd dabbled in today had likely angered God far more than anything he could say to her da. But her concern for his piety touched him.

74

'Well.' He thought of the men he'd left cutting his stretch of peat. 'There mightna be a need to say anything. I'll nae lie to yer da, but we could be thrifty wi' the truth, I'm thinking.'

She squeezed his hand. 'Thank you.'

It began to rain, fat drops falling sporadically among the heather making the tiny leaves tremble. The air freshened in their nostrils. They were almost at the track leading to Ballichmore when they heard the drum of hooves. He pulled her into the trackside undergrowth, crawling behind a screen of gorse. Jem followed but was so excited by this new game, she barked and ran in circles.

'Hush, lass.'

Rowena managed to quiet her. 'What is it, d'ye think?'

'Dragoons, mebbe. They use this track on the way to Inverness. I heard John Meldrum say so.'

'The men that took yer fish?'

'Or others. There're many o' the divils in the glen.'

They waited in the undergrowth, stroking Jem's head to keep her quiet. As the rain came in earnest, a detachment of redcoats appeared over a hump in the track. They rode two abreast, ten of them, armed with swords and flintlock muskets, a cart pulled by two sturdy garrons bringing up the rear.

These were not the men who'd taken his fish. The faces of those dragoons were forever ingrained in his memory. These soldiers were perhaps of a higher rank. Although clad in the same despised red coats, their facings were different, their hats, too. Notably, the two men leading the troop had showy gold braiding on their uniforms and wore ornate metal plates around their necks. He grew clammy, his heart quickening with fear. He despised himself for it.

Rowena gasped as the cart rumbled by. On their knees in the back, bloodied and roped together, pitching and rolling as the cart's wheels found every rut and hollow, two young lads were trussed like turkeys.

'Archie and Ewan Gordon,' she whispered. 'Donald's sons. They joined the rising, and Da said they were mebbe in a place called France now, though James said they were likely hiding in the glen if they were still alive. In woods and byres and malt barns.'

He made the sign of the cross as the cart rumbled by, thinking of Donald Gordon, the lads' father. The man was likely still working his peat bank for him, unaware his sons had been caught.

'Where're they taking them?'

'Inverness, mebbe, or south to London fer trial.' He turned to look at her, wishing to spare her the terrible truth. The young Jacobites would likely be hanged in the next few days at Inverness or wherever these dragoons were garrisoned. He'd oft-times fretted 'twould be Father Ranald's fate, but a notorious Jacobite priest like the father would receive special treatment. A show trial in London, public humiliation, a spectacle execution on the highest of scaffolds so all might see and be deterred.

They waited for the drum of hooves to fade. 'Are ye all right? Ye didna jab yerself in the whins?'

'I want to go home.'

He nodded, looking into her stricken face. 'Ye wished to tell me something?'

'It doesna matter. Only, thank ye fer keeping me safe.'

His chest tightened, and he looked intently at her. 'Ye can rely on me, Rowena. There's naught I'd nae do fer ye.'

He meant it, every word, even more fervently than he realised until now. Only, he'd once believed he'd do anything for his family—his mother, wee Eilish—but in the end, what had he done for them?

The rain became a downpour sheeting out of an angry sky, pelting their faces. Yet, even through the deluge, 'twas hard to stop looking at her, pale and touchingly vulnerable. He tugged her arisaid up to cover her head, trying to keep her as dry as possible, knowing even this was partly a ruse to keep looking at her a little longer. A tendril of hair had slicked to her cheek. He peeled it away, hoping he'd managed to impress his sincerity upon her.

'I know,' she whispered. 'Ye're my brother now.'

* * *

That evening, Duncan was even quieter than usual. Several times, Rowena caught his gaze upon her, but whenever she tried to engage with him, he glanced awkwardly away. Was he thinking of Archie and Ewan Gordon, fretting over what would become of them? She was. She could still see their pinched and hopeless faces as the cart clattered by, staring wide-eyed into the hills. Perhaps they hoped help would come from there or were capturing a final image, a cherished memory to carry with them wherever they must go.

Her da appeared to notice nothing out of the ordinary, likely supposing they'd been cutting peat all day. He seemed ill at ease, hunched in his chair with a dram in his hand, staring into the flames, the muscles of his throat working.

It bothered her that he didn't know the redcoats had taken their neighbour's sons. 'Twould grieve him sorely. Should she tell him what she'd seen? She agonised, knowing she didn't understand it all, and Da would be angry. They'd need to explain why they'd been at the trackside instead of cutting peat, and he'd think it foolish climbing a faeryhill to sit by a mysterious and, likely to his mind, worthless slab of rock. Learning Duncan had abandoned his work to search for her would only rile him further.

So, in the end, trusting Duncan knew more about these things than her, she took her lead from him. When he said naught, as was his way, feeling half guilty and half grateful, she did the same. Duncan was slowly winning Da's trust, but if he found Duncan had been less than truthful, that trust would likely be broken. Duncan hoped to be a priest one day. Didn't priests always tell the truth? God had a law about that as He seemed to about most things. Yet, Duncan had only wished to save her from punishment.

Secretly, she was relieved not to have to explain herself. How would she even begin? How would she describe the magic that drew her to Carn Liath? The comfort she'd found there? Especially when she didn't understand it herself.

With a sigh, she abandoned her thoughts. The reason for her da's unease had become apparent. He was about to climb Carn Liath, too, to attend the sinful thing Duncan had hinted at. She tingled with gooseflesh. Would he also sense Mam's spirit?

'Once I'm gone,' he told them, 'fix a rowan stick above the door and anither at the hearth. 'Twill deter troublesome faeryfolk. Witches are bothered by rowan, too, 'tis why the tree's known as witchbane.'

'I have some,' Duncan confessed. 'I have a great branch o' rowan-wood.'

He lifted a brow. 'I'm glad ye ken something o' Beltane, Duncan, and ye're prepared. I cut some mysel'.' He nodded at a pile of woody greenery in the corner. 'Dinna be opening the door to anyone.'

'We'll nae do that,' James assured him.

'Good.' He tried to coax a smile from Grace. 'I'll nae be awa' so long, ye'll see. But I need to be there if we're to hae any hope o' a decent harvest this year, never heed any fortune wi' the whisky. The glen's swarming wi' redcoats and rebel-hunters.' Clapping his bonnet on his head, he moved to the door. 'Mind and keep plenty fir-candles burning to chase the shadows awa'. I cut a fresh pile this forenoon.'

'I have them.' Grace glanced at the far wall; six or seven resinous pine knots poked from cracks in the drystone wall, each blazing with a yellow glow. More were wedged between the pot chain's links to deter cunning faeryfolk from coming through the hole in the thatch.

He nodded. 'I expect ye'll be abed when I return. I'll wish ye a guid night.'

Still, he loitered at the door, reluctant to leave them on such a night. Fear fluttered in her belly. What if he didn't come back? Beltane was as unchancy as Samhain. Everyone knew that.

'Ye'll protect yer sisters?' Her da aimed this at James.

'Of course.'

James blinked and turned to Duncan—they'd answered in unison.

Duncan dropped his gaze with an awkward twitch of his head, blushing furiously.

She imagined her da might judge it overfamiliar of Duncan to consider Grace and her his sisters, but he only chuckled.

''Tis good ye think on them as kin, Duncan. It eases my conscience kenning the lasses have two fine brothers watching ower them.'

Duncan blushed even deeper, his mouth twitching, something she'd learned meant he was pleased. She had the feeling he wished to say something, but he only nodded and glanced away.

'Till the morrow, then.'

'May the Lord protect ye, sir.'

Then Da was gone.

CHAPTER NINE

THE EVE OF Beltane passed without trouble, and when Rowena awoke, her da was there, as usual, acting as if naught had happened. The sinful thing Duncan had hinted at appeared not to have troubled him. As he moved about the cot-house, he whistled a jaunty tune, something she'd not heard him do since God took Mam away.

But there was little time to wonder over it; they were flitting to the shieling with the beasts, a move she'd been looking forward to for weeks. Tomachcraggen's shieling lay to the west of the cot-house on common grazing in the hills above the Lochy Burn. Away from the infield runrigs stretching around the cot-house, the cattle would fatten on sweet hill grass, leaving the new crops to grow unmolested.

After the long Highland winter, the cattle were little more than skin and bone. Keeping them out of the lush new barley was near impossible. 'Twas a relief to finally be moving them up to the pastures among the hills.

They set off early, a joyful cavalcade of lowing beasts, her da guiding the cart piled with churns and dairy equipment. Jem frolicked at Duncan's heels, barking at a cockerel crowing from atop the swaying cart.

'Twas one of those rare soft days, and as she walked, she breathed in the sap-fresh scent of meadow and heath, gazing upon all the wild places she yearned to explore. The land rose away, curved and folded, then rose again in steep wooded slopes and heather-clad summits, a dark slash of alder betraying the course of the river.

Alder was a magical tree. When cut, it bled and could foretell disease and, best of all, hint how it might be cured. 'Twas her mother's tree, she'd been named for it. The Gaelic name, *fearna*.

Leaving the rush of the river behind, they entered a straggling birch-wood. A song thrush trilled from a mossy stump, stopping to cock his head at them, wiping his beak of insects. James nudged her, pointing with his head. Deer stood among the trees, silent and watchful, moving slowly on, all the while looking back their way.

As the trees grew denser, they needed to wend their way through. Here the pine was king. After the peat smoke of the cot-house, the mountain air, fresh with the essence of pine, tingled in her nostrils, a green breath, and she felt bracingly alive. Around her, the trees seemed to whisper, lending her their wisdom. She sensed they had much to teach her, if only she knew how to listen. With a shiver, she thought of Morna living alone in the forest, but not alone. Never truly alone. Her journey to the symbol stone had changed her, but she sensed she must wear that change as tightly as her shadow. She hugged the feeling into herself, knowing Mam was always near, whether she could feel her or not.

As she walked, she stretched her memory back to last year's move to the shieling. The images were fleeting, willow-the-wisp things, hard to catch. They'd celebrated with a *ceilidh,* a feast with music and dancing, their neighbours joining them, and a deal of whisky had been drunk. Mam had said a blessing for the health of the land and herd. She remembered her kneeling, earnest-faced, in the grass before a freshly-kindled fire reciting the words.

There would be no *ceilidh* this year. 'Twas too dangerous for folk to be gathering together, and there was no appetite for celebration. They were under constant watch by government soldiers. Gatherings were deemed evidence of Jacobite plotting, and they needed no more attention from the redcoats, especially as Da's first smuggling trip of the year was to go ahead in a few days. Still, he'd hinted there would be something special, and she wondered what it might be.

She loved being at the shieling; it meant the long days of summer were finally here. 'Twould be late in the night before the sun finally slipped below Ben Avon in a blaze of gold, and hardly dark at all before a pearly glow heralded it rising again. 'Twas a time of sweet-scented blossom. It frothed like lace on hawthorn and rowan, dangled in creamy clusters from bird cherry and gean. Everywhere, broom and gorse blazed yellow.

Yet, despite being charmed at every turn, with the cattle to herd, their journey was a slow one. She was weary when they finally reached the stone hut to be her home over the summer months. The grazing land rolled away, a plush green mantle, clover and buttercup blossoms studded through it in their thousands, a sweet fragrance rising on the breeze. But without Mam, 'twas all dulled somehow.

She turned to Grace, seeing the tightness in her face, and knew Grace felt it too. James just stood, taking stock of the hut and the tiny dairy attached to it, and she sensed 'twas memories of past summers here made him look sad.

Remembering Duncan, she found him watching her, the familiar crease between his brows. He half smiled, trying to convey something with his eyes, aware he was trespassing in a painful place. His gaze strayed past her, focusing on something beyond her shoulder.

When she turned, a figure stepped from behind the hut—a woman, her head shrouded, carrying a wicker creel upon her back. She must have betrayed her excitement, for she felt Duncan's stare sear the back of her neck, and Morna glanced warily at him.

'Ye're here afore us, Morna.' Her da nodded to her. 'Welcome. Please.'

'Twas rare for Da to receive women visitors, especially an unmarried one. He seemed awkward and out of sorts. Freeing the pony from the cart's yoke, he muttered, 'James, see to the woman's burden, lad.'

James lifted the creel from Morna's back, casting her a curious look.

'I'm grateful fer yer trust, Lachlan.' Morna rubbed the top of her shoulders where the basket's straps had dug in. She seemed conscious of her appearance, that James might find it objectionable. He might judge her by it, deeming her a woman of bogs and pine needles and forest mulch; a woman who bedded down on heather or bracken, moss, or damp, mushroomy earth, waking to the rush of the wind in the trees. That her appearance might stir the word *witch* to the lips. Hag or draggle-tail.

'Thank ye, lad,' she muttered. 'We've met afore, you and I. Ye'll nae mind it, but I knew yer mother. Fearn was special; I'm sure ye'll agree.' She stretched out a loam-darkened hand. 'My name is Morna MacNeil.'

James blinked at her. She was undoubtedly an unusual sight, wrapped in an arisaid that must once have been beautiful. A vibrant plaid. Not now. 'Twas dark with decay. He took her hand and raised it gallantly to his lips. 'Mistress MacNeil.'

'James, then?'

He nodded.

'There's nae need fer chivalry, though I thank ye fer it. Morna will do fine.' She dropped her hand, extending her smile to them all.

She was smaller than Rowena remembered; finely-boned. Her eyes, the palest shade of blue, danced with life, striking against the silver threaded through her hair. She seemed ageless with an allure so subtle 'twas easy to miss, although Rowena did not. Morna's gaze lingered upon her face, and they shared a secret look.

'As I did say upon the hilltop,' her da muttered. 'Ye're welcome here. I wish I'd welcomed ye afore, when Fearn had sore need o' ye, but I let my judgement be swayed. I see that now. I worried ower-much on my immortal soul. Fearn's, too.'

He sighed as if he carried the woes of the world upon his shoulders and glanced at Duncan. 'I'm nae so sure churchmen ken everything there is to ken. Though, of course, the father's a decent man. A brave man, too.' His face tightened. 'But the auld ways and those who keep them shouldna be put aside so heedlessly is what I think.' He nodded to emphasise this. 'I think it, aye.' Stroking his beard, he eyed each of his offspring, challenging them to question this thinking.

'So,' he went on. 'Morna's come at my asking to bestow a blessing upon the land and beasts. 'Tis good o' ye. We need every kindness in these dark days. Fearn invoked this blessing every year, so 'tis only right I ask you now. That I do try to make amends.' He swallowed. 'Fer Fearn. My love.' Emotions flitted across his face, and he stiffened his jaw to contain them. ''Tis only right.'

There was a moment's silence, then Grace murmured, 'Welcome, Morna.' She began to cough.

Morna appraised her quickly. ''Tis a nasty cough ye have there, child. I've something will ease it.' She rummaged in her creel. 'And is that a burn on yer hand? A scald from a pot chain, I'd say. I'm thinking ye do the hearth chores now Fearn's nae here to do them. Ye miss her.' She glanced at Lachlan. 'As if ye've lost a limb. Yer sword arm.'

He swallowed.

She flicked her gaze to Rowena, her eyes softening. 'Or a piece o' yer heart's been torn out.' Turning back to Grace, she murmured, 'I'll prepare something to soothe that burn.'

Grace blinked, rubbing an angry weal on the heel of her hand. 'But how did ye—?'

Morna shrugged. 'I see much. What's yer name, child?'

'Grace.'

'Ye're well-named, I'm thinking.'

She shifted her gaze more warily to Duncan and nodded to him, then looked back at Lachlan. 'Ye've brought what I asked?'

He rifled in the back of the cart, returning with a piece of blackened peat.

'Taken from yer hearth fire?'

'From the smoulder this morn.'

She took it from him. 'Once I've kindled a blaze, I'll add it to the flames. As it burns, 'twill strengthen the blessing. Make it particular to you.'

She found a suitable spot a little way from the hut and set about raising a fire. Rowena squatted down to watch. Morna drew lichen and birch bark from her creel and formed it into a nest on top of some twigs. Rummaging in her basket, she drew out a folded leaf containing a green, resinous substance and whispered over it before setting it carefully aside.

Sensing eyes upon them, Rowena glanced up to find Duncan watching, his eyes narrowed in distrust. When Morna asked him to gather kindling and brushwood, he glanced questioningly at her da, who jerked his head in the direction of the nearest copse. He set off at once. Morna withdrew a piece of knapped flint from her basket and began striking sparks from it with her dirk, expertly aiming them into the pile.

'I'm that glad ye're here,' Rowena whispered. 'How did ye ken I wanted to see ye?'

'Mebbe I wished to see you, too.' Morna frowned, watching Lachlan unload the cart. 'But I came fer yer da. He wishes to make amends; I wish to help him.'

* * *

When Duncan returned, the fire was already in full blaze, and his brushwood would soon be consumed, he imagined, for this was no ordinary fire. No feeble, flint-struck flame could take hold so quickly nor burn so fiercely. He'd not been gone long yet already a flaming pyre crackled on the ground, stoked by this strange woman.

He looked uneasily at her. She was no cot-wife; he had an ill feeling about her. 'Twas not only her appearance that repelled him but her curious familiarity with Rowena. Already the woman seemed to have drawn Rowena under her spell.

Duncan had never known a real witch, only those Father Ranald called wretches, though he'd heard tales of witchery aplenty. Wretches were different. They were not willing servants of Satan but had been forcibly entered, body and soul, by his foulness.

To free these souls, Father Ranald performed a violent procedure called an exorcism. He'd once witnessed such a thing; the memory had stayed with him. 'Twould likely never leave.

They'd been summoned to the home of the possessed young woman during the hours of darkness, and in dim firelight, witnessed her violent throes trying to free herself from Satan's possession. The father had urged her shocked family to get on their knees and pray whilst he rolled the afflicted, a frail young lass, tightly in a length of plaid.

He'd gone down on his knees, too, praying with her kinfolk. The father then valiantly threw himself upon the crazed young woman, wrestling with the demon that possessed her, demanding it leave her body—threatening the wrath of God and fiery brimstone upon the evil that inhabited her. They'd thrashed and heaved upon the ground, her feet drumming, a bloody froth spewing from her lips.

With her tightly trussed, the father pressed himself upon her slender body, forcing her flailing limbs to the ground so she'd not harm herself. 'Twas neither a quick nor painless procedure and the struggle had gone on and on.

The relentless press of the father's holy weight, his pious summoning of the Lord's might, his use of consecrated water and a silver crucifix all combined to drive the devil from the afflicted and eventually, the unfortunate victim went limp. 'Twas how it was done. Some survived, some not.

The poor lass had not.

But this Morna was no more possessed than he was. What was she, then? A green woman? He'd heard of such creatures. They were said to be a dying breed, and rightly so, for they were heathen women shunning all dealings with the Lord. Primitive relics of an age-auld religion that worshipped trees and rivers, hills and stones. Much like the folk who'd set the devil's stone into the side of Carn Liath.

It seemed likely she was of that creed, for by his own account, Lachlan had met her atop the demon hill on the eve of Beltane. Highly suspicious. But what Duncan couldn't fathom was why Lachlan, a man he'd come to respect—particularly his whisky smuggling—would tolerate such a creature tampering with land on which he'd pasture his cattle.

Lachlan had asked the woman to come here, he admitted it quite openly, to bless the land and herd. But 'twas for the father to be conducting blessings. A man o' the cloth. All blessings came from the Lord; anything else was heathen superstition, Satan toying with the fears and weaknesses of mortal men. But worse was the way this leathered hag now whispered to Rowena. An innocent. The two were huddled with their heads together, stirring some noxious brew.

He approached cautiously, peering into the woman's pot.

'Welcome.' She shifted, making room for him. 'Thank ye fer yer trouble.' She indicated he should pile the brushwood he'd gathered at her side, and she began feeding it to the flames. 'What're ye called?'

'Duncan.'

'So, you're Duncan.' She studied him. 'Ye're a member o' Lachlan's family now; he's taken ye in.' She smiled. 'I'm glad.'

A wave of inexplicable shame heated his face, and he tightened his jaw but could think of naught to say in return. Rowena peeped up at him from beneath a sweep of dark hair, her secretive smile implying her pleasure at his inclusion in her family. Fondness for her prompted his mouth to twitch in a foolish grin.

'I'm nae kin,' he replied. 'I'll never be that. I have nae kin. I've naught in the world but my dog.' He whistled to Jem, and she bounded over, shying from the flames.

'Ye've the charity of others. Ye've sisters now. Nae in blood, but in other ways that matter as much. Two fine ones and an equally fine brother. Though what was done to yer ane folk,' she shook her head, 'that was beyond understanding, and I grieve fer yer sore loss.' Holding his gaze, she indicated he should sit with her. 'And ye've a friend in me, if ye wish it.'

Still peeping at him, Rowena whispered, 'Duncan's my brother now. I love him as much as James.'

He blinked, his face reddening. Never had she said such a thing. *She loved him as much as James.* James was loyal, principled, the kind of boy a grown man would be proud to call brother. 'Twas a privilege to be his friend, never mind join his family. But to be loved by Rowena as much as she adored James. A giddy sensation swooped through his innards. He should say something, try to describe how it felt to hear her say such a thing, but as ever, the words would not come.

'Thank ye,' he finally croaked. He was overwhelmed with an urge to embrace her, to show his mutual affection, but could hardly be doing that with this Morna here. Crossing his ankles, he sat down, peeking sidelong at her. She was so loving and loyal, brave too. Everything he was not. Swallowing, he tried to convey his devotion, but of course, words were needed for that. Words left no room for doubt. If only he had the knack of turning feelings into words.

He cleared his throat, again peering into the woman's pot, eyeing its pungent green depths. 'What're ye brewing?' A noxious aroma rose in the steam assaulting his nostrils.

'A tea fer Grace. Fer that cough o' hers. And this,' she unfolded a leaf, revealing a slimy concoction, 'is fer her burn. Fresh alder leaves, honey, and a few special things.' She winked. 'Pressed upon the skin, that angry scorch will soon heal.'

He wrinkled his nose, thinking it looked even more offensive than the tea, though smelled a shade better.

'Morna's teaching me how to make all this.' Rowena stirred the brew. 'Specially the tea. We all get coughs. 'Tis made from the stalks and berries of the bird cherry, the hackberry, fer Morna says it can cure a hacking cough.'

He reared back. 'Hackberry? Ye mean, *hag*-berry? 'Tis what the bird cherry's known as. My da was a wood-worker; he warned against using hag-berry fer any purpose. All parts are evil. Hag-berry's known to be a witch's tree.'

He stared at the green woman, looking for some reaction in her grimy face. Would she let something slip to confirm his suspicions? But she only chuckled.

'If by a witch's tree, ye mean it has many uses, many ailments it can cure, then aye, ye could call it so. Ague, cold plague, quinsy, croup, winter fever, the malignant sore throat, even chin cough can be treated wi' it. 'Tis a valuable tree fer a healer.' She laughed. 'But we'll ask Grace if she minds being healed by a witch's tree. I doubt she'll heed the name if it soothes her cough.' She nodded to Rowena. 'Fetch her, lass.'

Rowena scrambled away.

Alone with the green woman, Duncan was conscious she was studying him. He stared into the fire, refusing to meet her strange eyes. They seemed to bore into his soul. He tried to put his suspicions into words, but again, awkwardness tied his tongue.

'There's nae need to fear me. I want what you want.'

He blinked. 'What's that?'

'Rowena's happiness.'

He gaped at her.

'She's special. I ken it as well as you. She feels things more than common folk. I sense the promise in her; I hear it singing in her veins. Her gift. Her soul's voice. She cares fer her fellow man. 'Tis the purpose of her life, as 'tis mine. I wish only to show her how to use her gift.'

'She's a bairn,' he said in confusion. 'A broken, grieving one. Easy to mould, I expect, fer a woman like you. Ye should leave her be.'

'I mean her no harm.'

He held her gaze until her strangeness forced him to glance away.

'Listen to yer soul's voice,' she said softly. 'It speaks the truth. Souls never lie; 'tis folk do that. Even those who mean well.'

Rowena returned with Grace before he could form any response, but he brooded over her words while she treated Grace with her noxious green slime. Grace, always eager to please, gushed over much about both the woman and her treatments for his liking, claiming the pain left her hand at Morna's touch, and her throat felt better.

Too disturbed to sit idly by watching the creature worm her way into the hearts and minds of his sisters, he rose and left them to it. He returned for the blessing but kept to the fringes, confused and disapproving, his unease growing. Yet, he was careful not to betray any hint of disapproval to his new family. Lachlan's generosity, however grudging at first, and the warmth and welcome he'd received, meant too much to risk appearing rude or ungrateful. He hoped to one day repay that kindness. Yet this woman's blasphemy offended him to the core.

Her blessing was like no religious service he'd ever attended. There were no candles burning nor scent of incense heavy on the air, no altar cloth in evidence, nor the likeness of the Virgin Mary or any of the saints. No sign of a bible, either. Nothing comforting or familiar, only branches and green things that she hauled from her creel and spread around the pyre to represent the trees and plants that shared their glen. Nature's gifts for nurture or protection, medicine or cure, so she claimed. There was, in truth, nothing of God in any of it. 'Twas all heathen and ungodly.

Yet, she had a powerful gift, that much was plain. One he'd dearly love himself—a silver tongue. She charmed with the threads of her voice, casting a web of words that laced and interlaced, wove and interwove, until she held every member of his new family in her net. 'Twas an enchantment, for she had the glamour of witchery about her, and more than ever, he suspected she was of that race.

Looking at Rowena and the others, every soul appeared spellbound. All but him. She didn't fool him, though she worried him, for he sensed Rowena was her prey. The woman claimed she only wished to show Rowena how to help her fellow man. It sounded innocent, charitable. But how could it be? She was as ungodly as she was unwashed. She wished to mould Rowena to her ways. To make the lass like her.

He clenched his jaw. Nae whilst he still breathed.

CHAPTER TEN

YET, SHE KNEW how to use that silvered tongue, for the green woman spoke of the old ways and made them sound innocent, virtuous. She recalled the customs folk had once followed and held sacred, wisdom that shouldn't be put aside so quick, she claimed. Hadn't their traditions served them well through the ages? Until folk chose to turn their back upon the old magic, afraid of the Kirk and its sessions, of words like *heretic* and *witch*.

She made it all sound natural and wondrous, a magical force working in harmony through all creatures and all creation as if there were no God who'd created it, no Lord who guided it still. 'Twas all a force of nature, she claimed—earth, the moon, the stars—all realms had this elemental power flowing through them, unseen but connecting. Nature-magic stirred all things to life, in time bringing death, decay, and on the circle turned. All creation, she insisted, spun in this light.

Her words made him fearful for the souls of his new family, especially Rowena. He saw her blessing for what it was—a spell, a thing of witchery and deception. Crouched before her unnatural fire, Morna looked like any frail old woman, a *cailleach,* which perhaps she was. But she didn't fool him, beneath her innocence lay evil.

She poured buttermilk into a hollow stone, then whispered a spell to the faeryfolk—an appeal for Lachlan's milch cows. With witchery upon her lips, she lifted bannocks from her creel with earth-blackened fingers and broke them in two, flinging one half into the fire to sizzle and flare.

Each offering she aimed at a different enemy: eagle and raven, fox, hawk, and carrion crow. But she reserved her most potent spell until the last, levelling it at those in authority: soldiers and generals, the Duke of Cumberland, magistrates, kirk elders, the laird and his factor, those who raised taxes, rentals.

Her entreaties should have pleased him, but her neglect in mentioning the Lord God in any of it troubled him. She spoke of mother nature and her earth magic, not God. Heathen things. She made bargains with their enemies to spare their lambs and calves, whisky and menfolk. Above all, she wove a spell for the land: that it be fertile and provide for them, that Lachlan be allowed to work the soil tilled by his ancestors in peace.

Watching from the margins, he couldn't help but think of Father Ranald and all the prayers he'd heard the warrior priest recite. The father's blessings were as different from this as day is to night. His stomach tightened. It felt disloyal to be taking part in this abomination, however unwillingly. As if he'd turned his back upon the father and his teachings. On God, even. He wrung his damp hands and wiped them down the side of his breeks, wishing he were anywhere but here.

At last, the woman brought her ritual to an end and piled what remained of the bannocks she'd sacrificed on a wooden platter. His mouth dried. Would she commit the ultimate violation? Place a sliver of bannock in the mouths of her congregation as if it were the Eucharist, making a profanity of Holy Communion? She called Lachlan forward, and he got down on his knees before her.

Unable to watch, he flicked his gaze to the line of trees screening the hut from the south. His breath caught in his throat. A figure stood among the trees—a man, still as stone, watching unnoticed.

His cheeks began to burn, his stomach to churn. The figure was a familiar one whose presence under any other circumstance would fill him with joy. Not now. Shame sickened him to his stomach.

The man was bearded, his hair grown long. He was dressed in the simple garb of a cottar, but he'd know Father Ranald no matter what guise he took. Deeper in the shadows, a pony grazed, and he knew the father had come on urgent business.

He started forward, but the father held up a hand to stay him. He should wait, he indicated, until the woman had finished. Swallowing, he stepped back into place, relieved that at least the witch had not attempted to replicate the act of Communion.

Detecting movement in the trees, Jem scampered off to investigate, clearly remembering the father judging by her wagging tail. The man bent down to pat her fondly. Leading the pony, and with Jem trotting at his heels, he made his way out of the trees.

His sudden appearance stirred consternation.

Lachlan got to his feet, his face paling with horror. 'Father ... I wasna expecting ye.'

'Plainly not.'

'But ye're welcome. Always. The lad'll be pleased to see ye.' He glanced around for Duncan, roving wildly with his eyes, indicating he should come quickly forward and welcome their guest.

Duncan needed no telling. 'Twas plain from the father's expression, the priest was overjoyed to see him. Father Ranald had been his teacher as well as his saviour, a guiding light in dark days. Although he'd tried to keep his feelings hidden, he'd missed the man and his teachings with a fearsome ache.

'Duncan.' The father clasped the back of his neck, drawing him into his embrace. 'Duncan, Duncan.'

The familiar scent of candle wax, ink, and precious incense laced with a whiff of pony filled his nostrils. A heady mix and he breathed in great lungfuls of it, tightening his arms around the man. 'Twas long since anyone had held him.

'Ye're a sight for the sorest of hearts, lad.'

He shivered, savouring the sensation of being loved.

Conscious every eye must be upon them, even those of the green woman, he reluctantly loosened his hold, his heart brimming, seeking out Rowena. She'd understand.

She was standing a mite stiffly, staring at the father, her hands clenched into fists. For a moment, before she glanced away, he imagined her eyes flashed with anger. He was mistaken, of course, and drew a giddy breath, glancing to where the noxious woman was knelt. But she was gone.

'I've missed ye these last months.' The father stood back to appraise him. 'Ye've grown. Ye've colour in your cheeks.' He nodded, pressing his lips together. 'I made the right decision, hard though it was.'

'I've missed ye, too,' he mumbled. 'But what ye just witnessed, I wish ye to know—'

'Hush, now. Dinna fret. I see how things are. You're part of Lachlan's family now and must act as such. I lay no blame upon you. On any of you, in truth.' He drew a weary breath. 'In troubled times like these, folk turn to, well, to older ways. I'm disappointed, but I understand. I must work harder. With the Lord's grace, I must shepherd my flock gently into the fold.' Frowning, he pressed a finger and thumb into the flesh between his brows, turning to Lachlan, who squirmed, lowering his head.

'I would speak with you, Lachlan.' He smiled a mite indulgently at Duncan. 'Though, of course, 'tis not the only reason I'm here.'

'Come into the hut then, Father.' Lachlan flicked a hand at James. 'Find whisky, lad. And, Duncan, see to the father's mount. And keep a watch.' He forced a chuckle. 'We dinna want the red-backed divils creeping up on us as easily as you.'

'I did no creeping. Your attention was directed elsewhere. But the lad should hear this too—both of them. One of the lasses can keep a watch once you've seen your guest off.'

Their guest was gone, along with all her green mischief, although how she'd managed to vanish into thin air, Duncan could hardly fathom.

Looking shame-faced and a mite puzzled, Lachlan instructed Grace and Rowena to see to the father's pony, then perch on rocks at either side of the hut to watch for soldiers.

'Their brash colours do give them away,' he jested. 'Brazen as any strumpet.'

The father frowned, and the girls looked blankly at him. No one felt much like raising a smile, the father's drawn face deterring them. Duncan exchanged a look with James, who'd managed to source whisky and drinking cups, then followed him inside.

The hut comprised one room. Grace had lit a fire within a stone cairn in the centre. Smoke curled from here, pooling in a murky haze beneath the rooftree before seeping through the thatch. They sat cross-legged around it. In the gloom, Lachlan poured out the whisky.

Father Ranald brought his cup to his lips, his nostrils flaring as he inhaled, savouring the aroma before he tasted. It seemed to fortify him. Duncan was passed a dram, too, and sipped gingerly, gasping as the spirit burned the back of his throat. The burn was followed by a welcome glow that spread through his innards, and he instantly recognised whisky's allure.

Jem curled herself at his feet. For a moment, they just sat, enjoying the company and Lachlan's fine whisky, waiting for the priest to say whatever he'd come to say. The man was even thinner now, the state of repair of his borrowed clothing speaking of the hardships he'd endured since last they met. Aware of their anxious faces, the father cleared his throat.

'I pray your forgiveness. I am the bearer of tragic news.' He frowned into his cup. 'I bring the worst tidings imaginable.'

'What, Father?' Lachlan leaned forward.

'News of Archie and Ewan Gordon, Donald's sons. The lads were caught hiding in a bothy in the Braes of Glenlivet. Perhaps not the wisest of hiding places given the closeness of Scalan, or what's left of it, but Jacobites have long found loyal friends among the Glenlivet folk, myself included.'

He drew a ragged breath. 'I'm told the Gordon lads were taken to a place called Blacktown near Nairn on the Moray Firth where the Government army has a great camp, a place they're calling Fort George. They are to build a fort there named for the false king and replacing the old fort at Inverness Castle our forces destroyed last year.' He swallowed. 'It appears the lads were hanged there.'

James gasped, his cup frozen midway to his mouth.

'The bastards,' Lachlan growled. 'They were only lads. Oor lads. Fighting fer their king.'

'My friends,' James choked.

'I know, I know. I can scarce believe the army deemed those two a threat to their authority. Ewan was fifteen years of age. But it seems an example needed to be made, a message delivered. There will be no mercy shown, no stone left unturned until every rebel is rooted out.'

'Jesus God!' Lachlan hurled his whisky into the flames where it hissed and flared, releasing a cloud of whisky steam. 'There's no hope they might still be alive?'

'Notices were posted. Their names displayed. Archibald and Ewan Gordon, rebels late of Glenbuchat's Regiment. Hanged for treason.'

Lachlan sat back, visibly shaken. 'Naught could've been done then, even had we kent where they'd been taken?'

'Seems unlikely. Our prayers must be with Donald and his family now.'

Duncan stared into his whisky, seeing a rattling cart and two kneeling youths, their hands and feet roped together. He remembered their faces, stark as the rain began to fall and his craven self, hiding in the undergrowth. Guilt turned his lungs to lead, and he struggled for breath. He should've said something, at least told Lachlan what he'd seen. Maybe something could've been done. He should tell him now. But the moment passed, and still, he said naught. He only swallowed more whisky and rubbed Jem's belly, glad of the distraction, imagining how they'd look at him, judge him, how his whey face would surely betray him for a coward.

Whining, Jem lifted soft brown eyes to him.

'I hope to hold a service for the Gordon lads,' the father went on. 'We've not the bodies for burial. Doubtless, they've been left for the corbies and rooks to pick over. But I plan to hold a service to honour their memory.' He glanced at Lachlan. 'I hear you're leading a convoy south in the next day or two. To Edinburgh, I hear, with the MacRaes. So, once you're home?'

Lachlan swore softly. 'Does naught get by ye, Father? 'Twas meant to be secret. But aye, ye can count on me. Soon as I'm hame. Donald's long been a friend. I'd nae dishonour him by missing a service fer his lads.'

'I imagined as much.' The father sipped at his whisky, his face grim. 'There's more, I'm afraid.'

'Best be saying it.'

The priest rubbed his brow, drawing a draught of air into his lungs. 'I've received a letter from Bishop Smith. Sadly, it took some time to reach me. He speaks of new laws passed and other abominations—Protestant clergy ordered to give in the names of parishioners who took part in the rising. The Duke of Cumberland, the butcher himself, has ordered a proclamation read from every pulpit. All kirk ministers must discover and furnish the names of fugitives in their parish. Rewards will be offered. Worse, Cumberland has issued a proclamation against anyone harbouring rebels or concealing arms, munition, or anything belonging to the rebels. Hanging, the penalty. 'Tis, perhaps, what lies at the root of the Gordon lads' arrest.'

'They were betrayed, ye mean?' James choked.

'Perhaps. I've yet to ascertain the means of their arrest.'

'God's blood!' Lachlan exploded. 'What craven would do such a deed? Begging yer pardon, Father.'

'Have you not done enough blaspheming for one day, Lachlan? Inviting that woman here with her devilry.' The father's breathing was noticeably louder. He took a moment to steady himself. 'As ye've seen, more and more government troops are arriving in the glen, commandeering homes, plundering cattle, horses, sheep even, driving them south to sell to traders in the north of England. Burning crops in the fields. All manner of retributions carried out in the name of "pacification" of the Highlands. The name the German king has given it, fer these are the usurper's orders.'

'Ye mean thon great—'

The father held up his hand to prevent Lachlan's further blasphemy.

'They search this glen particularly for old Glenbuchat, Sir John Gordon, veteran of previous uprisings whose home at St. Bridget was pillaged and burned last year. And who, it's rumoured, has escaped to Norway or Sweden, or some such cold, mountainous place. I doubt his old bones will relish that, though perhaps his spirit is too crushed now to care. They hunt me too; a priest who dared draw arms for his prince, who fought next to Sir John on Culloden moor.'

He touched his hand to his left hip, and Duncan didn't doubt he kept a dirk or pistol hidden there. 'They say the usurper's still in fear of old Glenbuchat, that when our army reached Derby, he shrieked, "De great Glenboggit is goming!"'

Lachlan snorted. 'Pampered pudding o' a man! And to think he calls himsel' king. He wouldna recognise true principles supposing he choked upon them in his broth.' He frowned, sobering. 'Duncan's da was wi' ye at Derby, aye?'

'He was.' The father reached over and squeezed his hand. 'And conducted himself bravely.'

Duncan swallowed as they all looked at him.

'The bishop speaks of Jacobite ordnance taken from the field of battle and of the silver paid to government soldiers to collect it. For every stand of colours picked up on the battlefield, sixteen guineas were paid. In all, fourteen Jacobite standards were captured. All were burned at Edinburgh by the common hangman. Torched at the merkat cross after being carried in mock procession from the castle by a band of chimney sweeps!'

There were gasps from around the fire, and Lachlan let out another blasphemous oath. The father shot him a look.

'They made a mockery of the prince and his supporters,' James said in disgust. 'Those who gave their lives fer the cause.'

The father nodded bitterly. 'It seems every possible means was employed to discredit His Royal Highness and his God-given right to the throne of his own realm. But what I must explain, and yer safety depends upon it, are the new Acts now passed into law, for they will be ruthlessly enforced and aim to bring the Highlands to heel. To crush the clans and ensure there can be no more risings.'

Pouring himself another dram, Lachlan paused, his nostrils flaring. 'New Acts?'

'The Act of Proscription will be fully enforceable by the beginning of August and demands the delivering up of all arms.' The father pulled a scrolled letter from about his person and read aloud from what Duncan took for the bishop's letter.

'Every broadsword, targe, whinger, dirk, side-pistol and musket must be turned in. Anyone caught concealing arms will be gaoled and only released upon payment of a fine, a hefty one. Late payment will mean conscription into the army, and a repeat offence will see the culprit transported to His Majesty's plantations beyond the seas for a term of seven years. The playing of the pipes is now outlawed; pipes are judged instruments of war. This Act to apply to that part of north Britain known as Scotland.'

He looked up and nodded at their shocked faces.

'As I say, this letter took some time to find me. The law came into being last summer, but a period of grace was granted. A year until fully enforceable, although only three months remain. In any case, any leeway is wholly at the discretion of local forces.'

He looked back at the letter. 'There's more. A further clause forbids the wearing of traditional Highland garb by any man or boy in the Highlands other than those employed in His Majesty's army. No plaids, philabegs, kilts or shoulder-belts to be worn, nor tartan used for greatcoats or outer garments. Again, on pain of six months gaol and transportation upon a second offence.'

He lowered the letter to a stunned silence.

Duncan glanced across at Lachlan and James, noting their tartan plaids, Lachlan's broad shoulder-belts, then looked down at his own humble attire while he digested this shocking news. Judging by his companions' roving eyes, they were also considering their clothing and judging which parts of it were now forbidden.

'Of course,' the priest went on, 'having caught any man wearing the customary clothing of the Highlands, the authorities then have the perfect excuse for further investigations. Searching for arms, ransacking homes, rounding up livestock and other persecutions. I suspect little provocation would be needed for all manner of ill-treatment. And there are rumours of worse. Our language is to be forbidden—the ancient tongue of the Gael—and all Catholics are to be transported to the colonies. But these, as yet, are mere rumours.'

Lachlan choked with rage.

'I hardly expect you to give in all your weapons, Lachlan. No smuggler would set out without protection for himself and his contraband. But, perhaps, a token offering could be handed over, sufficient to satisfy the authorities for now and shift suspicion.'

Lachlan stared at him. 'Niver. Carrying arms is part o' what makes us Highland. If they wish my sword, my musket, they can come take them from me. Damned if I'll hand them ower. Nae whilst blood still flows in me.'

The father passed a hand over his brows, wearily rubbing the tender flesh around his eye sockets. 'This convoy you plan to lead, Lachlan, 'twill be your most perilous yet. The danger from dragoons and rebel-hunters is grave, never heed what other risks you might face. Smuggling whisky is considered treason. Avoiding taxes makes you a rebel. And what of your bairns? The lasses most especially. Are they to be left here unprotected whilst you risk your neck for whisky? Left to protect your cattle from rebel-hunters or reivers should they have a fancy to round them up and herd them Lord knows where? And what if something ill should befall you?'

A flicker of fear crossed Lachlan's face. He muttered, 'I thought they'd be safer up in the hills.'

'And you'll take James with you?'

'James needs to learn how things are done. Sooner the better. The safest routes to follow, how to assess the lie o' the land when it comes to hiding a train o' laden ponies, how to negotiate wi' blethermen, who to trust. 'Tis all part o' his education. Though it grieves me to leave the lasses, Father. And Duncan.' His face tightened. 'Everything's harder wi'out Fearn.'

His inclusion was an afterthought, Duncan knew, but he sensed Lachlan meant what he said. There was genuine angst in him, and some part of it, however small, included an unease at leaving him behind.

The father rolled the letter, concealing it amongst the folds of his coat. 'I'd stay with your youngsters myself, but should I be discovered here ....' He frowned into his whisky, still half full. ''Twould be the worse for you and your family. I'm taking a risk in coming here, as are you in sheltering me. Harbouring a priest is an offence. Harbouring a wanted Jacobite priest is certainly a capital one. The risks are too great. But I give ye my word.' He pulled his bible from his coat and clutched it to his chest. 'I'll stay close by and protect these youngsters as best I can. There are others I can rely upon, glensmen who'd rise to my call; only none could be here swiftly enough to prevent any real harm, I fear.'

'No, I see that, Father. Danger stalks yer every step.'

'But, Father,' said James. 'Should they catch ye, ye'd likely share the same fate as Ewan and Archie. Worse. Ye must mind yer own neck and keep hidden.' He turned to Lachlan. 'I should stay wi' Grace and Rowena, Da. They're my sisters and—'

'I could guard them.'

Duncan struggled to his feet as three pairs of eyes widened and focused upon him. He straightened his back, an idea taking form and gaining credence in his head.

'I could keep a watch fer the red-backed divils, sir, and hide the lasses if need be. 'Twould be my honour, a way to repay yer kindness.' He held

Lachlan's gaze, his heart thumping. 'I could find a safe place to hide them should the need come upon us. A bolt hole.' He sat back down, his cheeks burning, then reached over and gripped the father's bible. 'I'd make it my business to protect them, sir. I give ye my word.'

Sincere though he was, his heart fluttered, sweat prickling his underarms. He'd said all this without thinking, the notion of anything ill befalling Rowena or Grace filling him with dread. His voice had sounded tremulous even to his own ears. Doubt at whether he could do anything more than tremble in the undergrowth wormed its way insidiously through his innards.

'And how would ye manage that?' Lachlan grunted. 'What are ye? Nine years of age?'

'Nearly.'

Lachlan snorted.

'Duncan's loyal, Da,' said James. 'Brave, too. I've seen him be so.'

'When it comes to guarding a guddled fish, mebbe. And how did that turn out? Nae so well, if I mind. And 'tis hardly the same thing. We're talking o' tender young lasses, nae a dead trout.' Lachlan exhaled forcibly through his nose.

His bitterness was understandable, Duncan acknowledged. 'Twas fear and frustration sharpened Lachlan's tongue, his powerlessness to protect his own family. The man's anger was aimed principally at himself for having to leave them.

Sighing, Lachlan grudgingly softened his tone. 'Now see, lad, if I come hame to find my cattle still here, grazing contentedly, then I'll be mighty pleased. Let that be enough. After all, I need to keep you safe, too. I've no wish to see ye swing from a gibbet like Donald's lads.'

Duncan nodded, lowering his head, yet he was unwilling to give up. Lachlan had just acknowledged he'd be leaving his cattle in his care, so why not his daughters? From beneath lowered brows, he studied his companions: Lachlan's scowling face, James, sipping whisky, plainly disturbed at how casually his father had dismissed him; and Father Ranald, looking directly at him, considering him with a pensive expression.

He flushed and frowned into his now empty cup. The father was well aware of his failings; that he'd done naught but piss himself in the bushes while his first family burned.

'The lad'll be here anyway, won't he?' Father Ranald flicked his gaze to Lachlan. 'So, what harm is there in letting him help as best he can? His heart's in the right place, and I'll be close by should he need me. I see no harm in indulging him, Lachlan. What choice have you, anyway?'

Lachlan exhaled, rolling his eyes.

'And, while we're talking of Duncan helping, I believe 'twould be wise if he taught the lasses a little English. A smattering of the southern tongue, as I've taught it to him.'

Lachlan glanced sharply at him.

'I know what you're thinking, but 'tis not so much ye'd be giving in to the occupiers, admitting defeat, but looking to the future. Ensuring you *have* a future by bending a little to their ways. I see a need to speak English, inevitably, in the days ahead, whether the Gaelic tongue is forbidden or not. In truth, Scotland is two countries. One Highland, Gaelic in her speech and culture, the other Lowland, English-speaking and more closely linked to that realm than to our own in its wealth-building nature, in its faith and thinking.'

Lachlan scowled at the priest, not fully following the man's logic and instinctively disliking it. 'I dinna ken,' he muttered.

'Our southern rulers will never learn our tongue, Lachlan. They think it primitive, brutish.'

'As they think us,' said James.

'Aye, sadly. Such is their ignorance. But those who can speak the English tongue are held a little higher. Or at least, are not held in such scathing contempt. And to understand at least a little of what our rulers say, even supposing what they say makes our hearts sore, 'tis a valuable skill. Else, how are we ever to communicate with them? 'Tis a necessary evil, I believe, and the younger these bairns start, the easier 'twill be. What d'ye say, Lachlan?' He held Lachlan's sceptical gaze, then turned to Duncan.

'Lad?'

'If the lasses are so minded, I'd be willing to try, Father.'

'Splendid. So, Lachlan?'

CHAPTER ELEVEN

THREE DAYS LATER, her da and James were ready to leave. Rowena stood with Duncan and Grace to wish them a safe journey. The ankers of whisky had been spirited to the shieling in the dead of night. They were lashed to the ponies' flanks now, the garrons all tied together in a line.

As she watched her da check the ropes and fastenings one last time, her palms were damp, and she supposed the trembling thing in her middle must be her stomach. When she thought of the dangers they'd face, it churned even more.

The sun had already set, smuggling being a thing of the night, and the sky was a luminous pink, Ben Avon lit in a brilliant display. Shafts of light shone low in her eyes, making them nip and water and doubtless making her look tearful.

Seeing her so, James held her tight, murmuring into her hair. They'd be back in no time with the rental coin all counted out, and maybe some left for a new copper worm, a valuable piece of the whisky still. She had Duncan to protect her, and he'd do a grand job. There was no need for tears.

They held on to each other until Da came and cleaved them apart, but she allowed no tears to fall. Grace sobbed and wept, but she clamped her teeth together and lifted her chin. When Da looked at her, she knew better than to blubber like a bairn. He nodded in approval, then turned to Duncan, clasping him by the forearm, and they exchanged a look that meant something. He whistled to James, then led the first pony away.

She thought of Morna, of the things Morna had whispered whilst they prepared for the blessing. Morna had told her she possessed an inner strength, and she'd liked that. It filled her with hope and a longing to begin her learning. She'd wanted to ask Morna things, to tell her about going to the symbol stone, only Father Ranald came with his frowning eyes and chased her away too soon. Before she had a chance to ask her anything.

Duncan loved the father, and the others respected him. For their sakes, she'd tried not to show her anger, although she suspected she'd failed.

Before Morna vanished into the trees, she'd whispered to her, 'Spend time in nature, child. Notice the wee miracles around ye. 'Tis the way to ready yerself. I'll be back fer ye afore ye know it.'

That's what she planned to do. Yet as she watched the dwindling line of ponies and the two figures walking beside it, shadows melting into the gloaming, her heart beat heavy. 'Come back safe,' she whispered.

'They will.' Grace took her hand. 'I'm certain.'

Darkness pressed in, and they turned back into the hut, only three of them now to sit despondently by the fire. Duncan was quieter than ever, likely thinking over the last instructions Da had given him. Or, perhaps, as he rubbed Jem's ears, he was marvelling at her da's parting promise.

She'd not intended to listen in, but she'd heard Da make Duncan a promise: if Duncan protected his precious things, and by that, she knew he meant her and Grace as much as his cattle, he'd make Duncan a smuggler. A skilled one. He'd begin teaching him how 'twas all done—the malting and mashing, the distilling and the secret carrying of the mountain dew through the hills—as soon as he returned.

Pitifully grateful, Duncan choked his thanks. He wished to strike back at the redcoats and their masters—those who'd taken his family and peace of mind. He believed whisky smuggling would be his way.

Da nodded once to him, and so their bargain was made.

* * *

Despite her fears, Rowena's days at the shieling were strangely carefree, the pattern of her days set by the tending and herding of the cattle. Cattle had long been the mainstay of the Highlands. She'd heard tales of cattle raising and droving since she was a swaddler—stories told around the firestone of great trysts at Crieff and the arduous droving of mighty herds to market there from the farthest reaches of the Highlands. There'd been tales of reiving too, clans stealing cattle from other clans, and Rowena knew reiving was a real and constant threat.

She'd loved those tales, particularly Mam's stories of the troublesome faeryfolk who liked to shoot the beasts with their faery darts and all the ways glenfolk found to thwart them. But her favourite stories were of the benign beings, *Glaistigs* and *Gruagachs*, that made it their business to help care for the cattle.

Every day, as she milked the cows, she sang old milking songs, encouraging them to let down their milk. Highland cattle were fickle and could hold on to their milk if not soothed with a song. Once she'd taken what they could spare, she poured a little into a hollow stone as an offering to the guid folk for their kindness. 'Twas something Mam always did, so she made sure to do it, too.

As the days grew longer, she and Duncan spent almost every hour together, crossing and re-crossing the hills with the grazing beasts, Jem frisking at their heels. Grace, ever one for homemaking, preferred to stay at the hut baking bannocks and pressing cheese, but Rowena was happiest in the hills, while Duncan seemed to thrive in her company.

She loved the freedom of her days, breathing in that sweet, wind-blown clover smell, letting it fill her lungs. 'Twas glorious to be treading the pastures and deer tracks, gasping as a swift whistled by her head, watching it slice up through the air only to plummet earthbound with a cry so elemental it seemed to belong to the hills. They'd find a moss-lined nest of speckled eggs on a scrape of ground, and hear the wild *goback, goback* cry of a grouse warning of their presence. Almost every day, they were privileged to watch the lonely lope of a mountain hare, the effortless circling of an eagle, or the quiver of a ptarmigan as it flattened itself to the ground.

And they were watched in return. Deer, wary eyed, observed them from a ridge as they followed the cattle. They drank from mountain springs, savouring the icy sweetness, and knew the joy of a curlew's haunting cry. She especially loved to walk through long grass, wind-splayed into glistening waves, feeling it brush her legs. Warm rock, lichen-crusted, to sit upon, the changing light and shifting mists, even the rain—all of it gave her joy.

Just as Morna instructed, she couldn't help but revel in the tiny, unnoticed things, things Duncan seemed blind to until she pointed them out or he all but stumbled over them. 'Twas other things Duncan noticed, for he was ever watchful and alert to danger, scouring the hills with sharpened eyes. He monitored distant tracks and observed who used them. He skimmed heather-thatched cots crouched low on hillsides, watching for a splash of crimson among the trees, a blur of movement, listening for the drum of hooves. Vigilant. Ever vigilant.

But then, they were different. Each night, before they lay down to sleep, they prayed for James and Da's safe return, that the whisky would reach market safely and fetch a fair price. But they offered their prayers in different ways and to what seemed quite different gods.

Duncan clutched a rosary in his hands and prayed to a wooden likeness of the Virgin Mary, a gift Father Ranald pressed upon him on the day of the blessing. Though few, his words were full of Jesus and the saints, of God and his places, heaven and hell and likely the burning halfway place where Father Ranald said Mam had gone.

She needed no saints or idols. She gathered stones and flowers, cones and sprigs of trees, maybe a raven's feather, and knelt to pray to the creator of these things. Nature. Mother Earth. The universe, whom she sensed must be female, for her gift of balance and creativity, her ingenuity in fashioning every intricate part of creation and connecting them all with such beauty and perfection was too exquisite, surely, to belong to any man. Mortal or not. 'Twas what she thought, although she kept that thought to herself.

The first task Duncan undertook, and he was single-minded in it, was to look for a place they could flee to should soldiers threaten. The redcoats might fire their hut, but they'd not drive off the cattle that were Lachlan's livelihood. He'd given him his word. Nor would he let soldiers glimpse his sisters; he'd hide them away. They were innocent and trusting, too lovely for the likes of thon murdering scum to be gawping at.

He explained soldiers were wicked. They had no honour or decency and did shameful things to women and girls. Depraved, Father Ranald called them. They'd not hesitate to commit brutal acts toward any lass they chanced upon, believing all Highland folk were treacherous vermin living in stinking dung heaps, there to be used and abused. This was all well understood, he said, though not by Rowena or Grace. Hearing it, but understanding little, they shuddered, their imaginations running wild, trusting Duncan would protect them from these soldier-devils.

Good to his word, after much searching, Duncan found what he considered the perfect hiding place and named it the Shelter Stone. Rowena was proud of him and his discovery; she thought it the best hiding place in the world.

On the far slope of the hill where their hut stood, a fast-flowing burn cut a sharp gash through the hillside, where water hissed and gurgled on its way down, finally plunging over rocks in a thunder of spray. A shallow pool lay at the base, surrounded by rocks brought down by the force of falling water.

Among the slabs of granite and schist lay a single mass of rock, a giant boulder lifted off the ground at the front and held there by a natural arrangement of smaller rocks. Gaps in these rocks left a space big enough for a body to squeeze through and enter the depression made by the rock's impact with the earth. Once inside, a cavity was revealed, dark and damp-smelling but big enough for three people and a dog to hide in relative comfort. Once the gap at the front where they must squeeze in was disguised with branches and greenery, it was all but invisible to anyone passing by.

"Tis perfect,' Grace breathed, and Rowena nodded. 'I dinna ken how ye found it, but ye're a genius.'

His face twitched with pleasure. 'They'll nae find ye here, I swear.' And he clenched his jaw tight.

Fearing they might need to hide under the stone for some time, waiting for danger to pass, Duncan took great trouble to make their hiding place as comfortable as possible. He cut hoards of fir-candles and stashed them in the cavern to lighten the gloom. He cleared the ground of stones and laid down heather to keep them snug. They'd not be able to light a fire; the smoke would give them away, would likely choke them, but the glow from gently burning pine knots would illuminate their world, making it seem homely. And he remembered to store water there, along with a cache of pignuts so they'd not starve.

Before long, the Shelter Stone became one of Rowena's favourite places. There she could keep out of the wind and rain and conjure thoughts of her mother. She could coorie down on her belly and peer through gaps in the brushwood toward the forest surrounding Dun Sithean, the hill of the faeries—a place folk shunned. 'Twas said to be the home of faeryfolk. Yet, the more she gazed across at that wood, the more she felt drawn to it.

Mam had gone there once but hadn't allowed her young daughter to follow. She'd made Rowena wait at the tree line, warning of danger. She'd longed to follow Mam into the trees, and that same longing quickened again whenever she gazed across to Sithean Wood.

The Shelter Stone lived up to its name, for whenever the weather turned foul, she and Duncan could shelter there, watching the cattle graze within view. Duncan liked to pass the time going over the stiff-sounding English words, aware she was less keen to learn them than Grace. She worked hard to please him, sounding out the strange new words, trying to remember them.

She was gradually gaining more understanding but quickly tired of grappling with the unfamiliar sounds. They had no music to them like Gaelic words and brought her little joy. There was no word for the way a river sounded after a storm had passed, *tuil-bheum*, nor a phrase for a summer sky dappled with cloud, *breac a' mhuiltein*. The language of the Gael was one of poetry, she realised, everything named for nature in beautiful description.

On their fifth lesson together and tired of sounding out the English words, she decided she should tell Duncan about Morna and spending time in wild places.

'The green woman?' He frowned at her. 'She's a heathen. What does she want wi' you?'

'To teach me to be a healer.' She looked hopefully at him. 'A *draoidh*.'

He sat upright. 'To mak' ye a witch, ye mean? Like she is.'

'She's nae a witch. Ye make her sound wicked, but she's never that. Morna's kind. She helps folk. Did ye nae feel the goodness in her? It made me tingle.'

He stared at her, anxious to make her understand his repugnance at this but struggling with how. The crease appeared between his brows.

'She's taken ye in, Rowena, wi' that silver tongue o' hers. Her ways will only draw ye further from God. Folk shun her. What chapel has ever seen her face?'

'Ye dinna need to go to chapel to be a good woman. Who says ye do?'

'God. The church. The Holy Father.'

'I dinna like God. He makes stupid rules. He ... He riles me!'

'Ye mustna say that,' he stammered. ''Tis blasphemy.'

'God will damn me to hell, will He?'

'Yer immortal soul is in great danger, aye.' His face had whitened, and he blinked at her. 'Ye must pray fer the Lord's forgiveness. We can do it thegither. I'll help ye.'

She eyed him darkly and shook her head.

He didn't grow angry as she imagined he might. He'd never been ill-tempered with her. He stared at her all tight-faced, fearful for her but at a loss over what to do about it. She began to regret her words.

'I never wish harm to come to ye,' he said at last. 'Ye're innocent.' He frowned, and she saw his turmoil as he struggled for the right words. 'Have ye any notion how much you and yer family mean to me?' He swallowed. 'I suppose not; I've never told ye. I've nae the green woman's silver tongue—her gift wi' words. I stumble, and the right words never seem to come, but ye're more precious to me than ….'

He stared around, perhaps searching for something precious to compare her with, but there was naught but rock. He frowned harder. 'Ach, I dinna ken. All I know is that since I came here, since that night when ye sang to me.' He swallowed. 'All I've wanted is to shield ye from harm.' His face tightened, a muscle flexing in his cheek. 'To be worthy of you and yer family. Yer kindness.' He let his breath out. 'More worthy than I was o' my first family.'

She'd never seen him look so strange, feverish almost. He looked intently at her, willing her to understand.

'I know,' she whispered. 'Ye're decent. As loyal a brother as any lass could wish fer. Only we're different. As much as you want to be a priest like Father Ranald, I want to be a *draoidh,* like Morna.'

He stared at her as if his world had fallen about him, and she suspected it had.

She sighed. 'Ye saw how Morna healed Grace's hand. I wish to do that. And have ye heard Grace cough lately? I've not. Nae once. 'Tis a kind o' magic, the healing. Nature's magic. I wish to learn it.'

She lowered her voice. 'And Morna can sense folk's souls. What makes them who they are, even if they're dead and gone. Mam's gone, but she can still feel her.' She pressed her hands together, a quiver in her voice. 'I wish to do that, too.' Seeing his appalled expression, she canted her head. 'D'ye nae wish you could do that? It makes me giddy thinking on it.'

His face reflected his scandalised incomprehension. Discouraged, she looked down at her hands. 'And I wish to keep our story safe. The story o' our glen. What harm does that do? I dinna see the harm in any o' it.'

'But,' he stammered, 'others will. Dear God.' He let his breath out with a shudder. 'It all reeks o' witchery. Is healing nae just tampering wi' God's will? Most folk think so. 'Tis what I think.'

She drew back, giving him a pitying look. 'I'm sorry if ye think that.' She paused, wondering if he truly believed it, judging how best to change his mind. 'But if ye were sick or hurt, would ye nae want Morna to use herbs to heal ye rather than leave ye to suffer? Nature made the plant magic fer us to use. D'ye nae see?'

''Twas more likely the divil, Rowena.'

She sighed, sad they should quarrel about something so essential to her. She tried again. 'But if 'twere Grace or me. James, Jem even. Would ye nae want Morna to save us if she could? Even if it meant upsetting yer precious God?'

He blanched, his face quivering. 'Lord, I believe I'd go to hell and back to save ye.'

She nodded, and he stared at her.

The cavern darkened, a frantic scuffling and panting sound signalling someone making a hasty entrance. Grace almost fell on top of them, gasping for breath. Her face was blotchy, rain-streaked; her chest heaved as if she'd been running for her life.

'Thank the Lord ye're here! The soldier-divils are riding this way. Father Ranald's been rapping on our door to warn us. There's nae time to waste. They're rounding up the beasts. Ye must hide them, Duncan. We must all hide.'

He blinked at her, and she shook his shoulder. '*Duncan!*'

Rowena's heart began to race. 'Ye've seen them?'

'Nae yet. But the father says they'll be upon us directly. They've plundered a great herd—cattle, oxen, sheep—raiding every holding in their path. Taking the beasts to feed their troops. Or to sell. Any they find, they take. Anyone who stands in their way, they cut down. 'Tis the king's business; resisting them is treason.'

''Tis all right,' Duncan soothed her. 'I'll hide them. I'll drive the cattle into thon wood ower there and hide them amongst the trees.' He peered through the undergrowth to the cattle grazing stoically in the rain.

'Sìthean Wood?' A frisson tingled up Rowena's spine.

He turned to her. '*Sìthean*? Is it a faery place?'

She nodded. 'Mam went there once, though she came back safe.'

He looked across at the dark wood. From his expression, she could see the forest no longer seemed such a safe haven. 'We've little time. Hiding them in thon wood is the best we can hope fer. I'll nae let them take yer da's cattle. I swore to him.' He scrambled out into the rain with Jem at his heels.

When she moved to do the same, Grace caught her by the arm. 'What're ye doing? Ye canna go out there. The divils might catch ye.'

'He'll get the beasts hidden quicker wi' me helping.' She shrugged off Grace's hand and scrambled after him.

'Rowena!'

Out in the open, even above the hiss of sluicing rain, she could hear a strange rumbling, the ground trembling beneath her feet.

'Get back under the stone!' Duncan gestured wildly to her.

'What's that noise?' She stared at her feet.

'Cattle. Hundreds. Driven by dragoons on iron-shod mounts. So many the ground shakes. Go back to the Shelter Stone. Please, Rowena.'

She shook her head, helping cut switches of birch from a nearby sapling. With one in each hand, Duncan whistled and called, prodding the soaked and bellowing beasts, trying to gather them into a more manageable herd.

'Keep them calm,' she urged. 'Dinna affright them, else they'll scatter and go rampaging all ways. Sing to them.'

'Sing?' He shook the wet hair from his eyes. 'I ken no cattle songs.'

'Milking songs, then. Let me sing to them.'

'No, go back under the stone. Please, Rowena, go back to safety.'

The beasts were showing the whites of their eyes, ears pricked forward, snorting and milling, looking ready to scatter. She raised her voice, looking for Isla. Isla liked to be sung to. The other cattle trusted her, especially the calves.

As her voice grew stronger, carrying over the herd, she spied Isla in amongst the others, dark eyes peeping from under her fringe. She cautiously approached her. The others jostled and snorted, turning to face her.

Perhaps Isla imagined she would milk her, or perhaps she was just too frightened to run, but she let Rowena get close enough to stroke her neck. 'There,' she soothed. 'Bonny lass. *Neach-gaoil*.' Sweetheart. She ruffled the cow's long fringe, lifting one of her ears, and whispered to her, then gently tugged her by the horns. Walking ahead, she called her name.

Isla began to follow, the others too, calves first, slowly moving toward Sìthean Wood. Duncan brought up the rear, zig-zagging back and forth behind the herd, arms outstretched, cutting off any stragglers that looked ready to bolt. He hummed too, a mite frantically through clenched teeth.

The beasts halted at the edge of the wood, bunching together, confused and fearful. The ground quaked beneath their hooves, an ominous drumming filling the air. It grew louder, the eerie lowing of cattle coming to them as if from a ghost herd. The sound echoed off the hills, distorted by the heavy air—a menacing, disembodied din.

Her heart pounded; the urge to plunge into the trees was over-whelming. She was vulnerable out in the open, foolishly singing of all things, while an army of vengeful dragoons was almost upon them, riding hard, headed by a mass of charging beasts.

She glanced at Duncan. He was desperately trying to urge the cattle forward without alarming them. Should they stampede, they'd be lost, swept away by the approaching horde, while they'd both be trampled in the crush.

'Go back to the Shelter Stone,' he pleaded. 'Please, Rowena. They're almost upon us. I couldna bear it if anything happened to ye.'

'Nae till the beasts are safe.'

Stretching her neck out, Isla inched forward, snorting, smelling a patch of clover growing at the edge of the trees. Rowena swooped on it, tearing it up by the roots. It was drier under the trees, sheltered from the wind. The unnerving sounds were deadened a little. Shaking the rain from her eyes, she held out the clover. Isla wished to trust her; she could see it in her eyes. Should she enter the trees, the others would likely follow.

Yet it seemed there was an invisible barrier at the edge of the wood Isla was unwilling to cross. Woods likely held dangers for cattle that open ground did not. Wolves, for one. The beasts weren't to know the last wolf had been shot whilst she was still in her cradle. To them, the danger was ever-present. They'd never enter the wood; they'd always feel safer in the open.

She could hear the shouts of men now. Her heart hammered. Was it already too late? Jem began to bark, haring back and forth, nipping at the cattle's hind legs. She leapt onto the nearest beast's rump and bounced off, striking the ground before leaping onto the next. The cattle bellowed and kicked out, then swarmed forward, stampeding past Rowena into the forest, scattering in all directions.

Gasping, she leapt out of their way, running toward Duncan.

He scooped her up, sprinting with her under his arm, charging into the forest with Jem at his heels, leaping over roots and bushes, dodging trees, the terrible sound of the passing horde urging him on. Finally, he tripped over a clump of bracken, sprawling headlong into another, cursing and swearing. She found herself in the wet bracken, too, gazing up through the trees, her head spinning.

He sat up, staring at her as she lay on her back in the leaf mould. 'Are ye all right? I didna hurt ye?'

With his hair soaked and flattened to his head, his face splattered with mud, he looked so comical, and their escape seemed so miraculous, a foolish grin spread across her face. Sitting up, she giggled, then laughed so hard tears ran down her face.

He frowned in consternation. 'Are ye laughing or crying?'

'I dinna ken.' She flopped back, listening to the muted thunder of hooves still rumbling by, the earth shaking beneath her. 'Both, I think. We did it!' She laughed helplessly. 'And was that pious you, just now taking the Lord's name in vain?'

'Did I?'

She nodded, laughing at his mortified expression.

Jem licked his chin, smearing the mud, and she hooted again.

CHAPTER TWELVE

SHE WANTED TO take her time rounding up the cattle, for looking around now the danger was past, Sìthean Wood was surely a magical place. Nearly every tree was a giant, so gnarled and lichen-crusted, she saw what looked like faces in the creases of their bark. The face of an old man, a *bodach,* with curling hair and beard, seemed to watch her.

In the shadows beneath the dripping trees, she spied rare flowers: delicate twinflowers nodded amongst a drift of star-white daisies. Colours seemed brighter here. The air smelled earthy and fresh, a rich aroma rising from the dark soil with its blanket of leaf mould. The scent breathed light into the dark spaces in her soul that once her mother had filled.

What looked like paths curved through the trees, and she yearned to follow them, to feel the satisfying crump of pine needles beneath her feet. But as Duncan pointed out, they couldn't be real paths. Who could've made them? No one came here, did they? 'Twas a faery place, inhabited by devil's imps. 'Twas likely these imps who'd made the paths.

So, her time in the forest was short-lived, much shorter than she wished. Naught but a frantic search for the cattle and a hasty herding of them out of the trees. Yet she knew she'd return here. She'd felt something of her mother, as she'd done at the symbol stone.

* * *

Two days later, her da and James returned with the garrons. Both looked bone-weary but wore fat sporrans filled with coin. Never had she been so

109

overjoyed to see them. She launched herself at James, and he spun her around, whooping for joy. Beneath his bur-freckled clothing, she felt his thinness, the hardness of muscle and bone. He'd suffered, they both had, putting themselves in danger for their family, afraid to approach cot-house or steading for fear of arousing suspicion.

Da's unkempt beard all but hid his face, and they were both that mired with dirt and mud, and Lord knows what, she barely knew them, though 'twas naught an icy dip in the burn and a scrub with a handful of soapwort couldn't put right. James set her down and turned to wrap his arms around Grace, while Da gave her a rare smile, acknowledging the signs of hardship weathered in his face.

His gaze strayed over her shoulder, and he blinked, staring at the cattle grazing on the hill. His brows lowered, his face puckering, so she feared he was enraged, not pleased as she'd imagined he'd be. Turning to Duncan, he gripped him by the forearm, his breath rasping.

'Niver did I expect ....' He shook his head. 'I thought they'd all be gone, every last one.' He drew a quivering breath. 'I hardly ken what to say. Ye saved them. My lasses that are my heart's joy. My beasts.' His voice cracked, and he pressed trembling fingers to his mouth, shaking his head as if he couldn't quite believe his eyes. 'I'm indebted to ye.'

'Aye,' said James, staring too. 'We saw great herds being driven south and supposed ours must be amongst them. Da was that riled, 'twas all I could do to stop him taking a pot-shot at the thieving mongrels.'

''Twas my honour, sir,' Duncan muttered, 'but I did little.'

'Little?' Her da reared back. 'Dinna go putting yersel' doon.' He released Duncan's arm, looking back at the grazing beasts, wiping a wateriness from his eyes. 'I feared what I'd find here. I imagined there'd be naught but a smouldering pile, and there's all this.'

''Tis what they did to my hame, sir. Reduced it to a reeking pile.'

Her da grimaced. 'Forgive me, I'm forgetting. I'm in yer debt. And lad, Lachlan Innes pays his debts and marks well when they're warranted.'

'I'm beholden, too.' James gripped Duncan's hand. 'My sisters are precious to me. More than the beasts, I confess.'

'And to me,' Duncan said softly. 'Though, of course, the beasts are valuable, too.'

James rubbed a grimy hand over his face. 'We've hidden in bogs and ditches, under banks and in the most thorny places dodging the soldiers that infest every glen and township.'

Her da shared a look with him. 'Aye, seeing thousands o' plundered beasts, we imagined ours must be amongst them.' He shook his head. 'I should've kent better. I was mistaken to ever doubt ye, lad.'

'Thank ye, sir, but—'

'Now, dinna fret, I've nae forgotten what I promised. Ye've kept my precious things safe, and fer that I swore I'd mak' ye a smuggler. I stand by my word. If 'tis still yer wish, I'll start yer education as soon as ye're ready. There's a skill in making fine whisky. It takes time to master, but we've all the time ye need.' He frowned. 'Is it still what ye want, though? I'm thinking smuggling and preaching dinna sit so well thegither, what with ye wishing to be a priest.'

Duncan's mouth twitched as he tried to control the grin threatening to take over his face. 'I do still wish it, sir. More than ever.'

'Grand. 'Tis what I like to hear. Ye're a quick-witted lad, and ye'll be learning from a master.' He stepped back, running an appraising eye over Duncan's slight frame and twitching, fox-like face. 'And ye've something else. Something that might gie ye an edge, might mak' ye the most fervent smuggler o' us all.'

Duncan blinked.

'Ye nurse a hatred fer the authorities that rule us. Aye, I've seen it in ye; a need to strike back at them fer their cruelty. Fer what they did to yer kinfolk.' He shook his head. 'That was beyond terrible. But yer hatred's born o' injustice, and there's naught more powerful than that. Yer wish to smuggle doesna just stem from a need to pay the rent.' He smiled wryly. 'Yours, son, comes from a wish to settle scores.'

Duncan's cheeks flushed a subtle shade of pink. Looking over her da's shoulder, he sought her out, sharing a look of unbridled joy. She grinned back. Da had just called him 'son.' That fact had not passed Duncan by.

'Thank ye,' he croaked. 'Only, 'twas Rowena saved the beasts, nae me. She sang to them.'

'Sang?'

Rowena laughed. ''Twas truly Jem saved them. Just as well, she never went to the drowning sack. 'Tis no ill thing being a runtling. But Duncan was a hero, Da.'

Her da snorted, waving off mention of the runtling dog. He was too busy enthusing over the calibre of smuggler he'd make of Duncan; he'd no time for dog tales.

She cared not a jot. The look on Duncan's face was reward enough. He belonged at last. His brokenness would mend now, or so she imagined. Almost overnight, he'd become a valued member of her family and would find his rightful place in the glen. That she'd played some small part was reward enough. A warmth tingled around her heart.

'If it hadna been fer Father Ranald,' Grace pointed out, 'there'd have been nae time to hide anything. He risked his life coming to warn us, but Duncan found the perfect hideaway. Wait till ye see it.' She gushed on, praising every saint she could think of for her family's safe return, then ushered them inside for bannocks and broth.

Grace's food was almost as good as Mam's now; Rowena marvelled at how fast it went down. It barely seemed to touch the sides, so ravenous were her da and James. Between steaming spoonfuls of barley broth, James recounted their exploits evading redcoats and gaugers and negotiating with treacherous Edinburgh blethermen, her da adding his tuppence-worth whenever his jaws ceased chewing long enough.

Beneath the grime, James's face was animated. Rowena sat on the floor, curling her arms around her knees to listen, barely able to keep her eyes from his well-loved face. She couldn't remember when he'd talked so much, either of them. But then, they'd been stealthy so long, muffling the garrons' hooves so they could steal through the hills unnoticed, speaking in naught but whispers. 'Twas only natural words should come tumbling now.

Listening to their tales was a rare treat. Not usually privy to smuggling talk, she was quickly swept up in the daring of it all. Beside her, Duncan quivered with excitement. He'd soon be involved; she knew he could barely wait.

They'd glimpsed a detachment of dragoons just short of the Spittal of Glenshee.

'Malcolm MacRae drew them away,' said James. 'He cut loose his sturdiest garron and made a wild dash ower the hills wi' the redcoats on his heels.'

'Faith!' cried Grace. 'Malcolm did that? He's only a boy.'

'I met him when I was cutting peat,' said Duncan. 'He's nae much older than me.'

'He's young, aye.' Grace struggled to suppress a smile. 'But bold. Did he get away safe?'

'Aye, though damned if I ken how.' Lachlan laid down his spoon. 'He must hae mair lives than a barn cat. He swaggered into camp later that night looking like he'd spent the day toying wi' a mouse, then slept half the next day. We'd to douse him wi' water in the end to rouse him.'

'Faith!'

'We've nae just Duncan to thank.' Her da helped himself to more bannocks. 'But Father Ranald and John Meldrum. John warned where the soldiers would likely be camped.' He chuckled. 'The redcoats niver think to question where an exciseman's loyalties might lie. They assume his allegiance lies wi' the government that pays him.' He shook his head, pitying them their ignorance. 'John was born in the Cabrach, hardly known fer its allegiance to the Calvinist crown. Son of a Jacobite smuggler and as shrewd as they come, he joined the Excise Board as a way to protect his kinfolk, every one a smuggler.'

He loosened his sporran, weighing it in his hands. 'Thanks to John, we struck a fair price wi' the Edinburgh dealers. My pouches are fair choked wi' coin. There'll be no factor darkening my door come Lammas. We're safe fer a time from that.'

'I'm glad to hear it, sir.'

Lachlan laid his sporran on the table. 'I've still to pay John his share. I'm glad to. 'Twas on account o' John we had buyers in the capital. He arranged it all. He's wi'out question the most valuable member o' our smuggling ring.'

Duncan's brows rose. He was party to smuggling talk now. Her da trusted him with even this most delicate information, knowledge that could put Mister Meldrum in gaol, Rowena imagined, or worse. From the look on Duncan's face, he was keenly aware of his new status.

It dawned upon her she'd not see so much of him now. He'd be busy doing smuggling things—malting barley and working the pot-still, plotting with the others under the cot-house of an evening. And she'd be even freer to spend time in wild places as Morna directed—on her own. Yet oddly, despite realising she'd now have the freedom she'd yearned for, knowing she'd no longer have Duncan for company brought a sharp sense of loss.

* * *

She was right in her assessment; Duncan was soon much occupied with her da and James. The three of them worked together in all things, both on the land and in the secret bothy where the whisky was made. Duncan was now wholly trusted, and her da kept nothing from him. With his eagerness to learn, his gratitude for everything given him, he stirred no resentment in James, who'd never had much enthusiasm for smuggling. They became inseparable.

James soon confided Duncan was more a craftsman than he'd ever be. Not only did he take great care in learning every detail of the whisky-making, of thinking up imaginative ways to dupe the hated occupying troops, but he took great pride in the quality of whisky he produced.

Naught was left to chance or wasted. Duncan would sit up all night waiting for the precise moment the middle run of spirit which made the finest whisky would begin running from the end of the still's copper worm. He carefully re-distilled the oily foreshots and tailings, the first and last run of spirit, eeking out as much high-quality whisky from their precious malt as possible.

Her da was impressed. He spoke of Duncan often now and always with pride in his voice. The lad showed a single-mindedness to learn, to repay the kindness shown to him. He could ask no more of him. Whenever her da spoke that way, Rowena's chest crammed so full of feelings she had no name for, she wondered it didn't burst.

She spent the summer at the shieling with Grace, sleeping in the stone hut, the cattle now her sole responsibility. She'd never been to her da's whisky bothy and was not trusted with knowledge of its whereabouts. But in the rare moments she and Duncan still spent together, he described the interior and the genius of its location.

'Twas an earth-house, a stone-lined chamber built underground by long-ago folk likely for some wicked reason that escaped explanation. Her da had stumbled upon the place when he was a stripling and took care to store away the location of his find for future use, knowing he'd smuggle one day. Above ground, there was naught to see but a tussocky mound, the entrance concealed by bushes and scrub, but inside it opened into a cavernous chamber perhaps once used for storing food. Now it housed her da's still equipment, together with a range of barrels and casks for mashing and fermenting and for stockpiling the whisky before they could smuggle it away. A lime kiln was located nearby. They carefully diverted the smoke and steam there to disguise it.

Whenever he spoke of the secret bothy, Duncan's eyes shone, and Rowena could see the romance of the place had captured him.

'Is it as special a place as this?' she asked him as they took refuge from a downpour at the Shelter Stone.

He looked at her with a strange light in his eyes. 'It can never be that, Rowena. This is our place. Yours and mine. Where I teach ye the difficult Inglis words, and ye show me all the things I canna see fer myself fer being too blind and inattentive. The wondrous web o' life ye see all around us and that I barely see at all.' He laughed. 'Yer senses are sharper than mine, yer instincts keener. Mebbe ye hae an extra sense or two I lack.'

She blinked. Hadn't Morna said something similar? The promise she'd seen in her. Could Duncan sense these things too? But then, Duncan was sensitive—a deep thinker.

'Ye never go anywhere near Sìthean Wood, do ye?' He looked across at the forest with drawn brows. ''Tis a godless place, else why would it be named fer the faeryfolk, the *Sìth*?'

'No more preaching aboot God and the divil.' She laughed. 'Save it fer when ye're a priest.' Then, not wishing to admit she ventured a little farther into Sìthean Wood almost daily, somehow drawn there, she tried to deflect him.

'D'ye still pray as much, Duncan? Now ye're a serious smuggler, soon to go on yer first smuggling trip, d'ye pray fer God's protection the way ye'll pray fer folk's souls once ye're a priest?'

He sobered, his troubled expression making her regret asking.

'I still pray to the Lord,' he said at last. 'My faith's as strong as ever. But I fear I can never be a priest. The seminary hidden in the Braes o' Glenlivet wasna so well hid after all. Scalan lies in ashes. The Master and the boys training to be priests have scattered to the four winds. Father Ranald doesna speak o' it, and I've nae the heart to press him.'

He sighed. ''Twas the last place in Scotland boys could still train fer the priesthood. The last place upholding, in defiance o' the law, any spark o' the true faith, fer how can a faith survive wi'out priests? But even supposing 'twas still possible to train, to gain a place on the continent, perhaps, where the Catholic faith still flourishes, how can I?'

'Why nae?'

'I'm a smuggler now and plan to be a good one. And I'm landless, penniless, wi'out family or position.'

'What does that matter?'

'I'm nae worthy, Rowena.'

'Ye have a family. Ye're an Innes now.'

'But I'm nae. Ye know I'm not.' He lowered his voice, looking tenderly at her. 'Dinna imagine I'm nae grateful.' He swallowed, pain momentarily marring his features. 'I'm more grateful than I can say. But everything I have, everything I've become, has all been given me in charity. Naught's truly mine. I'm nae an equal to those other students, the true young priestlings. I'm a cuckoo in the nest.' He smiled crookedly. 'Now a criminal one.'

She frowned, not understanding. 'Does it matter? Having a position and family?'

'To be considered deserving of sending abroad fer training, I imagine so.' He sighed. 'But there's another reason I can never be ordained.' He turned troubled eyes upon her. 'I'm full o' anger. I've never forgiven those who burned and butchered. Those who gave the order.' He knotted his fingers together, searching for the right words. 'I dinna have it in me to forgive, so how can I be a worthy servant o' the Lord?'

'But I'd feel the same. Who *could* forgive such a thing?'

'A real priest could. A truly pious man would find a way to forgive, even that, I believe. But I'm nae that man. I know it now. Learning to smuggle has shown me what I am. I wish to strike back. I dream o' how it might be done.' He clenched a fist and drummed it hard against the rock-face with an anguished cry. 'So I'll never be worthy o' the Lord's work!'

She swallowed. 'I'm sorry. I ken how much ye wished to be a priest. But does it matter being a cuckoo in the nest?'

He sighed. 'When it comes to joining the priesthood, I believe so. But to smuggle? Nay. 'Tis just how I feel. I wish to prove myself. I believe smuggling will be my way.'

She nodded, not fully understanding but feeling his pain.

He forced a smile. 'So the whisky bothy can never be as special a place as this. This is ours, so special beyond measure.'

She nodded, glad of that much.

* * *

Although Rowena's days were sorely lacking without Duncan, they were still full in every other way imaginable. She spent her time almost entirely in nature, herding the cattle and foraging, often with Jem for company. Her da refused to have Jem at the whisky bothy. 'Twas too dangerous; she might bark or run out from cover, giving them away. Something Duncan assured him she would not. But 'twas her da laid down the law in all things whisky. Duncan understood, only he'd trust Jem to no one but her.

That first summer, they stashed more whisky under Tomachcraggen cot-house than her da could ever remember. Thanks to Duncan, principally, for James told her Duncan was so driven, he barely slept. 'Twas the reason she saw so little of him. On the rare occasions he spent the evening at the hut with Grace and her, he battled to keep his eyes open, and there were dark circles under them.

On the even rarer occasions he walked the pastures with her, going over her English words, he'd look wistfully at her, and she'd sense he wished to say something, though he always thought better of it. She consoled herself with the knowledge he still sought her out whenever he could, especially at the Shelter Stone.

When word came from John Meldrum of a quantity of whisky wanted by Sir Ludovick Grant to restock Castle Grant's cellars, Duncan could barely contain his excitement. Her da deemed it a fitting first venture into the world of smuggling for him. The distance they'd need to cover was not so great, and Duncan was beyond eager. Much more so, she judged, than James.

She came to realise that James was uncomfortable smuggling. His strong sense of honour meant he preferred to stay on the right side of the law, getting by raising cattle and working the land. He despised the unjust laws and taxes as much as any man but wished to live in peace.

She overheard a heated discussion on the subject, her da and Duncan not agreeing with James, although respecting his reasoning. James argued smuggling was wrong; he saw no future in it for any of them. 'Twould likely end badly, and they should give it up while they still could. Hearing that, her innards tightened. Yet, although James and Duncan held opposing opinions on the matter, they remained as close as ever, respecting each other's stance and the thinking behind it.

As for Grace, she cared little for smuggling or the politics of it. Her only thoughts on the subject were fearful ones. At night, when she lay down to sleep, Rowena would oft-times overhear her fervent prayers for her menfolk's safety. Grace also failed to understand Rowena's need to spend so much time in nature, doing Lord knows what as she put it, and Rowena's attempts to explain it to her never seemed to entirely succeed. Despite that, Grace was the most loyal of sisters. She seemed to understand Mam's death had affected her deeply, far more than the rest of them. Above all, she wished Rowena to be happy.

So, on the rare occasions Da questioned Grace over Rowena's whereabouts, although Grace fretted over her safety with the glen occupied with government troops, she'd fend his questions off with creative excuses. She even took some of Rowena's chores upon herself: churning butter, souring milk to make clabber, grinding oats. Grace didn't seem to mind; after all, she did tasks Grace was less keen to do. It seemed a fair exchange.

She gathered wild greens for the pot: nettles, silverweed and sorrel, wild garlic, dandelions, lovage and hoards of pignuts. Later in the year, she brought home guelder rosehips, blaeberries, cowberries, elderberries if she could find them, mushrooms and pine nuts. And always, she gathered fragrant herbs.

The bounty included delicious things Grace had neither time nor inclination to search for, but that made her food so flavourful, she began to blossom in the praise lavished upon her by the menfolk of the house.

Rowena also sourced all manner of crottle for dyeing wool. She spent hours scraping lichen from rocks and trees in damp woods, from old stone walls and dry moors and brought it all home bundled in her skirts. Once dried in the sun and ground up fine, she and Grace used it to dye their wool an array of subtle Highland colours ranging from a soft golden brown to the prized raw umber of winter heather. Come the dark winter evenings, she and Grace would spin it into yarn for blankets and clothing. Something Mam had done. She remembered Mam's voice rising in song above the whirr and creak of the spinning wheel.

It seemed every day now she discovered something new, growing and changing in all manner of ways. She learned to be still and silent, absorbing her surroundings, letting nothing pass her by. Following the cattle over the hills, she felt the wind as a tree does: at times a gentle caress, at others a raging battle to remain upright. Yet like a tree, she grew stronger, supple, able to bend a little. She loved to walk in the wind with her skirts billowing, watching the scudding clouds, listening to the snatched cries of mountain birds. 'Twas at these most wind-lorn times, she especially missed Duncan.

Often the cattle would take her to the Avon, a peaceful stretch fringed with alder and willow, and she'd sit on a driftwood log, watching the beasts drink what looked like mature whisky, so amber was the water's peaty flow. Rocks beneath the surface made the water sparkle and shimmer, an island of shingle forming a bridge where deer came to cross. 'Twas perhaps what heaven looked like—where Mam was, according to Duncan. But she sensed Mam was beside her, listening to the gentle rush of water and broom pods snapping open in the sun.

She loved the forests, too, walking in them with the air all cool and mossy. When the wind rose, it soughed through the trees, ruffling the bracken, teasing leaves into the air. In higher woods, pines rose vertical from the heather up hillsides, and every branch nurtured a thick fur of moss. 'Twas always treading in places like these, she remembered most clearly what Morna told her—to notice the wee miracles. Increasingly, she did.

She became a careful observer of nature, watching her world change day by day. When a flower budded then opened in the sun, she returned each day to celebrate the bloom's short life. She watched the bees with their delving tongues and bulging yellow legs and the delicate alight of a butterfly. Briefly, the insects revelled in the flower's sweet nectar, its heavenly fragrance, before the bloom changed again, becoming a seed to be blown or dropped or taken by a bird, only to emerge into another budding flower.

She followed the turning of the seasons, the vivid drama of autumn, the long sleep of winter, then the delicate dawning of new life and soon more green abundance. How did the trees and plants know to do that? Who guided them and told them it was time? 'Twas a kind of magic, and it fascinated her. Yet why did others not marvel at it? Why was nature's work so heedlessly disregarded when 'twas such a miracle? Surely it should be valued.

So, value it she did. She knelt to whisper her thanks to the gorse for her scented golden flowers, to the alder, her mother's tree, for her wood known to resist the rot of water. And to the rowan for her magical protection. Yet she sensed doing so made her strange and fey, but that it hardly mattered, not to her.

Was it what Morna saw that day by her mother's coffin? That day felt like a lifetime ago, yet more and more, she dreamed of Morna, the green woman, yearning for her promised return.

Then there was Sìthean Wood. A place that drew her as irresistibly as a bee to a nectar-filled bloom.

CHAPTER THIRTEEN

September 1757

WHAT DREW HER to Sìthean Wood? A feeling, she supposed—a magical one. An air of peace so profound, she sensed her mother everywhere. Here she remembered Mam's scent, the familiar timbre of her voice, the curve of her cheek when she smiled, her gaiety. And above all, how safe and cherished Mam had made her feel. Here the memories were so vivid, she seemed to relive them, those lost days.

Often, they made her cry, but here there was no shame in tears. Who was there to see them? Tears only meant she cared. As time passed, she'd found it harder to recapture the fleeting images, even to recall Mam's face, something that saddened her. But then, the memories were from her childish times, and she supposed she was no longer a bairn. As she grew toward womanhood, other things filled her head—chores, worries, and everyday things that mattered little. The cherished times were pushed into the cobwebby crevices.

From that first heart-stopping moment plunging into the trees with Duncan, she'd recognised the magic of the place. So, by age fifteen, she'd visited Sìthean Wood more times than she cared to consider, though never in anyone's company but her own. *Sìth* was a faery word, and the forest had long been linked with the faeryfolk. Coming here needed to be her secret. If discovered, her visits would be forbidden. She'd be chided for doing what she could no more stop herself doing than she could prevent herself breathing, loving her family, her glen.

Duncan would be especially fearful. He considered the wood a godless place, which was perhaps one reason she liked it so much. She had no love of God, but equally, she had no wish to worry Duncan, who only sought to keep her safe. He might love God, but he loved her too and had worries of his own.

He was swiftly gaining notoriety as a smuggler. Already his reputation rivalled her father's. His passion was to put Strathavon on the whisky map with their whisky ranking among the most sought after in the Highlands. He claimed a whisky's illegal origin only made it more desirable, and he hoped theirs would become prized. Da muttered they had no need of such attention. Only coin for paying the rent. He shouldna be getting too big fer his boots.

Soldiers were still billeted throughout the glen and now garrisoned at Corgarff Castle. The occupying army had converted the old tower of Corgarff, once held by the Jacobites, into an outstation of Fort George. From here, redcoats guarded the high passes and the new military road they'd built through Strathavon to Inverness. Part of the pacification of the Highlands, Duncan told her. His skill was to smuggle their whisky past these devils.

The redcoats still hunted down Jacobite sympathisers and now worked with excise officers, John Meldrum included. Smuggling was deemed evidence of the glensmen's traitorous nature. Smuggler and Jacobite were one-and-the-same to the authorities. Life was now perilous for Mister Meldrum. Her da warned John was in a damnable position, living in constant danger of discovery.

The redcoats' favourite occupation seemed to be persecuting local herdsmen, a pastime they engaged in with extraordinary zeal. They arrested any man who dared garb himself in tartan cloth or carry anything resembling a weapon. Yet, to defend themselves and their whisky, her menfolk needed to arm themselves.

Despite this, Duncan considered smuggling an honourable endeavour, as did most in the glen. 'Twas his way of carrying on the struggle his da died for, a way to settle scores and right injustices—although she shuddered when she thought of the danger he put himself in. But it seemed Duncan still needed to prove himself, to repay debts and make amends, although what for, she had little notion. Only she'd not add to his troubles by revealing she visited a place he considered dangerous. Some things were better kept to herself.

The bond between them had only grown over the years, and whenever she thought of Duncan, which was often, she'd fill with an inexplicable longing—a tenderness that puzzled her. She couldn't even explain to herself what she yearned for, but there was sadness in that yearning, a grief that frightened her. Hadn't she lost so much already? And Duncan even more? She couldn't lose again.

'Twas plain Sìthean Wood was immeasurably old, its sinister reputation protecting it through the ages from the woodcutter's axe. It had the feel of a place untouched since ancient times, which she sensed it was. Time seemed to move slower here, instilling a sense of calm so profound it entered her soul.

At first, she came only to gather berries and mushrooms, herbs, lichen. Witch's hair lichen, the colour of Duncan's eyes, hung from the branches of pine, and always a rich harvest could be found here. But soon, she came just to breathe in the beauty of the place, letting the forest weave its enchantments. Once soothed and sated, she'd be on her way, immeasurably enriched for coming here. But never did she venture too far into the trees.

The forest was a conscious place; it watched her, she sensed. The trees and the beings living amongst them seemed to follow her every move. Even the empty spaces were different here. Perhaps they were the lungs of the forest, for they appeared to breathe. Everything moved. The ground itself seemed to shift minutely, the opening of many unseen eyes, tiny movements glimpsed from the corner of her vision. But when she studied the earth and what grew there, the trees, the air itself, she saw naught. 'Twas only when she stilled herself and opened her heart to the forest's wonders, then things seemed to happen. Gifts were offered.

She sensed the forest had much to teach her, and she longed to explore farther, but she only ever skirted the fringes of the forest, needing to keep the cattle in sight. Still, they feared to enter the trees. Today, though, they'd followed her, sniffing out the last of the summer clover.

She'd come in search of rich jewels—blaeberries, rowanberries, elderberries. With luck, she'd find mushrooms. In autumn, they magically appeared from nowhere, pale cups sprouting overnight from decaying wood. Then there were the paths. They intrigued her, winding through the trees, teasing her to follow. But who or what had made them? Where did they lead, and how would she find her way back?

The rowans had begun to change colour. Golden now, their boughs hung with clusters of crimson berries. Although spring was her favourite season, 'twas such a joy after winter's dearth, autumn was nature's drama, her final flourish before winter clamped her teeth.

The wind rustled through the trees, the odd leaf spiralling down, but where she stood, it barely touched her. Ahead, a path stretched, undulating over root-cobbled ground, leading into a dappled glade where fallen birch leaves lay like scattered coins. Light filtered through the canopy, gilding the scene, inviting her to enter.

She knew better than to venture on, but today that golden light lured her. Her breath quickened, an earthy scent filling her nostrils, the ripple of water a siren call. The light changed, and her stomach fluttered. She was standing in that burnished glade, tingling, aware of a presence.

'Ye've grown, child, but I'd ken ye anywhere.'

She turned to stare.

'I should've come fer ye afore. I see that now. Ye're ready—poised upon the brink o' womanhood and wi' such beauty and grace. But I sensed disapproval amongst yer kinfolk. There's one there ill-disposed to me and my kind. Ever I'm wary o' that. But in the end, ye came to me.'

Her heart began to race. Morna had appeared as silently as the still folk. Standing among the trees, she seemed part of the forest. Other than a few more strands of silver in her hair, she was unchanged.

Her eyes nipped. 'I feared ye'd forgotten me, that I'd mebbe dreamed it all. 'Tis that long I've yearned to spend time with ye.' She bit her lip as the feelings welled.

The woman nodded. 'I, too, child. I've longed fer you, too. Let me see ye.' She moved out from under the trees. 'What a beauty ye are. The wee bairn has blossomed. Has become a bewitching young woman.' She fingered a lock of Rowena's hair, letting it slip silk-like through grimy fingers. 'Ye've a face o' such innocent perfection. And a mouth made fer kissing. I'm thinking ye'll break a few hearts afore ye're done.' She conceded this with a wistful smile. 'If 'tis yer wish.'

'It's nae my wish. I want to be like you. Just days ago, I heard ye saved Evie Lang from the child-bed fever. Ower the years, I've heard that many tales o' the lives ye've saved.'

Morna nodded. 'Evie came through the fever.'

'But her family despaired. Father Ranald told them Evie would meet her maker and leave her infant motherless. He prayed God would forgive her sins.'

Morna snorted.

'But nae willing to give up, her sister Mhari ran fer you. Herbs might help; a potion might save her. And this against the father's wishes. 'Twas his place to be tending a dying woman. A priest. But you saved her, and wi' naught but a few roots.' She shivered, her insides trembling. 'You. Nae God.'

''Twas nature's magic did the saving. I only applied it.'

She nodded. 'I wish to learn that. To save wi' nature's magic. Especially women and their bairns.'

'Why especially women?'

She frowned. 'Fer Mam, I think.' A pang of loss caught her. 'I've long sensed she'd have lived if ye'd been allowed to tend her.' She waited for Morna to confirm this, her chest tightening. ''Twas a conviction she'd long held, a belief that brought bitterness, turmoil.

Morna drew a long breath. 'Perhaps, but never do I make promises. What happened was a terrible thing, but a rare thing. If I'd tended her from the start, who's to say, but it wasna to be.'

'Who stopped ye, though? Was it Father Ranald? Mam would've wanted ye.'

'Yer da did what he thought was right. Like many, he's torn atween church ways and older ways. Churchmen can sway even the stoutest heart wi' their talk o' damned souls, though the priest ye speak o' is a decent man—one o' the more enlightened o' his kind. But Lachlan feared fer his immortal soul and fer Fearn's even more. Yer da's a good man. He did what he thought was right.'

'He let her die.'

Morna's eyes softened. 'Likely she'd have died anyhow. 'Tisna our place to judge. Lachlan feared my ways. Perhaps he believed 'twould be the worse fer Fearn if she died wi' my hands upon her. Her soul might burn forever, or some such nonsense. I've heard plenty foolishness o' that kind. But souls are nae bound by the laws o' church or man. They find their own way home guided by the goodness in them and by the greater good in all nature and creation.'

Rowena shivered, loving the perfection of that.

'Dinna punish yer da. He blames himself enough. Besides, Fearn and her child still live. Souls can never die.'

She nodded, not trusting her voice.

'As fer the heather-priest, he's a good man, if misguided. When he said 'twas God's will, he was mistaken. We have wills o' our own. Powerful ones.' She sighed. 'Ye see, while some folk heal, others dinna. Their own beliefs are too strong, too stubbornly held fer nature's magic to overthrow. If they believe they'll die, then die, they will, nae matter what I do. And if they believe my ways will finish them, then finish them they will, and mighty quick. But those are the rarer folk. Nature's magic heals in the most extraordinary ways, but only if the heart and mind allow it. We'll speak o' that, I promise. I've much to teach ye. But first, we must speak wi' yer da. Afore I teach ye anything, Lachlan must give us his blessing. Ye see that?'

She did, although she feared her da might not give it.

* * *

It had been a long night in the bothy. Duncan waited through the darkest hours for the final run of whisky to flow from the copper worm. Even now, after ten years perfecting his craft, the satisfaction of seeing that glistening liquid, something created from naught but barley, water and yeast, run into the waiting cask never failed to fascinate him. He sealed the anker, a ten-gallon keg made for Lachlan and bearing his mark, and rolled it to the side, stacking it with the others. Crafted by Angus Doull, a fellow glensman and skilled cooper, the cask of every Strathavon smuggler was marked in a particular way to identify its owner, ensuring no duplicity amongst smugglers. All Lachlan's ankers carried a small but beautiful carving of an alder leaf, the mark of his dead wife, Fearn.

Finally satisfied, he'd crawled home in the early hours so weary 'twas a wonder his legs could still carry him. Now he could hear voices. Lachlan and James would be discussing the harvest, the portioning out of labour, and he must do his share. He would gladly, for although James was undoubtedly the better farmer—'twas the smuggling that quickened his own heart—he still made sure to work equally as hard on the land as in the secret bothy.

'Twas the land that mattered. Every Highlander knew it. Each felt a deep connection to their glen, a powerful bond binding folk to the land and each other through shared ancestry and allegiance. Affinities were deeply felt, particularly now a new affliction was sweeping through the glens. *Eviction.* 'Twas a dreaded disease. Father Ranald brought regular word of its advance.

The father maintained correspondence with the bishop and men in authority, Jacobites principally, many in exile. He risked his life to do so. But in the doing, he gained a broader understanding of the world outside the glen, bringing word of changes, particularly to how the land was being worked. 'Agricultural improvements,' they were called. Common land was being enclosed, and sub-division discouraged while folk were being moved to the coast in great numbers, forced to become fishermen or kelp workers. During his secret ventures to coastal towns, he'd also heard rumours of this.

Smugglers kept no damning correspondence; most could neither read nor write. But Father Ranald risked all in his service to the humble folk of Strathavon. 'Twas one of the reasons he loved the man so much. To demonstrate his devotion, he'd taken a few risks himself. Under cover of darkness, he'd toiled alongside Gordons and MacRaes, McHardies, Chisholms, and MacPhersons, helping restore the father's chapel. Father Ranald had worked alongside them, almost feverishly, disguised as a common cottar.

To avoid the attention of soldiers and prying Kirk ministers, as well as the new factor, William McGillivray, said to loathe all Catholics, they'd rebuilt the chapel to look like a humble cot-house. Field-gathered stones and turf restored the charred walls, while the cruck-framed roof they'd reinstated with fresh timbers and thatched with heather. Slowly, the chapel had risen from its blackened bones.

The father was still forced to conduct Mass in the dead of night, the little chapel packed with the faithful, eager to hear the word of God. But the Lord must work in mysterious ways, for the father had finally been rewarded. The young duke, Alexander, fourth Duke of Gordon, had granted Father Ranald a rental of land.

Thanks to his grace, a young man rumoured to be sympathetic to the Catholic faith, Father Ranald now held the lease of the land his chapel stood upon. That hardly afforded him protection from arrest, naught could do that, but at least it provided a measure of respectability for a man of his standing. No longer must he bed down in barns and steadings, beholden to others for a roof over his head. He slept in the little chapel now, his vestments, vessels, and altar cloth hidden in a special chamber built into its back wall.

Of course, the land must be worked, and Duncan intended to help the father turn his soil, freeing him from the need to live off the charity of others like some beggar. He knew how that felt. Although more grateful to Lachlan than he knew how to say, being beholden had whittled away any pride he'd possessed. No ill thing, perhaps. Pride was one of the deadly sins. A cardinal sin, Father Ranald called it.

He had little cause for pride anyway; he knew the truth. 'Twas the reason he worked so hard. He wished to become deserving of his good fortune—James and Grace's friendship, Lachlan's trust, and Rowena. He desperately wished to make a better job of safeguarding them than he'd done with his first family. That failure he carried with him always, wearing it like a hairshirt. Never would he forget them—their terrible end. He would make amends. Somehow.

Perhaps 'twas a foolish notion, believing he could become deserving through hard toil, but he especially wished to feel worthy of Rowena, who was tender and lovely. Precious. In indulgent moments, he even allowed himself to imagine she might one day let him love her. Marry her. Though, of course, she deserved a better man.

Rising, he rubbed the sleep from his face, feeling the wispy beard he was secretly pleased now covered his chin. To be taken seriously by whisky agents, to negotiate with hard-nosed blethermen, he needed to look older than his eighteen years, although the fact he didn't had been useful at times.

His tender face had seen him through many a scrape. When the redcoats saw he was little more than a lean-limbed youth, they'd often dismiss his suspicious behaviour, putting it down to youthful high spirits. He could speak their tongue and did so with politeness and respect, something that stuck mightily in his throat, but he could do it when the need arose. Doing so saw him treated with a semblance of civility others less able to communicate were denied. 'Twas something he gave thanks to Father Ranald for near daily.

Yet, he must be a disappointment to the father if the father thought of him at all. He sighed; that was likely unfair. Father Ranald thought on all his flock. Even those he deemed most hopeless, he still prayed for every day. But, of course, the cherished dream of his younger self had been to become a priest—a Jacobite one.

Only, there were no battles to fight now. Not on an open field. All their struggles were lost. He waged his wars in bothies and back alleys, in slinking through peat bogs in the dead of night with a train of laden ponies, in crossing exposed hill passes guarded by redcoats. But he supposed that meant he was naught but a criminal—lowest of the low. Doubtless, the father considered him so.

Dressed now, he crossed to the table, halting mid-step with a hiss, wrong-footed by the sight that greeted him. Eyes turned toward him; one pair in particular fixed him with a cool blue stare. The green woman. He blinked. 'Twas years since he'd set eyes upon her or given her much thought, but 'twas undeniably her. In truth, she'd changed little. She was as repugnant as he remembered.

As she spoke, the witch's teeth appeared to flash. Likely her face had not been acquainted with soapwort in some time; her skin was the shade of old pipe tobacco. She was in conversation with Lachlan and James, doubtless beguiling them with her silver tongue. She gave the impression she was a welcomed guest. Kin, almost. Nodding warily to her, he sat down, murmuring his thanks when Grace slid a bowl of porridge to him.

Rowena was sitting at the green woman's side, her slender fingers laced together, steepled at her chin. From the whiteness of her knuckles, he could tell how tightly she squeezed them. This was no chance visit by the witch, then. Something Rowena held important rested upon it. His stomach began to churn.

Rowena glanced over at him. Her eyes burned brightly, and she wore such a hopeful expression, his heart squeezed, while his palms grew clammy. What did the witch want with her now? Could she nae leave her be? But something was plainly astir. Something worrying.

'I'm sure ye ken I'd do naught wi'out yer blessing and permission. Naught that wasna yer wish, Lachlan.' The crone pressed her lips together. 'Perhaps ye need to think on it some. There's nae need fer haste. We'll await yer decision and be hearing it when yer ready.' She sat back, looking from Lachlan to James, ignoring him.

'My sister will come to no harm?' James glanced at his father. 'Ye promise to keep her safe?'

'She'll come to no harm from me. That I can promise.'

'But there'll be no ....' He cleared his throat. 'Rumblings o' witchery and the like?'

'Come, James, the woman can hardly be promising that.' Lachlan pushed his chair back and poured himself a dram. 'We all ken what's oft-times whispered, but equally, we all ken Morna's a healer. *You* ken it more than most.'

A red tide spread up James's face. Mhari Lang was all he talked of, how fair she was, how the light picked out the gold in her hair. 'Twas said the green woman had saved her sister from the childbed fever. Though that seemed highly unlikely. Hadn't Father Ranald been there? God's miracle had doubtless been wrought through His servant, the father. The witch likely had naught to do with it.

'I wish Rowena to be happy. If this makes her so, helping others, then it makes me happy. I've nae wish to stand in her way.'

'Weel said, James.' Lachlan banged his cup down. ''Tis my thinking, too. Nay, I've little need to give it great thought. If 'tis what Rowena wants,' he looked sternly at her, 'I'll nae prevent it. In my younger days, likely I'd have done so. But I'm a changed man. I've made mistakes. One I'd give all I have to undo.' He exhaled, glowering at the whisky he'd slopped on the table. 'Ye ken I would.'

The crone nodded.

He rubbed his mouth. 'Father Ranald's done much good. I'm indebted to him, but even he doesna ken everything.' He frowned. 'I give my blessing, and any objection the father might have he can raise wi' me. Rowena's my daughter. *I'll* be deciding what's best fer her.'

'She's the Lord's child, too,' Duncan reminded him, though, of course, she was nearly a woman now. But his words were drowned by the clatter of Rowena's chair striking the floor as she launched herself at her father.

'Oh, Da!' She flung her arms around his neck. 'I dinna ken what to say. Thank ye, thank ye!'

She beamed at him over Lachlan's shoulder, and his heart fluttered.

'Now, now.' Lachlan prized her fingers from his nape. Displays of affection always seemed to make him uncomfortable.

'But,' Duncan stammered. 'What is it ye've all agreed to?'

CHAPTER FOURTEEN

February 1760

Drumin
Strathavon
13th February 1760

Father,

I arrived at the cot-house where I'm to lodge as the last of the light was dwindling and was too weary for much but seeing to my horse and bed. Today I see more, though it hardly gladdens my heart. Or mood.

Naught but wild hills and bogs, rocks and pine forests, and everywhere the smoking dung heaps these Highland villains call homes. Their hovels erupt like pustules from the heather. They particularly cluster by the river, like lice among the folds of collar and cuff. My own dwelling is little better— cold, dark, peat-reeking. I pray my stay here will be short, that I will soon have the means for better quarters. And I hope you will also pray for that, even be it I know I've disappointed you.

Some of these hovels might transpire to be illicit stills and bothies. This I will endeavour to determine on the morrow, although I've not yet my full authority. I ride to Elgin in two days to meet the Collector of Excise and receive my orders and allowance. The pity is, I must waste much of it paying

130

local rogues to interpret for me. I'm told the common muck-the-byres of these glens speak naught but the Irish, a primitive tongue. Few hereabouts can speak the King's English.

As Riding Officer, my ride will extend from Strathavon, where I'm to quarter, to Strathdon and all of upper Banffshire. A wild and lawless region infested with papists and Jacobites. Though, as you say, they are the same. Needless to say, the area is riddled with whisky smugglers—desperate types, dishonest by nature and lacking any respect for king or Kirk.

Even though this is my first real post, and I'm doubtless considered wet behind the ears, I'm to replace the infamous John Meldrum, who will shortly go on trial at Elgin. I think, Father, you will have heard of him. His infamy has spread far and wide, even, I expect, to peaceful Melrose in the bonny green hills of the Borders.

John Meldrum was a secret colluder. He carried orders for whisky to the smugglers, working with them and warning of raids. He alerted the villains to the whereabouts of army camps, receiving payment from both smuggler and exchequer alike, so mighty was his greed. His actions drew suspicion, however. When he worked alongside soldiers quartered at Corgarff, those soldiers smelled a rat. He was followed, and his fraudulent activities uncovered. Now I think he will pay for his duplicity with his neck. Do I hear you cheer? I expect so, knowing you as I do. So, this is the man I must replace.

As I sit here before my meagre peat fire, I think of you, Father. I imagine you drawn up at your pulpit, raging against papists and their false idols, against heathen superstitions, and particularly against the scourge of witchcraft. You are assiduous on that subject for my mother's sake, I know. God rest her soul. Lost to us at the hands of the hag paid to attend my birth.

Your diligence in rooting out these meddlesome women, healers and midwives they call themselves does you credit. All are cunning witches— devilish, potion-peddling crones. And I recall your industry in denouncing treasonous Jacobites, Father. Every papist is a Jacobite, you say, and in this godforsaken land, I well believe it.

They say the Duke of Gordon was himself a papist. The old duke who owned all that can be seen for miles here, albeit a secret one. Not a Jacobite— at least, not an active one. He knew better than to fall that way. The young duke is hopefully more discerning in his faith.

As I sit here alone with my task ahead of me, ridding these glens of the scourge of illicit whisky distilling, I can't help but think of Melrose and home.

Of the gentle river Tweed and the Eildon hills. Even of the stark grey walls of your kirk, Father, and I wonder what hellish place this is where I've been sent.

I hope you'll pray for me and my task, as I daily pray for you. I pray also for my brother. That army life is kind to him. As best it can be.

Despite your disappointment, it remains my hope to one day make you proud.

Ever your obedient servant and son,
Hugh

Hugh McBeath lowered his quill, folded and sealed the letter and put it safely inside his saddlebag, ready for his ride to Elgin. Despite his words, he doubted his father would ever feel any real pride in his younger son. At least, he'd never admit to such a thing. Andrew was the son who'd enjoyed what limited affection their father spared either of his offspring. And Andrew was gone, pressed into the army when recruiters visited Melrose and found him the worse for drink in the King's Arms. Easy prey for their wiles.

Their father had written letters, paid visits to the local lieutenant, even expounded from the pulpit, all to no avail. Andrew was gone. While Hugh, who'd killed his mother by his birth, remained—a poor substitute and a constant reminder to his father why his gentle-natured wife was dead.

He'd swiftly joined the Board of Excise, surmising that working for the Crown might save him from over-zealous recruiters, exempting him from taking the king's shilling. A masterly ploy, he imagined. Only, the Board had sent him to the Highlands, to this miserable place infested with Catholics and Jacobites where his predecessor would shortly be hanged.

He rubbed at his beard, pushing a flop of brown hair back from his brow. But then, had he no' always had to fight and scheme and employ cunning to gain anything in life? Cunning was his watchword. His way. Hugh had long understood life's comforts would never be handed to him. They must be taken when the opportunity arose, seized and fought for, then coveted and enjoyed. Presumably, all men thought this way.

Likely there would be opportunities for him even here—of sorts, leastways. There might be routes to advancement he could explore, lucrative ways to make his position here work for him without too much effort. Though he'd need to be wary, particularly with local troops. He'd no wish to follow John Meldrum to the scaffold.

With a shudder, he left the cot-house and saddled his horse. Once mounted, he urged the gelding to a rocky bluff where the tower house known as Drumin Castle stood. The derelict castle was the closest habitation to his hovel, although no neighbours lived there, thankfully. The keep, and to some extent his miserable cot-house, commanded a panoramic view in all directions. Stretching in the saddle, he surveyed the landscape he would soon control.

The position of his lodging was a strategic one. It afforded a sweeping view of the river Livet's confluence with the river Avon. From here, he could observe vast tracts of Strathavon and, perhaps even more notorious for its smuggling, Glenlivet. Little remained of the castle; it had long since been abandoned, likely fought over by warring clans, but its position was genius.

He nudged his horse on, carefully working his way down a steep embankment toward the river Avon. As he swayed in the creaking saddle, he observed a shrouded and indistinct figure crossing a distant moor. The man almost melted into the heathland so thoroughly did his clothing merge with the land. He lost sight of him for a moment before once more picking up the blur of movement. Suspiciously, the man appeared to be carrying something on his back.

His interest piqued, he drew his horse to a halt within the cover of trees where he could watch the man unobserved. It soon became apparent this was a woman, a small, swift-moving one, clothed in the tartan plaids all Highlanders seemed to favour. Being of the female gender hardly meant she was innocent. Women also smuggled. So he'd been told. Some of these glen women were as vicious as the men. 'Twas rumoured they'd think naught of carrying a weapon and using it, of cracking heads and slitting throats, and of course, being female meant they were twice as cunning as any man.

She skirted the edge of a wood, then began to climb a grassy hillside. He scrabbled in his saddlebag for the hand-drawn map he'd been given when first told of his position here. From the map, the hill appeared to be named Seely's Hillock. Something was marked upon its summit. He frowned. The words were in Irish, but the image appeared to be of a ring of some kind. His curiosity aroused, he replaced the map and urged his horse on, keeping within cover as best he could.

More of the hill was now visible. Another figure waited at the top, presumably for the woman, standing beside whatever had been erected there. Some manner of secret assignation, then? Lovers, perhaps? He snorted—the thought of the brutish primitives breeding was thoroughly offensive. Even so, watching them might be an education. Possibly a pleasurable one. Feeling a familiar stirring in his loins, he dug his heels into the gelding's flanks, creeping farther down the embankment within the cover of trees.

He forded the river at a broad stony bend and circled the hillock, approaching it from the west where a small birchwood concealed him. His horse made short work of the incline, and he was soon among bushes in a reasonably comfortable position to watch whatever entertainment might be on offer.

As he drew closer, it became apparent both individuals were female. The first removed a creel-like basket from her back, throwing off the rags that covered her head to reveal the face of a crone as he'd expected, then embraced the considerably younger waiting one. They clung to each other in an oddly touching fashion.

He dismounted and left his horse tied to a tree, afraid it might whicker and give him away, then crept as close as he dared, ensconcing himself behind a thicket of gorse. Peering through gaps in the prickly foliage, he could observe well enough whatever mischief was about to transpire.

The women's words he could not make out. They spoke in the Irish, whispering almost reverently as if standing before an altar or grave, acting like church elders, or whatever their heathen equivalent might be. Yet, there was no altar here, only a ring of devil's stones. At the crown of the hill, rooted into the rock and surrounded by billowing deer grass, stood a circle of upright stones, craggy and weathered and crusted with lichen. Unnervingly, they looked almost like human figures, aged and stooped. Squat old folk transformed into stone, as Lot's wife had long ago been turned to salt.

The hair on the back of his neck began to rise. Pagan sites like these were said to be littered all over the Highlands—evidence of the supernatural character of the place. And the women must be witches; why else would they come here? No God-fearing woman would visit such a place.

His breathing quickened, and he fought to stifle it lest the creatures hear him. He grew clammy, his bowels tightening, wishing he'd not followed the hag. If they found him here, what would be his fate? He swallowed, gripping the hilt of his sword, reminding himself they were only women. If the need arose, he'd soon despatch them to hell from whence they'd likely come.

Yet, the younger witch was beautiful; he saw that now. He could scarce take his eyes from her or remember having seen a more desirable creature. Dark hair billowed silk-like about her shoulders, and her face was delicate, perfect in every feature, as was her ripening young body.

Even through her drab clothing, he could see the slender curves of her shape. His gaze explored the burgeoning swell of her breasts set against her litheness, and his loins sprang to life. As she moved, spreading some manner of greenery from the crone's basket inside the stone circle, she displayed a sensual grace. He groaned softly, his breeches tightening over the swelling at his groin.

Surely no native of these parts, lower in both intellect and breeding, should look as she did: innocent and lovely with skin that begged to be caressed and a body that demanded to be undressed, explored, then swiftly plundered. He shook himself. There was some manner of bewitchment in the air, and he was falling under its spell.

Since adolescence, Hugh's appetites had been robust. They'd been shameful features of his life, things he'd needed to keep from his father, particularly his use of strumpets and whores. These were activities, business transactions he liked to term them, that he tried to deny even to himself. Watching the young witchling, he was reminded of his hunger for female flesh.

Compensatory pleasures might be found here, then, in this wild place. Pleasurable distractions might come with his position, one of power, especially if all the glen women looked like this one, although that seemed unlikely.

Standing in the prickly bushes, the exotic scent of gorse flowers filled his nostrils, though oddly, few buds had even opened. The spicy aroma seemed to belong to the young woman, for she was exotic, too—a mysterious inhabitant of a strange and dangerous land.

With the spreading of the greenery complete, the women sat inside the stone circle holding hands with their eyes closed. They wore earnest expressions, whispering what seemed to be a heathen prayer of some kind.

Strangely, he was glad the crone he'd followed had not transpired to be a male lover come to dance the goat's jig with the young witchling. He'd still have watched their coupling as closely, but his pleasure would not have been the satisfying kind he sought. More likely, their rutting would've roused his anger and jealousy, for he desired the witchling himself.

The women completed whatever devilment they were about and rose to their feet, sharing a sad smile. The girl's smile took his breath away. By God, he wanted her, and more fervidly than he'd wanted any woman in his life. Only, who or what was she?

She removed a strip of material from around her neck, bringing it to her lips before tying it to one of the stones. The older woman stooped to touch the offering too, then slung the now empty creel upon her back, and they turned to go, making their way swiftly and sure-footedly back down the hill.

He trembled as he emerged from his hiding place. Standing before the entrance to the stone circle, he half expected a burst of fire and brimstone to blast him to the bone, but there was naught but a gentle, gorse-scented breeze. He released his breath and stared at the strip of fluttering material.

It didn't cross his mind to venture into the devil's circle. He skirted the perimeter until he stood before the chosen stone, then untied the offering and brought it to his nose, inhaling deeply. It smelled of herbs and green things, an exotic scent but a pleasing one. It smelled of her, he suspected, and again his loins throbbed.

Examining the piece, he found it had been intricately stitched, depicting entwining stalks of grain. Barley, he thought. He pocketed the item. If he saw the witchling again—nay, *when* he saw her, for he planned to discover who she was—he'd return the item. 'Twould be a way to subtly warn her he was aware of where she'd been and what she'd been doing, so therefore, what she must be. She should have a care and keep in his good favour if she valued her freedom. Fingering the scrap of cloth in his pocket, he knew it was his passage to bedding the young temptress. He chuckled. No' every man was as tolerant as Hugh McBeath. If she played his game right, he might even forget about reporting her to the authorities.

* * *

In Morna's company, Rowena no longer felt any hesitation in penetrating deep into the very heart of Sìthean Wood. Morna seemed to know every path and glade, almost every tree, which was only natural since she'd made her home here. There was no danger of becoming lost in the company of such a guide or of riling the faeryfolk. Morna was respectful and seemed to possess an innate understanding of that race.

'Twas two and a half years since she'd begun her apprenticeship with nature, as Morna put it, and she was now almost as versed in plant magic as her teacher. She'd spent those lost years well, waiting for Morna's return. Without realising it, she'd learned much on her own. When Morna showed her the many ways herb magic could ease suffering, it all made intuitive sense, the pieces falling quickly into place.

She'd learned that the plants thriving in the wildest, most extreme places and conditions possessed a magical essence enabling them to survive in their harsh world. That essence could be captured or extracted and used to ease people's suffering, for Highland folk lived in places just as harsh as mountain plants, and their lives could be just as cruel. Since the last rising, their lives had been blighted by all manner of hardships. Easing suffering was more important now than ever.

She'd learned that to heal, the plant's substance must be ingested, generally in a potion or elixir. Morna showed her how to concoct all manner of potions, explaining that nature provided a remedy for every affliction of man. To Rowena, this was the true miracle of creation, not God, and certainly not his ministers. Nature had done this since the dawn of time.

Morna also explained, and again Rowena intuitively recognised this, that for the magic to work, nature's help must first be respectfully requested by connecting with sacred places. Most importantly, gratitude must be expressed and deeply felt; naught was simply taken.

As her knowledge and respect for nature's ingenuity deepened, so did her eagerness to put it into practice. Now, whenever they attended a sick glensman or woman, she treated the patient. Morna only advised. She learned quicker that way, and folk grew to trust her.

As they neared Morna's home deep in the forest, her troubled heart began to lift. They'd prayed at one of the most sacred sites in the glen, leaving an offering for the life of John Meldrum. Yet they both knew their plea was likely a forlorn one. John's fate was doubtless sealed.

Her da had gone to Elgin with Duncan and James to attend John's trial and petition for his life. Many more would also make that journey, eager to show their support. John was trusted and respected. She sensed the glen was holding its breath, unable to believe the life of such a man might end so cruelly.

Yet, entering the place Morna had made her home was always a delight to the senses, and even today, she felt it. Morna had fashioned a simple wooden bridge over the Altnachoidh Burn adapted from a fallen tree. Crossing it, the ripple of water reached them as they entered an ancient wood within the greater forest.

Here the trees were true giants fringing a tiny lochan where the dangling heads of snowdrops nodded on a scented breeze. Bracken unfurled under pine trees growing down to the water's edge, butterflies flitting between their trunks. They followed them, mosses and liverworts cushioning their feet.

As they neared Morna's home, a dragonfly swooped by in a purr of wings, and they passed beneath a bower of flowering hawthorn that frothed and perfumed the air. Only here did it flower so early. Nearby, a spring bubbled crystal water to the surface guarded by an ancient oak. Looking up through the oak's twisted boughs, scraps of cloth fluttered in their hundreds. Before the wood was feared, this was a place of pilgrimage—a clootie well. Here she would leave another offering for the life of John Meldrum.

Yet, a heaviness in Rowena's heart told her John's soul was bound for the next realm, only first he must endure the jerking minutes of writhing limbs and drumming feet. The choking moments. She hoped they'd pass quickly, that her mother would be waiting to welcome him.

Inside the home, every imaginable scent mingled, for Morna spent much of her day crushing herbs and boiling potions, and the essence of green things from the earth lingered in the air. Herbs hung drying from the timber frame above their heads, while piles of berries, dried roots and mushrooms covered every surface. She breathed it all in.

Always she was conscious of how privileged she was, the one chosen to carry on the wisdom. Morna had begun to share tales of long-ago ages now, back when their glen first formed. 'Twas ice, she said, had shaped the contours of their beloved glen.

'I've something fer ye, child.' Morna turned to her with a tense smile, then rifled amongst some pots, finding a small object wrapped in calfskin. She pressed it into her hand. 'I wish ye to have this.'

Puzzled, she removed the wrapping, revealing a delicate silver ring, one she was accustomed to seeing on Morna's finger. She turned it to catch the light. Tendrils of ivy and mistletoe had been exquisitely etched into its surface.

'I canna take this,' she stammered. ''Tis beautiful, likely worth more coin than I've seen in all my life, and it's yours.'

Morna's eyes clouded. 'It's worth is beyond measure, but nae so much in coin. In what it betokens. 'Tis the lore-keeper's ring, passed to me when I was given that role.' She met Rowena's puzzled gaze. 'Now I must pass it to you.'

'But,' unease stirred in her belly. 'You're the lore-keeper, Morna.'

'My days as lore-keeper draw to an end. I chose you long ago when ye were a grieving bairn. Ye're nae that now, though I still call ye child, but that's from affection. I love ye like my own. But ye're a woman now—a wise and thoughtful one. I chose well.'

'I dinna want that honour, Morna. Nae yet. Nae till—'

'I'm gone?'

Anguish tightened her throat, and she nodded, not wishing to speak of such a thing.

'But, ye see, I feel it, child: my end. I know it comes.' Morna slipped the ring onto her finger. It slid on easily—a perfect fit.

'Yer end?' She dragged her gaze from the glistening ring. There were new lines on Morna's face. She seemed to have aged, to have grown old overnight.

'I sense a new threat in the glen.' A catch came into Morna's voice. 'A danger I canna yet put a face to. 'Tis born o' ignorance, intolerance. What isna in this world? 'Twill find rich soil here and grow strong, wielding great influence. No sufferance will it hold fer me—'twill root me out. But you it will tolerate fer its own designs.'

She gasped. 'I'll nae let it harm ye, Morna. Whatever it is. I swear.'

Morna squeezed her hand, rubbing the ring that already seemed part of her. 'I fear there's little you or I can do.'

She drew back with a whimper.

'But while there's still time, I must speak the lore. We must speak it thegither. They are but folktales, but there's wisdom in every one. And they must bide here.' She tapped the side of Rowena's forehead. 'Naught's ever put to paper. That was never the *draoidh* way. Tales are told, nae written. Tell them to whoever will listen; that way, our story will endure. Once our story's forgotten, our folk will fade from this Highland land as surely as I will.'

Stricken, Rowena stared at her. 'Please, dinna speak as if ye'll soon be gone.'

'Child, one end is only ever another beginning, fer life is but a turn o' the seasons. In the autumn o' my life, I'm content. My harvest's been fruitful. I've reaped what I've sown, as do we all. Every soul must cycle through its seasons, connecting wi' many souls and all o' creation as it learns and gains wisdom. Anyhow,' she shrugged, 'I may be wrong in what I foresee.'

Rowena swallowed; Morna was never wrong.

'Telling tales has been man's way since ever he had wit enough to tell them, and wisdom enough to grasp their message. 'Tis so, aye?'

She nodded, feeling the tightness in her throat that brought tears.

'There's something else I need to show ye.' Morna turned to the hearth-cairn at the centre of the room. Bundles of herbs were stuffed between the stones. She removed what filled the largest gap, then crouched to draw out what was hidden behind.

'My talismans.' She blew the dust from the package. 'Given me by my mother. Never have I used them. There's danger in working their magic.' She used the word cautiously. 'They can only be used once, and whatever ye wish fer ye must do wi' a pure heart. Naught but faith in the goodness o' creation will render ye pure enough, else whatever ye evoke will be visited back upon ye a hundred times ower. D'ye understand?'

She nodded, although so many fearful emotions crowded in, there seemed little room for understanding.

Morna left the bundle unopened, carefully replacing it in its hiding place. 'Should anything ill befall me,' she held up a hand to stave off Rowena's protest, 'they'll be here fer ye. Mind and come fer them. I bequeath them to ye, though I pray ye'll never need them. There's an ancient invocation in a long-forgotten tongue, though the meaning is clear enough. It must be committed to memory. We'll nae speak it now; I can see ye've nae the heart fer it, and I ken I've not. But 'tis important.'

A powerful energy seemed to emanate from the bundle. Rowena's stomach churned.

'All I'll say more, and I mean this well.' Morna looked steadily at her. 'Ye love too much. Ye must guard yer heart.' She retook her hand. 'Such a heart ye have, such love fer yer fellow man. But have a care who ye give it to. Love's dangerous. Man's love.'

She blinked in confusion. Did she mean Duncan? Had Morna guessed her secret? But she'd always loved Duncan, since that night on the floor when she'd vowed to heal him. Yet her feelings had changed. There were the new longings, though she'd spoken of them to no one.

'Love will tear ye apart. All love dies or is taken from ye.'

She thought of her mother, of her enduring love for her. She'd been taken, and it had torn her asunder.

''Tis the way of man's love, but nature's love never dies.' Morna squeezed her hand. 'Nature's laws are the true laws, nae man's. Man's are designed fer some want in man's black heart. Nature has no want, other than to see harmony in all creation.'

'I dinna ken what ye mean.' She rarely saw Duncan, though always, deep down, there lived a yearning for him.

'I think ye do.'

She whimpered. Da had urged her to harden herself, yet she was still that lost child. The empty days still haunted her. Would Morna be taken?

Duncan, even? Oceans weep, nae Duncan.

'What must I do?' she whispered.

'Be strong.'

'Strong?'

'Harden yer heart. Protect it. Put yer love away. Then I can go to meet whatever awaits me knowing I've little need to be worrying about ye.'

Her heart shrank, but eventually, she nodded.

CHAPTER FIFTEEN

AS HE DREW close to the old town of Elgin, approaching it from the south, Hugh McBeath was surprised to learn from the signpost the ancient settlement was a Royal Burgh. Rising in the saddle, he surveyed the township spread before him. Elgin was a market town, possibly prosperous, even civilised, although that would be astonishing for a place so far north of the educated south. Yet it looked an agreeable place.

Clustered around a bend in the river Lossie, the ancient town was dominated by the castle hill to the west; Lady Hill, according to his map. It was clearly a ruin. Another much larger and more impressive building lay to the east. Elgin Cathedral, the Lantern o' the North, had once been the glory of the Catholic faith in the north. Thankfully, it, too, lay in ruins—a casualty of the Reformation and the coming of the true Presbyterian faith. Along with the Wolf of Badenoch, who'd burned the great cathedral in a fit of anger. His father had explained this to him when he'd learned his youngest son would be under the control of the Customs House in Elgin.

He would meet with the Collector shortly, one Samuel Farquharson, and receive his orders and allowance. From that allowance, hopefully substantial, he would need to finance all his expenditure. He would require hirelings, violent types accustomed to dealing with the ruffians of these parts and fluent in both English and Irish. These men must be armed and provided with mounts, which would doubtless eat up a sizeable portion of his allowance.

Then he'd need some manner of housekeeper or drudge. He could hardly keep his own house or prepare his own sustenance—'twas women's work. A dog might be useful, too. A vicious type he could set upon suspected smugglers. A bulldog, perhaps. A hound he could train to seize smugglers' ponies by the nose, forcing them to rear up and spill the barrels from their backs. He chuckled. The villains of these parts hardly knew what awaited them now a real exciseman had landed in their midst.

Riding along the cobbled High Street, he approached the parish church of St. Giles. The crowstepped profile of Elgin's tollbooth with its impressive spire filled his field of vision. There was a deal of activity around its entrance; a crowd of raucous men had gathered, women, too, with a mutinous look about them. Muck-the-byres, he judged, as he termed all common farming folk, wearing homespuns, and speaking the Irish in strident tones.

He shifted his gaze to the structure being erected nearby. Gangs of tradesmen were raising a wooden platform, the work accompanied by crude shouting and a general commotion of hammering and sawing. Clouds of sawdust filled the air. Grimacing, he rode through it holding his breath and squinting to save his eyes.

Once in the bustling marketplace with its lion-topped Mercat Cross, he brushed the dust from his coat, looking around at the respectable merchants and townsfolk going about their business. The sight reminded him a little of home. The stench of horse dung wrinkled his nose, but even gentle Melrose sometimes smelled that way.

He passed a coaching inn to his right where painted women loitered in the doorway, disdainful townsfolk pretending not to see them. Hugh smiled wickedly as he read the sign—Mrs Geddes's Accommodating House. If Mrs Geddes or any of her bawds wished to accommodate him, 'twould suit him fine. It might be an agreeable place to bed down for the night with the added benefit of a strumpet to warm his bed. Better yet. He liked this Elgin, pity he'd no' been sent here instead of godforsaken Strathavon.

As he neared the Customs House, crowds of townsfolk were flocking back the way he'd come. Puzzled, he considered stopping to ask what was afoot but thought better of it. He should concentrate on his meeting with the collector and make a good first impression.

Reaching the elegant building that served as the administrative headquarters for the local Board of Excise, he tethered his horse, taking the steps to the entrance with confident strides, two at a time. The door stood slightly ajar. He raised his hand to rap upon it, only to be met by a red-faced and officious man who bustled past him, almost knocking him off the step.

'I'll be at the Burgh Court.' The man aimed this back over his shoulder. 'They'll return their verdict within the half-hour, I expect. I've no intention of missing it. Though why in God's name it needed to take all this time, the Lord only knows. His guilt is evident even to a child.'

'Aye, sir,' came the reply.

The man frowned, eyeing Hugh warily.

He extended a hand. 'Hugh McBeath. Riding Officer for Strathavon and Strathdon.' His left eyelid twitched as it dawned upon him he should have addressed the man as sir. This was evidently a man of some importance.

'McBeath, eh?' The man snorted. 'Your timing's impeccable.'

Did he detect a hint of sarcasm in the man's voice?

'I'm at this moment, on my way to the courthouse to hear the guilty verdict returned on your predecessor.'

Hugh blinked. 'Mister Farquharson, then?'

The man nodded, shaking his hand. 'I've no time fer the niceties now, McBeath.' He pursed his lips. 'But perhaps you'd care to join me? We might speak in the courthouse. I think you'll find the spectacle an education.' He eyed him darkly. 'A warning, too. Well, what are ye waiting for?' He scurried off down the street.

At the tollbooth, they fought their way through the crowds into a medieval hall with galleried seating and a packed public area. As they squeezed their way through, Hugh grimaced at the reek of unwashed flesh, the squabbling Highlanders offending both his nose and his ears.

'Samuel!' boomed a voice from across the hall. The voice belonged to a bloated but impeccably dressed man in silk breeches and frilled, knee-length coat. The man made his way over, folk instinctively moving aside as he shooed them away with his tricorne.

'Come up to the gallery, Samuel. A finer view we'll have from there. These scoundrels have scuffed my shoes. Who's this?'

Farquharson introduced him with a sardonic smile. 'The treacherous exciseman's replacement. Hugh McBeath's his name. And this fine gentleman,' he indicated the newcomer, 'is William McGillivray of Inchfindy Hall, his grace's factor in Stratha'an and Glenlivet. A gentleman, I'm confident in saying, soon to be appointed Justice of the Peace.' The Collector beamed a mite fawningly at McGillivray. 'You'd do well to make each other's acquaintance.'

His interest aroused, Hugh extended a hand to the factor. 'An honour, sir.' The man appeared a buffoon of the highest order, but still, he was plainly a man of wealth and position. Making his acquaintance could prove profitable.

The factor ignored his hand. Sweeping his hat from his wigged head, he bowed extravagantly, jowls swinging. 'A pleasure.' He replaced the hat. 'Shall we?' He indicated the staircase leading to the upper gallery.

The upstairs area was clearly reserved for gentlemen and prosperous merchant types; there were no ruffians here. They had an excellent view of the floor below. More and more unsavoury characters were attempting to gain entry, armed soldiers searching everyone and physically preventing more from getting in. Tempers were fraying. Only respectable-looking folk were being permitted to enter now. Residents of the town, he imagined.

'Has the whole of Strathavon swarmed down from the hills to support this brazen thief?' McGillivray whined. 'The wretch should've been charged with high treason. Were I on the bench, I'd have had the felon transferred to the High Court in Edinburgh on that very charge.'

'Aye,' Farquharson observed, 'I fear a number of the man's fellow conspirators have travelled down from the hills to cause trouble. Take a long hard look, McBeath. Many of Stratha'an's most hardened smugglers are in this room. Mark them well. Commit their faces to memory. I expect to see them in the dock where Meldrum stands in the shortest of order.'

'I'll do my best, sir.'

Looking down on the packed public area with fresh eyes, he attempted to burn the faces of the common muck-the-byres into his memory. There were many, and they all looked much the same. What was there to differentiate one miserable, pock-marked villain from another? Naught he could see. They wore the same rags, and in an attempt to feign respectability, had altered their outlawed Highland plaids to resemble Lowland breeks. Damned if the law wasnae letting them away with it.

Looking closer, Hugh saw they wore similar expressions. A desperate kind of anger marked each face. It gleamed darkly in their eyes, and they used that shared expression to communicate some common feeling, grief, almost, as if they believed the law had wronged them. Or that this corrupt exciseman, who was clearly one of them, had been unjustly treated. He exhaled in irritation. Rebellion must be bred in these rogues from birth.

He flicked his gaze to the accused, a small, surprisingly benign-looking man standing white-faced and stoic in a metal cage guarded by four soldiers, each with fixed bayonet at the ready. Oddly, the soldiers appeared more nervous than the prisoner, even though the man was clad in irons and shackled to his cage.

Folk pressed forward, crying out to the disgraced exciseman, trying to reach a hand through the bars to squeeze his shoulder or grip his manacled hands. He nodded tightly to them. 'Twould almost have been a touching scene, Hugh supposed, were not those thronging to support his corrupt predecessor treacherous smugglers likely as guilty as the prisoner. As more of them flocked forward, the guards swung their muskets, aiming at any who came too close.

'This Meldrum was always a Jacobite, was he not, Samuel?' McGillivray declared. 'Does the man not hail from the Cabrach, a hotbed of popery and the treasonous Jacobite cause? 'Tis what I've heard. Of course, I always suspected the man. I have a nose for these things.' He sniffed loudly to demonstrate his skill in the field of detecting Jacobites by their peculiar smell. 'And isn't every papist a Jacobite, and every Jacobite a smuggler? So, why were your suspicions not raised before, Samuel, as mine were?'

Farquharson snorted. 'You never mentioned your misgivings, William, and such a connection is too great a leap to make. Many smugglers are Jacobites, I agree, but not every Jacobite smuggles. Many are simply rebellious—despisers of what they see as the usurping king and his German court. Still more resent the union of the parliaments and the taxes the union brought their way. Though, of course,' he smiled pragmatically, 'I'm employed to collect those taxes and prosecute those who fail to pay. I deem that task an honour. But understanding the workings of the smuggler's mind is the key to catching them, in my humble opinion. John was an agreeable sort,' he added, 'and made many seizures, though, of course, few arrests.'

McGillivray's words were a thinly veiled jibe at the Collector, Hugh recognised, questioning why Farquharson had failed to detect Meldrum's criminal activities. Seeing an opportunity to ingratiate himself with the factor, he leapt in.

'Nay,' he gushed. 'Ye're right, Mister McGillivray, 'tis what my faither always said, and he's a churchman. A Kirk minister in the border town of Melrose. He knows more about these things than most. Every papist is a Jacobite, he says, and all Jacobites are disloyal to British rule. He preaches Heilanders are naught but savages, rebellion a disease they carry like the plague. It spreads like contagion whenever they gather together, infecting others if no' rooted out.'

'Well, said!' McGillivray guffawed.

'He, and I,' he added lest the factor think him incapable of independent thought, 'have naught but praise for the arrests and executions, the burnings and banishments that followed our glorious victory at Culloden.'

Farquharson exhaled, raising his brows at him.

'Bravo!' McGillivray pounded him on the back. 'Your father is a wise man. A man of faith, as you are, I can tell. I am a Kirk Elder myself. I assume your father despises idol-kissers as much as I do.' He chuckled. 'I like his thinking.'

To Hugh's delight, the factor was now looking him up and down, appraising him with genuine respect in his eyes.

'Your name again?'

'Hugh McBeath, sir. New Riding Officer for Strathavon and Strathdon. An area well-known to ye, I think.'

'How extraordinary! I am factor there. His grace's representative in that lawless land.' McGillivray waved his hand with a flourish, then bowed in a gesture of mock subservience. 'And his close acquaintance, of course.'

Hugh stifled a smile. A personal friend of the duke; a fortuitous meeting, indeed.

'Ye'll be well acquainted with the criminal tendencies of the place, then?' he flattered McGillivray. 'Will be versed in the petty politics of the area. Who pays their rent on time, and who is in arrears? Who smuggles to pay that rent?'

'I like to think so.' McGillivray's meaty face creased in a self-satisfied smile. 'Although who there smuggles whisky is for you to determine, I think.'

'We'll soon see if he's up to the task,' Farquharson observed.

'I am, sir,' Hugh assured him. 'More than up to it, assuming that my work is adequately supported.' He swallowed. 'I've a wish to discuss that matter with ye, sir.'

'Have you.'

'And sir,' he turned back to McGillivray, 'I believe we might be of service to one another. I imagine his grace wishes rid of the scourge of whisky smuggling from his land. Would look kindly upon those who work to achieve that end?'

'The duke wishes the outrage that is whisky smuggling strangled at the root.' McGillivray flicked an invisible speck from his frill-lined cuff. 'That it should be going on upon his land is a slur upon his good name.'

'Of course,' the Collector put in. 'Extinguishing smuggling is what we all want, I assume.'

McGillivray nodded, jowls wobbling. 'The Highlands must be

brought to heel, shown where its loyalty must lie. Jacobite support lives on here, and we all know smuggler, papist, and Jacobite are one and the same. Isn't that so, Samuel?'

'Do we? Hmm, I'm not so convinced. Anyway, whisky's been distilled on the duke's land for centuries. Since before there was a duke. 'Tis considered a tradition. A difficult thing to strangle, as ye put it.'

'I doubt I'll find it so difficult,' Hugh contended. 'And I believe Mister McGillivray is right. These elements all combine to mark the rebellious character of the Heilander.'

'You see!' McGillivray thrust his chin out. 'Even your lackey sees things my way, Samuel. The correct way.'

'And, of course,' Hugh added, 'I plan to make it my business to strangle it at the root.' He suppressed a smile, sensing he'd won the factor over, although less than pleased at being styled a lackey. 'Ye can depend upon it.'

'Humph,' the Collector muttered. 'We'll see. But I doubt you'll find it as easy as you imagine. And you're wrong, both. For a start, not every Highlander is a papist. Many are Episcopalian, and a few belong to the established church.'

'Pah,' sneered McGillivray. 'Papists by another name.'

Judging it best to say no more, Hugh sat back, assessing the two men. McGillivray, with his haughty airs, was of the class of man who considered only his views the correct ones and tolerated little dissent from others. He delighted in being right in all things, and in his arrogance, assumed he was. He smiled inwardly. 'Twould be child's play indulging this man. Farquharson, however, might prove trickier game.

'What matter was it you wished to discuss with me?' Farquharson squinted suspiciously at him.

'Aye.' He fidgeted, rubbing his beard as he considered how best to phrase his request. 'Hailing from the Borders, sir, I've little knowledge of the primitive tongue spoken in the glens—the Irish.'

'Gaelic, you mean.' Farquharson tutted priggishly. ''Tis a tongue commonly spoken in these parts, even in Elgin you'll find. I'd swiftly acquaint myself with its basics if I were you.'

'But, sir,' he tried again. ''Tis not something I'll master overnight. Yet, my wish is to knuckle to my task in short order, as you say. To that end, perhaps you might afford me a more generous allowance than is customarily the case. The extra coin to fund employing hirelings. Local men fluent in Gaelic and with an understanding of the mind of the smuggler. Men of a similar disposition, ye could say. These men would need to be armed and mounted, and,' he held his breath as he pushed his luck still further, 'as I am, as yet, unmarried, I fear I will also require the services of a housekeeper.'

His left eyelid twitched, an affliction that plagued him whenever he found himself in an uncomfortable position. He was now painfully aware of how greatly his request had displeased the Collector of Tax.

'A housekeeper!' Farquharson exploded. 'What about a manservant or two? A footman, a valet perhaps?' He snorted.

'Allow me to be of service,' McGillivray put in. 'As Samuel intimated, I am shortly to be elevated to the position of Justice of the Peace.' He visibly inflated, an indulgent smile stretching his jowls. 'But as factor, I am sufficiently familiar with the misdemeanours of those living in Glenlivet and Strathavon. Languishing in Elgin's Tollbooth at this very moment, awaiting trial for the crimes of carrying arms and poaching the duke's salmon, are two unsavoury characters from the Inchrory area. Both can speak English adequately, albeit with a thick Highland brogue, and are, I'm certain, of the violent disposition you mentioned would be required. I believe upon payment of their bail, they would make adequate assistants.' He smiled with a patronising air. 'I could arrange their release as hirelings if Samuel here were to pay their bail.'

'Excellent, excellent.' Hugh beamed at his employer. 'Is it no', sir?'

'Their names?' Farquharson growled.

'If my memory serves, Charles Stuart and Dougal Riach, although the former goes by another name, which escapes me.'

'I know of them,' Farquharson grunted. 'A pair of half-witted villains.' He exhaled with a hiss through clenched teeth, a mannerism Hugh cared little for.

'All right,' he grudgingly agreed. 'I daresay 'twill be my cheapest option.' He eyed Hugh darkly. 'I'll agree to it, McBeath, and think yourself fortunate. But, as for a housekeeper, if you're so incapable of keeping your own house, I suggest you find yourself a wife with all haste.' He sat back, cheeks flushed.

Hugh considered pressing him a little harder but was distracted by an odd sound emanating from the floor below. The general din had ceased, replaced by a hushed tone, a collective intake of breath almost, followed by a strange wailing. Peering down, he saw what he took for the men of the jury filing back into the room.

Composed of fifteen men, carefully selected Hugh assumed, the jury made their way into the back of the courtroom preceded by the wigged sheriff. All were grim-faced. Silence fell as the jury took their seats on a pew-like bench to the right of the sheriff. More soldiers poured in behind them, taking up positions around the room, plainly expecting trouble.

Even the most rabble-raising of the crowd had fallen silent now as tension thickened the air. Incredibly, the muck-the-byres were gripping each other's hands, even hardened menfolk. Bunching together, they clutched fearfully at each other.

The sheriff took his seat and waited for silence before recounting aloud the prisoner's alleged crimes. There were many, some so obscure Hugh doubted their authenticity. Looking around at the impressive military presence in the room, it dawned upon him these were likely the same soldiers the exciseman had duped.

Meldrum had let the army believe he was an ally working alongside them to achieve shared ends. He'd made dunderheads and fools of them all, and the authorities intended to make him pay. Every legal means possible had therefore been employed to bring him to ultimate justice. A message would be delivered today—one not easily forgotten. Not usually sensitive to such things, Hugh could almost taste the authorities' eagerness to ensure Meldrum found no legal means to slip the noose.

His list of charges complete, the sheriff turned to the men of the jury.

'Have you come to a majority decision?'

The foreman assured him they had.

'And how do you find the accused? Guilty or not guilty?'

'Guilty, sir.'

The prisoner showed no reaction, but a roar of anger erupted in the room.

Hugh winced, the din bruising his ears, and glanced at McGillivray. The factor grimaced, clapping his hands over his wig.

Below them, redcoats thrust their muskets forward, bayonets at the ready.

'Shame!' one woman cried. 'Ye call this justice? Shame on ye!'

The crowd cheered her, taking up her call. A stripling of a lad climbed onto the shoulders of another, shouting out in a tolerable attempt at English. The rabble quietened to listen, though Hugh doubted many would understand his words.

The lad wore a fervent expression, his pale eyes flashing. His face bore a hint of the fox, yet for all that, he was handsome—for a Heilander. Even balanced upon another lad's shoulders, he carried himself with dignity, his youth lending him a vulnerable air.

'Shame it is!' he cried. 'Shame upon a government that forces a man to smuggle to feed his family. To keep a roof ower their heads. That sanctions a thousand outrages against decent Highland folk. You charge this man?' He pointed an accusing finger at the sheriff. 'Then, by God, I charge you. All o' ye.' He swept his gaze around the room, picking out the soldiers who stared back open-mouthed.

Another roar went up, and his face twisted, a muscle jumping in his throat. 'I find ye guilty o' crimes against innocent Highland folk. Burning homes, butchering whole families, acts o' savagery carried out against defenceless people. Crops burned, herds plundered, women violated.' His voice cracked, but he struggled on. 'Every cruelty devised by the British government to persecute poor Highland folk.'

The sheriff was on his feet. 'I'll have that man arrested. Guards, for the love of God!'

Soldiers shoved their way through the crowd, the stripling continuing to blast the sheriff until the last. As judge, he represented a king and government every villain in the room clearly despised.

'Ye condemn a man whose only crime is to possess a guid heart. A wish to help his fellow man. Shame, forsooth, fer John is a man o' principles. A true glensm—'

The lad was wrenched from behind and forced to the ground, then swiftly gagged and bound. He struggled furiously, outraged redcoats taking turns to bury their boots in his vulnerable midsection, viciously jabbing him with their musket butts, laying about his companions with fist and musket. Any who tried to shield him, they struck down.

'Who is that preposterous young Jacobite?' McGillivray spluttered.

Farquharson shook his head. 'I regret I have no notion. He was in the company of Lachlan Innes, so I fear he's likely a smuggler as Innes is rumoured to be. Pity. He put on an admirable performance. Let's hope they don't disfigure him. He was pleasing to look at, I thought—spirited young fellow.'

It was now McGillivray's turn to snort.

Once order had been restored, the sheriff donned his black cap to pronounce the sentence. Farquharson ushered them down a back stair and out a side entrance onto the High Street.

'Is that—?' Hugh stared at the wooden platform he'd seen earlier. Soldiers were raising a gibbet upon it.

'The scaffold for the exciseman's execution. 'Tis to be completed by the morrow for Meldrum's hanging,' the Collector confirmed.

'Surely they dinnae mean to hang him on the High Street?'

'The Gallows Green is judged too far away. More will come to witness the spectacle here. Will be deterred by it is the hope.'

151

'Good God!' exclaimed McGillivray. 'On the Plainstones? One can scarcely imagine anything more barbaric.'

Swallowing, Hugh turned away, walking back up the now deserted High Street with his new companions. He'd shortly receive his orders and take command of the hapless Meldrum's territory, and with luck, Farquharson would grant him a sizeable allowance. Looking back over his shoulder, he reflected the day's spectacle had indeed been a warning as Farquharson had foretold.

CHAPTER SIXTEEN

VEXINGLY, THE COLLECTOR had not been quite as generous as Hugh had hoped, but it was still a bulging purse that filled his pocket as he approached Mrs Geddes's Accommodating House with an eager spring in his step. Provided the drudge he employed had little expectation of being generously paid, he now had funds to ensure his hovel would benefit from a woman's touch. At last, he might fill his belly with a half-decent meal. Thus far, Hugh had concluded Highland food was fit only for horses. It would need to be a woman of humble expectations, and if she possessed a face none too offensive to look at, better yet, though doubtless that would prove too much to ask.

Business in Elgin was clearly good, for Mrs Geddes was the fattest whore he'd ever seen. Several chins propped up her head, a furry mole sprouting from the largest. Her pudgy face was slathered in so much paint, it caked in the creases of her nose and chin, giving her a grotesque, caricature-like guise. She waddled along the hallway, skirts rustling, leaving a trail of cheap French cologne in her wake.

'Niver fear,' she breezed. 'I'll gie ye my best room, Mister McBeath, wi' a view onto the Plainstones and the Mercat Cross. And wi' extra-thick walls fer privacy.' She chuckled. 'Ye must be a gentleman from the prosperous south.' She turned back to ensure he was following and tapped the side of her nose. 'I can tell from yer speech ye're nae from these parts. Ye're a cut above the folk we mostly get and will be wanting my best girl, I expect.'

At least the woman was perceptive, despite her ridiculous appearance.

153

'Someone young and comely,' he confirmed. 'And clean.'

'All my lasses are clean,' she informed him in an injured tone. 'But I've a new lass. Isobel's her name. She's nae experienced, if ye catch my drift, but I can gie ye experience mysel' if that's what ye're efter.'

At his horrified expression, she laughed uproariously.

'Her da's in debtor's gaol fer unpaid rent. They've been evicted from their hame up in Stratha'an. D'ye ken the place?'

He grunted that he did, his interest raised.

'She needed a roof ower her head and a way to pay their debts. Being the soft-herted type, I've given her baith.' She stopped at the door to his room and fumbled with the lock, opening it to reveal a veritable strumpet's boudoir swathed in crimson silk. The bed, which dominated the room, did, at least, look comfortable; the rest of it was of no interest to Hugh.

'My best room,' she gushed. 'Furnished wi' silks from the Orient and every comfort fer my best clients.' She indicated a china chamber pot and washstand in one corner, then with a crude chuckle, nodded at a full-length mirror placed at the foot of the bed. 'Would it be to yer liking?'

'More than adequate,' he assured her. 'As for the strumpet, ye're saying this girl is untouched? A virgin, in fact?'

'Pure as the driven snow, though there'll be a wee extra charge fer that, as I'm sure ye can appreciate.'

He snorted. Had he a shilling for every girl pushed upon him, he'd been assured was a virtuous maiden, he'd be a rich man by now and would hardly be wasting his time chasing tax-dodgers.

'Can I be sending her along to ye?'

'I'll no' pay above the going rate. Virgin or no'.'

'Heaven forbid.'

* * *

After dining, he returned to his room to find the girl already there, perched on the edge of his bed. She was young, at least, younger than he expected, although that hardly meant she was chaste. She was a Heiland creature, after all, and looked every inch of it. Dowdy as a dunnock, her hair hung lank on her shoulders, her eyes round and fixed upon him as a deer might appear in the hunter's sights. He smiled to himself, imagining the sport he'd shortly have with her.

Removing his coat, he thought of the dark-haired witchling he'd observed on Seely's Hillock and the powerful desires she'd stirred within him. She'd tormented him since that day, an image of her lithe young body constantly filling his head, not to mention his breeches. Feeling a familiar stirring there now, he turned and locked the door, stifling a smile as he anticipated what he'd do with this purportedly chaste young trollop.

He began by introducing himself, thinking it the thing to do considering he was about to be as intimate with her as 'twas possible to be with another body. She swallowed and muttered something unintelligible. He'd forgotten she'd have naught but the Irish. No matter. She was hardly here for her conversation.

Shrugging, he raised her to her feet and peeled off her clothing, removing layers of a dense woven material. He grimaced at the peat-fire smell of it, the coarse texture. 'Twas the same garb every Strathavon muck-the-byre wore. Hardly what he'd expected a young woman schooled in entertaining gentlemen in the finer arts of her gender would wish to wear. Still, parted from her clothing, her body looked tender enough. Patting the end of the bed, he indicated she should lie upon it.

She did so cautiously, staring up at him, her legs draped over the end of the bed. He stripped off his clothing and stood at the foot; doubtless, a magnificent sight to behold. Still staring at him, her gaze slide from his face down to lower parts of his anatomy, where, being ready for imminent activity, he was at his rampant best. Her eyes widened, and she glanced away, cheeks reddening.

He laughed harshly. 'If ye're thinking ye'll no' manage to accommodate me, *all* o' me, ye being a scrawny wee piece, I can assure ye otherwise. I've no' met a strumpet yet that couldnae take me inside her, every inch.' His face hardened. 'And I'm paying good coin, so take me ye will, and as many times as I please, fer I intend to have my fill.'

He relented a little, remembering his latter school days and the many ribbings he'd received, the teasing references to his resemblance to a male horse that always amused him. A mocking smile touched his lips. 'Or maybe ye're looking forward to the lusty stretching I intend to give yer flesh. If so, let's no' waste any more time.'

She looked blankly at him.

Once more, he'd forgotten she was a Heiland half-wit. No matter.

Reaching down, he fondled her breasts, no more than swelling buds, crushing her nipples between his fingers, then grasped her by the ankles and forced her feet up onto the bed. Parting her knees, he groaned at the sight of her rosebud of flesh which he fully intended to plunder to the hilt.

She looked up fearfully, or so she contrived, for being a Heiland creature 'twas inconceivable she'd not been tumbled in every byre between Delnabo and Ballindalloch. Even before she came to this place of employ, she'd likely been bent over many a steaming dung heap, her skirts thrust over her head.

Grimacing in distaste, he looked at her hair straggled over the bedsheets, a brown, nondescript colour. He thought of the satin drape the desirable young witchling possessed. It had floated like silk about her shoulders, framing her slender curves and concealing so much he dearly yearned to explore. Another surge of hot blood whetted his loins. With a grunt, he jerked forward, forcing himself upon her with a savagery that even took him by surprise.

She flinched, eyes flying wide, adopting a ludicrously alarmed expression. He grunted in amusement; evidently, she was practised at play-acting. Coital games were a particular favourite of his.

Having some unexpected trouble, he forced himself hard upon her until brute force prevailed, and the strumpet gasped sharply. With a grunt of triumph, he pushed on, feeling her flesh cleave to accommodate his girth, and began thrusting vigorously.

The strumpet gave a series of little whimpers, prompting a further rush of blood to his manhood. Pleasure pulsed through his body, the sensations mounting as an image of the witchling blotted out the strumpet's face, and blind lust took over.

'Holy God,' he groaned. A bewitchment was surely upon him, for never had he known such arousal. He clambered onto the girl, half flattening her, all thought driven from his head but the urgent need to furrow female flesh.

The bed creaked wildly, his breath rasping in his throat, sweat running from him, a sense of mastery driving him on, along with a perverse desire to punish her for not being the girl he wanted. She turned her head away, and without her face below, 'twas easy to imagine another. The exquisite features, the molten dark eyes. He groaned, his hunger for the mysterious witchling so mighty there could be no satisfying it with this strumpet, no matter how hard he used her. He tried, though, rutting like a bull, only just managing to stop himself from bellowing like one.

His furious onslaught quickly brought release, and he collapsed upon her, fighting for breath. She whimpered beneath him. Shifting his weight, he turned her over so he might continue his pretence. A smear of blood stained the sheets, some trick he imagined. He could hardly have used her any harder than a hundred men before. He would use her again in a moment as soon as he'd recovered his vigour sufficiently. Perhaps from this angle. Aye, she could raise her rump, and he'd make great waves surge across her buttocks.

Incredibly, in moments he was aroused again, and as soon as he'd caught his breath would be upon her afresh. If he angled the mirror correctly, he might view his performance, gaining maximum pleasure for coin. His appetite seemed insatiable. Yet oddly, he sensed he'd find no real satisfaction here. 'Twas the witchling he wanted.

* * *

Come morning, although a little fatigued from his many exertions throughout the night, Hugh had failed to experience the customary relief such encounters usually brought. He felt unsatisfied, his appetite for female flesh undiminished even after the night's many indulgences. His craving for one particular female still tormented him. He feared even supposing he possessed the luxury of a whole week to plunder the young strumpet's body, near rupturing himself, true satisfaction would continue to evade him.

When finally spent and drifting into sleep, he'd felt the creep of the girl's arm come around him, followed by the caress of her fingers on his damp skin. The sensations were unfamiliar and should've displeased him, yet he'd fallen into a deep sleep and come morning found his own arm wound around the girl. He even left it there until she woke, although upon detecting her movements, swiftly removed it.

Now, as he dressed, a thought occurred to him. On settling his bill with the fawning and even more gaudily painted Mrs Geddes, he voiced it with her.

'I've decided to give employment to the girl I bedded last night. Isobel, I believe she's called. If you'd be willing to release her from her duties here, I could offer her employment closer to home. Strathavon, I mean. I live and work there. I would, of course, pay her ... adequately.'

She raised heavily pencilled brows. 'The lass musta pleased ye richt fine, Mister McBeath.' She smiled knowingly, rouged lips peeled back to reveal horse-like teeth. 'Did I nae say she was innocent?'

He grunted.

''Tisna every man that's comfortable tak'ing a lass's innocence, but others, like you, will pay fer the privilege. I'm thinking ye're the type o' man who likes to be the first.' She chuckled. 'And wishes to keep it that way. Weel, far be it from me to deprive ye. If ye wish the lass all to yersel', I'll nae deny ye that pleasure.'

'You misunderstand,' he said in irritation, although in truth, the woman had been uncannily astute. 'I wish to employ her as a scullery maid and cook, naught more. My cottage requires a woman's touch. I could give her respectable work. No one need know of her whoring of last night. Her reputation might be saved.'

She regarded him with a teasingly sceptical expression.

'Well,' he snapped, 'will you release her to me?'

'Noo, then,' she chuckled, 'I micht.'

Embarrassment flushed his face. He was offering to save the girl from prostituting herself to pay her father's debts. A charitable offer, surely? Yet this ridiculous woman was looking at him as if he were some lecherous goat intent on keeping the girl for his own perverted use. He clenched his teeth. His ire was irrational; his reasons for wanting the girl were no concern of this madam.

'If 'tis Isobel's wish,' she looked him pointedly in the eye, 'I micht let ye hae her fer yer *scudgie*.' She stressed the word with a Highland twang that sounded suspiciously like a sneer. ''Twill be better fer her, I'm thinking, haeing but one man a nicht instead o' ten or mair.'

He blinked, his left eyelid convulsing.

* * *

It was all swiftly arranged, the girl appearing content to leave with him for Strathavon that very day. She travelled light, apparently naught to her name but the peat-reeking clothes he'd removed from her the night before.

He'd arranged to meet the Collector at the tollbooth entrance where Farquharson would pay the bail money necessary to release the hirelings. These men would be required to make their mark on contracts binding them to work for the Board of Excise until they'd repaid the money advanced to free them. It seemed a favourable arrangement for all concerned.

As he waited for Farquharson to emerge from the cells under the building, he studied the girl who was now his maidservant, thinking how unsuitable for the position she looked. She was on the young side, plain as porridge, and had no speech but the Irish. What in God's name possessed him? But he knew what. Her biddable nature, her unquestioning acceptance of his every lustful demand, her tender young body and his now almost unlimited access to it.

Sensing his gaze upon her, she looked up shyly as he sat on his horse. Their eyes met, the first time they'd done so beyond the bedchamber, and she blushed furiously, looking nervous and out of place.

A crowd was beginning to gather. Isobel seemed to know many among them. They were waiting to witness his predecessor's hanging, he supposed, and were likely from the same glen as the girl. Some women spoke to her, and she murmured in response, moving to stand at his horse's flank. Mrs Geddes had plainly explained he was her saviour, and she wished to show gratitude and loyalty. He smiled inwardly. She could demonstrate her gratitude later once he'd gotten her home and she'd cooked him a decent meal. He doubted his stomach could tolerate any more oats.

Farquharson eventually appeared with the two cut-throats in tow, the men blinking in the weak sunshine, staring up at the gallows. The Collector folded and pocketed some paperwork Hugh took for the contracts he'd mentioned, regarding him cynically.

'I've explained their duties and where their loyalty must lie if they wish to stay out of gaol.' He eyed Isobel with suspicion. 'Both men have made their mark to show they accept those terms.'

'Thank ye, sir.'

The Collector nodded at the first man, a weaselly streak with shifty eyes. 'Charles Stuart, known as Ghillie for his supposed skill as a laird's gamesman, though in truth, I fear the man has poached more of his grace's game than anyone in living memory. And this,' he turned to the younger of the two, a man with vacant eyes and a face as red as a freshly skelped arse. 'Is Dougal Riach, a man of limited intellect I fear, who likely follows his accomplice in all things, having not the wit to think for himself.'

Hugh nodded to them. They were both filthy and looked vicious and sly, yet he doubted either could better him in combat. Branded a bully at school and always of a muscular physique, he had unfaltering faith in his skill with sword, pistol and fist. He smiled grimly; few men would attempt to challenge his position. Still fewer had a hope of succeeding.

Farquharson frowned at Isobel. 'Who's this lass you've acquired? Don't tell me you've squandered your allowance employing this lass as a scullion?'

'Of course, no',' he lied. 'I believe she's here to see her faither. In gaol for unpaid rent.'

Farquharson questioned Isobel in Gaelic, and she nodded, answering him timidly. With a grateful smile, she disappeared into the building.

'I've allowed her a few moments with her father, Willie Gow.' Farquharson glanced up at the scaffold. 'She's no wish to witness the hanging. I confess I've no heart for the spectacle either. I once considered

Meldrum a friend. He may have betrayed the authorities that paid him, but I've little wish to witness his painful end.' He glanced around uneasily. 'And there's a chance of trouble, I fear. Many have come to show support for him and opposition to the powers that will execute him. 'Tis said they've come from as far as the Cabrach, Speyside, the ports of Banff, Cullen and MacDuff, and of course, from rebellious Stratha'an and Glenlivet. There's even a concern of rioting.'

Hugh glanced around in alarm, noting a number of verminous types beginning to appear like rats from the sewers. They muttered together, grim-faced and dark-eyed, forming into mutinous packs.

'I suggest you move swiftly along,' Farquharson advised. 'Should they see the gauger's garb, who knows what they'll do. I intend to do likewise to avoid inciting trouble.'

'I'll do that, sir. Once I've arranged mounts for the hirelings and armed them, we'll be on our way back to Drumin.'

''Twould be advisable.'

Isobel reappeared from the tollbooth in conversation with two men who were half-carrying another. Between them, the men dragged a youth, bolstering him under the arms, his feet scrabbling to gain purchase on the cobbled street. Hugh recognised the youth as the young Jacobite from the day before, his face swollen and bloody.

Farquharson also recognised him. His brows puckered, a look of concern darkening his features. He stopped the men and questioned them intently.

'Aye, sir, thank ye fer yer trouble,' the younger of them replied. 'But he'll be right enough once his sister sees to him. She's a healer. A skilled one. She'll nae let his bonny face be spoiled if 'tis in her power to prevent it.'

'Glad to hear it.' Farquharson stood back to let them pass. The men nodded to Isobel, then made their way slowly up the High Street dragging their semi-conscious companion.

Watching them, it dawned upon Hugh this Isobel might know many of the smugglers of his ride. The cogs of his mind began to turn. She likely knew who in the glen smuggled, maybe even where their bothies were hidden. She might know when convoys were leaving and where they were headed, and if not, could perhaps find out. Excitement bubbled up. She might prove even more useful than he initially imagined.

Smiling inwardly, he envisioned how this might work, but almost immediately, a difficulty reared its head, and his smile soured. For his plan to work, the girl would need to understand and speak English so he could interrogate her and give her instructions. And he'd need to understand whatever she had to tell him. Damnation. He'd need to teach her English. He muttered an oath under his breath, causing Farquharson to glance sharply at him. Being of a lower intellect and race, 'twas highly unlikely the girl possessed the wit to learn such a refined and complicated language. And how many pointless hours might he waste trying to teach her? The thought of mastering the Irish himself briefly crossed his mind, but he swiftly dismissed it. 'Twas a primitive tongue fit only for heather-lowpers. Lowering himself to learn it would be beyond his endurance.

He smiled thinly at Farquharson's questioning frown. The Collector appeared ill at ease, anxious to put as much distance as possible between himself and the gibbet where Meldrum would swing. Far be it from him to detain him. Murmuring an assurance that smuggling would soon be a thing of the past in Strathavon, he took his leave, the hirelings trailing in his wake.

* * *

By midday, he was riding south to Strathavon, the girl sitting behind him astride his horse, her arms around his waist and her warm young body pressed into his back. She'd uttered not a word since leaving Elgin, but several times had lain her head against him. He'd felt the hard press of it between his shoulder blades and the timid grip of her fingers at his waist, prompting him to imagine how hard he'd press himself upon her later.

The two hirelings were now armed with flintlock pistols and cutlasses and rode sturdy garrons. They swayed on their ponies, looking suitably pleased with their sudden and remarkable elevation in life. He wondered how long they'd been languishing in gaol. Both looked raw-boned and pale. To be of use to him, they'd need to fill out in muscle and brawn. He could hardly take on packs of vicious smugglers on his own. God forbid. Others would be required to put their lives on the line. Not him. 'Twas what these hirelings were here for.

Wondering how much they knew of the smuggling activity in his area, he turned to the man he judged the less witless of the two.

'So, Ghillie, I imagine ye've been a smuggler most of your days, and the most notorious offenders in Strathavon are well known to you. I require their names.'

The man blinked, looking shifty, frowning ahead at the forested slopes of Ben Aigen.

'Come, man, word will soon spread of your change of occupation. I suggest you relinquish any lingering loyalty. 'Tis entirely misplaced. The rogues will think naught of turning upon you like the rabid dogs they are. Ye know that, I assume.' He squinted at the weasel, feeling no affinity with him or his witless companion. 'So, then,' he coaxed, 'the names of the worst offenders will suffice for now.'

Ghillie frowned in confusion, evidently struggling to follow his Lowland speech and inflexion.

'Their names,' he repeated.

'Err, would it be Lachlan Innes ye're wanting to ken aboot?'

'Lachlan Innes?' He'd heard the name. 'He's the ringleader, then?'

'Weel, he micht be. He's a masterly smuggler if 'tis what ye mean. But ye've little hope o' catching him.'

'Is that so?' Hugh snorted. 'A masterly smuggler, is he? We'll see. And where might he be found, this Lachlan Innes? Which holdings does he work?'

'Far aboots does he bide? That'd be Tomachcraggen. But he's nae there noo. He's in Elgin. Ye seen him earlier, mind? Wi' his lads. The youngest was looking the worst fer wear. Beaten aboot the face and body from what I saw. Duncan's his name. He's a bonny smuggler, too.'

Hugh stared at him. 'You mean, the men we saw with the injured youth? *They* are the most notorious smugglers in Strathavon?'

'Thon's aboot the size o' it, sir, aye.'

'Christ, man! Why on earth did ye no' say so?'

'Weel, I didna ken 'twas so important. 'Tisna like they had any whisky on them at the time. D'ye nae need to catch them in the act, then?'

'Well, of course,' he snapped. 'I'll need proof of their guilt, that goes without saying, but to simply let them stumble by without so much as a nod to me.' He let his breath out in exasperation, eyelid twitching. 'As I said,' he muttered, trying to master his vexation. 'I'll need proof of their guilt. Perhaps you can help me there? Either of you.' He flicked his gaze to Dougal, swaying absently on his pony, scratching at himself.

'Eh? Oh, aye, Mister McBeath. Mebbe.' Dougal chuckled. 'I'm thinking Lachlan's eldest is soon to wed. He's smitten wi' Mhari Lang, and she's agreed to wed him.' He scratched himself a deal more vigorously, his tongue poking out. 'A lucky man, though I'm thinking she could do better.' He laughed wickedly, his scratching growing ever more vigorous. 'She coulda had me, after all.' He broke into a wheezing laugh. 'Anyhoo, what Highland wedding did ever ye go to that didna hae whisky at it? Gallons. Thon's the time to catch 'em. They'll nae hae their wits aboot them then. They'll be too busy haeing a wee *ceilidh,* getting roaring drunk on Tomachcraggen's whisky.'

Hugh sat back on his horse, whistling softly. How in God's name had the noxious simpleton thought of that? Inexplicably, the halfwit had stumbled upon a genius idea.

'Dougal,' he grunted, 'ye might just be a genius. Find out where and when the wedding's to take place. Only, do it discretely.'

They both looked blankly at him.

'God's teeth! I mean in secret.'

'Aye, Mister McBeath, we'll do that.' Ghillie glared at Dougal, sitting back smugly, basking in the unexpected praise.

Another thought occurred to Hugh. He leaned over in the saddle, fixing his gaze intently on the pair.

'I saw a girl in Strathavon.' A quiver came into his voice. 'A young lass who's comely in an unconventional way. She was in the company of an old crone. She looked ....' He frowned. How to describe the enchantress who'd taken possession of him? 'Intriguing,' he ventured. 'Who might she be?'

The hirelings exchanged looks. 'That'd likely be Rowena,' said Ghillie. 'When ye say she looked "intriguing", d'ye mean ye fancied a wee roll in the heather wi' her?' He hooted at Hugh's expression. ''Twould be Rowena, right enough. The crone was likely Morna MacNeil. Some call her a healer, though kirk folk hae other names fer her like witch. Rowena's her apprentice, though she's hardly a witch. Nae looking the wey she does.' He sniggered. 'I wouldna mind a wee roll wi' her mysel'.'

'I'd do mair than roll wi' her,' Dougal put in. 'I'd pound the living bejesus oot o' her.'

'You'll leave her be,' Hugh snapped.

Rowena. An unusual name, though somehow fitting.

'So,' he continued, his excitement growing. 'If I wished to approach this Rowena. On a private matter, ye understand, where might I find her?'

Ghillie waggled his head, considering. 'If 'tis a private matter, as ye say, and ye wish to meet the lass on her own. Just the two o' ye.' He looked Hugh in the eye, unsuccessfully stifling a smirk. 'Then, ye'd do well to look fer her oot on the hills where she tends the beasts, or in woods, or mebbe doon by the river where she gathers weeds and things. Healers do a deal o' wandering ower the land, searching oot roots and herbs fer their potions. 'Tis what she does. Only, she oft-times does it wi' the auld witch. Or her brother. The younger ane. Ye'd need to watch the lass secret-like, mak' sure the MacNeil witch wasna lurking in the bushes. Ye'd nae be wanting the auld hag watching yer private matter, I'm thinking.'

Hugh's face reddened. 'I've no wish to be acquainted with that creature. She's fit only for the scaffold. But I'd likely just find this Rowena wandering the hills, or skulking in woods, then?'

'Thons aboot the size o' it, sir, aye.'

The quivering in his innards had spread to his face; his eyelid twitched. Other parts of his anatomy had also jerked to life. His breathing roughened with excitement. He'd find her. Supposing he had to tramp over every Strathavon hill and pasture, search every bog and tangled wood, he'd track her down. The searching would only make the finding sweeter. He saw himself returning the item in his pocket to her with a meaningful look. She'd recognise her danger at once. Any threats could likely be left unsaid. Just as well, as she doubtless spoke no English. But he'd make his intentions clear enough, as he'd done with the strumpet. Sitting back on his horse, he inhaled deeply. Already he could smell the sweet scent of success—it smelled of gorse flowers.

This Rowena would presumably be flattered by his attention. A respectable government officer, a man of power and influence in the area. He'd always known he was attractive to women, had used the knowledge to his advantage. This occasion would be no different. And even supposing it was, the threat of exposing her devil-worshipping would likely be enough to ensure she played his game. He'd be rolling in the heather with her in no time. Or anywhere else he chose for the deed.

Feeling the tentative press of Isobel's fingers around his waist bracing herself against the roll of his horse's gait, he glanced at the hireling's sturdy but diminutive ponies. Their garrons had no hope of matching his horse for speed, and with the strumpet pressed up against him and thoughts of the witchling filling his head, not to mention his breeches, he felt the need to reach home as swiftly as possible.

'You two can catch me up,' he grunted. 'No need for haste. Report to me at Drumin the morrow's night.'

Urging his horse into a gallop, he left the hirelings in his wake, showering them in flying clods of wet heather and sod. The morrow would do fine. He'd be busy with the girl later. He'd no intention of sharing her with those two misfits.

CHAPTER SEVENTEEN

ROWENA STOOD BACK as her da and James carried Duncan in and laid him on the table, gasping as she caught sight of his face. One eye was shut, the other little more than a slit, his face bruised to an angry shade of purple. The gaping gash on his forehead would need stitching, but from what James had told her, the worst injuries were to his body.

'I'll need boiled water,' she instructed Grace. 'And broth to nourish him once I've finished wi' the herbs.' She turned away to fetch her pestle and mortar and select the best herbs, using the time to gain mastery over her emotions. White willow bark first to deaden his pain, then she'd be able to examine him without hurting him too much.

As she worked, a voice spoke in her head. 'Twas her healer's voice, and she was glad of it. It spoke of herbs and what she must do with them. It talked calmly, giving her industry instead of shock, fuss to dampen her anguish.

An infusion o' yarrow and wormwood fer cleaning his wounds, then compresses fer the bruises and swellings. Calendula and marshmallow leaf, witch-hazel if she had it. Poultices of these would draw out infection. If bones were broken, knitbone would be needed. 'Twould speed the binding together of bone as well as flesh.

As she worked, she trembled, dreading what she'd find when she cut away his blood-stiffened clothing. The worst injuries would be inside his body, not evident to the eye. They'd be felt on examination, by Duncan as well as her.

Despite her industry, tears scalded, and she struggled to swallow them away. She must be strong. Yet a tightness in her chest told her she was not that strong woman, no matter the promises she'd made. Not when it came to Duncan. The tightness was the crushing of her heart, the pain of it, knowing what the soldier-devils had done.

Clenching her teeth, she pounded witch-hazel leaves to a pulp. How could any man treat another wi' such savagery? To beat a lad, and one more loyal and God-loving than anyone she knew. 'Twas beyond comprehension. She swiped sparks of green paste from her cheeks. Were all men nae the same underneath, nae matter what tongue they spoke or where they'd been born? Surely every man was born as naked and helpless as the next?

Yet Morna was right; what use was there in letting her hurting show? Who did it help? Duncan needed a healer, nae a weeping child. She must put her love away.

As she worked, Duncan watched her through his one crack of an eye, a tiny glimmer of blue-green reminding her who this mash of flesh really was. He didn't speak, but she felt his gratitude. It was in the gathering of his brows, in the dip of his throat as he tried to thank her through lips so swollen and split, they'd sealed themselves shut. She sponged his mouth with yarrow water, gently unsticking his lips, then cradled his head, holding the willow bark tea for him to drink.

'Try nae to speak. This will ease yer pain.' She looked intently at him, a vein of steel stiffening her voice. 'I will heal ye. I swear. Everything I've learned, I'll harness to mend ye.' She turned away lest tears should come.

James was pacing the room.

'In all the years we've kent him, Duncan's aye been frugal wi' words. Even as a boy, he was more a thinker than a talker. Words came sorely.' He exhaled. 'But when he finds himself in a courtroom crowded wi' soldiers and government men, what does tongue-tied Duncan do?' He halted, his face working. 'He lets loose a storm o' words. A lifetime's worth o' bitterness and delivers it in the most impassioned way.'

He drew a ragged breath. 'Both in defence o' John and in condemnation o' the government's cruel treatment o' Highland folk.' His face twisted. 'Ye shoulda heard him. Ye'd have been that proud. A lad o' few words, a pious man and loyal to a fault, yet when he speaks out, dear God, he stirs a whirlwind and does it kenning full well he'll be punished fer it. Yet he put into words what none o' us could do, even had we the courage.'

He moved to the table, looking down at the purple, swollen face. 'Ye're a rare man.' His face tightened until it quivered. 'I'm proud to call ye brother.'

'A damn fool,' Lachlan muttered. 'They coulda killed him. 'Tis a wonder his carcass isna hanging next to John's.' He crossed himself. 'Forgive me, John. God rest yer soul.' He threw himself into his chair. 'Ye met yer end wi' quiet courage, as I kent ye would, but the glen's a darker place wi'out ye, my friend.' He clutched his head in his hands.

'Poor Mister Meldrum.' Grace stood rooted at the hearth.

'The water, Grace. I must work fast. Infection sets in swiftly when wounds are left untended.'

With a supply of boiled water to hand, she cut away Duncan's sark, easing it from an oozing wound beneath his ribs where the fabric had become almost part of his skin. A tapestry of bruises was revealed. Angry lumps and swellings patterned the once smooth contours of his body, one on his side as big as a goose egg.

Working slowly, she cleaned his battered body, sponging him with handfuls of moss soaked in a warm infusion of wormwood. Few herbs could surpass wormwood for its power to soothe and speed healing. Once she'd cleaned the blood and grime away and the willow-bark tea had done its work, she drew a trembling breath.

Jem had been whining since they brought Duncan in. She hushed now, seeming to understand the need for stillness and quiet. She licked Duncan's hand, then lay under the table to guard him. Rowena closed her eyes, and with tentative fingers, began her examination.

Taking immeasurable care, she inched her hands over his body, stopping to feel around hot areas where the skin was shiny and taught. Applying gentle pressure, she worked over muscle and bone, searching for injuries to vulnerable inner tissue, feeling for broken and splintered bones. 'Twas easier to sense discord with her eyes closed, to feel the distorted flow of energy in his body, the areas thrown out of harmony and to establish the cause. Every one of her senses she honed to his body.

With the softest touch, she moved her hands over his shoulders and neck, gently palpating, then slid them over the swell of his chest. Tentatively, she found his nipples, feeling them harden at her touch, then traced each rib, verifying its wholeness. With caressing fingers, she moved to the plane of his abdomen, working around to his back. Her fingers circled in their thoroughness, touching what she'd never touched before and keenly conscious of it. Every one of her senses, she attuned to his hurting, all her awareness. Never had she experienced such intimacy with another soul, nor been more mindful of it. Her skin tingled, her senses heightened to a rare intensity.

Duncan's breathing quickened. She heard it catch in his throat.

Swallowing, she opened her eyes, feeling a new tension in his body and an answering one in hers. He would heal. Two bones were broken—ribs, not splintered but cleanly snapped. They would mend given time, the bruising inside his body, too. She covered him with a blanket. Compresses would ease the swollen and inflamed areas where he'd been kicked and punched, but first, she must sew torn flesh together. She turned away to heat a needle.

He caught her by the hand, pressing her fingers, murmuring something. She squeezed his hand in return.

* * *

Over the next few weeks, Duncan healed quicker than Rowena had dared to hope. 'Twas a miracle, Grace declared, and her da admitted he'd never have believed it possible the lad could recover so swiftly from such a vicious beating. He looked at her with new respect.

Once she'd completed her initial ministrations, they'd moved Duncan to his box-bed near the fire, and she drew the drape, allowing him privacy to sleep. Morna had oft-times told her sleep was the best of all healers. 'Twas when the body did its mending. All healing came from within, from the invisible force powering life. So, in truth, everything she did, all the herbs and nature-magic she used, were but ways of assisting that force, and it worked best during sleep.

Other than going out to forage for herbs, she stayed by Duncan's side at all times. No sooner did he stir than she was on her feet, preparing fresh herbs, encouraging him to sip soothing teas. She changed his dressings often, altering the herbs to stimulate further healing, anxious to ensure no poison festered in his wounds.

Yet, watching his remarkable recovery, she couldn't help feeling 'twas love healed him so fast. Perhaps love prompted all healing, the greatest healer not sleep, but love.

Within a few days, Duncan wished his drape opened, and she managed to prop him up so he could watch Grace and her go about their chores. Often, she just sat quietly with him and 'twas almost like old times before he became a smuggler. She thought of the many hours they'd spent together at the Shelter Stone when he'd shown inordinate patience teaching her the difficult English words.

But then, those were their childish days, and she supposed that lent them a magic they could never recapture. There was little magic in the world for Duncan now, not with John Meldrum hanging from a gibbet on Elgin's Plainstones as a deterrent to them all.

She wondered if he'd continue to smuggle but thought better of asking him. James no longer wished to, not once wed. Leaving Mhari to struggle whilst he languished in gaol, or worse, was his greatest fear. John's fate had coloured his decision, but James had never been comfortable smuggling. Keen to give his bride-to-be a home of her own, and the bairns he laughingly claimed he'd soon give her, James had signed his name to a rental agreement on land at Druimbeag.

Druimbeag was a beautiful holding on the far side of the Avon. Rowena went there often to forage for red clover and nettles, to harvest a little bark from the white willow growing among alder and pine. But the cot-house needed re-thatching, and there was work needed doing on the land. James and her da now worked there most days with Donald Gordon.

Donald was skilled at thatching and was keen to pass his skills to James. They spent their days cutting heathery divots from high moorland, scalloping them and arranging them in overlapping rows upon the roof timbers. More bundled heather finished the roof. When done, James looked upon his new home with shining eyes. He wished the cottage to be perfect, ready for his wedding night when he'd carry Mhari over the threshold.

Donald was fond of James, Duncan too, and never tired of telling her da how fortunate he was. His own sons had been hanged by the soldiers more than thirteen years ago, just boys, yet he always spoke of them as if they still lived. For Donald, they did, she supposed. 'Twas how he got through his days. But he liked to help his neighbours, particularly the lads who'd been friends of his sons, and he wished James and Mhari well.

Once part of the Avon's floodplain, Druimbeag land was fertile, the soil rich and dark. James would grow oats and barley and keep a few beasts, building up a herd, but he'd no longer break the law by smuggling or making whisky.

Duncan went quiet when James told him, but he respected James' decision. Her da was less understanding. He tried hard to change James' mind, eventually winning a small concession. James would accompany them on their next smuggling trip. 'Twould be sore work with Duncan injured, but they'd split the spoils, James putting his share toward establishing his herd. Then he'd turn his back on smuggling forever. He hoped to show the rest of the glen 'twas possible to meet the steep new rentals with naught but a scrape of land and a few beasts.

As he healed, Duncan tried to thank Rowena for everything she'd done for him, although she always brushed his attempts aside with a blushing half-smile. Healing was what she did. Yet she felt his gratitude, for his eyes told her everything. As she moved about the cot-house, crossing from hearth to table to his box-bed and back to the hearth, she felt his gaze upon her.

There had always been a vulnerability in Duncan—a consequence of the suffering he'd endured. But she sensed a new poignancy now, something that troubled her. 'Twas as if his heart lay open and raw, and she couldn't help feeling strangely responsible. His experience had changed him, his courage in speaking out and the beating he'd taken, and she knew he'd witnessed John's execution. Da and James had, too. 'Twas badly done, her da said. Deliberately so, he believed.

James had always jested there was a hint of the fox about Duncan's face, even more so now he'd taken to wearing a close-cropped little beard. Yet, there was naught sly about him. His was a candid face, and she'd long been able to read it. Now, when she treated his wounds, she couldn't help sensing a new restlessness in him. He'd swallow and close his eyes, a tightness in his jaw, a pulse beating in his throat. And when she'd finished, he'd fix her with such a hopeful look, she'd need to glance away, hiding the answering longing that raged in her own heart. Duncan's brows would rise and tighten together, and she'd sense he wished to say something, only, whatever it was should remain unsaid. 'Twould be better for them both. So always, she'd move away, making much of busying herself with tinctures and salves.

Duncan's recovery was also aided by an endless string of visitors. His actions at Elgin Burgh Court and his treatment by the soldiers was soon well known throughout the glen. Already a respected smuggler, to his embarrassment, folk came from far and wide to look upon his battered face. They wished to capture his hands, clutch him by the forearm, or just press a hand upon his shoulder and thank him for speaking up for them all, no matter that it changed nothing.

Father Ranald came, too. She found him on the doorstep one morning, clutching his bible and rosary. He seemed unsure of his welcome, eyeing her warily from the threshold. She greeted him with as much warmth as she could muster, and whilst he knelt at Duncan's bedside to offer prayers for his recovery, she escaped to the hills and forests in search of fresh herbs. And to whisper her own thanks at the sacred stones on Seely's Hillock. Church ways would never be her ways; she sensed they both knew that.

Once the swelling had gone down enough for Duncan to be once more recognisable, James delighted in making fun of him.

'If it's nae, Duncan,' he laughed. 'Ye've returned to us. I worried ye might frighten my bride away on my wedding day wi' that battered face.' He grinned. 'I see I needna have worried. Rowena has restored yer handsome face and wi' a few new scars fer character. The glen lasses will be pleased.'

James and Mhari were to wed in three days, and there was still much preparation to be done. Grace was the busiest she'd ever been, spending her days with Mhari and her mother helping prepare the wedding feast. Tradition dictated the wedding take place at Lagganvoulin, the bride's home, although Da muttered 'twas too soon after John's death. They should be putting the wedding off for now. 'Twas disrespectful to be celebrating after such a tragedy. A slur on John's memory.

Yet, Father Ranald argued it should go ahead as planned. John would wish them to celebrate as Highland custom decreed. They shouldn't allow his death to darken their lives. He'd wish a dram of illicit whisky raised in his memory, and her da and James were keen to do just that. Duncan wanted to be on his feet to honour John's memory too, and to toast the health and happiness of his brother and his bride. When Rowena prescribed fresh air and gentle exercise, he quickly agreed.

So, with his chest protected by a fresh strapping, she helped him out of bed, and he swayed in the doorway, blinking in the watery sunshine as he admired their oats and barley rippling in the breeze. They'd grown tall since last he saw them. When he lifted his gaze to the distant Cairngorms, a catch came into his voice.

'Lord, I give ye thanks wi' every fibre o' my being.'

She looked curiously at him. 'Fer what?'

'Fer allowing me to return to all this. And to you.' He looked at her with such a softness in his eyes, his meaning disturbed her.

'Where else would ye go?' She slipped an arm around him for support.

'I feared I might never leave the stinking hell o' the tollbooth wi' its clanking chains and scurrying rats, except to join John on the scaffold. That I'd niver see all this again.' He swallowed, turning to look at her.

She tightened her grip on him—*all love is taken from ye*. Those had been Morna's words.

When she said naught, he whistled to Jem, and they crossed Tomachcraggen land together, slowly making toward the Avon.

They heard the river before they saw it, finally glimpsing the shimmer of water through the trees, silver dark, a breeze sweeping across its surface, splaying it into glistening waves. She led him to a shingle beach where the air was so fresh it chilled their nostrils. Boulders littered the beach like petrified seals. They found one to sit on, Jem content to lie at Duncan's feet watching the antics of probing oystercatchers. Here the water rushed through a narrow channel, then smoothed its flow, bubbling into a deep pool where something beneath the surface disturbed it again, sending ripples splaying out. She thought the word water-horse and shivered.

'I feel that fortunate to be here.' Duncan rubbed Jem's ears. 'Yet, guilty. What they did to John.'

'Dinna think on it,' she urged. ''Tis only his body died on that gibbet. His soul still lives. Ye'll meet him again one day, and all yer kinfolk that ye've lost, as I'll find my mother. 'Tis long I've dreamed o' that.'

'In heaven, ye mean?'

She hesitated, not wishing to speak of God's places. Morna said they were naught but church inventions, though Duncan held unfaltering faith in everything churchmen said. 'How d'ye feel after yer walk?' she asked instead. 'I've nae ower-taxed ye?'

'Tired,' he admitted, 'but glad to be in the light after the dark o' the cot-house and breathing air that's nae reeking o' burning peat. And always I'm happiest when I'm wi' you.' He looked steadily at her, and that uncomfortable feeling crept over her again.

'I'll leave ye fer a moment.' She got to her feet. 'I need more wormwood. Jem can keep ye company.'

'Take her wi' ye,' he urged. 'Dragoons could be patrolling. Ye saw what they did to me. Should they find you ....' He shuddered.

'I'll be moments. I can look after myself.'

'Please, Rowena.'

But she turned away and was soon out of earshot, searching along the shingly riverbank for the silver leaves and acid yellow flowers of the wormwood plant. A tender herb, it preferred stony ground, only growing among the trees and bushes fringing the river. She knew where to look and quickly found a patch.

Before pinching off any aromatic leaves, she knelt and whispered her thanks for the healing properties of this powerful herb. Satisfied her intentions were sincere and she'd not waste anything she picked, she set about harvesting enough to make another batch of healing tea.

Almost at once, she sensed danger, and her skin prickled. Glancing up, she stilled her breath to listen. A twig snapped behind her, then the rattle of disturbed stones. Spinning around, she drew a fearful breath, scanning the bushes. Jem began to bark in the distance. Her nerves skirling, she bundled her things together and hurried away.

When she returned to Duncan, Jem had quietened, only growling sporadically. Duncan's relief was palpable. 'Jem heard something.' He slid his dirk back into its place. 'Stay aside me, Rowena. Please, so I can protect ye.'

'I'm fine. I need no protecting.'

But he continued to search the alders and whins for signs of danger, his face pale and tense. Feeling guilty, she sat at his side.

'Ye misjudge the danger.' He skimmed the bushes behind her, then focused on her face. 'Ye're an innocent. I couldna bear it if anything happened to change that. To hurt ye.'

She met his gaze, and he swallowed, glancing awkwardly away.

'Ye're a trusting soul wi' those great dark eyes. Too trusting, fer I see how men look at ye.' His jaw tightened. 'God help me, I know why they look, fer I canna help looking too. Ye're lovely beyond words, unaware o' yer beauty. Uncaring. Yet ye should care.' His gaze returned to her face. A soft sheen of sweat had beaded on his brow. 'When menfolk follow ye wi' their eyes, 'tis because they desire ye.'

'It hardly bothers me.'

'But it should. There's disrespect in—danger even—especially from soldiers. They're wicked men wi' nae respect fer Highland women. They take what they want, and always in the most brutal way.' He looked steadily at her. 'I couldna bear it if that happened to you. Never could I forgive myself.'

'I'll be heedful, I promise.'

He nodded, and she sensed his tension ease a little. His gaze moved over her face. 'I dinna say this to frighten ye, but because ye're precious to me. And ye're a woman now.' His gaze moved to her mouth, lingered there. She felt herself flush.

He swallowed, looking back into her eyes. 'A beautiful one wi' eyes darker than a winter river and just as deep. As treacherous. I could drown in them and nae even notice. Nor care, I think.'

Dropping her gaze, she leant back against a rock. She mustn't let this happen. Duncan was a man now, taller even than James, finely muscled with a grace to his movements and manners. A man who considered deeply, who showed respect to all. There wasna a lass in the glen didna flutter their lashes, blush and grow tongue-tied when he entered a room, though he seemed nae to notice.

Her skin began to tingle, aching for his touch. The wanting made her shiver but frightened her, too. She must be guarding her heart, nae giving it away to be maimed and broken, and especially nae risking Duncan's heart. She must be the strong woman she promised Morna she'd be. Without love, there can be no loss, no living those lost-child days. 'Twas how to stay whole. To be a true healer.

'Rowena.' He cut through her thoughts. 'There's something I need to ask ye.'

She looked up to find him regarding her intently, holding himself very still.

'What happened to me,' he drew a ragged breath, 'and most foully to John. It showed me how fleeting life is. This moment we're sharing thegither,' he captured one of her hands, 'we'll never live it again. 'Twill be gone in a heartbeat.'

'We can come back here again the morrow, if ye like,' she said uneasily.

'But it'll nae be the same. It'll nae be *this* moment. This moment will be gone.' He frowned. 'What I'm trying to say, and I'm making a poor job o' it, is life is a fragile thing. It can be taken from ye,' he snapped his fingers, 'in the blink o' an eye.'

She flinched.

'So, it must be treasured. Lived to the full wi' nae regrets ower what mighta been. There should be nae waiting fer better times, fer life to begin. It began the day we were born, and we should be living it. Every moment.'

Her discomfort deepened, and she withdrew her hand, letting her hair fall forward, half hiding her face. 'Are we nae doing that?'

'Aye, but there's more. I wish more, though I've nae right to ask it. But I'm changed, grown bold, perhaps, and there's something I must ask ye. 'Tis that long I've wished to say it, I fear if I dinna do it now, I'll never find the courage.'

He retook her hand, caressing her palm, and her heart choked with sadness, knowing she must disappoint him. Since their first meeting, she'd wished to shield him from hurt. He'd been hurt more than anyone she knew, but now she would hurt him, for she must. Her chest tightened. Only, was it nae better to sting a little now? To ache, perhaps, than to be crushed in heart and spirit in the future? Surely this way was better for them both.

He swept her hair aside, draping it over her shoulder, then, with gentle fingers, lifted her chin and looked into her eyes. The sun picked out the gold in his hair, making it glisten. His eyes were bright, too, shining with hope and an ardency that pierced her heart.

'While I've the courage—'

In a desperate bid to forestall what she sensed was coming, she blurted,

''Tis that peaceful here, Duncan. I'm thinking I'd like to be buried here when 'tis my time.'

He frowned in consternation. 'Dinna speak o' such things, Rowena.'

A dipper flew down to the water's edge, flitting back and fore, twitching its wings, calling to others of its kind. Desperate in its search.

'I'd feel as lost as thon wee bird.'

She knew all about feeling lost. 'We all die. Each one o' us in our time.'

His face tightened. 'I canna think on that, on ye dying, fer I'd wish to die, too. But while we're both still living, young and,' he swallowed, 'aching wi' powerful longings.' He glanced away. 'I've never told ye how I feel. Lord knows, I'm nae one fer words, but I must say it now.'

'There's nae need—'

'But there is. I can keep this in me nae longer.' He rose and stood before her, gingerly taking her hand. She sensed the tremble in his fingers. Stepping back, he lowered a knee to the shingle, his gaze steady upon her face.

'I've always loved ye, since that night long ago when ye laid yer wee self down on the cold floor aside me. But my love's deepened. I feel it in my heart and soul, and now, God forgive me, I feel it in my body. I'm nae worthy o' ye. I'm a penniless criminal, landless, kinless, as undeserving a wretch as ye could come across. Yet, still, I find I must ask ye.'

'Ye're mair worthy than anyone I know.' A sob came into her voice. 'And only penniless in that every penny goes to help yer family. Pays rent on land we're bound to more fiercely than any rich man's deed could hope to match.'

'Ye flatter me,' he said tensely. 'But I ken what I am.'

He cleared his throat, looking as though he couldn't quite believe what he'd say next. Tight-faced, he pushed on.

'If ye'd let me love ye, Rowena, I swear I'd do whatever's in my power to mak' ye happy. I'd give my life fer you, and gladly, fer I'm hopelessly in love with you.'

'Ye shouldna say such things,' she croaked. 'Ye're my brother.'

'But I'm nae. Ye know I'm not. There's no blood atween us.'

'And ye wish to be a priest.'

She saw the pain behind his eyes at that and wished she'd not said it.

'Aye, God forgive me, I'm the weakest and worst o' men. Though I love God and wish to serve Him, I'm unworthy even o' Him, fer I love you more.' He swallowed, willing her to understand.

'Marry me, Rowena. I ken I've nae right to ask, but I canna help myself. I swear, no one could love ye more or be more faithful. Ye mean more to me than wealth, or life, or even the Lord Himself.' He swallowed, aware of the enormity of what he'd said.

She stared at him, dismay tightening her throat, tears brimming. She should stop this, but he was unstoppable.

He squeezed her hand, and her heart squeezed, too. 'Ye'd mak' me the happiest man in all the glens if ye'd agree to be my wife.'

The word seemed to hang in the air between them, cutting the bonds that bound her to nature, to Morna, and all the wild places she loved, lingering for what seemed an eternity before falling flatly to the stony riverbank. She swallowed, wishing to be gentle but not knowing how. Tears burned, and she pressed her lips together, fighting a desire to take him in her arms.

The silence stretched until finally he blinked, looking at her mouth, and she sensed he longed to kiss her. She longed for it, too. Then he glanced away, a tiny frown marring his features, revealing his pain as he lifted his gaze to the Cromdale hills, watching the slow circling of a hawk scanning the ground below. In his expression, she saw the crumbling of his world.

'I'm sorry,' she whispered.

'Nay.' He shook his head, his face closing to contain his pain. 'Dinna be. 'Tis me should be saying that.' He rose to his feet. 'Can ye forgive me? I dinna ken what came ower me. I had nae right. You deserve a better man. I hope one day ye'll find that man, and he'll give ye what ye seek. I was foolish, thinking ye might want what I want. Might want me when I've naught to give ye.' He looked down at Jem, and she whined, somehow sensing his pain.

'Duncan—'

'Please.' He stopped her with a tender look. 'I've no wish to mak' ye explain. I understand. I should never have asked ye. 'Twas unforgivable.' A muscle in his throat convulsed.

''Tis only—'

'If ye can find it in yer heart to forgive. To forget I said such things, that I ever imagined mysel' worthy, then mebbe in time we might find a way back to where we were afore I spoke so out o' turn.'

'There's naught to forgive,' she sobbed. 'Naught's changed.' Though, of course, everything had changed. 'Ye're my brother. Ye always will be.'

His eyes clouded with grief.

'And ye're nae unworthy. Never were ye that.'

He gave her a crooked smile, believing none of it.

'We should go back,' he croaked.

CHAPTER EIGHTEEN

HUGH WAITED IN the bushes until the witchling and her spurned lover had vanished from view, taking the growling dog with them. He let his breath out with a quiver. He'd been holding it so long the blood pounded in his head. He'd nearly been discovered, but the dog was old, hardly a keen-nosed guard dog, and he'd moved with a stealth he scarcely knew he possessed. He raised a hand to his mouth, seeing that it trembled, and he marvelled at that. Never had he been so affected by a woman—a mere slip of a lass. Yet, by God, she was the most bewitching creature.

He crept back to the tree where he'd tied his horse. Here, after endless hours of searching, he'd finally stumbled upon the witchling kneeling in the shingle, praying to a yellow-flowered bush. He approached cautiously, trying to determine what had made her do such a thing. Did it mark the entrance to a faery knoll? Did she pray to the beings that walked between worlds? His skin prickled at the thought, but he could see naught out of the ordinary.

He was untying his mount when the rattle of displaced shingle made him start. He glanced up to find the crone he'd seen on Seely's Hillock standing directly in front of him, blocking his route out of the bushes.

'She's not for the likes of you,' she said in perfect English.

He gaped.

'You must leave her be.' She came a step closer, blue eyes boring through his soul. 'They'll call you the Black Gauger. You'll be my undoing, but I fear 'tis your own appetites will be yours.'

His jaw dropped open. She dared to threaten him. A witch. He drew

177

his sword, but she was gone in an instant, vanishing into the undergrowth with barely a rattle of riverbank stone.

He blinked, trying to gather his wits, but all he could think of was the witchling. How much he wanted her. Yet, he was not alone in wanting her. What had he just witnessed? The young Jacobite, one of the most notorious smugglers in Strathavon, trying and failing to woo her. It seemed so, for although their words had been beyond his deciphering, the lad's actions had not. They'd been clear enough. He'd gone down on one knee, desire written all over his face.

She'd rebuffed him, of course, though in a gentle way that roused his jealousy. There'd been some wanting on her part, too. Yet, that was perhaps a pleasing sign. She was a woman of appetites, as he was a man of all-consuming ones. But the young Jacobite, remarkably recovered from his beating, had no' been to her liking. The gall of the lad. To try his hand with what was plainly not for him. She'd put the upstart in his place, though, so all was well. She likely remained innocent of the ways of the world—ignorant for him to teach. He smiled, relishing the prospect of educating her.

Yet, the muck-the-byre could not be allowed to try his luck again. He clenched his teeth, blood pulsing through his temples. He'd deal with him. He wiped his mouth, a quivering excitement growing in his flesh. If only the witchling had been alone; he'd have made her his already.

Murmuring to his horse, he remembered the rustle of her skirts as she heard him in the bushes and took flight through the trees. With a shiver, he laid his forehead against the animal's neck and closed his eyes, seeing her look back coyly, inviting him to chase her. In his mind, he crashed through the trees after her, the light playing tricks upon him, duping him to take a wrong turn. She giggled to alert him to his mistake. The birds gave him away, as did the undergrowth with its snapping and crunching and snake-like roots that tried to wrap around his boots.

Yet, neither the trees nor her female wiles were a match for him, and he soon caught her, hearing the rustle of her skirts again. This time as he thrust them out of his way. Briefly, he felt their softness against his thighs as he pressed himself upon her, then he was lost in the silken thrill of her, hearing again the tinkle of her laugh.

Trembling with desire, his loins on fire, he mounted his horse and urged it into a gallop. Whatever chores Isobel was about could wait. He had a powerful need of her. The most biddable of creatures, not once did she question what he expected of her but strived to please him and satisfy his needs.

He supposed she was a natural trollop, as he'd heard all Heiland women were. From the start, she'd seen what he required of her, other than to keep his house and feed him like a lord and submitted to him whenever he desired it. He only needed to look at her in a certain way, and she'd stand still, blushing, waiting for him to undress her.

Her unquestioning compliance, the little sounds she made when he readied her with his fingers, her urgent moans when he furrowed her hard, all heightened his pleasure. He'd even managed to teach her some English words. He chuckled. Not ones a respectable woman should be fluent in, but that hardly mattered. She was naught but a whore anyway, and a heather-lowping one at that. But at least he now knew she could learn.

Hugh hoped all glen women possessed the same desire to please. 'Twould bode well for future encounters with the witchling, although Isobel's persistent attempts to demonstrate her affection were disconcerting. As were the great calf eyes she lifted to him whenever he enjoyed her face to face. But he supposed his virile nature, his robust stature and rugged good looks had such effects upon women, even common muck-the-byre types.

He flogged his horse harder, hearing the foaming of its breath. With his blood up, along with other parts of his anatomy, he'd likely be enjoying her any way he pleased for much of the afternoon.

* * *

Duncan was even quieter than usual that night. The others imagined him weary, Rowena supposed, this the first day he'd ventured from his sickbed since he'd been carried there. Sensing his gaze upon her, she struggled to look him in the eye. Regret that she was the cause of his misery lodged in her chest like a musket ball. His believing himself unworthy of her seemed the saddest thing. Never was there a man more deserving of happiness and love. Only, she couldn't give him what he wanted—her heart was already pledged. She'd given it to nature and creation. 'Twas better that way. It safeguarded his heart as well as her own.

Yet, the next day, helping Grace with the wedding preparations at Lagganvoulin, Grace glanced across at her. 'Have you and Duncan rowed?'

'Rowed?' Her heart fluttered. 'Why would ye think that?'

'I thought, mebbe, ye'd quarrelled.' Grace was churning butter and pressed her plunger home. 'He seems that low in spirits. Anxious to be out from under yer feet now his injuries are healing. Yet, I ken he likes to stay close by ye if he can. Ye're the centre o' his world. Ye ken that, aye?'

She frowned, keeping her head down.

'Ye musta noticed, Rowena? I mean, every other lass in the glen surely has.'

She daren't look up but could feel Grace assessing her. Her cheeks burned. 'I dinna ken aboot that.'

'Mebbe I'm wrong, then.' Grace snorted.

Thankfully, there was too much to do for Grace to assess her for long. The whole glen was coming to celebrate James and Mhari's wedding. 'Twas considered the greatest of slights not to be invited, and James had ridden over every hill and bog in an effort to ensure he'd not missed anyone. Even Morna was invited. Not to the chapel, but she'd come to the *ceilidh*. She'd saved Mhari's sister and was considered an honoured guest.

Throughout the day, glenfolk came with gifts for the feast: bannocks by the score, eggs, cheese, venison and hare, salmon freshly poached from the Avon. The MacPhersons of Lochy Mill brought the rump end of a cow, butchered and ready for Mhari's mother to roast and braise for the feast. A gift beyond measure.

Most of the cattle were driven south at the end of summer, the coin they brought needed for paying rents. Even after all these years, cattle were still less numerous in the glen than once they'd been. On that fateful day of rain, when she'd helped Duncan hide their herd in Sìthean Wood, government soldiers had driven away more than half the cattle in the glen. Those remaining were shared out amongst neighbours and kin, but it had been a long road back for many a herdsman. Some never recovered, leaving the glen to board ships bound for the New World, never to see the wild beauty of Strathavon again.

As the groom's father, her da would supply the whisky. A great deal would be required. Every guest would sup from the Loving Cup: a quaich filled with whisky and passed to each guest by the bride. There'd be toasts to the newlywed couple's health and happiness as they danced the first reel and to the memory of John Meldrum. After that, there'd be a deal of merriment, as was generally the case at Highland weddings.

Tradition dictated the bride's mother bake the bridescake. Ismay had made an enormous sweet bannock, a portion of which she'd break over Mhari's head before the feasting began, hopefully to shatter into many small pieces signifying a fruitful union.

Her da expected the celebrations would pass in peace. The authorities were unlikely to choose John's replacement from the local area with sympathies known to lie with the smugglers. And even if a replacement were found in the south and sent north, 'twas doubtful the new gauger could be in place in time for the wedding.

Soldiers were always a threat, however. The whisky would be hidden in a secret chamber in the back wall of Father Ranald's chapel. 'Twas only a short walk from there to Lagganvoulin. The ankers could be lashed to the sides of the bride's pony and concealed beneath her wedding gown. Should soldiers chance upon the wedding train, there'd be little to raise suspicion.

* * *

On the day of the wedding, Rowena rose early to climb the Haughs of Cromdale in search of white heather for Mhari's bouquet. 'Twas said to bring luck, and she sensed they'd both need much of that. It had rained during the night, and she'd lain awake, her mind turning, listening to the steady drum upon the thatch and the occasional hiss as droplets found their way in to sizzle on the hot peats. When the day finally dawned, it came fresh and bright with an earthy aroma.

As she trod over rock and heather, avoiding tender mountain plants, a sadness seeped into her heart. She missed James already, despite wishing him joy. Unable to shake her sadness, it followed her into the hills. From the top of *An Sgòran*, she looked down on the chapel yard where her mother was buried. Chance had not taken her here but a wish to be close to her mother.

Fearn's eldest was grown to manhood, would take a wife and make his way in the world. How would she feel about that? She had little notion. Mam had been gone so long, she struggled to remember her face. Would she be sad but wear a blithe smile, or be heart-glad for her son? Maybe a little of both. She was torn herself, sensing something dark lay ahead for James.

Since learning the lore of her glen, she'd discovered a battle had been fought right here on the Haughs of Cromdale and not so long ago. One where Jacobites died in their hundreds. The knowledge had stirred strong feelings—such a bitter story they had. Morna said Highland folk were perhaps a dying race. Her ancestors' deeds spoke of honour and fierce bravery, yet glenfolk were considered a lower breed, vermin to be civilised or removed. Looking around, she saw only beauty, both in the breath-taking expanse of mountain and glen and in the faces of those who belonged here. She saw an ancient people with generous hearts, men like Duncan, women, too, who needed no civilising.

Her sadness deepened, and she was suddenly on the verge of tears, struggling to banish her thoughts. She mustn't spoil James and Mhari's day with red eyes and a pinched face, and it felt good to be in the hills.

Below her, the river with its verdant fringe snaked through the glen, twisting through an undulating tapestry of mountain and moor, forest and mire, all stitched together with the unmistakable pattern of folk's toil. Heather-thatched homes of turf and field-gathered stones, runrig strips and patches of lush pasture hard-won from the heath spoke to her of her folk and their hardiness. Life had always been a struggle here—with the elements, warring clans and invading settlers—now with the landowners and their rents, their foreign rulers and their plans.

Her sorrow deepened. With an effort of will, she resumed her search. White heather was rare, luck needed to find it, but eventually, she spied a patch sheltering among the more common purple and mauve. As she knelt to whisper her thanks, the light caught the ring on her finger, making it glisten. 'Twas her own wedding ring, she supposed, the entwining tendrils binding her to nature, to the hills and Sìthean Wood and all the wild places she loved. She would never wed. She'd remain a maiden all her life, giving herself to the land and its people. Clutching her precious find, she picked her way down the hillside, her sadness following as tightly as her shadow.

* * *

Hugh glowered darkly at Ghillie and even more sourly at Dougal. The hirelings had proven themselves incapable of finding suitable cover from which to observe the miserable hovel where the wedding festivities would occur. Hence the three of them now lay on their bellies in the wet heath atop a small hillock.

Prostrate, his head raised just enough to peer over the heather, Hugh was deeply uncomfortable. Dampness seeped into his bones, a tightness at the back of his neck sending waves of pain to his head. It throbbed, and his back hurt. His horse and the hireling's garrons, they'd tethered in bushes on the far slope. The occasional forlorn whinny came from there. Midges swarmed around his head, making him itch. He fought a desire to sit up and swipe at the blood-suckers, stretching his aching back.

He'd slept poorly, tossing and turning, dreaming about the witchling lass. In his dream, he'd revelled in her lithe young body, in the feel of her skin beneath his hands with the scent of gorse flowers upon it, had held her molten gaze as he brought her to rapturous heights of pleasure. But the dream had become a nightmare when he rose from her to splash his face. Upon returning, he glanced in the mirror at the foot of the bed. Only, 'twas the face of the young Jacobite that looked back at him. Mocked him. And 'twas the Jacobite's lean young body, naked and finely muscled, beautiful in truth, that once more joined with the witchling, vigorously bringing her to even greater pinnacles of pleasure with low, drawn-out gasps.

'Damn this Godforsaken place,' he cursed. 'What in God's name is taking so long? How many hours does it take to repeat a few vows?' He spat into the heather. 'And will one o' ye explain why two locations are needed? In civilised centres, a simple church ceremony is enough.'

'Aye, sir,' muttered Ghillie. 'But they're papists. They've nae church to go to—only Father Ranald's secret chapel. I'm thinking there'll be bible readings, prayers and blessings as well as the exchange o' vows. All that could take some time.'

'Mebbe some hymns,' added Dougal.

'Aye, 'tis only efter that will they come here fer the *ceilidh*. To feast and dance and sup a muckle spate o' whisky.'

Hugh stared at Ghillie, the midges and his aching head forgotten. 'A secret chapel? Here in Strathavon? Are ye saying a papist priest is hiding here? An idol-kisser living here in the glen?'

'A famous priest. Father Ranald Stewart.'

'Infamous,' Dougal put in. 'A wanted Jacobite. Chaplain in Glenbuchat's regiment.'

Hugh gasped, too shocked to even swear.

'But he doesna do so much hiding these days. He holds a rental from his grace. Land and a cot-hoose that serves as chapel fer the papists o' the glen. 'Tis all secret, though.'

'But,' Hugh stammered, 'why on earth did ye no' mention this before?'

Ghillie frowned in confusion. 'Tell ye aboot the priest? I thocht 'twas smugglers ye was efter, sir, ye being a gauger. Nae priests.'

'But papistry is banned—all preaching of it. Even attending a papist service carries the penalty of banishment. And a *Jacobite* priest ....' Hugh's innards trembled with excitement. 'There's likely a price on the man's head. A reward for his capture. The duke would—'

'Likely nae thank ye fer interfering.' Ghillie turned to look at him. 'He did grant the man a tenure o' land here, efter all, and permission to rebuild upon it likely kenning full well what he'd build.'

'You mean, he *knows*? His grace, the young duke, has sanctioned this atrocity?'

Ghillie swallowed, looking shifty. 'Thon's aboot the size o' it, sir, aye. 'Tis said the duke holds sympathy wi' the auld faith, a mark o' respect fer his father who was known to be a papist.' He shrugged. 'Or mebbe he follows the auld faith himsel'. In secret, like.'

'You mean the Duke of Gordon, the young Cock o' the North, educated and cultured, wealthy beyond imagining, is a papist?' Hugh's voice rose incredulously.

'I niver said that, sir. 'Tis just what I've heard. But if 'tis true, I doubt there'll be a reward fer the priest's capture, nae from his grace. He'd nae thank ye fer that. And if he learned 'twas you reported the man ....' Ghillie sucked his breath in through his teeth, making a hissing sound. 'I'd nae like to be in yer shoes. Ye might just find the tenure o' yer own hame ended right sudden-like. His grace isna the sort to rile, I'm thinking.'

Hugh gaped at the weasel. 'But what of McGillivray?'

'What o' him?'

'Surely he knows naught of this. The factor despises papists as much as I do. He'd have a fit if he knew a Jacobite priest was on the rent-roll.'

Dougal shrugged. 'Likely he doesna ken, then.'

Hugh's mind began to whir. How could such a foul creature be permitted to preach here with impunity? It beggared belief. He recalled his father's many sermons on the subject of popery and priests. Popery was a disease that infected others if not rooted out. Catholic priests carried it. McGillivray would agree and would need to be told. His left eyelid twitched. There might be some profit in bringing McGillivray the information, despite the duke.

'Sir!' Ghillie nudged his elbow.

An eerie sound came to them on the breeze—a plaintive droning like the wind wailing through a mountain pass. His heart fluttered. What in God's name was it? It grew louder, becoming a hideous skirl. He squinted into the sun, scanning the landscape. A dark mass appeared on the horizon, swelling, advancing toward them.

'Holy God,' he breathed. 'A horde of villains.'

Ghillie grunted in amusement. 'Lachlan Innes is weel-liked hereabouts, and James is a popular lad. I'm thinking there's nae a cottar nor herdsman, nor smuggler,' he added, 'who's nae been invited. And 'tis a rare one wouldna wish to celebrate wi' the lad and his new bride. Drink their health and wish them a fruitful marriage.'

'You mean the whole of Strathavon is about to descend upon this miserable cot-house?'

'Looks that wey,' Dougal chuckled. 'Glenlivet, too. Fer a *ceilidh* and a sup o' Tomachcraggen's finest.'

Hugh's heart began to pound. He glanced at the hirelings; they carried a pistol and cutlass apiece. He wore a sword himself and a flintlock at each hip, but against such a horde ....

'They'll nae be armed,' Ghillie grunted, 'if 'tis what ye're thinking. And there'll be womenfolk among them, bairns, too, whole families. They might seem a horde, as ye say, but 'tis a *ceilidh* they're coming fer, nae a battle. Nae unless ye wish to mak' it one.' His lips thinned as he looked at his employer. Not for the first time, Hugh wondered where the man's true loyalties lay.

Ghillie turned back to watch the approaching crowd. 'So,' he muttered, ''tis just Tomachcraggen and his eldest we take? The bridegroom and his da?'

'And the Young Jacobite. Particularly him.'

'Young Jacobite?'

'The lad they dragged out of the tollbooth. He'd been beaten if ye remember.'

'Duncan.' Dougal smirked. 'Tomachcraggen's youngest. Said to be a master smuggler in the making. A handsome lad, or he was afore the soldiers gave him a seeing to. Popular wi' the lasses.' He reached down and scratched at himself.

'Is he?' Hugh's face reddened. 'Much good it'll do him in gaol.'

'So.' Ghillie rolled onto his back, massaging his neck. ''Tis just thon three we arrest? And we take the whisky.'

'Of course, we seize the whisky. 'Tis evidence and a bounty will be paid for its seizure. But aye, those three will do for now. The others can wait for another day. Any whisky discovered, and I expect to find a great deal, Innes and his sons will have distilled illegally, yes?'

Ghillie nodded, glancing at Dougal. 'Let's hope they gie it up quiet-like, along wi' themselves. 'Tis hardly the best start to a marriage, I'm thinking, arrested on yer wedding day.'

Hugh snorted. He cared not a jot about that.

The eerie sound transpired to be a lone piper playing a poignant ballad on an outlawed instrument. If Hugh's memory served him, the Act of Proscription meant the playing of the pipes had been illegal for some time. The piper led the way ahead of what appeared to be the bride, clutching a meagre bunch of flowers and her smuggler-groom, both mounted on garrons.

Behind the bridal couple, a host of villains followed on foot, creatures of all ages, presumably wearing their best clothes. They looked like filthy savages, many bare-legged, living up to the term 'redshanks' given to Highlanders with their legs exposed to the elements year-round. The men were mostly wearing proscribed garb: blue bonnets and belted plaids of checked mountain colours. The women wore similar colours, though they at least had thought to cover themselves with semi-respectable shawls.

On they came, their voices raised in an incomprehensible babble, eager to celebrate with the young couple, Hugh supposed, though just as careful to cast a wary eye over the surrounding moors. Doubtless, most intended to be roaring drunk by the end of the day, if not sooner. They'd be out of luck there.

As the head of the procession drew level with their hiding place, all three instinctively crouched lower in the heather, holding their breath. Eventually, the swarm reached the cot-house, milling outside, apparently waiting for the groom to lift his bride from her mount. They cheered when he did so and cheered even louder when he bent his dark head and pressed a kiss upon her lips. Then they all filed inside or dispersed to the byre. The festivities would plainly spill over a considerable area if they were all to feast and dance the day away.

Once most had gone inside, a thick-set man, bearded and faintly familiar, removed two bulky objects from the flanks of the bride's pony. Another smaller man came to help him. Between them, they carried the items inside.

'What's that they're doing?'

'Removing the ankers o' whisky from the bride's garron, by the looks o' it.' Ghillie cocked a brow at him. 'They musta hid them under her skirts, fearing dragoons might chance upon them on the wey here.'

Hugh chuckled. 'Clever o' them, but no' clever enough. We'll give them time to fill their cups and sup some peatreek before we burst in on them. Time enough to hang themselves.'

Fifteen minutes later, reunited with their mounts and with pistols loaded and primed, they exchanged taut looks from the corner of the cot-house. Hugh dismounted, nodding to the hirelings to do likewise. He moved to the door with drawn pistol, put his shoulder to the timber, and burst in, followed by the hirelings.

CHAPTER NINETEEN

DUNCAN COULDN'T HELP but follow Rowena about the room with his eyes. She was wearing the gossamer-soft gown Lachlan had bought for her role as bride's attendant. Never had he seen her look more beautiful, and his heart ached as he watched her. The gown was of a checked material in shades of blue. It set off the darkness of her eyes, the cream of her skin, and sheathed her slender form, accentuating every angle and curve. Coiled atop her head, her hair was decorated with a single white dog rose, almost a white cockade, a tendril trailing at her neck. Accustomed to seeing her hair loose, he found the effect striking and swallowed, trying to avert his gaze. His eyes rebelled, though, and would not leave her be.

She smiled shyly at him as she followed behind Mhari, squeezing through the crush of bodies, refilling the Loving Cup with whisky as Mhari passed it to each wedding guest in turn. He blushed and looked away, his heart contracting, aware he was likely embarrassing her.

She didn't want him as a husband, only as a brother. He couldn't banish from his head the stricken look she'd been unable to hide when he'd brazenly asked her to be his wife. That look now haunted and shamed him. Too tender-hearted to tell him the truth—that his proposal shocked and repelled her—she'd struggled to answer but hardly needed to. Her face had answered for her.

He still couldn't fathom how he'd imagined himself deserving of her. Perhaps 'twas the beating he'd taken, or his fury over John's death. Those things had changed him but were only excuses. He'd been fooling himself for long now, hoping she felt as he did, sometimes even imagining she did. She'd captured his heart from the start. From his first sight of her, wretched and forlorn yet bravely weathering her grief, she'd given purpose to his life. She *was* his life.

When younger, he'd wished to serve God. He'd thought that by following Father Ranald into the priesthood, he might somehow repay the man for all his kindness. He'd even believed 'twas his calling. But he was not the man the father was. The father was brave, and over time, he'd seen his mistake. He couldn't be serving God when all he thought about was Rowena. She'd fascinated him from that night of dreams when she'd soothed his worthless skin and then when she'd shown him kindness on the sad walk back from her mother's grave. She'd been a healer even then, for she'd healed his spirit. Perhaps he even hoped to redeem himself through her, through the loving of her, if she'd let him, for her heart was pure. But, of course, and deep down, he'd always known it, he wasn't good enough.

He supposed a decent man would be content to be her brother. To love and protect her as a brother should. Nae him, though, curse his ungrateful skin. He'd wanted more. Not satisfied with all the Lord had given him, he'd wanted Rowena, too. Whenever she was near, his heart trembled, and though he tried to fight it, God help him, wistful yearnings quickened in his body. He wanted her as fiercely as any man desires a woman. No brother should feel like this. Though he wished to keep her safe, he longed to love her, too. Every inch of her. To look upon her knowing that, in the eyes of God, she was his to cherish and to hold, and to never stop holding. To please her if he could. To drown in her, God help him.

He gulped at his whisky, the spirit burning the back of his throat. Only, he was still a coward even now, for he'd never found the courage to tell her the truth: everyone he'd ever loved, he'd failed.

So, she was not for him. Another man, a better one, would someday love her, wed her, make her happy, he hoped. Only, he resented that man already, so fervently did he long to be that man himself.

He drank more whisky, glad of its effects. With the formality of the service over, tongues were loosening, voices rising in anticipation of the feasting and dancing to come. Mhari's mother carried the bridescake from the hearth, holding it above her head for all to see. A great cheer went up. She waited for the commotion to die.

'Andrew and I wish to thank ye all fer coming to celebrate James and Mhari's union.' Her cheeks coloured. 'We wish to thank Father Ranald fer the Nuptial Mass, and we especially wish to say what a fine young man oor Mhari's found in James Innes.'

Another cheer bruised Duncan's ears. When things had quietened, Ismay beckoned to Mhari, who stood shyly before her, searching the crowd for James. He nodded to her, his eyes bright with pride. Smiling, Ismay kissed Mhari's cheek, then raised the slab of bridescake purposefully above her head. There was a deal of giggling, and a press of girls flocked forward, jostling to snatch a piece. 'Twas considered lucky, a sign they'd soon be wed, too.

'All ye halfling women,' Ismay cried, 'I wish ye luck finding guid husbands.' With that, she broke the bridescake above her daughter's head, Mhari laughing as pieces of bannock showered over her. She shook her head, fragments flying across the floor amid a wild scramble to secure a piece.

He glimpsed Rowena then, watched her step back into the shadows and take no part, but there was no time to wonder why she'd do that. Suddenly the girls were screaming as three armed men pushed their way in, shouting and brandishing pistols.

He recognised two of them, desperate types Lachlan had warned him not to trust, but the third, the leader, he'd never seen before. Muscular in build, the man wore a short beard and side-whiskers. His face was striking, all sharp lines and angles, his eyes hooded, a grim smile playing at his lips. But 'twas his garb that most alarmed Duncan. He was wearing the tailed black coat of an exciseman.

'Stand ye still!' the man bellowed. 'Still, I say.' He turned to his companions, beckoning one of them with his head.

Duncan knew the man as Ghillie. He addressed them all in Gaelic.

'This here's Mister Hugh McBeath, new excise officer in these parts. Here to uphold the law and replace John Meldrum, lately hanged.' He swallowed, looking uncomfortable. 'Best be doing what he says.'

This McBeath nodded to Ghillie, then swaggered back and fore, crushing pieces of bridescake beneath his boots. 'Now that you all know who I am,' he said in English. 'You'll understand that, as Riding Officer, I act for the king and government and hold great power over the likes of you.' He curled his lip. 'Muck-the-byres, heather-lowpers, smugglers and tax-dodgers. As such, I demand respect.'

He halted, surveying them all, a calculating gleam in his eyes. 'Yet, I could be persuaded to let you continue in your villainous ways provided you pay me the respect I'm due. And when I say pay, I mean pay, for I'm talking hard coin.' He inhaled, puffing his chest out. 'In return for this respect, I may let ye carry on outrageously defrauding the treasury.'

He nodded, glowering around as if they'd all come to some agreement, one acceptable to all, even though most of those he glared at looked back blankly, understanding none of this.

'Henceforth,' he went on, 'smuggling goods out of the glen will mean crossing my ride and paying passage to do so. Fail to pay, and you'll be up before the magistrate quicker than ye can blink. And be warned, William McGillivray's an acquaintance o' mine and has recently been made magistrate.'

While Ghillie translated this into Gaelic, McBeath stalked back and fore, a grim smile acknowledging the now stricken faces around him.

'So, if ye wish to remain here working your miserable runrigs, you must learn to play my game. Agreements must be reached. The situation accepted, but make no mistake—those who fail to pay will be shown no mercy.' He squinted at Mhari's father. 'But so long as payments are made, you may carry on with your villainous lives.' He ceased pacing and spread his hands wide. 'Well? Am I no' a reasonable man?'

Once Ghillie had translated, folk exchanged dark looks. Dougal sniggered.

'So,' he went on, 'to the matter in hand. Much as I hate to disturb your wee celebration, if I were to search this hovel, I expect I'd find a quantity of illegally distilled whisky. Spirit for which no duty or passage has been paid. 'Twas being handed out as we arrived.'

He fixed his gaze on Malcolm MacRae, still clutching the Loving Cup and staring incredulously at him. 'Was being *drunk* as we arrived. Like pigs at the swill.' He snorted. 'I fear, therefore, an example must be made.'

Folk looked fearfully at each other, the festive mood gone, replaced by a tension so thick it might be sliced. Duncan swallowed, watching this fearsome new exciseman. The man resumed his pacing while Ghillie translated, flicking his gaze from one shocked face to another. With swaggering disdain, he measured and dismissed each face in turn, finding its owner lacking in some way. Donald Gordon, old Alexander MacRae and his son Iain and grandson Malcolm, the McHardies, the MacPhersons, Andrew and Ismay Lang, even Father Ranald disguised as a cottar; all were scrutinised, then sneeringly discounted.

As he strutted, the man oozed self-importance, his disregard for glenfolk evident in the contemptuous curl of his lip, hostility radiating from his every pore. Watching him, Duncan felt the apprehension around him grow. But what did the man intend to do? John Meldrum had aided his fellow glensmen. Possessed of a good heart, he'd never been anything but scrupulously fair. Yet this McBeath, sent here to replace him, had none of John's fibre. He was enjoying himself, relishing the signs of fear in folk's faces, knowing he was the cause. He was an insult to John's memory.

Still surveying the room, the gauger flicked his gaze over Lachlan, whose face was flushed with anger. James and Mhari were at Lachlan's side, but there was no sign of Rowena. Next, he raked Duncan's face, pausing to focus sharply upon him. The gauger reddened and went very still. They measured each other for what seemed an unconscionable time until one of the gauger's eyelids began to twitch, and Duncan was aware the man was in a towering rage. Mystified at how he could have riled a man he'd never set eyes on, he stared back.

McBeath turned abruptly to his men. 'Find the whisky. It shouldnae be so hard to find, and since you're both more familiar with Lachlan Innes than I am, I'll let you arrest him. Bind his hands and tie him to a garron for his ride to Elgin. His eldest ye can treat likewise, the young bridegroom. But this one,' he turned back to Duncan with a piercing stare. 'You'll leave to me.'

Dougal and Ghillie exchanged looks, then leapt into action, ruthlessly shoving wedding guests aside to reach their quarry. With a growl, the crowd closed ranks, grappling to hold them back, fists and elbows flying, bare legs hooking trousered shins, the air thick with curses.

In the midst of the fray, Duncan glimpsed a slight but determined figure battling to reach the exciseman. His heart lurched. McBeath saw the threat too; he raised his pistol, cocked it, and took aim.

'NO!' He flung himself forward, throwing himself between the enraged exciseman and his assailant, his heart in his mouth.

In the skirmish, Rowena's hair had come loose. As she stumbled from the fray, it flowed over her shoulders in a glistening river of silk. He thrust a hand out to stop her, but she ducked under his arm and stood in front of the exciseman, the man's pistol pointed into her face. His heart near exploded.

'Please,' she said. 'We meant no harm.'

At the edge of his vision, he saw Lachlan, backed into a corner at Ghillie's gunpoint, frantically signalling for her to keep quiet.

'Please,' she repeated in perfect English. 'I beg you, sir, don't arrest my kinsmen. The Loving Cup is our tradition, the whisky, too. 'Tis a marriage custom, an old one.' Seeing the gauger's extraordinary expression, she swallowed and pressed on. 'I pray your forgiveness, sir. Your leniency for my kinsmen.'

The gauger could not have reacted more astonishingly had one of the faeryfolk manifested out of the air in front of him. '*The witchling,*' he breathed. His pistol now hung limply in his hand. Rowena reached out and gripped the barrel, then slowly lowered it to point at the floor.

To Duncan's profound relief, not to mention astonishment, the gauger allowed this. He stared open-mouthed at her, wearing the strangest expression. Only he'd seen that look before; menfolk oft-times wore it when they looked at Rowena. Maybe not as markedly as this, but in a way similar enough to diagnose the cause. He even understood it. 'Twas hard not to look at her. A single look was never enough. Most men looked and looked, never having their fill. Perhaps he did, too, though he sincerely hoped not.

He moved closer, trying to draw the gauger's attention, to spare her the man's crudeness. The exciseman was looking her up and down— undressing her with his eyes.

'Get away!' McBeath swung toward him.

But Rowena half-smiled, acknowledging his attempt to spare her the man's unwelcome attention. With a shiver, he caught her familiar herb-rich scent.

The gauger's countenance darkened.

'My brother.' Rowena looked back at McBeath. 'Duncan.'

'Your brother? This man is your brother?'

She nodded. 'The younger, while James there is the older. A married man now.'

McBeath blinked at her. 'Then you are?'

'Rowena Innes.' She curtsied awkwardly.

'Innes? Of course, I hadnae ....' He shifted his gaze back to Duncan, giving him another hard stare. 'So, you are the same family? You and he are ... what I mean.' Less sure of himself, he uncocked his pistol, still staring at her, then seemed to come to a decision and chuckled unconvincingly.

'I was, of course, only jesting just now. Was I no', Ghillie?' He glanced around for the hireling, trying to communicate something to him.

Dishevelled and disgruntled, Ghillie frowned back.

'Come, man, you know I only jested. Never did I intend to arrest anyone today. No' at a wedding.' He gave an incredulous laugh. 'What d'you take me for?'

'Sir?'

The gauger was suddenly the image of calmness and reason. 'Now, Ghillie, dinnae go acting obtuse. You know my mind well enough.'

The hireling frowned harder. 'Are ye saying ye nae longer want Tomachcraggen and his lads? Nae to arrest them?'

'But,' Dougal spluttered. 'Ye telt us—'

'Never mind what I said.' He glared at Dougal. 'You know very well I meant no harm.'

Dougal's mouth dropped open. 'But I thocht—'

'Never mind what you thought. God's blood, when did you ever think anything worth hearing?'

Dougal's eyes dulled as he tried to make sense of this. Finally, he saw the light and brightened. 'Oh, aye.' He smirked. 'Ye're still efter thon wee roll in the heather!'

'You'll hold your tongue.' McBeath raised his hand as if to strike him, then thought better of it. 'Your days in Elgin's tollbooth have addled yer brain, Dougal.' He patted him on the head.

Dougal was unabashed. Still smirking, he winked at Ghillie, who shrugged back with a warning shake of his head, indicating Dougal would be wise to keep quiet.

McBeath ignored them both. 'So,' he reluctantly shifted his gaze from Rowena. 'Please, everyone, resume your festivities. I've made myself known to you; that was all I intended. My apologies for any misunderstanding.'

He crossed to the door, indicating Ghillie should translate, and again locked eyes with Duncan. While Ghillie attempted to explain what he plainly struggled to understand himself, McBeath stared coldly at him. They gauged each other, Duncan again aware of the man's strange animosity.

When Ghillie had finished, McBeath nodded at the bewildered faces, and with a last lingering look at Rowena, turned to go. Only his way out was blocked. He stumbled, wrong-footed, drawing back with a curse. The green woman stood squarely in the doorway. Swathed in her customary decayed old arisaid, her face half-hidden in its folds, she clutched a thickly twigged birch branch in her hand. An object not unlike a broomstick, almost giving the impression she'd flown there upon it.

She was unchanged, ageless yet ancient, and he couldn't help wondering how old she truly was. She seemed otherworldly, her expression unfathomable, something about her reminding him of the mysterious stone set into the side of Carn Liath. She seemed part of the landscape, too, craggy and weathered. Never had she more keenly resembled a witch, yet, for the first time in his life, he was genuinely glad to see her. His heart gave an odd thump, while beside him, Rowena made a joyous sound.

Morna showed no surprise at coming face to face with three armed men. She stood her ground, noting McBeath's violent recoil with some satisfaction. He recovered and attempted to shove her aside, but she hissed, and he jerked back, side-stepping her with a shudder. Hurrying away, he shouted for his mount, his hirelings scurrying at his heels.

Rowena rushed to embrace Morna, unconcerned who should witness their affection. Glancing at Father Ranald, Duncan saw the priest stiffen. Perhaps for Rowena's sake, the father swallowed his revulsion and came forward to greet the woman.

'All are welcome here,' he murmured. 'But it seems you and I finally have a thing or two in common. A fondness for Rowena, of course, and if I'm not mistaken, an instinctual distrust of our new exciseman.'

Morna blinked at him, astonished he'd even acknowledge her existence, Duncan supposed, never mind welcome her, but visibly touched he'd done so. Blushing, she thrust the birch branch behind her skirts.

'Thank ye, Father. I expect, in our own ways, we can both see into the blackest hearts. Thon gauger's is blacker than a raven's wing.' She quirked a brow. 'Mebbe ye now see that our faiths are nae as different as ye imagine?'

'Are they not?' His expression hardened.

She sighed. 'I came here only fer I was asked to come. I wish no trouble.'

'None will you find, then. You'll excuse me.' He moved away.

Duncan turned to Rowena. 'Are ye all right? When the gauger pointed his pistol at ye ....' He shook his head, unable to put his agitation into words.

'I'm fine.'

'I think ye just saved yer menfolk from arrest. Likely a beating, too.'

She nodded. 'Only, I dinna ken how. But I confess I care little fer John's replacement.'

'Nor I. He seemed ... ower-taken wi' ye.'

'He made me fearful fer ye, Duncan.'

He frowned; the gauger had made him fearful, too, though for reasons he'd no wish to voice.

Her face tightened, and he longed to hold her. Knowing she wanted no more expressions of love from him, he muttered, 'I'm yer brother. I'll nae let him harm ye.'

'Likely, he meant nae harm.'

'Perhaps.' But looking at her, he suspected they both knew better.

Lachlan recovered quickly from the strange incident and appeared keen they should put it behind them and resume the festivities.

'Niver fear,' he announced. 'My mountain dew is unmolested. Dinna ask me how, but I thank the Lord fer it. And I intend to share it wi' all my neighbours.' He rolled out an anker to a great cheer.

Ismay filled cups while Andrew gathered his pipes and began a stirring melody accompanied by Ewan Munro on the fiddle. Grace appeared in the doorway to announce the feast was ready and laid out in the byre. More cheering accompanied this news, folk heading away, following their noses.

Morna hung back, waiting for the other guests to take their places. To Duncan's surprise, Lachlan took her by the elbow.

'I've niver right thanked ye fer teaching Rowena yer healing ways. I wish to remedy that. The lass healed Duncan, and I love that lad as if he were my own.'

'I ken ye do.'

'I'm grateful. I wish ye to ken that. The lad's mended, or as near as damn it. Had I nae witnessed it wi' my own eyes, I'd niver have believed it possible a body could heal so fast.'

'Nature's magic works swiftly, especially when love's a powerful ingredient in the mix.'

'Weel, I dinna ken aboot that, but I gie ye my thanks and my respect fer yer ways. They may be far from church ways, but to my mind, if a puckle weeds can work such miracles, that's as close to the creator as I can see. Was it nae the Lord put all the herbs here in the first place?'

She nodded. 'Mother Earth provides a remedy fer all that ails us, nae matter what ye wish to call her.' She half-turned, following Rowena with her eyes. 'Duncan's nae the only one she's worked her magic upon. Rowena does most o' the healing in the glen these days. Already she's as able as me. She was born to it.'

Lachlan watched Rowena move about the room, righting chairs and restoring order. 'I used to worry ower this need in her to be learning the plants and lore, her strangeness, forever ranging the hills and forests, but I dinna worry so much now.' He shook himself, shouting to James, then turned back to Morna.

'Would a drop o' whisky be of use to a healer? Fer cleaning wounds or numbing the pain o' setting a bone or stitching torn flesh?'

'Any spirit is a valuable addition to a healer's medicine kist.'

''Tis what I thought. James!'

But James was already approaching with a little barrel under his arm. This keg was much smaller than an anker, holding only half a gallon. For healing purposes, Duncan supposed its contents would go a long way. James righted the keg and placed it at Morna's feet, the carving of an alder leaf cut into its side a clear indication of its original owner.

''Tis a mite heavy to be carrying on yer back.' Lachlan shuffled his feet. 'I could bring it to ye the morn, if ye like. To the edge o' Sìthean Wood.'

Beneath the grime, Morna's face coloured. 'I dinna ken what to say.'

'Then say aye, and we can go join the feasting.'

'Thank ye, aye. Only, I need no help getting it hame.' She smiled, bringing the birch branch out from behind her skirts. 'I'm stronger than ye might think, and I have my own special means o' travel.'

Lachlan hooted. 'Noo, that I'd like to see.'

Rowena explained the birch stick was a gift for James and Mhari. A symbol of fertility, not so much for them, but their small herd. 'Twas said a pregnant cow herded with a birch stick would unfailingly produce a healthy calf, while a barren cow herded with one would magically become fertile again.

Duncan smiled doubtfully, and she laughed, offering him her arm.

CHAPTER TWENTY

July 1760

NOW JAMES HAD moved to Druimbeag, Rowena felt the loss of him, missing his ready wit and his gentle, teasing ways, but she missed Duncan even more. Duncan was fully recovered from his beating and spent much of his time helping James and Mhari establish their holding at Druimbeag or working in the whisky bothy, building up a stock of ankers for their next smuggling trip. And staying out of her way, as she'd been staying out of his. 'Twas easier, she supposed, no longer seeing so much of each other and maintaining an awkward distance when they did, but it saddened her. She'd often catch his gaze upon her, but always he'd glanced away, shamefaced and confused.

Grace was far too love-struck to miss James. Though coy about it, 'twas rumoured Malcolm MacRae was wooing her. She spoke of little but Malcolm's freckles and fiery hair, his daring as a smuggler and his clumsy attempts to win her favour. Rowena was pleased for her, but the thought of Grace leaving Tomachcraggen too was a heavy burden to bear.

In the four months James had been married, Rowena had seen naught of their new exciseman, the Black Gauger as he was being called, referring to the tailed black coat he wore and the black heart Morna claimed he possessed. She'd heard plenty about him, though, enough to curl her toes. Near daily word reached them of the gauger's exploits. He and his hirelings had waylaid the last few convoys leaving the glen: Archie Fraser and his sons, and brothers Donald and Arthur Milne. These glensmen they'd taken to Elgin for trial. Easy pickings for the gauger, her da said, for they'd foolishly attempted the route in daylight. Still, he was puzzled how the gauger had caught them so easily. How had he known where they'd be and when? It seemed doubtful he could simply have struck lucky like that, not without foreknowledge.

McBeath had also been brutal in Glenlivet, where a fierce battle had arisen between smugglers and government men. There'd been cracked heads and bloody noses, though, thankfully, the smugglers had escaped. These were desperate glensmen needing to smuggle to feed their families and afford the steep new rents. Her da grumbled McBeath had already extorted a fortune in coin from folk who could ill afford it. There'd be trouble at Lammas when rents were due. The coin needed to pay those rents now lined the Black Gauger's pockets.

Everywhere she went, she heard talk of McBeath and his hirelings. Even old Angus Grant wasted his last breath upon him. 'Twas plain the old saddler's time had come, and she could do naught but hold his hand as he slipped through the cleft between realms. But on the verge of passing, and with scarce breath left in him, old Angus had gripped her hand and wheezed, 'The Black Gauger's upon us!'

It seemed the whole glen was in fear.

Her da had never paid passage in his life and made no bones of the fact he'd not be starting now. 'If he thinks to mak' a living from me,' he told her, 'he'll need to catch me and my haul fair and square. 'Twill be a cold day in hell afore I hand that rogue a penny o' my hard-earned coin.' He fixed her with a grim look. 'I've nae been caught in near thirty years, though there's many have tried. I wish him luck trying. And if he imagines he'll simply arrest me and hand me ower fer trial, he can think again. I've nae intention o' coming quiet-like.'

'Nor I,' Duncan assured him, and her heart fluttered.

Her heart fluttered a deal more only a couple of nights later when Duncan returned in the dead of night, wakening them all, his face and clothing blackened with soot. In the dim light from the fire, all she could see of him were the whites of his eyes and a flash of teeth, but she could smell him from the doorway. He coughed and retched, a pungent reek of wood smoke wafting from him.

'Christ in heaven! Is it a fire at the bothy?' Her da was pulling on his clothes.

'No, Jock McIntyre's sheep-cot at Ardbreckan. I heard the commotion on my way hame and ran to help. It seems McBeath imagined a still was hidden there, and wi'out even looking inside, set fire to the thatch wi' all Jock's sheep inside.'

Grace inhaled sharply, hastening to stir the hearth-fire into life and light some fir-candles. Her da was already searching for his pistol, cursing the exciseman in the foulest of language. Duncan pressed a blackened hand on his shoulder.

'There's naught to be done. The lambs that could be saved are wi' McIntyre's wife, and the flames are out, though there's little left o' the cot but smoulder and ash.' He sat down heavily. 'McIntyre's neighbours heard the bleating commotion, and on seeing an eerie glow in the sky, came rushing to his aid. They found the gauger searching fer whisky amongst the scorched remains o' Jock's lambs. He was unrepentant, a flaming brand still clutched in his hand. Jock was that enraged, he and his neighbours set upon him.'

'And killed him?'

'No, leastways, I dinna think so. But they gave him a beating he'll nae forget.' He shook his head a mite grudgingly. ''Twas some brawl. McIntyre knocked the pistol from his hand and kicked it into the pyre, and though the devil drew his sword, they took that from him, too. He bellowed like an ox, lashing oot wi' fist and boot, though he'd little chance against so many. As the fight went on and he refused to stay doon, I feared they might kill him.'

A shocked sound came from Grace.

'He likely imagined the same, fer though beaten and bloody, he hauled himsel' onto his horse. Jock charged efter him in a roaring rage, swinging a spade. The gauger's horse took fright and bolted toward Sìthean Wood.' He glanced at Rowena. 'There's nae a man in the glen would follow him there, even in daylight.'

Lachlan swore softly. 'Let's hope he still lives, then. If murdered, every one o' those mixed up in this will swing.' He looked at Duncan. 'Every man there, I'd say.'

There was silence as this sank in. Rowena's heart lurched.

'What o' his hirelings? What happened to them?'

Duncan snorted. 'He must think himself untouchable. He fired the hut on his own. Likely thought the bothy, or what he imagined was a bothy, would be deserted at night, and he'd seize a few barrels of Ardbreckan's whisky.'

Lachlan raised a brow. 'Then, mebbe he told no one o' his plan. Let's hope so. Should he die in Sìthean Wood, who'd ken? Who'd even find him in thon haunted, impenetrable place?' He glanced at Rowena, still huddled in her blankets. 'But if he blabbed o' his plan, there'll be hell to pay should he fail to return. We'll be overrun wi' soldiers and government men by the morrow's night, I'd say, searching fer him, ransacking hames to find him. Arresting whoever takes their fancy.'

'Lord!' Grace's hand flew to her mouth. 'Should they discover his beaten body—'

'Aye, by Christ.' He turned back to Duncan. 'Was he hurt bad, then?'

'Looked that wey.'

'Weel, if he telt nae one, divil take him, let's hope he dies in thon faerywood where 'tis likely he'll never be found. But if he did tell, we'd best be praying he lives. Better yet, the beating scrambled his wits, and he remembers naught o' this.'

Duncan nodded grimly.

Grace clambered onto the bed beside Rowena, and they clung to each other. Rowena tried to soothe her but was trembling herself, her mouth dry and head aching. She glanced up to find Duncan watching her, his face strange under its layer of soot.

Oh, please, nae Duncan. Mother Earth, nae him.

* * *

Come morning, her head ached even more, for sleep had evaded her. She rose before dawn and gathered what herbs she kept to hand, wrapping them in a blanket. Pulling the door softly behind her, she crept into the darkness, her stomach churning.

By the time the dark outline of Sìthean Wood came in sight, dawn had spread a pearly mist across the land, jewelling every tree. The glen was wreathed in a gentle light, yet inside her, a storm raged. Her heart and head battled each other, her head telling her to leave well alone. Leave the exciseman to his fate, whatever it might be. He frightened her, and she'd no wish to come upon him in the woods. But her heart told her she must do something. Duncan's life was in danger. If the gauger's beaten body were found, what might that mean for Duncan?

Lying awake through the night, she'd imagined his arrest. She pictured his hands roped together, him made to run behind a dragoon like a dog on a leash, his face stricken as he looked back. He fell, was dragged, twisting as he tried to right himself, the breath knocked from him. The hopeless look in his eyes brought back memories of the Gordon lads from years ago.

Tears streaked her cheeks, and she whimpered, stumbling half-blind through the heather. Drawing to a halt, she clenched her teeth. She must be strong. Yet, without first establishing where the exciseman's panicked horse had entered the trees, 'twould be futile to go searching in such a vast forest. She combed along the margin of the trees, searching for signs left by a charging horse as it crashed through the undergrowth and on into the forest.

At last, her search was rewarded, and she came upon the place. Trembling, she sank to her knees in the wet grass to whisper her thanks, then dried her tears. Drawing a quivering breath, she rose and followed the trail.

Beneath the trees, the air was cool and mossy, and even as she penetrated the darkest reaches of the forest, she was able to follow the path left by the fleeing horse with relative ease. Snapped branches and twigs, broken bracken fronds, a dark trail of churned moss and leaf litter were signs no one familiar with the forest could miss. She strained her ears for any tell-tale sounds, but the forest was uncannily silent, the air lush with the scent of crushed vegetation.

Entering one unfamiliar glade after another, she tried to calm the wild beating of her heart. What if he were dead already? Her da would be pleased, would judge it the best outcome for Duncan. For the whole glen. And she would do what? Leave his body to the forest? To the creep of ivy and bramble, the slow moulder of the forest floor, unburied and unmourned? It seemed disrespectful, a sorry end for any man. And perhaps, even more disrespectful to the forest and especially the *sithiche,* the silent folk she oft-times sensed, and who gave the wood its name. A desecration in a place such as this, particularly if the man's heart was as black as Morna believed. Yet, she would need to do so for Duncan's sake. In truth, she'd need to bury him. She shuddered. 'Twas the only way to be sure no one would ever find him.

But if he were still alive, what then? To save the exciseman meant danger, peril for Duncan, and her heart trembled. Duncan, who was as precious to her as this forest, the mountains, the glen that was her home. More. Much more. And there'd be danger for Jock McIntyre and all those who'd come to his aid. Maybe even for herself, though she pushed that thought away.

Only, to do naught. She was a healer; who deserved to live and who to die was not her decision. 'Twas what Morna taught. As she kept moving, these thoughts wrestled in her head.

At last, a plaintive whinny sounded eerily through the trees, and she came upon both rider and mount. The man lay on his back in the leaf mould, one foot still attached to his horse by a stirrup. Not dead, his chest moved faintly, but close to it. His skin was grey, a bloody seep trickling from wounds packed with earth and forest mulch, festering already.

She pushed the hair and leaves from his face, revealing a jagged gash above his brow, his hairline crusted with blood. His horse had likely taken him under a low bough, and he'd been knocked from its back, then dragged by one foot. How far 'twas impossible to tell. Far enough to do damage, a deal of it. More, even, than Jock McIntyre and his neighbours had done.

His horse shivered, chestnut flanks trembling, a magnificent animal, taller than the Highland garrons she was used to but flighty and highly-strung. She moved to stroke its neck, and it shied from her, snorting in loud rasps through flared nostrils, yet its dark eyes betrayed a wish to trust her. Whispering, she dug in her pockets, producing a handful of pignuts. It took them from her with a ripple of velvet lips. She stroked its nose, and it shivered, pricking its ears forward to listen to her voice.

Quickly, she secured it to a tree lest it take fright again, then worked at disentangling the exciseman's foot. Once free, she lowered his leg to the ground, knowing it would cause him pain and he might waken.

His eyes flicked open, and he looked into her face. With a suck of breath, he struggled to rise, then grunted as a wave of pain caught him. He slumped back. *'The witchling,'* he croaked. He stared at her, then at the creaking ranks of oak and pine towering over him. She nodded, aware the trees appeared to watch them, their trunks knurled with knowing eyes.

'Try not to move,' she said in English. She wet his lips with a little water, and instinctively he swallowed, clutching at life. 'I will help you. But first, I must take you from here.'

She imagined his fearful night alone in the forest, cold, bleeding, disorientated as he flickered upon the edge of consciousness. He'd been at the mercy of his horse's nerves. Had it bolted again, his brains would likely have patterned the next rock or stump. Human lichen. At some level, he'd perhaps been aware of the *sìthiche*, of being in their presence. Had likely been more afraid than he'd been in his life.

She tucked the blanket around him, then searched for moss to pack into the wound on his head. It would staunch the bleeding and strengthen his flesh against infection. Once satisfied she'd stemmed the blood loss, she hunted for branches suitable for making a litter. She would drag him through the forest behind his horse. Once free of the trees, she'd hide him under the blanket, pile logs around him to make it look as if she hauled firewood. 'Twas how she'd get him home.

As she worked, she prayed they'd meet no one on the way. The chestnut gelding was likely as recognisable as the man, and she'd no wish to draw attention. Few in the glen would understand her helping him. Most would wish him dead, or leastways, gone from here. Her chest tightened; she wished for that too, but the inherent compassion at her core meant she couldn't just leave him to die.

The exciseman held the rental of the cot-house at Drumin, that much she knew. 'Twould take most of the day to drag him there. With trembling fingers, she fashioned a makeshift litter from foraged wood, binding it with strips of birch bark, then used the blanket to drag him onto it. She piled more logs around him, then guided his horse through the forest, a tortuous undertaking, the injured man jolted over every tussock and root.

Finally, they emerged from the trees into daylight. His face was grey, but even in his semi-conscious state, he grimaced at the change in light. She deemed that a good sign and loosely covered him with the blanket.

From here, the route she chose had by necessity to be a winding one, avoiding bogs and sloping ground and any small settlements or farms. The man groaned but did not speak again. At the river's edge, she stopped to water his horse and let it graze, trickling water between the gauger's lips. He swallowed, his eyes flicking open, and he repeated what he'd said before. She shivered. Leaving him, she gathered moss for making dressings, tucking it under the blanket. As soon as his horse was revived enough to go on, they did so.

It did not cross her mind the exciseman might not live alone. When finally they reached Drumin, her heart gave a jolt when Isobel Gow came running from the cot-house. No one followed her out, thankfully. She drew a quivering breath and pulled back the blanket.

Isobel's hands flew to her face. 'Lord! What happened? Who did this?'

She shook her head, eyeing Isobel curiously. 'I found him like this. D'ye live here wi' him, then, the gauger?'

'As his housemaid.' Isobel blushed furiously, pressing a hand to her mouth. 'His poor face.'

In the unforgiving light, the exciseman's face looked shocking. His lip was split and weeping, the flesh around his eyes so angry and swollen, his face had all but swallowed his eyes. He was filthy, grimed with soot and blood and forest mire, mud clumped in his beard, but his face was the least of Rowena's concerns.

'Help me get him inside,' she urged. 'He's lost a deal o' blood, and I feel a fever brewing.'

Isobel sobbed, clutching at her wrist. 'Most folk woulda left him where he lay.' She squeezed her hand. 'Bless ye.'

She nodded, hoping she'd not live to regret not doing that.

They unhitched the litter and used it to drag the gauger inside. He was solidly built; lifting him onto the table was beyond their doing. They made him as comfortable as possible on the flagstone floor, Isobel fussing over him with blankets and pillows. His men would carry him to bed later, she said.

'Sir.' Isobel tried to force water between his lips. 'Mister McBeath, sir.'

Exhausted, Rowena looked down at him. 'I'll need warm water, plenty o' it, and clean linen. Soapwort if ye have it.'

When Isobel hastened away, she began cutting off the shreds of the man's clothing, then fetched the peat moss she'd gathered. Soaked in warm water, moss was the best material for cleaning wounds. Dry, it made an effective dressing; truly nature's gift. She piled it in readiness. But until the man was clean, 'twas impossible to tell what horrors lay beneath the layers of mud and ash.

By the time Isobel returned, she'd stripped the man to his sark and cut that away, too, leaving only enough for decency. Isobel gasped, slopping water from her bowl onto the floor. Squinting up at her, she imagined the lass had never before seen her employer in a state of undress. Or any man. She wondered what the girl's father made of her living here with an exciseman—a ruthless one. But from Isobel's stricken expression, 'twas not the gauger's naked and heavily muscled body that made her stare, but the state of it.

Laying her bowl down, Isobel knelt gingerly at his side. 'Sir. 'Tis Isobel, sir.'

Rowena offered her a handful of moss. 'Ye can help me if ye like.' She stirred the herbs she'd brought into the warm water.

The girl was as gentle as a fawn, looking anxiously into the gauger's face whenever she touched a raw area, working slowly but surely around every mud-packed wound. Rowena nodded in approval.

'I heard ye can heal as well as the witch o' Sìthean Wood.' Isobel glanced sidelong at her.

''Twas Morna taught me,' she confirmed. 'But she's nae a witch, only a woman. A wise, far-seeing one.'

She wished Morna were here now; she'd know what to do. Yet, deep-down, she recognised this must be her secret. Having witnessed McBeath's reaction to Morna, 'twas plain what he'd judged her to be. He was a danger to her.

Isobel's hands stilled. 'Is he going to die?' She kept her head bent.

''Tis possible. All I can promise is I'll do what I can to prevent it.'

'But, 'twould be better if he did? Fer yer kinfolk. The smugglers o' the glen?'

She hesitated, seeing in her mind's eye a row of limp bodies hanging broken-necked from a scaffold. 'I doubt it,' she said bitterly. 'But be careful what ye say. 'Tis possible he can hear.'

They'd replenished the bowl of herb water many times before the man was clean. Every inch of him was bruised or lacerated, his ankle broken. But the worst injury was to his head. 'Twas this damage to flesh and bone, and the soft tissue within, that gave him his grey colour and robbed him of his senses.

She sat back, rubbing her brow. She could heal his wounds and lower his fever, mend his broken bones, but damage to what lay within his skull was a mystery beyond her understanding. Time and tenderness were abiding healers, but beyond that, only charms and herb magic, and likely luck, would decree if he emerged from his stupor with his wits intact. In truth, if he emerged at all. She knew not if she wished him to, but if he died, Duncan and those others would doubtless have to pay.

She dried her hands. 'I must search fer more herbs. Try to keep him comfortable, talk to him, give him water. I'll be back to stitch his wounds.'

Isobel nodded, taking the gauger's hand. She was loyal. If he died, at least one soul would mourn him.

She returned with comfrey root, wormwood, purple coneflower and witch-hazel, and set about making infusions and pastes. The light was fading, and she was weary, her head aching, her heart, too.

The gauger was still unconscious as she stitched his wounds. He lay in the nest of blankets and pillows Isobel had made for him, insensible to the stab and draw of needle. A blessing, but afterwards, she must try to rouse him.

Had she done the right thing? Only time would tell.

* * *

Over the next five days, Rowena battled the fever in Hugh McBeath's body, returning daily to Drumin. He was delirious, crying out to God, to his father, oft-times confusing the two. He spoke of his mother, how his birth had brought her end and raged against the cunning witch who tended her. He begged forgiveness for his sins, particularly those of the flesh, and hearing his ravings, Isobel wept.

As a healer, Rowena oft-times heard folk ramble so whilst in the grip of fever, particularly those who neared the end and craved absolution. Some even confessed their sins to her as if she were a priest. But the gauger grew fearful and agitated, greeting like a bairn. He grasped her wrist with a strength that made her wince, whimpering of an endless forest alive with devil's imps.

When she tried to soothe him, he hissed of a witchling, his glassy gaze roving the room, and she held her breath. More than once, he'd called her that.

Isobel prayed fervently for him in Gaelic and faltering English; the gauger had taught her the rudiments of his tongue. She believed her employer possessed, and it seemed so, but Rowena knew his demons were of his own making. They lived in his fever-fuelled mind, born of the trauma to his head and body and the swelling and heat his body created to fight it. 'Twas the swollen matter inside his skull that most tormented him. Mysterious flesh she must somehow heal.

Murmuring a heartfelt, 'Amen,' Isobel unclasped her hands and rose from her knees, her face drawn. 'Is it nae time we fetched the minister? I could ask Ghillie or Dougal to ride fer him. Reverend Dundas will thump his bible and rage against Satan like he does in kirk. He'll soon drive out the divil from Mister McBeath.'

She sighed resignedly. 'Yer concern does ye credit, Isobel, but this isna the divil's work. If such a creature exists.'

Isobel gasped at her blasphemy. 'I could run fer him mysel',' she muttered.

'He's nae possessed, Isobel.' She squeezed the girl's hand. ''Tis his own body he battles—a mighty struggle to heal the harm done to him. See the wet seep from his ears? 'Tis a sign fever rages inside him, that it reaches a crisis. We must keep him cool, use herbs to help him fight it. Once his fever breaks, the delirium will pass. So, too, his demons.'

She hoped that were true, yet all she knew for sure was she must reduce the swelling inside his head. She stirred strips of linen into a cold infusion of willow bark and nettle, adding rosehip seeds for their potent power to soothe. Lifting out the dripping strips, she wrapped them around his head.

Isobel watched her with troubled eyes but eventually nodded. The girl was a God-fearing Presbyterian like her father. She could only hope Isobel had seen enough of her healing skills to trust her. The gauger's wounds were healing; a healthier colour had returned to his face. He'd even spoken some words, though naught that made any sense.

She pressed a hand to his forehead, feeling the burning heat radiating

206

from within. By day's end, they would know if he'd live. But whether his mind would survive and he'd be the man he'd been before was another matter. They'd know more once his fever broke. Yet, with his recovery would likely come his memory, and with it, doubtless a desire for revenge.

She sighed, praying for Isobel's trust, knowing no minister would ever be her friend. Any who came would see only her herbs and potions, the hollow stone filled with healing water from the clootie-well in Sìthean Wood placed by the man's bed and would judge it all witchery. Sniffing the bubbling pots at the hearth, he'd denounce her for a witch.

CHAPTER TWENTY-ONE

FLAMES LEAPT INTO the darkness, the foul reek of burning wool filling Hugh's nostrils, his lungs. He could taste it, overlaid with an even more offensive stench. Muck ran from the backside of every panic-stricken lamb. He slipped on it, cursing, covering his mouth and nose with a corner of his coat, shoving the bleaters out of his way. With a roar, he grasped the most damnable of them and hurled it into the flames. There was whisky here, he knew it, only he'd no' expected all these sheep.

The heat and choking smoke became unbearable. Blundering out of the bothy, he was struck hard from behind. He bit his tongue, and his teeth rattled, but he managed to stay upright. Whirling around, he drew his pistol. It was knocked from his grasp. Out of the darkness, the faces of Highland savages emerged. They ringed him, cursed him in their barbarous tongue, their faces choked with anger. Some tried to beat out the flames while others moved in on him. He drew his sword.

He tried to hold on to that memory, to recall what came next, but the images were fleeting and scattered. He was careering through the darkness, the wind in his face, clinging to his horse's mane, the animal lathered and snorting, pounding the heathery ground. His jaw ached, his knuckles, too. A metal taste filled his mouth.

Trees loomed, then all the world was blackness and a chill as sharp as glass bit into his soul. The forest revolved, blurred past, the swish and whip of leaf and branch in his face as he grappled with his runaway mount. Then the crack of timber on bone resounded through the forest, and his head must surely burst, his leg be torn from its socket. Still he hurtled on, through bracken and bramble, pummelled and whipped, dragged over hummock and root, the stink of moulder and rot in his nostrils, the wet slither of it up his back.

On and on into blackness.

Later, from that blackness shapes formed, dark shapes like men. A presence came, then many. From the trees, the ground, he felt them come. Soundless. But he could smell them; their breath, the tang of iron.

He awoke cold, his clothing soaked in blood and mire and urine, for he'd pissed himself. His lips were cracked, his head throbbed, and one leg no longer belonged to him, that numb was it. But finally, a grainy light began to penetrate the blackness, pushing the shadows back. Trees slowly came to the fore, creaking and swaying as they watched him. Creatures scurried by his head, a swarm of flies feasted upon him. The forest shifted in the changing light. A crow hopped down from a stump, head slanted, eyeing him.

And a witch came.

Water, he tried to suck it in, and her face came into focus. 'Twas a face he knew, or thought so, but in his head a cauldron boiled. He groaned, tried to rise. Pain lanced his skull.

'Ye must rest,' the witch said, and she placed something cold upon the cauldron. 'Here, I've made a potion to quench your fire.' She angled a cup of poison for him to drink.

He squinted, tried to see her face, but the light was behind her, haloing her head. She was no angel, though; he knew what she was. No angel would come here.

Only, when he looked again, he was in his own home. The miserable hovel at Drumin. In his own bed. He tried to hold on to her face, but blackness rose again.

When next he woke, she was still there, smiling at him, only the light was different, and she was, too. Her hair was tied up, revealing the perfection of her face, her expression composed, unfathomable. Her eyes looked deep into his soul, and he knew 'twas a different day, maybe even a different century. And she was surely a witch.

'You've returned,' she said and placed a cool hand on his forehead.

'Where was I?'

'In the grip of fever.'

He blinked, aware she spoke the truth, but there was more he needed to know. He raised his head, and a jolt of pain took his breath away. His vision blurred. He put a hand up, feeling something fungus-like growing from his forehead.

'A peat moss dressing. 'Twas my doing. I'm a healer.'

'What's been done to me?' he choked, angry now.

'You don't remember?'

'There was fire ... and a forest, an abominable one.'

'I found you in the woods, injured, insensible, you and your horse. I brought you here. You've many wounds, but a blow to your head robbed you of your senses.'

'Who are you?' Staring at this alluring spectre, Hugh was aware that information already existed somewhere in his splitting head.

Her gaze moved over his face. 'Rowena Innes of Tomachcraggen.'

Frowning, he remembered a devil's ring atop a hillock and a girl and her crone-like companion. He recalled hiding in the bushes and the pleasure he'd derived from watching her. His response to her had been robust, red-blooded. He'd wanted her, and with a fervour that staggered him. He'd desired many women—had enjoyed almost as many—but never had he been so consumed with the want of one woman. Even now, in his diminished state, he recognised something alluring about this witch and struggled to look away. She might act innocent, but she didn't fool him.

'You're the witchling.'

'Why d'you call me that?'

'Are you no'?'

'I'm a healer.'

'A healer?' He slanted his eyes. 'Where did you learn to speak English?'

'From my brother. And he from a churchman.'

'Your brother?' There was something about that, but he struggled to remember what. 'Why are ye here? Did Isobel send for you? Where is Isobel?' He remembered the strumpet at last.

'She sleeps. She sat up all night tending you, waiting for your fever to break. Ye're fortunate to have her; never have I seen a maid more loyal. But she was dead on her feet when I came to visit this forenoon. I sent her to bed. She's no use to you exhausted.'

She smiled, and his pain and confusion receded. They no longer seemed to matter. Naught did but her smile, that it was for him. He slumped back, remembering she was a witch—she was casting a spell upon him.

'Are you hungry? You've eaten naught in days.'

He found he was hungry, but not for food. For her company, her smiles, the touch of her hand, but he nodded and let her fetch him broth.

'Why did ye help me?' This troubled him. He knew it was true; she'd saved his life. 'If you're of this glen, you'll know who I am, what I do. You could just have left me. Finished me yourself.' He shuddered, remembering the poison.

She laughed, a tinkling sound he wished to hear more of.

'Healers heal, they don't harm, no matter who needs their help.'

She tucked a lock of hair behind her ear and perched on the edge of the bed, spooning broth into his mouth as if he were a hatchling. He began to feel better. He sensed her relax in his presence; that pleased him. A lilting, Gaelic tone had crept into her voice. He found he didn't mind it from her. He wished to hear more of her voice, to know more about her, but when the broth was finished, she rose and left him.

Over the next few days, he began to recover his strength and wits but found Isobel's constant fussing and praying vexed him beyond endurance. Confined to bed, weak, swathed in linen and God knows what else, his right leg in a bark and resin splint, his face a swollen obscenity, he grew restless and frustrated. His days and nights blurred together, tormented by confusing dreams.

Threaded through dreams of a haunted forest, he fantasised about the witchling, dreaming his vigour and prowess were restored to him. On chancing upon her in the woods, he begged a kiss. When she laughed, he quickly overpowered her, hearing her tinkling laugh again. The sound both stung and aroused. On an impulse, he deflowered her, brutishly plundering virgin flesh, exchanging her laughter for his rasping breath and groans of pleasure, exhausting himself in the sinful thrill of her. Finally, he enshrined the act in all its detail and sensation within himself as if it were real.

When he awoke, it was always to find Isobel at his bedside, usually praying. As she moved about the room, he followed her with his eyes. When she leaned over to fuss with his blankets and pillows, he slipped his fingers inside the bodice of her gown and pinched her nipples until they hardened, imagining the many ways he'd enjoy her as soon as he was able.

She blushed, letting him do as he pleased.

But he was only content for the short time each day when Rowena came. She visited at some point every day, bringing potions and noxious green brews she called tea. She pulled his blankets back and gazed upon his lacerated flesh, touching him with a tenderness that made him shiver. When she stretched over to examine the wound on his head, he breathed in her fresh green scent, itching to slip his fingers inside her bodice, too. The desire was so intense, a surge of blood flushed his face, and he near swooned.

'Ye're healing fast.' She nodded in approval. 'These sutures can come out the morrow. Ye'll feel better then. What about the headaches? They're still as bad?'

They hardly bothered him now, but he nodded and affected a pained expression, stifling a smile when she pressed her cool fingers to his brow. In the last few days, his memory had begun to return, and he now remembered exactly who she was. In the pocket of an old coat, he kept a scrap of material belonging to her. He'd not use it now. She'd saved his life; he didn't doubt that. To repay her by using the item to coerce her now held little appeal. She was the daughter of the most notorious smuggler in Strathavon, one of her brothers was none other than the Young Jacobite, a man he disliked intensely, but despite that, he desired her as fiercely as ever.

Her strangeness was part of her attraction. Her darkness lent an edge of danger to any intercourse he'd have with her. A notion he found intoxicating. Arousing. She'd likely been sent by the devil to tempt him, and he should resist, but he had no defence against her. Confined to bed with little to occupy his mind, he knew she'd taken possession of him, body and mind.

Curiously, he no longer wished to force her roughly in the heather as he might any heather-lowping whore. Where was the thrill in that? What he wanted now, and with a hunger that took his breath away, was that she give herself to him willingly. Better yet, respond to him with an appetite that rivalled his own.

Only, for that, she'd first need to trust and respect him. Admire him, even. During his twenty-eight years on God's earth, Hugh had observed how women were attracted to men of position and power. Only, he sensed that, as a healer, she would be swayed more by compassion and a sense of empathy. He smiled inwardly, knowing how he'd play her. He'd force her to imagine his plight—a gauger in this clannish glen of smugglers. He'd make her feel for him, knowing his position to be a damnable one. No' an easy task, but the rewards would be worth the trouble.

'Doubtless, ye think ill of me,' he ventured. 'An exciseman working in this glen of smugglers.' He drew a wary breath. 'What with your kinsmen in the smuggling trade.'

She went very still.

'I'm hated here. D'ye imagine I don't know? I'm a tax collector. Like those in the Holy Bible, I'm feared and despised.' He laughed bitterly. 'I strike terror into bairns.'

212

Her dark eyes flickered.

Being despised had never troubled him before, but the thought of this beauty despising him galled. 'Yet, I do only my duty, Rowena. Strive to make a decent living, as any man must do.'

She swallowed and glanced away. He sensed he was making her uncomfortable and deemed that good. He must force her to question her loyalty, but carefully, or he risked turning her against him. 'I'm an honest man, Rowena, something I believe cannae be said of my predecessor.'

Her eyes flashed. 'John Meldrum was a decent man. Loyal to his fellow glensmen.'

'I meant only, in doing my duty, I live under constant threat of violence.' He glanced down at his body with its bruises and bandages. 'And no' just the threat of it. As you see, I'm a target for smugglers' anger. I represent a king and government most Heilanders despise. Daily, my work brings me into danger.'

As he spun his tale of woe, he began to enjoy himself, lies tripping blithely off his tongue. 'In the past, I've been held captive by smugglers. Merciless men wishing to prevent me giving evidence at a trial. While they held me, those villains amused themselves, tormenting my flesh. I'll no' distress ye with the details, but you see, they punished me for doing my duty.'

She lowered her head, unable to look him in the eye. Pleasure rippled through his innards. His fiction had aroused her sympathy, shamed her even, though he'd perhaps overdone it. He did, after all, enjoy it when she looked at him.

'You're sure 'twas smugglers did this?' She indicated his recent injuries. 'I thought you'd little memory of what happened?'

'I recall enough.'

She swallowed, looking faint. 'Then, I'm sorry.' She rose to go.

'Please,' he captured her hand to detain her. 'I dinnae say this to discomfit you or solicit sympathy, but so you might understand.' He affected a wistful smile. 'Might better tolerate me. It grieves me to be so hated. Especially by you.'

'I don't hate ye.' Her brows came together. 'But I'd have ye know, Highland folk want only to be understood. We wish our glens left unpillaged, our folk unoppressed. We're different, Highland and Lowland folk, our speech, our dress and ways, but beyond those outer things, our differences are few. Beneath our plaids, your breeches and silks, are we nae the same? Yet we're granted little tolerance.' She grew breathless. 'Since the last rising, we've seen naught but tyranny. Burnings

213

and hangings, land plundered, beasts and crops—'

She pulled her hand free. 'Forgive me. I speak out o' turn. I'll see to your sutures the morrow, sir.'

'Hugh. You must call me, Hugh.' Her passion was quite magnificent; his buttocks tightened with want. Only, as he'd gripped her hand, he'd felt something hard. Looking down, she wore a ring. A silvery thing. His face grew hot. 'Twas on her wedding finger.

She nodded and began gathering her herbs and potions together.

'Tell me,' he blurted, 'have ye a husband, Rowena?'

She flinched, a muscle in her cheek flexing. 'I've not.'

'Then,' he let his breath out in relief, 'then, there's still hope.'

She glanced up sharply. 'I'm wed to the earth. To nature and her magic. Pledged to heal and keep the lore of my glen.'

'But you're no' pledged to a man?'

She shook her head, hastily wrapping her herbs in linen. 'Nor ever will be.'

'Ever's a long time.'

'A lifetime, aye.'

As she turned away, a sense of dismay overwhelmed him. All had not gone as he'd hoped. Yet, perhaps he'd at least given her something to think about. If only she'd no' run away so fast. If she tarried a while, he might undress her with his eyes. But she moved to the door and, without a backward glance, was gone.

Good to her word, she returned the next day and with an unexpected air of gaiety. Hugh indulged himself, imagining this welcome change was down to him. Isobel soon shattered his delusions.

'What gladdens ye so, Rowena?'

The witchling blinked, her expression charming in its awkwardness. ''Tis no longer a secret, I suppose. James is to be a father. Mhari carries his child, has done for a time, though she kept the secret till she was sure. A child will come with the first snows.'

'Oh, Rowena! How wonderful. I'm delighted fer them.'

'Thank ye, Isobel.'

'They didnae waste much time procreating,' Hugh observed. 'But I wish them well.'

She nodded to him, then set about unpacking her things: more herbs and moss, along with a wicked slip of a blade. Isobel eyed the knife uneasily.

'Have ye no chores?' he growled at her. 'And tell Ghillie and Dougal I wish to see them. I expect to hear what they've been doing whilst I lingered at death's door. If they've neglected to collect passage, I'll flay the living flesh from their bones.'

'Aye, sir.' She scuttled away.

Lying back, Hugh presumed the young witch would need to remove most of his clothing to take out his stitches and would, of course, have to touch him, place her hands on his skin and concentrate her attention solely on him. It would evidently involve the use of a knife. Nevertheless, he shivered with anticipation. As he settled back, he struggled to suppress a smile. With the witchling absorbed, he'd be free to admire her delights. The smooth lustre of her skin, the slender curve of her hips visible through the wool of her gown. And, as she bent to work on him, the ripeness of her breasts. He'd distract himself, envisioning how he'd enjoy those delights once he'd won her over.

Having received few injuries in his life, Hugh knew little of how they healed. He preferred any risks to life or limb to be taken by others, not him. But even with his limited knowledge, he recognised his wounds, though severe, were healing with astonishing speed. Other than his ankle in its splint that still troubled him, he felt almost wholly recovered. In truth, he felt invigorated. Isobel had told him she'd feared he'd die. She'd snivelled infernally over the point, but Rowena had saved his life. His soul, too, for he'd been possessed.

He smiled inwardly, knowing he still was. Only, 'twas not Satan that possessed him now but this bewitching young she-devil. He supposed the notion should trouble him. He should hear his father's doom-laden voice in his head raging against the scourge of witchcraft, but 'twas hard to hear that voice when he lived in an almost constant state of arousal. Hugh knew of only one remedy for lust. He looked forward to indulging in that remedy as soon as he was able.

Sadly, the witchling removed the neat rows of stitches quicker than he could have believed possible, and he derived little pleasure from her touch. 'Twas all over in moments. She sponged the angry weals with a fragrant concoction and stood back.

'I didna hurt you?'

'A little.'

'Forgive me, I meant to be gentle.'

She had been, but he enjoyed toying with her. Canting his head, he considered how best to proceed toward his objective. 'I'm indebted to you, Rowena. How can I ever repay you?'

''Twas naught. A snip, a gentle tug.' She shrugged, packing her things.

'I meant for saving my life. I know you did, although how, I can hardly fathom. How you found me in that dark, tangled place is a mystery, never mind how you moved me here.'

She smiled, ignoring his questions. He began to fear she might not return after today. She might deem him healed enough to no longer need her. The notion was unthinkable. 'What about my ankle?' he whined. 'When can this whigmaleerie come off?'

'A few weeks yet, sir. But ye mustn't lie in your sickbed longer than's needed. I've brought oxter-staffs to help ye walk. Moving will keep ye strong.'

At least she'd noticed he was strong, although what oxter-staffs were, he had no idea. Doubtless, as she'd tended his wounds, she'd admired his muscular body. Perhaps she'd even imagined how it might feel when pressed upon her, as he'd similarly imagined.

When she left the room, he stifled a groan. Had she known a man before? Been defiled by one? He remembered the Young Jacobite, how his eyes had glazed with desire when he looked at her. Only he'd turned out to be her brother. Although she was patently a witch, she possessed a face of such clear-eyed perfection, her manner so gentle and without guile, he sensed she had not. That she was, as yet, untouched.

She returned carrying two rustic wooden crutches, items he suspected she'd made herself and that touched him.

'Will I show ye how to use them, sir, or do ye need to rest?' She eyed him uncertainly.

'Show me, aye. But I'll need help getting out of bed.'

She proceeded to peg-leg comically about the room, demonstrating how the crutches should be used, then slid her arm around his shoulders and helped him upright.

'I'm no' entirely decent,' he warned her, and she spun around, blushing.

'I'd forgotten.' With her eyes covered, she passed him his breeches and stood with her back turned while he struggled into them with his splinted leg.

Finally, feeling light-headed and flushed, he put his hand out to her, and she slipped her arm around his waist, letting him lean on her as he struggled to stand. He was weaker than he'd imagined. His head throbbed, and he feared he might swoon.

'I have ye, sir,' she murmured. 'I'll not let ye fall.'

He briefly wondered how on earth she would prevent it, but he managed to stay upright, and slowly, the room ceased spinning. Still a mite light-headed, he was overcome with the scent of her, subtle but unimaginably sweet, the electrifying tingle of her fingers at his waist, the sweep of her hair as it brushed his shoulder. He yearned to push her onto the bed, to possess her with powerful, plundering strokes. But as he could barely stand, that would need to wait.

She groped for the crutches and fitted them under his arms, then, to his regret, stepped away, swapping her weight for the sticks. He managed a few hobbling steps, then sank onto the bed.

'Tis too soon, I fear.' She took the crutches from him and propped them by the bed. 'You must go slow, but once ye're stronger, ye should take as much fresh air and exercise as ye can.'

The crutches, although crude, had been fashioned with his welfare in mind. Wiping the sweat from his brow, he considered her. 'What do your family make of you coming here?' They could hardly be pleased.

She swallowed. 'They don't know of it, sir. But if they did, they'd likely try to stop me.'

'Thinking I'd harm you?'

'Thinking me ... foolish to make myself known to ye.'

'Because I might harm you?'

She nodded, avoiding his eyes.

'And you believe I would?'

'I don't imagine so, but my kinfolk are fearful of ye. Of the power ye hold over us, and how ye might use it. Especially after what ye said on James' wedding day.'

'But I jested! Surely they know that?'

Her dark gaze roved the room, searching for a prudent way to frame her answer. 'My kinsmen are hill-farmers, sir, herdsmen and,' she swallowed, 'whisky smugglers, as I'm sure ye know. 'Tis how we afford our rent, for it must be paid in coin. Finding that coin is sore work. Sorer still now the rents have risen so steep. Should that rent go unpaid, I imagine ye know the penalty.'

He nodded, using the pretext of contemplating this situation to stare blatantly at her. Her face was pale, vulnerable, her dark eyes full of fear. Having confessed such dangerous information, he could easily force her to his will. Only, he no longer wanted that. What she'd admitted could be used more gainfully.

'I had wondered how I might repay you.' He exhaled with a frown, affecting to search his soul. 'But, God forgive me, I believe I see a way.' He paused, watching her slender throat dip as she swallowed. 'I cannae repay you directly; there's the pity of it. But I can do so through your family by ... ignoring certain activities they might be engaged in.'

She blinked, confused. 'Ye mean—?'

'I mean, I will leave them be. Your faither and brothers. James and ....'

'Duncan, sir.'

'Should I come upon them with whisky or malted barley, whether they're distilling the spirit or smuggling it away, provided I'm no' in the company of dragoons or infantrymen, I'll no' interfere. You have my word.'

She stared at him, her face lighting with hope. 'Oh, sir!'

'Hugh. My name is Hugh.'

'I hardly know what to say.'

'Then say naught, for this will need to be our secret. I believe my predecessor was hanged for similar behaviour. Colluding with smugglers.'

The smile froze on her lips as the truth of that dawned upon her. She sank onto the bed, her eyes clouding. 'I can't ask such a thing of ye, Hugh. 'Tis too dangerous. What if you should be discovered? I couldn't bear it if anything befell ye on my account.'

He shivered at the tenderness in her voice, at his name pronounced in her soft, Highland way. A generous feeling kindled inside him.

'Let me worry about that.'

The reassuring smile he offered her was measured, for he fought with all his might to stifle the triumphant twitching of his lips. She trusted him now. Was pitifully grateful. Perhaps she even considered him an honourable man. Admired him. His eyelid twitched, and he soothed it with a subtle movement. How might she reward him? Would she allow him close to her now, let him take certain liberties? Perhaps as her lover? He no longer imagined himself her plunderer or abuser. Hugh now wanted so much more.

CHAPTER TWENTY-TWO

Drumin
Strathavon
15th September 1760

Father

I hope this letter finds you in robust health and that you will forgive my tardiness in not writing sooner. I have been incapable of such a task. Even now, weeks after the assault, I am kept to bed with my splinted leg. It galls me to tell you I have been assailed here in this villainous glen, attacked with murder in mind, and in the course of my duties for the king. I was beaten and left for dead in a dark wood—a haunted place alive with devil's imps where I feared I would die.

Only, a Highland girl rescued me, a halfling woman I cannot hope to describe; her grace is beyond my words. She took me from that fearful place and delivered me here, to the hovel I'm obliged to call home. She healed me with herbs and tenderness, for I was fever-ridden, possessed by demons.

Do I hear you exclaim, Father? Choke, even, pronouncing her a witch? She is not. A bewitcher, then? Aye, she is that, for she has bewitched me.

But, so you understand, I must go back a little if you will indulge me. I was obliged to attend my predecessor's trial, and there had the fortune to meet the local factor, Mister William McGillivray. It will please you to know I conducted myself admirably in his presence. McGillivray has since been elevated to magistrate and is a man of position and wealth. He is also a Kirk Elder, and I feel you would esteem him, as he admired you when I enlightened him of your views (and mine) on the matter of papists and traitorous rebels.

But we have more in common, for we have become acquaintances, he and I, working toward a shared purpose. That purpose is the removal of the scourge of whisky smuggling from the Duke of Gordon's lands. It is to that end I put myself in danger. Yet, as I continue to extend my authority across this miserable land of hills and bogs, I can say with some certainty, I have found a powerful ally in this man. Any smuggler I bring before him he finds guilty without exception, swiftly fining or imprisoning every one.

He also shares your views on the bane of witchcraft, which I can confirm is rife in these parts. I have myself discovered an evil crone living here on his grace's land, and even more gallingly, she does so rent-free. McGillivray has no entry for her on his rent-roll. It seems the blood-sucking leech prefers to haunt woods, feeding off the superstitions of witless locals. I will remove her. The law, with my help, will deal with her as she deserves.

So, before I was fiendishly attacked, I had achieved considerable success here, both financial and within the limited society that exists in these wild parts. My name had come to the duke's attention, and wealth was, at last, flowing my way. It will again, I have great confidence, as soon as I regain full health. On that note, my headaches are much improved. Only my ankle remains to heal completely.

So, I come to the crux of my letter. With my increasing prosperity, I believe I need no longer concern myself with securing a favourable marriage. As such, I have decided to take a local woman to wife. The woman I have chosen is the young halfling who nursed me.

I appreciate you will not approve, and I regret that, Father, but I have set my mind on her. Rowena is her name, and she is as alluring a creature as her name suggests. If you could but see her, I'm convinced you'd be as captivated as I and would welcome her into your affections.

Yet, knowing this news will disappoint you, I pray you will not think too ill of me. Indeed, I hope you will pray for me and my bride, as I daily pray for you. Here in these barbarous lands, my mind often strays back to gentle Melrose, and I see myself sitting quietly in your congregation. I fancy I hear your voice reading from the holy scriptures, bringing the word of God. It *sustains me in this heathenish place. But mostly, Father, I pray I have not disappointed you too sorely.*

It is still my hope to one day make you proud.

Ever your obedient servant and son,
Hugh

* * *

Hugh lowered his quill and wiped his mouth with trembling fingers. Crossing the room, he slopped a sizeable measure of seized whisky into a glass and swallowed it down in one gulp. His ankle barely troubled him now, although he was careful not to let Rowena know. She might stop coming; he could hardly have that. Already, he'd been forced to appeal to her tender heart. She'd pleaded the excuse of needing to help bring in the harvest, claiming every hand was needed when clearly no need could be greater than his own—especially among the den of rogues she called kin. Their need was only for grain, hardly a necessity since they'd only distil it into whisky.

Admittedly, he'd grown partial to the fiery liquor, particularly now he had so much of it. Only yesterday, the hirelings had brought in another haul, although this he would hand over to Farquharson. The Collector was aware he'd been grievously assaulted and would likely be impressed by evidence of his continued dedication to the work despite its perils.

As he sealed the letter, Hugh imagined his father's reaction to the tidings it contained and was thankful at least two hundred miles of mountain and moor separated them. His father's anger would doubtless be explosive and would be conveyed to him in short order. At least it would come in letter form and could swiftly be burned. But in truth, it was only once he'd put pen to paper that he'd conceived of this course of action. Now, with his decision made, he quivered with excitement.

It made perfect sense. He would wed her, turn Rowena from her witchery and make her respectable. A dutiful and desirable wife. Already she spoke English adequately, and when dressed in the finest silks and satins, would look as decorous as any gentleman's wife. More, for what woman possessed the power to stir the loins the way the witchling did? Not one Hugh had ever met.

Thinking further on the matter, he anticipated buying her an array of flimsy undergarments. Fripperies to tease and tantalise and make the ultimate deed he'd commit with her all the more thrilling. He groaned. He'd have her slowly reveal her delights to him on their wedding night, teasing him to new heights of arousal before the consummate act the night would bring. He expected that night to be a long one.

Of course, with her living with him, every conceivable urge might be indulged whenever he desired it, and the fierce wanting he'd long endured would finally be at an end. He smiled. At least until it arose again. Why in God's name hadn't he considered marrying her before? After all, Isobel made a poor substitute with her incessant praying for the Lord's forgiveness after every pleasurable act. Not to mention her childish attempts to demonstrate her affection, something he found insufferable.

Yet, he would be magnanimous and keep her in his employ. She wished to repay her father's debts. The man could rot as far as Hugh was concerned, but Isobel, far more than the hirelings who were idle, witless creatures, acted as his eyes and ears in the glen. She was the real reason for his remarkable success here, for although her loyalties were torn, thus far, he'd had little trouble convincing her where her allegiance should lie.

The occasional tender word or endearment was not beyond his capacity, and like the child she was, Isobel responded to such manipulations with predictable results. She betrayed every smuggler she had knowledge of. Indeed, she actively sought knowledge of smugglers' movements so she could report them to him and shine in his eyes. So, aye, Isobel would be staying.

* * *

Over the weeks of the exciseman's recovery, as Hugh grew stronger in both body and mind, Rowena continued to visit him, despite sensing he no longer needed her. He expected it, so she came. She did so to show her gratitude and to safeguard the precious assurance he'd given her. She still couldn't quite believe he'd given her that promise, an almost unimaginable gift, and hugged the wonder of it into herself, knowing she couldn't share it with another soul for fear of putting him in danger.

The man was still a mystery to her, and she couldn't help distrusting him, yet he'd shown her extraordinary kindness. Continuing to visit him seemed a small price, although she was eager to wean him from the habit.

In truth, she should be helping with the harvest. The infield might all be stubble now, corn stooks pimpling the land, the oats and barley ready for threshing if only she'd helped more. Even pregnant Mhari had done her share. Only last night, she'd rubbed Mhari's chafed hands with calendula balm, knowing 'twas her own hands should be reddened and sore. As each day passed, it became harder to explain her absences, her unease deepening at the secrets she must keep.

Needing to steal away again, she pulled the door softly behind her and hurried away. Yet something made her look back. Duncan was watching her from the byre, tight-faced, knowing she no longer confided in him. She'd refused him; he had no hold on her, but a distance now separated them, a remoteness filled with longings and regrets, and the spectre of a love denied the soil to grow.

It saddened her. Everything she'd done had been for him, but her feelings for him were dangerous. Her heart was so vulnerable to him, she kept it locked away in a place she tried not to visit. Only, she failed miserably in that. There was scarce a moment of any day she didn't think of him. Duncan, whose faithfulness was never in question. Who, even now, would toil to the ends of the earth for her if only she'd let him. But at least she'd kept him safe. As she passed the Shelter Stone, a place poignant with memories of him, she knew she must let that be enough.

At Drumin, she found Ghillie and Dougal loitering outside in a soft rain, apparently grooming McBeath's horse. They lifted their bonnets to her. Ghillie's look was sly, while Dougal's slow smile, directed everywhere but at her face, unnerved her.

Inside, Hugh was pacing the dark interior. There was no sign of Isobel, and even more surprising, no sign of the sticks she'd fashioned for him. He moved unaided and without even a suggestion of a limp. A dog uncurled itself at the fire, a black, bulldog type with a blunt face and muscular shoulders. A creature she'd not seen before. Snarling, it crept toward her, fixing pin-like eyes on her throat. Hugh jabbed his boot into its underbelly, and it whined, skulking back to the fire. Unlike the dog, Hugh showed no sign of pain despite using his injured ankle.

'At last.' He drew her into the room.

She eyed him warily. He seemed uncommonly buoyant, a strange excitement pulsing in his veins. His presence dominated the room, his masculine scent, all leather and gunmetal overlaid with whisky. He came closer, his nostrils flaring.

The bruises had faded from his face. The comfrey she'd lately used had done its work, and other than the angry scar at his brow, there was naught to suggest he'd recently been beaten. He'd trimmed his beard, his hair gleamed in the firelight, curling at his nape where he'd laced it, flopping on his brow in a casual but charming fashion. He was an attractive man, his features strong, rough-hewn. A far cry from the pitiful creature she'd found in the leaf mould of Sìthean Wood. He exuded confidence, and she caught a sense of what Isobel found so intoxicating. That the lass was in love with her employer, she had no doubt.

'Ye're feeling better, sir?' She directed her gaze from his face. 'Ye're not using your oxter-staffs.'

'Hugh; you must call me Hugh. Dear God, especially now with the tidings I bring. I have news that will shock you.' His eyelid twitched. 'But delight you, I trust. Indeed, I hope my decision will inflame you as much as it does me.'

Her innards tightened. What might this decision be? He was an unpredictable man; she must remember that.

Watching her, the muscles of his face worked. 'I've made a decision, one that will benefit you greatly—will lift you from poverty, elevating you above the other wretches of the glen.' His eyes flashed. 'I've decided to make you my wife.'

Rendered speechless, she stared at him.

He beamed back.

'But, sir,' she finally stammered, 'I've no need of a husband. I'm wed to the earth, to nature and her wisdom.'

He seemed not to hear, was talking again.

'I'll protect you in this villainous place. You need never want again. You'll share my home, soon to be a fine one. I plan to build a sizeable house at Balintoul. The duke has plans to lay out a village there, on the top of the hill, and I have plans, too. To own the foremost house in that village. I'm on my way to becoming a wealthy man, Rowena. I'll buy you dresses, silks, perfumes from France. You'll sip the finest claret, dine like nobility. Whatever you desire.' He paused to catch his breath, locking eyes with her. 'Provided you agree to be my wife.'

She could only blink back. What had made him think she had feelings for him? His recent familiarity had made her uneasy, but she'd thought it born of gratitude. She'd saved his life. Already he'd repaid her in the best, the only way he ever could.

He continued to scrutinise her face, a warning gleam in his eyes. 'I'm offering you a new life—a position in society. Ye need never go ferreting in tangled woods again. Digging up weeds, convening with Satan, risking your immortal soul, by God. It goes without saying you must give up all witchery. Put the vocation behind you and particularly sever any connection with that crone I've seen you with.' He shuddered.

She paled, staring at him.

'But that's hardly a great ask, is it? Giving up a sinful craft that'll only

224

damn you anyway.' His gaze moved over her face. 'So, I await your answer with great ardour. If you judge it necessary, I will, of course, seek your faither's permission. But, for now, I long to hear your answer.' His gaze wandered south. 'Your sweet acquiescence.'

She swallowed, guessing what that meant. Unable to give it.

'I desire you, Rowena. Surely you know that? I *burn* with the want of you.' One of his eyelids spasmed. 'You've bewitched me.'

She struggled with all her will to keep the horror from showing upon her face. Yet, horror prevailed—an appalled grimace stretched her lips.

'I amuse you?'

'Oh, no, sir. 'Tis only, I've no need of those things. I belong with my folk. Keeping them hale and hearty. I'm grateful fer yer kindness; I'm honoured. Only, I've no wish to wed ye, sir.'

He exhaled in disbelief. 'Ye cannae mean that? Good God, I'm offering you the world when all I require in return is what's due me as your husband. My rights. I ask naught more.'

''Tis more than I can give, sir.'

'God's blood, 'tis no more than I could take. Right now, if I chose!'

She stumbled back. 'Forgive me, sir. I should be getting away hame.'

'Hugh, God damn it! Call me, Hugh.'

She backed to the door. 'I hope in time you'll understand, Hugh.'

'You'll reconsider, then? I meant naught ill. I was disappointed, but if you need time, I'll give you that.'

She fumbled for the door latch, the dog growling. Hugh's stunned expression stirred a pang of guilt. He wished to repay a debt that needed no paying. He did her a great honour. Only, her heart was already given.

The door yielded, the rain welcoming her, the freshness on her face.

'Rowena!'

* * *

Duncan glanced at Father Ranald, watching him wield a scythe as he imagined he'd once wielded a sword, with bold, slashing strokes, confident the Lord was on his side. The light shifted, darkened, rain threatening the harvest as it had many times over the past week, and he bent to gather and bind. Women's work, Lachlan called it, but he didn't mind.

Father Ranald was more than capable, but during the harvest, when time was against them, even the father needed help bringing in his crop. Duncan was grateful for the opportunity to help him, to spend time in his company. Since his confession of love to Rowena, his arrogance in assuming he was in any way deserving of her, little had gone right.

Rowena now avoided him. Most mornings, she left the cot-house before dawn to make sure of it. They rarely spoke, and when they did, there was awkwardness, a tension so brittle, he sensed they tiptoed around each other, fearing a miss-step could shatter the closeness they'd always shared. His fault, but how to mend it?

He was no longer privy to her thoughts and dreams. He knew neither where she went nor what she did. She was more a mystery to him than ever she'd been; hence the light had dimmed in his world. Keeping her safe was all he'd ever wanted, so he'd told himself, but of course, he'd selfishly dreamed of more. Yet even protecting her was beyond his doing now. She wished no part of him.

'Should you nae be harvesting at Tomachcraggen, lad?' The father wiped the back of his neck with his kerchief. 'Lachlan will be cursing me for stealing ye away.'

'He'd have come himself had he nae business in Banff.'

'Banff?' The father raised a brow. 'Illicit business?'

'Wi' smuggler merchants in the town. They and their coastal fleet.'

The father drew a weary breath. 'So, I take it another string of laden ponies is about to leave Stratha'an, this time for Banff?'

'Soon as the hervest's ower, Father. 'Twill be James' last. He's sworn he'll smuggle no more now he's a marrit man.'

The father nodded thoughtfully. 'And what of the Black Gauger? He's alive, I hear.'

'He's been seen, aye, he and his men. Unharmed, though I can hardly fathom how. I saw him beaten wi' my own eyes.'

'You'll have a care, then? Will be wary?'

He nodded, watching a pair of lapwings drum the ground with their feet, calling their peesie call, listening for a tricked worm. Jem watched them, too, her bones too stiff now for chasing birds.

'Lachlan will never pay him passage. Nor will I.'

'Many have.'

'Aye, and more still regret nae doing so as soon as they're up afore McGillivray.'

'And you? You'll continue to smuggle? You seem ... weary of it, Duncan. Weary of life.' The priest laid down his scythe, leaning on the shaft as he considered him. 'I listen well, ye know, should ye care to try me.'

He banded the sheaf he'd gathered. 'I worry fer Rowena, is all.'

226

The father continued to study him. 'She's fascinated you since first you saw her, but she's a dark one. In many ways, I feel I'm to blame. She was a sensitive child; her mother's death distressed her greatly. Damaged her, perhaps. I trod clumsily with her. I fear I turned her from God, yet I see more of our Lord in that young woman than I do in many of my flock, though she's yet to cross my chapel door. I live in hope, though.'

'As do I.'

'I sense the Lord works through her as surely as He does through any ordained servant. Her healing's unquestionably a gift from God, but there's more.' He frowned. 'Her gentleness, the joy she derives from helping others. She's filled with the Holy Spirit. She's as spirit-filled as any churchman I've ever known, only she doesn't recognise it. She calls it by another name. I hope one day she'll see her mistake.'

'She's wise, Father, her heart's ....' Duncan shook his head, as ever struggling with words when it came to Rowena.

'Compassionate?'

'Aye, she's tender-herted, though I doubt she'll see things your way. 'Tis the hills and forests are Rowena's church.'

'Is that why you love her so much?'

He paused, bound oat sheaf in hand, his face reddening.

'I've eyes in my head, lad. Any fool can see how you feel about her.'

He raised his gaze wretchedly. 'But she doesna feel the same.'

'You're sure?'

* * *

To Duncan's surprise, the next day, the last of the harvest if the weather stayed with them, Rowena joined him and Jem in the infield at Tomachcraggen. Prepared to toil, she'd bound her hair up, exposing her slender neck, and had forsaken her arisaid, knowing the work would make her hot. She wore only a simple gown of heathland colours. Her beauty was devastating, cutting his heart to ribbons. Having her beside him, solely his for the whole day, stirred so many emotions, his legs trembled.

Yet she was changed. She seemed troubled, her sober mood tempering his happiness at having her to himself. He longed to ease her burden.

She smiled shyly at him, her head canted in a gesture so redolent of her childish self, so poignant with familiar yearnings, he blushed and glanced away, fearing his longings must show upon his face. But he couldn't keep his gaze away for long. As they toiled under a gravid sky, the hills echoing to the roar of red deer in rut, his gaze was persuaded back to her time and again. A starving man drawn to nourishment.

'I've missed ye, Rowena,' he said at last. 'I nae longer know where it is ye go each day. I worry about ye. Ye're wi' Morna, I suppose.' But he knew that wasn't true. He'd been at Druimbeag when the green woman came to tend Mhari. She came alone. When he asked after Rowena, she grew uneasy. She'd seen little of her, and he'd no reason to doubt that, but something about the way she said it made him anxious.

'I've missed ye, too.' She seemed reluctant to meet his gaze. 'I'd have helped more wi' the hervest had I'd been able.'

'I didna mean to chide ye.'

She nodded, and he knew she'd not share her troubles.

'I'm hoping Morna will come to bless the cutting o' the last sheaf.' She swept her gaze across the land, skimming pasture and rig, searching among whin and birch for a glimpse of the green woman. 'I long to see her.'

Cutting the last sheaf was a dangerous thing. The final sheaf was known as the *Cailleach*, the Old Woman. To the superstitious of the glen, which was almost everyone, it symbolised the Spirit of the Corn. Cutting it conferred ill-luck on whoever did so, although someone must. He knew he would cut it. But the green woman's rite was said to counter any ill-omen.

The custom was old, steeped in fable and fear, something Father Ranald frowned upon, yet Lachlan set much faith by it. The green woman came every year to perform it, somehow intuitively knowing when they'd cut their last sheaf. He supposed that, in her way, walking widdershins around the stooks, whispering ancient, forgotten words, she blessed the harvest and those whose livelihoods depended on it. Herbs and roots, bones, crystals from the Cairngorm mountains, all manner of things Morna deemed precious were employed. Finally, she anointed the *Cailleach* with water from a mountain spring and worked it into the top of the last stack to protect it.

The ritual had scandalised him once. He'd been ashamed to be associated with such heathenism, even as a reluctant onlooker, yet he accepted it now, judging it benign. He supposed the ancient rite had a sanctity of its own, and Rowena seemed to draw comfort from it. Knowing she did so made it tolerable.

Throughout the day, he swung his scythe in wide, arcing strokes, resting little, driven on by the rising wind and dark sky. Rowena gathered and bound what he cut, the relentless stoop and rise of her body echoing the flow of her song. Her voice, the sweetness and melancholy of it, roused him to join her, and together they lifted their voices, paying tribute to the land in the age-old way of the Gael. Their melody was a balm, soothing the tension between them, easing them into a shared rhythm. Only, the green woman did not come.

As the last of the light died in the west, and the shadows lengthened, he laid his scythe down, massaging his aching shoulders and stood before the final swathe of barley. With a sigh, he took up the scythe again.

Rowena gripped his hand. 'Nay, 'tis unlucky. Let me cut it.'

He shivered at her touch, then brought the blade swinging across his body, and in one stroke, it was done. He rubbed his face, dislodging husks from his beard, and half smiled in apology.

She stared back fearfully, a hand pressed to her mouth. Jem began to bark, and over her shoulder, away to the north near the ruin of Drumin, he fancied a dark figure watched them from among the trees.

CHAPTER TWENTY-THREE

Drumin
Strathavon
27ᵗʰ September 1760

Father,

I pray this letter finds you in sound health and trust my recent tidings have not overly displeased you. You may be relieved to learn my marriage has yet to take place. A minor obstacle presented itself, one I expect to surmount with only the slightest trouble and delay. The exchange of vows will take place in the local kirk, and you are cordially invited should you wish to venture north into these lawless glens. McGillivray has agreed to bear witness. He has become a useful acquaintance, as I will shortly elucidate.

I hope it gladdens your heart to know I am now fully recovered from the heinous assault upon my person. In writing again so soon, it is in the expectation the news I now bring will predispose you more warmly to my impending marriage.

As promised, I have been instrumental in the seizure and arrest of the witch I spoke of in my last letter. The crone now awaits trial for her crimes in Elgin's tollbooth.

The likely location of her lair was revealed to me by an informer in my employ. A girl claiming the hag had made her lair in the same evil wood where I was left for dead. As you can doubtless imagine, I was reluctant to return to that diabolical place. But, on informing McGillivray of the existence of this creature squatting on his grace's land, he swiftly marshalled the aid of a detachment of foot soldiers from Corgarff.

Together with my own hired men and a savage hound I recently procured, we made an impressive force, and I ventured into that wood with righteous steel in my veins. The dog finally tracked the witch to a secret lair deep in the forest, an ungodly place of giant trees and dark water.

Let me tell you of the evidence of wickedness we uncovered there. We caught her in the act, crouched over her fire, brewing some noxious potion. Her home, if her lair might be called that, was filled with the unmistakable evidence of her craft. Roots and bones, crystals, toadstools, poisonous greenery, faery-darts—she is unquestionably a conspirator with that race—charms, even a miniature keg of illicit whisky which I promptly confiscated. Her bed was a nest of hides where she doubtless committed carnal acts with the horned one.

Sadly, since the misguided Witchcraft Act of 1735, McGillivray informs me her offence can at best be only 'pretended witchcraft' as if she were some charlatan, rather than a true disciple of Satan. Yet, I tell you, Father, she is the real thing. If you saw her, you would instantly recognise that fact.

As you so vividly describe in your sermons, we found evidence of the ceremonial use of tools for making spells. Her loathsome appearance, her ungodly home and ways, the items we took away as evidence—Father, the proof was overwhelming. Yet, incredibly, she gave herself up without resistance, only with a barbed tongue in her head, for she believes herself innocent. Even unjustly persecuted, can you countenance!

She will certainly serve at least a year in gaol, likely much longer, for the fine levied upon her will doubtless be beyond her means to pay. In addition to the witchcraft charges, McGillivray has accused her of unlawfully occupying his grace's land. She had made her lair in that haunted wood without possession of a legal rental agreement, squatting there for years. The witnesses I will procure will testify to that fact.

So, there you have it, Father, I have been blessed with another victory here. In truth, this is a major coup for both McGillivray and myself. With our shared moral and religious values, we make a formidable partnership, and upon the witch's conviction, anticipate the duke will demonstrate his gratitude.

Likely my name will become well known to him. I hope he will equate it with loyalty, for I acted in his service. I believe I can rightly expect him to bestow his favour upon me. I'm left only to imagine what form that favour might take.

In carrying out this odious task, I hope I have demonstrated my regard for you and your work. In my darkest hours, I often comfort myself by conjuring your image. I imagine you relaying this tale to your congregation in the form of a sermon—a cautionary one. The thought sustains me in this barbarous land.

The light dwindles, Father, so I will close, but rest assured as ever it remains my intention to one day make you proud.

Ever your obedient servant and son,
Hugh

* * *

The daylight had gone, its afterglow merely a fiery memory and the sky was clear and crammed with stars. The moon, a full harvest moon, had already risen and would relentlessly illuminate her kinsmen's route through the hills with its cold, pearlescent light. Hardly a smuggler's friend. Rowena shivered. Darkness was a welcome accomplice on any illicit venture, but tonight, as her da and brothers prepared to lead the garrons north to Banff on the Moray Firth coast, they would be denied its collusion.

The wind rose, the air sharp in her nostrils, the birks whispering farewell to the last of their leaves. As she watched her kinsmen make their final preparations, her mouth was dry, her stomach leaden. Their safety troubled her. She'd not been back to Hugh since his disturbing proposal and could only pray he'd keep his promise. She'd sorely disappointed him, so she couldn't be sure, but even more worrying—where was Morna?

She'd found Morna's home empty that morning, her peat fire cold. No flame had burned there for days, something unthinkable. Hearth fires were never allowed to go out. Folk smoored them with ashes at night and kindled them into flame again come morning. Not only for superstition's sake but to keep the inside of the home dry, especially the sods of the roof. Once waterlogged and heavy, they soon collapsed in. Searching Morna's home for clues, water had dripped onto her head, slithering down her neck.

Shivering, she discovered herbs and mushrooms left to blacken on the bench, rank with the smell of decay. A layer of peat ash covered everything. In it, she recognised boot prints studded with hobnails and the prints of an animal. A dog. It had snuffled amongst Morna's possessions, leaving evidence of its snout and muzzle smeared in the dust.

Items were missing: the herbs that hung drying from the roof, the faery-darts Morna collected and held precious, crystals, notably the beautiful cairngorm Morna used for divination. She searched among the rocks of the hearth cairn, discovering the cherished crystal half hidden behind one of the larger stones. The blood drained from her face. Morna went nowhere without it.

Picking it up, she cleaned it of dust, polishing it until it gleamed with its smoky quartz fire. The knot in her stomach tightened—Morna had dropped it there as a message to her. Alarmed, and remembering Morna's chilling prophesy, she scrabbled in the hearth cairn with her fingers, delving into the crumbling crevices, pulling out roots and resins, then finally the calfskin package Morna had left there for her. Her talismans.

With trembling fingers, she tied the package in her arisaid along with the gemstone and took a last look around. The room was cold, unfamiliar. No birdsong came from outside; even the sacred spring seemed to have ceased its bubbling. All that had once been joyful here, all wisdom and insight, had gone. Had somehow died. Desperate to be gone too, she stumbled away.

She spent the rest of the day crisscrossing the hills and high pastures, the mountain passes, visiting every symbol stone and cairn, every sacred grove. Trees were Morna's greatest love. She scoured the places where special plants grew, circling back to the Avon, trawling among alder and whin where precious wormwood sheltered. Warily, she approached cot-house and byre, stopping folk in their fields, only to be met with blank faces. No one had seen her.

Finally, she forded the river to Druimbeag. In her absence, while she'd battled to save the exciseman, Morna had instinctively taken over Mhari's care. But Mhari had seen naught of Morna either. Not for days. She sank to the ground and wept. Mhari knelt beside her, gingerly stroking her shoulder, waiting for her grief to exhaust itself. When spent, she let Mhari help her up, and together they'd trudged back to Tomachcraggen.

* * *

Since John Meldrum's death, smuggling had become more dangerous. Now that Hugh had replaced him, smuggling was uniquely perilous. John had shared invaluable information about the redcoats' movements and revenue collectors' ploys. He'd understood the glen and its people, appreciating their need to remain on the land of their birth, their enduring love of that land, for he'd shared it. 'Twas a love born of knowledge of the harsh upland hillscape, of working it, watching it change through the seasons, shaped by wind, water and ice. Of the blood and toil given in homage to it. The kin lain to rest beneath it. He'd known that for most, leaving this glen was unimaginable. But to stay meant finding coin. Whisky-smuggling was the surest way. Those were her thoughts as she watched her kinsmen's final preparations.

Grace nudged her elbow. 'You tell them, they'll nae listen to me. Tell them to be heedful. Nae to be taking foolish risks. Especially James. He's Mhari to think on, and the bairn he's put in her belly.'

She swallowed. 'Likely, he kens that.' From the set of James' jaw, the tightness in his face, he seemed aware of little else.

'Cease yer fussing,' her da growled.

Mhari stood quietly, watching James, her fingers laced over her abdomen shielding the innocent inside. Her devotion was a living thing, it radiated from her, but there was fear there, too, though she'd not shame James by giving it a voice. They loved each other, so he'd be careful, her expression said. Duncan was the rash one. James was sensible, peace-loving.

Watching Mhari, Rowena struggled to swallow down her fear. She must be strong. Seeing her anguish, Duncan came to her at once.

'What is it?' He drew her aside, his gaze moving over her face. The battle to keep her tears away grew harder.

'There's something I would ask ye.'

'Anything.'

'Never would I put ye in danger, and I ken ye've nae great love fer her, but will ye listen fer word o' Morna?' A tremor came into her voice. 'She's gone. Her home's been violated. Soldiers had a hand in it; I saw the signs.' She pressed trembling fingers to her brow. 'I fear fer her.'

His face softened, and he took her trembling fingers and moulded them with his own. Shyly, he raised them to his lips, his eyes seeking communion with her. 'I'll find her. I promise.'

'I shouldna ask but ... thank ye.' She pressed his fingers.

He moved closer; she inhaled his earthy scent, knowing he wished to hold her. Reluctantly, she let him go. 'Ye'll have a care?'

He nodded, tight-faced.

* * *

The moonlight troubled Duncan, the cold brilliance of it, the shadows it made. He'd known stormy days darker than this. Leaving Tomachcraggen, they followed the course of the Avon, keeping to level ground, no one daring to speak. His thoughts were reflective, jostling to the creak of leather, the rhythmic thud of hooves on sod, the slosh of whisky against the sides of the barrels. The air was cold on his face, yet his flesh, warmed by exertion and the thrill of the night's mission, was clammy, flushed.

Nearing Drumin, they veered east, wary of the exciseman's home, climbing through the heather to skirt Carn Liath and Gallowhill and ford the Livet near Inchfindy before heading north-east.

Always the smuggling quickened his heart, both the danger and the thrill of outwitting the authorities. Tonight was no different. Buoyed by his added purpose, an opportunity to ease Rowena's heart, he quivered almost with fever. He conjured her face, heartbreakingly beautiful, and his heart ached. She'd entrusted him with this mission. He couldn't fail her. Thoughts of the danger she might now be in knotted his stomach. If soldiers had taken the green woman, mightn't they now turn their attention to her apprentice? The notion brought a wave of nausea.

Reaching Inchfindy, they passed the factor's home in silence, its cluster of steadings ghostly in the moonlight. As they neared the Livet, the rush of water grew loud in their ears, the riverbank thickly wooded. Aware of potential danger here, of the steep banking crowded with trees, the boulders waiting in the shadows like selkies, he drew his dirk. They would cross in single file, a man at the head, another taking up the rear, the third man midstream ensuring no garron slipped on weed-slimed stones or panicked and plunged into deeper water. Lachlan nodded to signify he should cross first.

Guiding the first pony into the water, he murmured a reassurance to it, moonlight silvering its back. The first three garrons were safe across when a flicker of movement between the trees made him stiffen. A figure stepped out of the shadows, its ghostly silhouette stretching to the water's edge. Two others joined it, and another, a low slinking thing, crept from the bushes.

'*Christ!*' Lachlan appeared at his shoulder. ''Tis the Black Gauger and his men.'

His heart hammered. Some in the glen now considered McBeath the

235

devil himself. He possessed uncanny foreknowledge of smugglers' move-ments, had reappeared in their midst unharmed after his beating at Ardbreckan—risen from the dead with his black heart.

'Well, well.' The exciseman raised his musket to his shoulder. 'If it's no' the Innes smugglers. A fair tally ye have there. Only,' he stepped into the full glare of the moon. 'I dinnae recall receiving a penny in passage from ye. No' a shilling for all these barrels ye seem hell-bent on spiriting away.'

White-faced, James joined them on the riverbank, the garrons bunch-ing together, whickering. Duncan translated for Lachlan.

'Nor will ye,' Lachlan growled. 'If ye want my whisky, ye'll need to tak' it from me.' He drew his pistol.

McBeath laughed harshly. 'Reckless words, Innes.' He lowered his musket. 'Hasty words. I've a proposal I wish to put to you. Something you'll doubtless prefer to gaol and a crippling fine. Drive the garrons up here so I can put it to ye face to face.'

Lachlan quirked a brow at James, who shrugged back, mystified.

'Dinna be trusting him,' Duncan warned.

'I trust him nae further than I could hurl him,' Lachlan muttered. 'But any skirmish will more likely go our way up there, on flatter ground.'

After a whispered exchange, Duncan agreed. With tight fists and a pounding heart, he drove the garrons up the banking onto pastureland, the hirelings observing him with feigned indifference, lounging against a tree.

The ponies bunched together, wary of the circling dog with its powerful, jowl-swinging jaws. He knew the type—bow-legged, bred to bait bulls, seizing the beasts by the nose. It kept up a furious growling, making the ponies snort and swish their tails. He tried to calm them, feeling the exciseman's hard stare on his back, the same inexplicable resentment emanating from him that he'd felt before. When he turned to meet it, the gauger shifted his attention back to Lachlan.

'We meet in earnest, Innes. This day's been long in coming.'

Lachlan snorted. 'We met afore, if ye mind, at my son's wedding. Ye'll forgive my lack o' enthusiasm on meeting ye again.'

'But I jested with you on that occasion.'

'Did ye? Well, what is it ye want now if it's nae my whisky?'

'I've a proposition for you, one that'll serve us both, smuggler and revenue man alike.'

'What would that be?'

In the full glare of the moon, the gauger's face was greased with sweat.

236

He wet his lips with a flick of tongue. 'What if I said you could smuggle unhindered and for the rest of your days with only a small condition attached?'

Duncan frowned. 'That being?'

'I've a fancy to take myself a wife, Lachlan.'

'Have ye? Weel, I dinna fancy ye mysel'.' Lachlan blew him a kiss. 'Ye're nae my type.'

Dougal sniggered.

'Someone winsome. Easy on the eye, ye could say. No' just any woman, but your daughter.' The gauger's eyelid twitched, a mannerism he seemed unable to control. 'I wish Rowena for my wife. Might we come to an arrangement?'

'Ye want us to sell her?' James gasped.

'Your words, no' mine. Convince her is how I'd put it. She'd be contributing to her family's welfare. Freeing her kinsmen to smuggle unmolested. There'd be little need to fear the factor, to worry over the next quarter day's rent. I'd let you smuggle to yer heart's content.'

'But,' Duncan croaked, too stunned to think clearly. 'How d'ye know Rowena? I mean, have ye even met beyond briefly at my brother's wedding?'

An indulgent twitching of the lips now. A smile barely contained. 'Of course, we've met.'

'When?'

'Let's just say I've observed her peculiar allure.'

Remembering the man's unhealthy interest in her on James' wedding day, his offensive staring, Duncan's blood ran cold.

Confused, Lachlan turned to his sons for a translation. Through clenched teeth, James attempted to give one. Lachlan loured at the gauger.

'So, Innes,' McBeath went on. 'You understand what I'm offering? A thing of great value. You may smuggle like there's no tomorrow, pilfer from the treasury in the most outrageous fashion, and I'll no' interfere. All I ask is Rowena for my wife.'

'She's nae fer sale,' James said bluntly.

'Did I ask you?'

'My sister's nae a chattel to be bartered and sold. D'ye imagine my da would sell his own daughter? And to a gauger? Ye're insane.'

'I conduct my business with the auld dog, no' the whelp.' The gauger's tone was cold; his hand moved to the hilt of his sword. 'It's no' as if there'd be little profit in it for Rowena. I'd protect her. She displays some unwise traits. I refer to her witchery; I'd soon stamp that out. 'Twas because of me they arrested the old witch in Sìthean Wood. The crone awaits trial in Elgin thanks to *my* pious efforts.'

Duncan paled.

'Surely, that demonstrates my integrity. I'll return Rowena to God. Save her immortal soul. And, of course, as my wife, she'll enjoy every comfort. Wealth, an elegant home, the finest fashions. She'll want for naught, including a position in society. Things *you* cannae give her.'

'What makes ye think she wants those things?' James' tone was scornful. 'Gain acquired through the suffering of others.'

'What woman does not?'

'Many, and Rowena's nae like other women.'

'I'm aware of that.'

At Duncan's comment, McBeath turned to him with his hatred laid bare. A cold enmity. The only thing still unclear was the reason for it. Yet, what the man said was true. He could never give Rowena any of those things. He'd always understood they held no value to her, but did they? The seed of doubt was a potent germ—it rooted easily.

'Well, McBeath.' Lachlan fixed him with a murderous glare. 'Ye've had yer answer. My daughter's nae fer sale at any price.'

'But should ye need that answer reinforced,' James drew his dirk, 'I'll gladly oblige. Ye've insulted my sister. Sullied her name.'

'Wait, James.' Duncan drew his dirk, too. '*I'll* take on the blaggard. He'll nae blacken Rowena's name.' Fury boiled inside him; the man would bargain with a woman's life, expected her delivered like a lamb for slaughter. And nae just any woman, but the most innocent and loving one imaginable.

At the edge of his vision, Ghillie and Dougal jerked forward, drawing pistols. He turned to face them, hurling his dirk into the grass. 'And I'll do it wi' naught but what the good Lord gave me.' Bunching his fists, he began to circle the exciseman.

McBeath exploded with laughter. 'I could take on the pair of ye bare-fisted and no' disturb a hair on my head. I could beat ye both to oblivion and no' even raise a sweat.'

James was also circling the exciseman, moving his dirk from hand to hand. 'Stay out o' this, Duncan. I'll nae have ye hurt again. She's *my* sister; it needs to be me.'

'Ye've Mhari to think on,' he reasoned. 'She'd nae thank ye fer this.'

'God's blood!' McBeath spluttered. 'You mean this upstart's no' even her brother?' He gaped at Duncan. 'Who are ye, then?'

'Thon's aboot the size o' it,' Ghillie confirmed. 'Tomachcraggen took him in. As a lad, an orphan. From the priest I telt ye aboot. Redcoats fired his hame.' He glanced uncomfortably at Duncan. ''Twas a well-known nest o' Jacobites.'

McBeath's mouth fell open. 'Then he doesnae even share a drop of blood with Rowena? He's a trickster with no connection to her. No claim on her affections, other than her pity.'

Duncan faltered, the insecurities crowding back. He was an imposter with no right to prevent Rowena bettering herself if she wished.

'You want her yourself,' the gauger accused. 'Deny it. I challenge you.'

'No man calls my brother a trickster,' James growled.

'Duncan's my son.' Lachlan picked the discarded dirk out of the grass and handed it back. Their eyes met briefly, Lachlan's unflinching. 'He mightna share my blood, but he shares my heart. He's my son in every way that matters.'

'I beg to differ,' whined McBeath. 'He gives himself airs. Harbours designs of his own for Rowena.'

'D'ye love my daughter?' Breathing hard, Lachlan nailed the exciseman with his eyes.

'I ... possess strong feelings for her.' Again, the veiled smile. 'She's bewitched me.'

'I didna ask if ye wanted her, I can see that. D'ye love her?'

'I—'

''Tis a simple question.'

'I'm consumed with passion for her, yes, easily enough to fulfil my role as husband.' He laughed. 'Have no fear on that account.'

Lachlan snorted. 'My daughter's a free woman. Since ever she was a bairn, I've allowed her a deal o' freedom. Duncan's right, she's nae like other women. I doubt the things ye offer will sway her, but she's free to choose her own match. If ye love each other, I'll nae stand in yer way.'

'Then you see the advantage in this match? The profit in it for you?'

'I do. I'm nae a fool.'

McBeath exhaled in triumph. 'I knew you would. This union would be in your interest. Convincing her, your wisest course.'

''Tis fer you to be doing that. If she loves ye, it shouldna be so hard.'

The exciseman's face twitched with irritation. 'But you see the benefit to you? The gain?' He stared at Lachlan, eventually muttering, 'Of course, you do.' He nodded slowly. 'But it sits better with you, a hardened smuggler, to make a show of opposing me.' He jerked his head at the hirelings. 'Let them through.'

Lachlan's eyes widened.

'You'll persuade her.' He stepped back to let them pass, his face stiffening as James swept him a mocking bow. 'I know ye will. Ye'll no' be able to help yourself.'

* * *

Elgin held no warm memories for Duncan. He'd been here only once before, for John's trial, spending that night in the 'black hole', a vaulted cavity beneath the council chambers where petty criminals were kept in a dank cell. Given neither food nor water and denied medical attention, he'd lain bleeding in a filthy corner, his eyes swelling shut, listening to the scurrying of rats and the foul-mouthed banter from the guardhouse next door. Every inch of him had hurt.

Looking at the tollbooth now, its sandstone walls stained with the contents of latrines emptied from the battlement parapet above, a handcart abandoned by the tower, he shuddered, searching for the place where the scaffold had stood. There was no trace of it now—no evidence of the injustice committed here. Nothing to mark the life valued and respected in the glens, but cruelly extinguished here. Perhaps 'twas as well; he'd half-feared John might still be hanging. Or at least, what the corbies had left of him.

He'd taken leave of Lachlan and James by the Burn of Tervie, and with a heavy heart, had skirted the boggy eastern slope of the Hill of Deskie and headed north to Elgin. There'd been little quarrel from the others; they all agreed one of them must go there. That he would wish to do so perhaps surprised them; his dislike of the green woman was no secret, but they accepted his desire to help her without comment. What mattered was Morna, that whatever could be done for her was done.

Strangely, despite his views on her unchristian ways, he felt an overwhelming sadness at her arrest, while the thought of bringing Rowena news of it caused him physical pain. He hoped he'd be permitted to see her, that he might bring her some comfort. Rowena would wish it, James and Lachlan, too.

His kinsmen had carried on to Banff, they and their cargo perhaps now protected to a degree. At least, he prayed so.

His journey to Elgin took the best part of two days. Snatching an hour or two of sleep wherever he could, he'd trudged mile after mile through forest and heathland with naught for company but the voice in his head. A voice that refused to be stilled and was obsessed with one subject—the Black Gauger's desire for Rowena.

His thoughts turned feverishly, his head aching, his heart, too. Rumours abounded of McBeath's cruelty. How might he treat Rowena? The question consumed him. Was she aware of his passion for her? Did she perhaps return it? His imagination played cruelly with him. He'd seen little of her lately; how had the gauger become so familiar with her? McBeath was a forceful man, certainly in temper, perhaps in charm if he chose to be. Attractive to women, he supposed. Yet 'twas hard to believe Rowena would be taken in by him.

As he neared Elgin, he began to question how the authorities there might treat the green woman. A telling weight in the pit of his stomach told him he already knew. Having been arrested on witchcraft charges, the soldiers and townsfolk would be quick to judge her. Particularly her appearance. They'd view her with disgust and loathing, that loathing would colour her treatment. Trudging on, it occurred to him he'd done the same. In truth, what harm had she ever done him, other than to draw Rowena under her spell? Something he'd always despised her for. His harsh judgment of her now appalled him.

Looking up at the tollbooth's prison tower now, he sincerely hoped she was not incarcerated in the infamous third floor. Here, inmates were said to be fettered to an iron bar, a hole high in the wall admitting a tiny square of sky. Naught to keep the rain and skirling winds out, no hearth to give comfort or warmth.

How to get in to see her, though? 'Twas barely dawn, the sky no longer clear but threatening rain, the wind rising. He'd not be welcome at the guardhouse at this hour. He stepped back into the mouth of a narrow wynd, within its shadows, wrapping his plaid tighter, and prepared to wait.

The prison tower was reached by an external stone staircase. As it began to rain, he observed two men negotiate their way down the stair carrying a cumbersome bundle. At the foot of the stairs, they heaved their burden into the waiting handcart, stopping to rub aching muscles. Watching them manhandle the object, his heart faltered. The bundle had unravelled, revealing limbs that flopped over the sides of the cart. He broke into a sweat.

The men folded the limbs back in, then, taking a shaft each hauled the cart and its contents along the High Street. Stepping out of the shadows, he followed them. The High Street was cobbled, the cart's wooden wheels unevenly worn; as it rattled along, he fell in behind it. The body was wrapped in a length of tattered material snagged with moss and shards of pinecone. So familiar was the garment, the shock of recognition brought

241

a surge of anger. With a hiss, he jerked forward and yanked it away.

What lay beneath was repugnant. Her mouth hung open, the flesh shrivelled from her face, her eyes sunk in their sockets. The life that once so animated her had gone. In death, Morna looked older than the hills.

'Hey!' Dropping the cart, the men whirled to face him, drawing weapons: a small dirk and a *sgian-dubh*.

'Who did this?' he choked.

'What's it to you?' the dirk-wielder hissed. 'She was a witch. Look at her!'

'*Who did this?*' His dirk had materialised in his hand.

The younger man eyed his foot-long blade with alarm. He was only a youth. 'Nae us. She just died. Eh, Willie?'

'Aye, 'tis what she did.' The older man removed his bonnet. 'Doubtless, the soldiers had a play wi' her, but they didna kill her. She was fer trial; they darena be doing that. She died o' ....' He frowned, considering. 'Grief, I suppose. She whimpered and keened, rocked herself, wailed o' needing the forest around her, the trees and their spirits, the wide skies and hills.' He shrugged. 'Like Archie said, she was a witch.'

'But no one just dies. Especially nae her. She was vital, full o' life.'

'Then likely, she took it harder than most being confined, specially in a dark cell. She took naught to drink and niver touched a morsel, just muttered in Gaelic. Summoned the divil fer all I ken. But she lived in filth. Disease stalks those that do so.'

'Ye mean,' he glanced up at the prison tower, 'she died up there? Slowly. Alone. Of disease or ... or a broken spirit?'

The man replaced his bonnet. 'Seems so. I'm sorry if she was kin.'

'Twas unimaginable. Too cruel to contemplate. Swallowing, he spread her arisaid back over her, covering what remained of her dignity with the tattered old thing, tucking it in as if to keep her warm. 'Twas all he could do for her now. 'Where are ye taking her?' he croaked.

Archie looked curiously at him. 'Fer burial.'

'But where?'

'She wasna a Christian.' Willie frowned. 'No kirk will hae her. She's to go in the common pit.'

'The common pit?'

'Where criminals go,' Archie supplied. 'Efter they've been hanged. Wi' a spadeful o' quicklime to stop 'em from reeking too bad.'

'Oh, God.'

''Tis how it's done.'

Never could he tell Rowena this.

CHAPTER TWENTY-FOUR

October 1760

JAMES AND LACHLAN rode in with the garrons as the light slipped from the day. Their shouts flushed Rowena from the threshing barn, brushing chaff from her face and hair. They were in high spirits, clasping each other by the forearm, but there was no sign of Duncan.

Having seen their whisky safely stowed aboard a fishing boat bound for Leith, they'd left Banff with bulging pouches. James had enough coin to meet his first rental payment due at Martinmas in six weeks, but he'd decided not to use the money for that. If he bought cattle fattened over the summer months and drove them south to the drover's tryst at Crieff in three weeks, he could perhaps double his money. He could make enough to meet his rental and have coin left for buying breeding stock to build up his herd. 'Twould be tight getting there and back in time to meet the quarter day's rent, but he was convinced he could do it.

Her da was more sceptical. James was no drover, and the droving routes were dangerous. Reivers and cattle thieves stalked the drove ways, waiting for any man fool enough to drive his own beasts. 'Twas why drovers banded together and bristled with arms, driving herds of up to a thousand head. They were hardened, ferocious men. They needed to be.

But James was insistent. This way, he could secure a decent future for Mhari and their unborn child. In one journey, perilous and punishing, he could make enough to prove his worth as a tenant and also grow his precious herd. He need never smuggle again. He planned to show the rest of the glen it could be done.

'That's grand, James,' Rowena whispered. 'But where's Duncan?' With all this talk of cattle and coin, why was there no mention of Duncan? Where was he?

Her da cast James a dark look, and he fell silent. Leaving rubbing down the garrons to Grace, he took her gently by the arm. 'The thing is, lass, we heard ill news on our way to Banff. Morna's been arrested. Duncan's gone to Elgin to see what can be done.'

'Arrested?' She stared at him.

'On witchcraft charges. 'Tis troubling news, I ken, but try nae to worry. Whatever can be done, Duncan will do. Ye mun hae faith in him.'

'I do,' she whispered, her chest tightening. ''Tis soldiers and magistrates I dinna trust.'

He nodded, looking ill at ease.

'There's more, Da. I ken there is.'

'I've telt ye all I ken o' the healing woman.' He frowned, searching her face. 'We had a run-in wi' the Black Gauger, is all. Fer reasons best known to himsel', he let us through untouched.'

'Oh!' She blushed furiously. 'I believe he's a fair man, Da. I doubt he deserves his black reputation.'

He grimaced noncommittally and turned back to the garrons.

Duncan returned the next day.

He was sitting at the table when she came in, Grace plying him with bannocks and broth. They stopped talking when she entered. Duncan rose with a scrape of chair, clutching his bonnet.

'Would ye mebbe tak' a walk wi' me, Rowena?'

She nodded, not trusting her voice.

They crossed the stubble together, the bracken golden now, the birks too, and she thought of her mother, how she'd loved this dying time of year: the splendour and brilliance before the months of aching cold. She could feel Duncan's pain as he walked beside her. He'd never been able to hide his feelings, and she knew what he'd tell her before he said a word. Morna had gone to the next realm—she'd never see her again. Tears burned; she stumbled, her vision blurring.

He caught her by the elbow, guiding her to the dead birch tree her da had refused to cut down. Storms had stripped the bark from its bones, and its mushroomy old trunk was almost on the ground now. By law, it belonged to the duke, every tree in the glen did, but Da said the factor could come for it if he must. He'd nae be cutting it down himself. Fearn had loved it too much.

They sat apart, aware of the new distance between them. Grief tightened her throat. Knowing this was the last news he'd wish to bring her, she tried to spare him.

'Was it a good death?' she choked. 'A soft, slipping away?'

'*Ye know?*'

'My soul did, I think. Morna foresaw her own end. She tried to prepare me.'

He swallowed, struggling for words as he'd done as a boy.

'Just tell me no one hurt her. Please tell me that.'

'I give ye my word; if any death can be gentle, I believe hers was.'

'Bless ye.'

Despair surged, and she rocked and keened, struggling to stay afloat. Even over her sobs, she could hear Duncan breathing, wrestling over what to do. When he spoke again, his voice sounded strange.

'She may be gone, but she doesna leave this world unchanged. She touched folk. She touched you. I was envious once, wretch that I am, but there are folk living in this glen, a great many I think, who only do so because o' her.'

'Oh, Duncan.'

'If I could tak' yer pain away, if I could tak' it upon myself, I'd do it a hundred times ower.'

The sobs came harder; she hid her face in her hands.

He moved close, bringing an arm awkwardly around her, and she leaned into him, breathing his familiar scent. With a groan, he pressed her to his chest. She gripped him as fiercely, knowing she shouldn't, 'twas unfair, but the comfort was profound. For long moments she clung to him while he stroked her back and whispered things only a lover should say.

When finally she twisted herself free, he made a small bereft sound.

* * *

The hills and forests were her solace now. In her grief, Rowena turned to the earth and her healing arts with a desperate devotion, ranging over hill and heath, striving to ease suffering wherever she found it.

Often Mother Earth placed bounty directly in her path, and she shivered with the knowledge 'twas never by chance. So it was with the nettles. Nurture for the blood, Morna called them. She found the patch sheltering by the ruins of an old cot-house, a rare find in the hills, especially at this time of year. Whispering her thanks, she knelt to take what could be spared. She'd make a tonic to fortify Mhari for the approaching birth and another for Evie McHardy. Evie was over the worst of her fever but was still gravely ill.

As she filled her creel, her thoughts turned to Isobel. She'd met her only the day before. She met Isobel often and in all manner of unusual places. Hugh sent her on many errands, she supposed. The lass was popular, always finding time to ask after folk's troubles. A blatherskite her da called her, too free with her talk of whisky for his liking.

Isobel had been in high spirits. Her da had been freed from gaol, his debt paid in full. He was back working the land near Croughly. 'Twas all thanks to Hugh, she claimed, for he was surely the best employer.

To Rowena, the man was a puzzle, his cruel reputation well-founded, according to Duncan. James and her da were scornful of him, too. But for all his reputed heartlessness and his troubling proposal which she'd tried to put from her mind, he'd kept his promise. He'd turned a blind eye to her menfolk's smuggling.

She got to her feet, looping the creel's straps around her shoulders. Straightening, she gave a start. The exciseman was sitting astride his horse only feet away, his dog skulking at its tail. He dismounted and strode purposefully toward her.

A prickle of alarm fired along her spine. How had he known she was here? The old cot-house lay in a desolate spot. But of course, he'd not known. His reason for being here likely had naught to do with her.

He was all smiles, walking without a limp.

'Rowena! What a welcome surprise.' He took her hand and brought it to his lips as if she were royalty, then seemed loath to release it. 'I'm sorely wounded you've no' been to visit me.' He regarded her sternly, pulling a woeful face. 'Your neglect cuts me to the quick.'

'Forgive me, sir. There was the harvest to bring in, then dreadful news came, and I thought ye'd little need o' me, anyhow.'

'Hugh, you must remember to call me Hugh. I had no *need* of you, Rowena. I'm healed. Renewed, in fact.' He whacked his afflicted leg with his riding whip to demonstrate. 'But I *wanted* you!' He laughed wickedly.

Wary of him, she drew back.

He tightened his hold on her hand, caressing her captured palm. 'I've missed you and your gentle ways.'

Aware she could not truthfully say the same, she slipped her hand free, struggling for something to say.

He let his drop. 'You're well, then? Your family?'

'Well, sir, aye. And I wish to thank ye for what ye did for us.' Her cheeks flushed. 'You kept your word. 'Tis no small thing ye did. I'm grateful si ... Hugh.'

His smile broadened. 'You know of that? Well, I'm glad. You kept your word also, I think—our secret. Ye've told no one of our arrangement. No' even your family?'

'Nae a soul, sir. I'd not put ye in danger.'

He nodded, considering her, the corners of his mouth twitching.

'And my kinsmen will be less trouble in future,' she added. 'Leastways, one of them. James has given up the whisky. He means to farm the land at Druimbeag, where he holds the lease. To raise cattle, but not break the law. Not with a wife and bairn. Banff was the last of it. He means to buy cattle. Fine beasts he'll drive to Crieff.'

'I see.' He frowned.

'He's away with Duncan now, searching for such beasts.'

'Commendable,' he muttered through clenched teeth.

'My only worry is whether he'll make it to the tryst in time, then home for Martinmas to meet his rental.'

McBeath fell silent while he digested this. 'Your brother has set himself a formidable task, Rowena. He must be back by the eleventh day of November, yet I assume he has no droving experience.'

'He believes he can do it.'

'Well, I warn you: McGillivray holds no sympathy with those who miss payments. Lease agreements are binding documents. Failure to pay will no' be tolerated.'

''Tis what I thought.' Although hearing it put so bluntly sent a shiver down her spine.

'Anyway.' He seemed to brighten. 'I hope you've given thought to our last conversation. Have been persuaded of the benefits our union would bring. I'll soon be a wealthy man. I can give you things no man in these parts can match. You know that, I assume?'

'I do, sir.' Would he make her refuse him again? Her stomach churned at the prospect.

'Then, I hope you've allowed yourself to be convinced.'

She swallowed, not entirely sure what he meant. 'Forgive me, sir, but I've no need of a husband. I'm a healer, and since Morna's gone ...' her voice betrayed her with a quiver, 'my skills are more needed than ever.'

'Morna?'

'My teacher and guide. Morna was wise; folk called her a *draoidh*. But she's passed to the next realm.'

'Dead?'

She nodded.

He looked startled, then his expression hardened. 'I cannae say I've heard of her, but I fail to see the connection.'

'She was a gifted healer. 'Tis her work I do. Only, now she's gone, there's more work than ever.'

A muscle tightened in his cheek. 'Married to me,' he rasped, 'there'd be no need for such work. Demeaning yourself.' He flicked his hand at the creel on her back. 'Laden like a pack-horse. Pandering to these muck-the-byres.' He gestured with his head, encompassing a great sweep of hill and glen. 'Dabbling in the black arts.'

'They're my folk, sir. I do it for the love of them. There's naught ill in it.'

He exhaled, nostrils flaring in frustration. 'The Kirk would see it otherwise. Surely you know that? My faither is a minister. I know more about these things than most. What you speak of is witchery. And I fail to understand your stance. As my wife, I'd protect you. I'd give you whatever you desire. A perfect arrangement, I suggest, as you'd doubtless satisfy every one of my desires.' A twitch of a smile threatened, but he quickly censored it.

'I desire only to be a healer, sir.'

'Hugh, God damn it!'

'Forgive me, I do forget, Hugh.' She swallowed, her mouth dry.

He paced back and fore, swishing his riding whip through the air, his boots churning the grass, crushing what was left of the nettles. Their green scent nipped her nostrils. Finally, he slowed to study her. For long, uncomfortable moments, he prowled her body, lingering at her breasts, his gaze ranging south. His face worked with passion, his eyes dark with it.

She flushed, sensing his desire and the effort required to master it. A vein throbbed in his neck. She tensed, heart fluttering. 'Twas this potent sense of power, of arousal barely restrained that she fancied Isobel found so intoxicating.

Finally, he flashed her a smile, a fleeting ghost of a thing as he regained control. 'I'll no' argue the point. I see you've yet to be convinced, despite my efforts. I hope your brother hasnae poisoned you against me. He'd doubtless prefer you wed to the Young Jacobite.'

'Young Jacobite?'

'Never mind.'

Confused, she murmured, 'I'm sorry if I've displeased you.'

'I'm no' displeased, Rowena.' Although his black countenance suggested otherwise. 'But I dinnae give up so easily. Whatever I desire, I usually get in the end.'

Her face must have betrayed her alarm, for he gentled his tone. 'Forgive me; I'm disheartened. In my desire for you, I'm easily grieved.' He retook her hand and pressed it to his lips, inhaling deeply as if she were snuff. She flinched at the scratch of his beard. 'Be assured of my continued ardour and affection.'

Releasing her hand, he swept her a bow, then with a curt cry to his dog, turned on his heel and stalked to his horse. Mounted, he nodded to her and rode away.

As she watched his retreating figure, a wave of relief swept over her. Only, her relief was tempered by contrition. Despite all he'd done for her and would hopefully continue to do, again, she'd disappointed him.

* * *

As the days shortened, moving toward Samhain, the only cattle left in the glen were those kept as breeding stock or deemed too weak to survive the arduous journey to market in the south. Only robust beasts would survive such a journey. It involved wending through mountain passes, crossing moors, negotiating forests and bogs, fording rivers, often in spate. The herd must be kept together, continually on the move, and guarded at all times, especially at night.

There were routes to follow, ancient droving tracks where thieves known as reivers lurked—armed, vicious men who made stealing cattle their business. But without a sturdy herd to catch the buyers' eye, any droving venture was destined to fail.

To find such a herd, James and Duncan were forced to travel far and wide: north into Moray's fertile lands, east through the Corryhabbie hills and the Blackwater Forest into Aberdeenshire, then south to Strathdon.

They were away many days, and Rowena fretted. James carried on him all the coin he owned in the world. At least he had Duncan, but whenever she thought of what he planned to do, a dark cloud settled over her.

Her da had been against the venture from the start but did naught to stop it. James was a grown man. He'd be a father soon. She supposed he judged it hardly his place to be telling his son how to live his life, but she shared his misgivings. Keeping a roof over their heads had always been Da's first concern.

Despite her fears, James returned with choice beasts. Hard bargains had been won, according to Duncan. James had spent every penny he owned, along with Duncan's share from Banff. Coin Duncan gladly gave him.

Her da was impressed. He ran his hands over solid flanks, examined teeth and hooves, peering under long fringes into liquid brown eyes.

'Tolerable beasts,' he muttered. 'Let's be praying they still look that wey by the time ye get them to Crieff.' But there was genuine respect in his voice.

'I'm glad ye approve.' James' smile stretched wider than the sky. 'Ye'll agree there's coin to be made from these beasts, then?'

'Mebbe. If ye're nae robbed blind on the wey there. Or on the road back.'

'We'll be vigilant, eh Duncan?'

Duncan nodded tightly.

James' enthusiasm was hard to keep down. When Grace wished him all the luck in the world, he grasped her by the waist, whisking her around until she shrieked to be put down.

'Bless ye,' he beamed. 'I've a good feeling about this. Wi' my profit, I'll add to my own herd.'

'Pay yer rent first,' her da warned.

Thus far, James' herd comprised only two scraggy milch cows as far as Rowena was aware. She glanced at Duncan, and they exchanged an uneasy look.

Then James was away, whistling, urging the beasts on with a switch of hazel, eager to get home to Mhari and show her what he'd given up the whisky for.

'I'll be back fer ye just efter dawn,' he called to Duncan.

But he was back before dawn. The new day was barely a glimmer when he burst into the cot-house, breathless, his eyes wild and clothing dishevelled. Her da was splashing his face and stared at him.

'What is it?'

'They're gone. The cattle. Every last one.'

'Gone?'

'Taken in the night.'

Her da blinked. 'Plundered, ye mean? Ye're certain? They've nae just wandered?'

The firelight made shadows of James' face. 'I was bone-tired and slept like the dead, but Mhari heard naught either. A few dung-pats among the weeds, that's all there is to show they ever existed.'

Grace clapped a hand to her mouth. 'Faith! Who'd take them?

Reivers?'

He shrugged, making a despairing sound.

Duncan stared at him. 'But James, how would reivers ken the beasts were there?'

'Aye, lad.' Her da dried his face. 'Who kent ye had them?'

James stared back blankly. 'Only the hill farmers I bought from. I bought a cow here, anither there. I explained what I planned to do, of course.' Aghast, he turned to Duncan. 'Ye dinna think they imagined I boasted, do ye? Bragged o' proving 'tis possible to keep body and soul thegither wi'out smuggling? Dear God, did I only rouse them to prove me wrong?'

'Nay, James.' Duncan frowned. 'They were glensmen. They wished ye well. Even those wi' nae cattle to sell hoped ye'd make it. Ye could see it in their faces. They admired yer boldness. We'll find the beasts; they canna be far.'

But that was supposing they knew which direction the thieves had taken. Rowena pressed James' hand, a small gesture, and he looked wretchedly at her. If reivers had stolen his cattle, they both knew they'd be long gone.

Her da dressed quickly, tucking his pistol into his belt along with a pouch of shot. He tested the keenness of his dirk on a strip of leather and sheathed it at his girdle, then hung his powder horn from his neck. 'Let's away. If the cattle are to be found, by God, we'll find them.'

But they returned at day's end with drawn faces. James slumped at the fire, despair dragging his features. He should be getting home to Mhari, she'd be fraught with worry, but he needed time to steel himself. Returning to his pregnant wife to tell her he'd let their future be stolen was the last thing he wished to do.

'There's a foul stink about this,' her da muttered.

'I sense the Black Gauger's hand in it,' Duncan agreed. 'There's little love lost atween him and James. Or any o' us.'

Such a judgement seemed unfair. Hugh had helped them, though they hardly seemed grateful. 'Ye're wrong,' she blurted. 'I canna believe Hugh would do such a thing. Even being he's a gauger and must do the most despised work, I believe he's a decent man.'

Duncan stared at her.

'What d'ye ken o' him?' Her da squinted suspiciously at her.

'Little.' She drew back. She must say naught to put Hugh in danger. 'He might seem black-hearted, but I imagine 'tis how he paints himself. So folk dinna think him soft. Likely he's a fair man. I mean, did he nae allow ye safe passage to Banff?'

Duncan exchanged a look with her da, who twitched his brows at him. Frowning, her da laid a hand on James' shoulder.

'Ye mun go to the factor, lad. Tell him what's befallen ye. If yer cattle were taken last night, chances are others were, too. Be respectful, nae matter what the man says, and let's be praying ye find McGillivray in a lenient mood.'

James swallowed. The factor was hardly known for his forbearance.

'I could come wi' ye,' Duncan offered. 'If 'twould help.'

'I'd appreciate yer company.'

'Just dinna go saying anything to inflame the man.' Lachlan frowned at Duncan. 'Mind what happened last time ye stood up to the authorities.'

James gave a bitter laugh. 'I doubt there's anything Duncan could say could make things any worse.'

* * *

Duncan had never set foot inside Inchfindy Hall. He'd accompanied Lachlan to the estate office located in one of the steadings on quarter days to pay their rent and witness the formal recording of their payment in the great ledger McGillivray kept. But the house he'd only ever viewed from a distance through curious eyes.

The factor was a keen huntsman and enjoyed entertaining like-minded gentlemen at his home—a home more hunting lodge than house, far grander than anything nearby. Expansive lawns sloped to the river, hard-won from heather and pine. The sandstone building itself was three-storied, twin turrets flanking the grand entrance. It bore no resemblance to the squat, heather-thatched dwellings of stone and turf clustered amongst the surrounding hills. The only homes Duncan had ever known.

Making their way up the birch-lined track, he felt his palms clammy and innards restless. He glanced at James, dressed in his best clothes and walking with the natural grace of the Highlander. James bore himself with quiet dignity, despite coming to admit he lacked the means to pay his rent and wished to plead clemency. His thoughts would be with Mhari and their unborn child; guilty thoughts, he supposed, full of shame and remorse. He knew such thoughts. He'd lived with similar regrets since boyhood and prayed McGillivray would show compassion.

Poised at the massive, iron-studded door, they turned to each other, bonnets clutched in hands. James's eyes were dark, fearful. A deal of wrangling ensued with a dour-faced man in gaudy livery who opened the door and squinted suspiciously at them. They were finally admitted and passed beneath ranks of mounted stag's heads with glassy eyes to a plush, book-lined study.

Never had Duncan seen so many books. He owned a copy of the Holy Bible Father Ranald had given him and that he'd learned almost word for word, but never for a moment had he imagined so many books existed. Whole worlds were likely contained within them. Waiting beside James in the centre of the room, he longed to explore.

After some twenty minutes, the factor appeared dressed in checked breeches and doublet and accompanied by another dour-faced manservant, apparently brought as interpreter. McGillivray wore a petulant expression, his face registering his displeasure.

'Now, see here,' he whined, flicking a hand at them. 'If you've come to proffer excuses for failure to pay, Donnell will escort you out. I've heard every pretext and excuse. None will I countenance.' He stood with his back to an enormous fireplace, hands clasped behind his back, and stared them down. 'I possess neither time nor tolerance for such ploys.' He jerked his head at the manservant. 'Donnell.'

When the man attempted to rephrase the factor's words into Gaelic, James held up a hand. 'We both speak passable English, sir, if ye'll grant us a moment o' yer time.'

'One minute, then.'

'Thank ye, sir. I wish to report a theft. Cattle were taken from my infield last night. Reivers took them is my belief.'

'You have proof of this?'

'Other than an empty field, no, sir.'

'An empty field.' McGillivray guffawed. 'Hardly damning evidence. You lack understanding of the law, I fear.'

'We wondered if other cattle had been reported stolen,' Duncan said.

'None to my knowledge. And I would know, being Justice of the Peace.'

'Aye, sir.' He frowned, surprised by this. Why would only James' beasts be taken?

'I trust this tragedy will not affect payment of your rental.' McGillivray flicked an invisible speck from his sleeve while he waited for their allotted minute to expire. 'You are tenants, where?'

'Druimbeag, sir. Not Duncan, he still lives with my father and sisters at Tomachcraggen.'

'Tomachcraggen? I believe no rent is in arrears there, although I've heard the tenant is a smuggler. Notorious, I believe. His grace's tolerance for such behaviour wears thin.'

'Aye, sir,' said James. 'I've no wish to smuggle. 'Twas my intention to sell the cattle at Crieff and pay my dues from the coin made there.'

The factor rolled his eyes. 'And now you cannot, is doubtless what you propose to tell me.'

James looked at his feet. 'To my great regret, sir.'

'If only I had a shilling for every similar tale. Your name, then?'

'James Innes.'

'Innes? Tenant at Druimbeag? Did I not recently draw up your lease agreement?'

'You did, sir.'

'And you intend to default almost immediately? I fear I smell a rat.'

Duncan cleared his throat, aware their time ticked away as swiftly as the factor's patience. 'My brother bought the beasts in good faith, sir, in the days before the theft. He pastured them in his infield overnight, ready for driving south come morning. Only, when he awoke, the cattle were gone.'

McGillivray frowned. 'To be clear, only the cattle belonging to Mister Innes have been taken.' He glowered at James. 'Whilst every other cow in the area miraculously remains, happily chewing clover, or safely housed in byres. All but those of Mister Innes. You see why I smell a rat?'

'I do, sir,' Duncan admitted. 'Only, 'tis the truth.'

'And you expect what from me? An extension to your brother's quarterly payment? You take me for a fool, I think.'

Duncan lowered his head. His palms were damp, his mouth dry. 'We know you're no fool, sir. We ask only for a period of grace, respectfully, that James might—'

'Ha! Well, I'll tell you what I think. It seems, by his own admission, your brother is a charlatan and had the money to pay his lease but rather spent it. On cattle, he says, which have vanished into thin air. Or perhaps, if they ever existed, he's concealed the cows thinking to delay his payment by spinning me a tale. Or the trickster gambled the money away. Lord knows, the best of us enjoy a flutter.' He allowed a smile to crease his fleshy face. 'But when we've not the means, we must resist.'

'I've never been a gambler, sir,' said James.

McGillivray glanced at his manservant, who'd been standing expressionless throughout. 'How many similar tales have we heard, Donnell?'

'Many, sir.'

'And when have we entertained them?'

'Never, sir.'

'Just so. Your next payment is due at Martinmas, Mister Innes. Do you need reminding of the amount? I can have the ledger—'

'No, sir.'

'Then be sure to pay it. I shall be particularly vigilant in noting your payment. Default, and I'll have removal papers served against you. Do I make myself clear?'

'You do, sir, but I dinna seek leniency for myself. 'Tis for my wife, Mhari, who's soon to have our child. I wish to keep a roof over their heads.'

The factor made an exasperated sound. 'Good God, man, honour the articles of your lease agreement, and you shall.' He stared hard at James and shook his head.

'Sir,' said Duncan. 'If ye'll let me explain—'

McGillivray hissed to silence him, flicking his hand at the door. 'I've more pressing matters.' He nodded to Donnell to show them out.

Duncan stood his ground, incensed by the man's bovine indifference, but James looked askance at him. To protest further would only shame him, his look said. Would likely accomplish naught, maybe make things worse.

Remembering Lachlan's warning, he nodded, sick to his stomach, and followed James out.

CHAPTER TWENTY-FIVE

JAMES WAS SILENT on the walk home. He trudged doggedly, his gaze on the heathery ground. Duncan felt his despair.

'What'll ye do?'

'Damned if I ken. But I'll nae wait fer the factor to put us out. The shame o' that—'twould finish Mhari. She's done naught wrong. The blame's mine.'

'But what wrong did ye do? Ye tried to do the right thing.'

'Right or wrong,' James laughed bitterly, 'I'm nae so sure the difference matters. I should've followed yer lead. Ye've never trusted the authorities. What they did to yer kinfolk ....' He exhaled, clenching his hands into fists. 'When've those in authority ever cared fer Highland folk?'

They walked another half-mile in silence.

Finally, James said, 'Only, I find it does matter. I made a choice to give up smuggling. By God, I intend to honour it. We'll do what so many afore us have done and leave the glen.'

Duncan's stomach lurched. 'And go where?'

'I could try fer work in Inverness. Anything. I'd do anything. 'Tis what's best fer Mhari and the bairn that matters.'

'Lord, James, I dinna want ye to go.'

'Nor I, but what choice have I? Subdivision of holdings is forbidden. Ye heard McGillivray; if we stay, he'll have us evicted.'

Duncan shuddered; he'd not wish that on any man. 'There must be another way.'

'Damned if I ken o' one.'

They walked on, Duncan struggling for something to say. Stratha'an was all James knew. He belonged here as much as the duke or his factor. When had they ever pushed their hands into the earth and breathed its peaty scent, drawn water from a mountain spring and staggered home under its weight, nursed shoots from the meagre soil? They had others to do such things. Yet, Lachlan had not the coin to pay both rentals, and he'd already given James all he owned himself. His heart thumped in his throat. Life without James was impossible to imagine. 'Twould be endlessly bleak.

'Please,' he choked. 'Give it some mair thought afore ye decide.'

James sighed. 'If it'll mak' ye feel better, Duncan. But what'll it change?'

* * *

James left for Inverness in search of work a few days later.

As he took his leave of them, pale and grim-faced, Rowena pressed him close. 'Dinna worry about Mhari,' she whispered. 'I'll stay at Druimbeag. Wi' the birth close, she shouldna be on her own.'

Pitifully grateful, he drew her arms from around his neck and kissed her fingers. 'Bless ye, Rowena.' Then he was gone.

She watched his trudging figure until her eyes watered, then turned back into the house. She could feel Duncan's pain, Grace's too. Slumped in his chair, her da fumbled for whisky with trembling fingers.

'Twas worse at Druimbeag. Mhari dragged herself from table to hearth, out to the byre, the infield, then back, the child heavy in her belly, her face no longer blithe, but fearful, contemplating leaving behind the land and folk she loved.

Rowena watched her uneasily. Mhari's pregnancy had gone smoothly thus far, but she looked drawn now and pale. She slept poorly, pining for James. Her mother came whenever she could, and knowing she could safely leave Mhari with Ismay for a while, she escaped to the hills and forests. The women would cleave to each other, reflecting on happier days, conscious their time together slipped relentlessly away. She would give them as much time together as she could.

Wild places were her solace. Only in the hills and forests could she find the peace to think clearly. She gathered what she needed for the birth: moss, cramp bark, skullcap, self-heal and valerian. Then, inexplicably drawn to the ancient symbol stone, she made the punishing climb up Carn Liath.

Frost had cast a glistening net across the land, and on the surface of the stone, a delicate crystalline web had grown, casting the marks etched into its surface into deep relief. The air was cold and clear, shimmering with the cries of geese flying overhead. In the lucent air, autumn colours glowed like living fire. Deer-grass and bracken, heather, bog-cotton blazed against the verdant green of pine. Her innards swooped, giddy with it. The glen was bewitching, but knowing James would no longer be part of it tinged the scene with sadness. Moved to tears, she stumbled away.

On her fourth day at Druimbeag, Duncan came bearing a cradle he'd fashioned from willow. She opened the door to find him standing on the doorstep with it tucked under his arm. Jem lay at his feet, the old dog greying now, her eyes misty as she looked up at her master. Duncan seemed doubtful of his welcome. Refusing him had made them awkward strangers, yet all she'd ever wanted was to make him feel he belonged. That he perhaps no longer did hurt deeply.

Mhari beckoned him inside, exclaiming when she saw what he carried. 'Oh, Duncan! However can I thank ye?' Her eyes glistened with tears.

He shook his head, blushing. ''Tis naught. A wee gift to remember me by.' He set it by the fire, giving it a push to demonstrate its motion. 'Twas a charming piece with curved legs intricately carved to resemble the head and neck of a heron.

Mhari swallowed, her voice choked with sadness. 'What'll I do wi'out ye both.' Her gaze moved back and fore between them. 'I confess, I once imagined you two would wed. Ye're both that tender-hearted, that handsome. I thought ye'd mak' the perfect couple. I still do. Was I foolish to imagine such a thing?'

Duncan squirmed, his ears flaming. Neither of them could answer such a question. How would she feel if 'twas Duncan leaving? His earnest face she might never see again. But the thought was too much to bear.

Fearing she'd said the wrong thing, Mhari struggled out of her chair to admire Duncan's handiwork, wincing as a wave of pain caught her. She waited for it to pass before kneeling on the floor.

Rowena touched her shoulder. 'Yer pains havena started, Mhari?'

She glanced up in alarm. 'I feared 'twas that. Only, is it nae too early?'

''Tis nature decides when. How long've ye been having these pains?'

'All last night, but they're fiercer now and come quicker.'

Rowena sat back, laughing at Duncan's expression. Mhari had hidden her labour well. 'Looks like ye brought the cradle just in time. We'll be needing it sooner than I thought, and you'll be an uncle all the sooner.'

'Lord,' he stammered. 'What might I do?'

She shook her head, helping Mhari to her feet. 'Away and fetch some whisky to wet the bairn's head. 'Tis all the use a man is at this time.'

He leapt to his feet, startling Jem awake, and she gave a bewildered bark. 'D'ye need anything? I mean, can I do anything?' He swallowed. 'Forgive me, I suppose ye ken what to do.'

'Well enough, but if ye know more,' she winked at Mhari. 'Ye're welcome to show us.'

'Heavens, no,' he stammered. ''Tis just I dinna like leaving ye.'

''Tis alright, nature guides these things. Ye can bring a drop o' whisky if ye like.'

He nodded, flashing them an uncertain smile, and moved to the door. With a last anxious look, he ducked under the lintel and was gone.

Mhari's labour was already well advanced. 'Ye should've told me,' she chided. 'There's nae need to suffer. I've things will help. Nature has ways to soothe the pain o' labour.'

'I didna wish to be a burden.'

'Ye're never that, Mhari. 'Tis a privilege to help bring yer child into the world.' She rummaged among her supplies, finding a small hessian sack she'd filled with barley husks and valerian herb. She laid it on the hearthstone to warm. Pressed into the small of the back, or wherever pain was severe, it would warm and relax tight muscles, releasing its soothing vapours.

'I thought I'd be afraid, but I'm braver wi' you here. Even wi' James gone.' Mhari bit her lip.

'There's nae need to be afraid, Mhari. Ye're young and strong. Yer child's ready to be born. He'll be here soon.' She filled a cup with cramp bark elixir. 'This will smooth yer contractions and ease yer pain.'

'He? Ye think 'tis a boy?'

She considered. 'I've always imagined so, but we'll know soon enough.'

Mhari circled the room, sipping the elixir, stopping whenever a pain gripped. After a few ragged breaths, she walked on. 'I thought 'twould be bitter,' she said once she'd drank it all. 'But 'tis honey-sweet.'

'Nature likes to sweeten her cures. Where she doesna, I always do.'

'Twould be a swift labour. The contractions were powerful, coming in quick succession—a blessing. Mhari had already suffered in so many ways.

She loosened the girl's gown, urging her to sit astride a chair so she could massage her back. She was sweating, whimpering through each contraction. Smoothing her hands over tight muscles, she kneaded and soothed, humming an old lullaby. When another pain clamped, Mhari clenched her teeth, trying to hum along.

As she anticipated, the child was born within the hour. She encouraged Mhari to make slow circuits of the room, stopping to lean heavily against her whenever a pain gripped, breathing through it as instructed. Remaining upright and on the move, the girl's progress was rapid. As the moment of birth approached, she encouraged Mhari onto the bed, spreading layers of sacking under her. When the baby's head crowned, Mhari wailed like a banshee, wild-eyed, clutching at her shoulder. Within moments, the infant slipped into the world.

'A boy,' Rowena gasped. 'Wi' dark hair like James.'

The baby gave a pulsing cry. She wrapped him tightly and handed him to Mhari.

'Oh, Rowena, he's beautiful. But his dear face is all puckered. I fear he thinks little o' this world.'

'He'll soon smooth out, ye'll see. He's come a mite early, is all.'

The infant opened his eyes and blinked, his face uncrumpling, and began to mewl.

'He's James in miniature.' Mhari laughed. 'So strange to think he was inside me, and now here he is. Already I love him that fiercely.'

Rowena's throat tightened. Mhari was born to be a mother, while she, wed to the earth, would never be one. Her eyes nipped, and she choked back tears; she mustn't think on that. She must deliver the afterbirth, and it must all come away.

* * *

Duncan touched his ankles to his garron's flank, urging the pony to quicken its gait. He'd only half-filled his water skin with whisky, doubting they'd need a full flask, but as the garron thudded through the heather to the slosh of whisky, he wished he'd filled it to the brim. Folk would come from far and wide to wet the bairn's head, to wish James and Mhari well. He should've brought more—a great deal more.

It hadn't felt right just leaving them. Childbirth was a mysterious process, oft-times dangerous, a private, female thing thus barred to him. All the long ride to the bothy, anxiety had wormed through his innards. 'Twas with trembling fingers he'd unsealed a cask and drained off some whisky. *Uisge-beatha.* Water of life. 'Twas to celebrate the miracle of life that he fetched it. But like any new life in the glens, that miracle could swiftly become a tragedy. For mother and for infant. Decanting the whisky, he'd rambled like a lunatic, trying not to think on that.

Too old now to keep up with his pony, Jem was curled in a sheep's fleece in his lap, the garron's motion lulling her to sleep. He murmured to her, her warmth a welcome counter to the frigid air, and she stirred, ears pricking, then sat up and growled.

'Hush, lass.' But he gave a start as the reason for her alarm rounded the bend in front. Mounted on his chestnut gelding, the animal snorting great clouds of steaming breath, the Black Gauger fixed him with a scornful glare. He flicked a corner of Jem's fleece over the whisky.

'Well, well, if it's no' the Young Jacobite. What have you there?' Drawing his sword, McBeath urged his horse closer, using the sword's point to lift the covering fleece. 'No' whisky, I hope. Lucky for you I'm feeling lenient.'

His heart pounded. What did the black divil want now? At the edge of his vision, the gauger's dog crept from the bushes.

'On your own, eh? Where's your foolhardy brother? The brother that's no' a brother.' He chuckled. 'Oh, aye, he'll be away to Crieff, to the famous cattle tryst. Or maybe no'. I mean, what would he sell?' He snorted.

'What d'ye ken o' that?'

'Everything, I think ye'll find.'

'I doubt that.'

'Try me. Your sister has disclosed the whole sorry tale.'

'Rowena? She'd nae do that.'

'Though, of course, she's no' your sister. No' any more than she's mine. Just as well since I plan to make her my wife.'

Anger flushed Duncan's face. 'I doubt Rowena will ever wed, but I'm certain she'll never wed a gauger.'

'Even one paid as well as me?' The exciseman sheathed his sword with a flourish. 'What would you know? A whelp plucked fresh from the teat. You've yet to appreciate the whims of the fairer sex.' He laughed bawdily. 'While I possess an exhaustive knowledge of that species.'

At the inherent disrespect, Duncan tightened his hands on the reins.

'I know how to please a woman,' McBeath went on. 'I'm just returned from Aberdeen's Merchant Quarter, where I acquired certain items for Rowena's fancy. And mine. Silken dainties to replace the weeds she commonly wears. To make her feel like the desirable woman she is. Perhaps you'd like to see?'

'I'd not.'

Heedless, McBeath turned in the saddle, drawing a fat package from among others bundled at the rear. 'I bought undergarments, too. Frill to show off her ripe young figure, though they're no' for your eyes. Lord, no. Only I'll ever gaze upon these fripperies, and no' for long.' He chortled. 'I doubt I'll be able to leave them on her long.'

'Ye spin a fanciful tale,' Duncan hissed through clenched teeth. 'Only, yer fiction speaks far more o' you than o' her. I dinna recognise my sister in this fable. She's a beautiful woman nae matter what she wears, and ye're a liar. An offensive, foul-tongued—'

'You'll watch your mouth. You want her yourself! Deny it, and we'll see who lies.' The gauger stuffed the package back behind his saddle. 'You imagine I invent this, do you?'

'I know ye do. What makes ye think Rowena cares a jot for you?'

McBeath smirked, delving in his coat pocket, and drew out a folded strip of fabric. It unravelled with a flutter. 'Her favour, given me as a token of her affection. A sign we have an understanding, she and I. It shows she cares for me a deal more than a jot, whether you like it or no'.' He handed him the scrap. 'You'll recognise it, perhaps?'

He smoothed the piece out on his thigh. 'Twas of woven wool dyed in mountain shades and delicately stitched to resemble swaying heads of barley. A nod to the whisky that supported them all, both distiller and, he supposed, exciseman. An ache ripped through his heart, his mind reeling back to the night he'd watched her stitch it.

Sitting at the hearthstone, firelight picking out the lustre in her hair, she'd bent her head diligently to the task. When he'd asked her what it was she worked upon, she'd smiled sadly. 'Just sumhin and nothing.'

'Where did ye get this?'

'I told you; she gave it me. A labour of love to demonstrate her affection. Perhaps you dinnae know Rowena as well as you imagine.' The gauger whipped the piece from his fingers, sitting back in the saddle with an amused smile.

Doubt gnawed. Why would she stitch this fairling for McBeath? The man was known for his cruelty. Rowena would never mistrust without cause, yet the grief in his heart told him there was more to it. Inexplicably, she cared for this man.

'I ken her love o' wild places,' he said slowly. 'Her passion for healing, and that her passion doesna include being wed. Especially to a gauger.'

'You know her passions, do ye? Well, I know them too. There's scarce an inch of my flesh that's no' trembled under her touch. But then, being a witchling, there's sinful magic in her fingers. The power to arouse to exquisite heights.' The gauger allowed a provocative smile to curl his lips.

'I look forward to my remaining inches receiving her attention on our wedding night.'

Duncan recoiled, staring at him.

The gauger smirked back.

He moved without thought, incensed by the man's crudeness, wishing only to wipe the leer from the gauger's face. With a howl, he lunged at him, dragging him from his horse. Jem jumped down, barking in excitement as he slammed his fist into the gauger's startled face.

Caught unawares, McBeath landed heavily, the blow finding its mark with a sickening crunch. He was on his feet again at once. Blood spurted from his nose. Panting, he gaped at Duncan, then shoved him violently into the undergrowth.

Propelled into the trackside heather, he landed on his back. His teeth rattled, and the air wheezed out of him. He fought to drag in more. Then the gauger was upon him, straddling his midsection, cursing him in the foulest language. Beefy fingers tightened around his throat, the hated face purple, spitting snarl, stippling his face with bloody spittle.

The sudden weight squeezed what breath was left from his lungs, ruthless fingers crushing his windpipe. At the edge of his vision, the bulldog appeared. McBeath head-butted it away. Jem tried to defend him, barking furiously, nipping McBeath's elbow. When he paid her no heed, she sank her teeth in. He screeched. Excited by her barking, by the blood and rage in the air, the bulldog clamped its teeth into the back of Jem's neck. She was old and frail—no match for it.

The pressure in his lungs was now unbearable. His vision dimmed. Yet even through the torture, he could hear Jem's agonised yelps as the demon hound shook her in its steel jaws. Writhing desperately, he jabbed his knee into McBeath's groin. The man groaned, loosening his grip to clutch at himself. Dragging in lungfuls of air, he wriggled from under him.

The bulldog had lost interest in his Jem; she lay still in the heather. He crawled to her side, his vision swimming, but one look told him what he feared. All the years they'd spent together were coming to an end.

She lifted soft brown eyes to him, and in their depths, he saw all the devotion she'd given him, all the faithfulness, and desperately wished to hold on to it.

'Jem,' he sobbed. 'Dinna leave me. Please, Jem.'

But her eyes grew heavy. Whining, she licked his hand, thanking him for all the years the drowning sack would've taken if not for him. He lay down beside her, weeping, stroking her silken head, feeling the blood trickling there. The life left her then, its gentle sough brushing his cheek.

Her eyes stilled to polished glass. In them was reflected all the beauty of the glen.

'Here.' Something landed beside him. 'Wrap it in that. And think yourself lucky only your dog's a corpse.'

Jem's fleece. It smelled of her. As his sobs came hard, he buried his face in it.

* * *

It was warm at the fire; a thin film of sweat beaded on Duncan's brow. Glancing around, most folk were busy with their jaws, engaged in conversation, whisky quaich in hand. They'd come to wet the baby's head and would likely pay him little heed. He cautiously removed his neckerchief and used it to mop his brow.

'What're thon bruises?'

He swallowed, throwing James a dark look.

'Christ, the gauger did that? He mighta killed ye.'

Retying the neckerchief, he muttered, ''Twas only thanks to Jem he didna. She gave her life fer mine.'

'Poor Jem.' James rubbed his brow. 'I still canna believe she's gone. Ye seem naked wi'out her.' He downed a mouthful of whisky. 'Can Rowena do naught fer the bruising?'

'She doesna ken o' it. I couldna tell her what happened—nae the full truth. The divil said crude things about her.' He swallowed. 'I believe she must care fer him.'

'Does she nae care fer everyone?'

'But especially fer him, I think.'

'Nay. Why would she?'

'He kens things. Things he maintains Rowena told him. He knew ye planned to drive yer cattle to Crieff, and he kent they'd been taken. It amused him knowing ye'd been paupered. He's involved, I ken he is. Only, how can I tell her that? Especially when 'twas mebbe her careless words gave him the chance to hurt ye.' He squeezed his eyes shut, blotting out the world. 'He claims they have an understanding.'

'And ye believe that?'

'I ....' He shook his head.

'He's sown enough seed to mak' ye doubt?'

He nodded.

James drew back, studying him. 'Ye love her. Have done most o' yer days. I've long known, afore ye go denying it.'

'Mair than my life.'

'Then, ye must tell her.'

'That I love her?'

'Aye, that too. But that ye suspect McBeath. Ye must warn her. 'Twas McBeath had Morna arrested.'

He nodded, hatred darkening his face. 'But will she listen? She kens how I feel about her. Mightn't she doubt my motives?'

James blinked in surprise. 'She knows how ye feel about her? And?'

He shook his head, his heart too sore to explain.

'Christ, Duncan, I'm sorry.' James grimaced. 'But she's carved herself in Morna's image. A self-made woman skilled in her craft. She doesna see what's under her own nose. She'll be away on that business now, I suppose?'

'Gathering herbs fer a bairn wi' croup.'

James nodded. 'Dinna gie up on her. Her heart's been a guarded place since Mam died.'

He swallowed, looking wretchedly at James. 'Since yer da took me in, all I've wanted is to keep her safe.' He sighed. 'Till I foolishly wanted more.'

James looked upon him with pity. 'She was young when Mam died. She didna understand what happened. Perhaps she's afraid to risk her heart, but she's always been closer to you than anyone.'

'Mebbe once, afore I acted the brazen fool and asked her to be my wife. How I ever imagined myself worthy ....'

James' face softened. 'Ye mean mair to her than she's willing to admit. I'd stake my life upon it. As fer the gauger, that he kens my business isna to say 'twas Rowena told him. He runs a network o' spies. He must do. Ye ken as well as I, there's little escapes him. Ye're nae suggesting Rowena spies fer him?'

'Lord, no, but she defends him. Ye've heard her. I canna help feeling there's something atween them.'

The baby snuffled in its cradle, and James turned to look at his sleeping son. Since his return, he'd scarcely taken his eyes from the infant, gazing at him in wonder. When he looked back at Duncan, his face tightened with grief.

Duncan understood. Everything had gone wrong for James. He was responsible for losing the home he'd made with Mhari, pride his undoing, he believed. He'd hoped to prove it possible to survive these harsh times without smuggling. To fail so disastrously and then be rewarded with this priceless gift was more than he could bear. The infant was a blessing from

God, but James felt undeserving of such a blessing.

'Forgive me,' he murmured. 'I shouldna be burdening ye wi' my troubles. Ye've enough wi'out mine.' He sipped at his whisky, the spirit burning his injured throat. He endured the pain for the soothing effects on his troubled mind. Although James blamed himself, he knew better. He'd once imagined reivers responsible. He no longer thought that. He knew who was to blame.

Donald Gordon worked his way through the crowd. Clearing his throat, he peered into the cradle. 'A bonny bairn. What's he to be called?'

'James,' he croaked. 'Efter his father. Though he'll be known as Jamie.'

'A fitting name.' Donald pressed James' shoulder. 'Ye'll be missed, lad, and nae just by yer kinfolk. When is it ye'll go?'

'Day efter next, Donald.' He looked up tightly. 'I'll miss folk, too—the bond we all share. Already I've given up Druimbeag, fearing the factor and his men. The shame o' being put out.' He swallowed, searching for Mhari in the crowd. 'I've found work in Inverness.'

'As a burye-man,' Lachlan choked, appearing with the McHardy men in tow. 'My son. A finer herdsman and tiller o' the soil 'tis hard to imagine.' There was a rumble of agreement, and bitterness darkened Lachlan's face. 'Nae longer will James be digging the earth to sow oats and barley. 'Tis what's left efter the hangman he'll be planting from now on.'

Angus McHardy shook his head. 'James, a grave-digger? 'Tis a crime.'

'Someone must do it,' James muttered. ''Twill put food on the table till I find something better.'

A superstitious murmur rippled through the room, the door opening to admit another body. Duncan didn't need to look; he knew it was Rowena. She came to him at once, placing a bundle of thyme on the hearthstone, an ingredient in her cure for croup. She had yet more greenery with her and knelt to arrange it. Looking up at him, her smile was stiff, her fingers trembled.

She'd never recovered from her mother's death; he knew that now, and his heart grieved. She'd lose her brother now, too, for when would she see James again? Or Mhari and the child she'd help deliver? None of them would get to know wee Jamie. He'd grow up far from here, in Inverness or wherever James was forced to go. The lad would never know the land that bred him, the beauty of it, or the kin whose blood he shared. One thing was certain: McGillivray would never grant a new lease to a tenant who'd defaulted.

He sighed, watching the tender way Rowena worked with nature's bounty, so reverent in her touch. With the skill of an artist, she blended winter heather with delicate thistledown, adding crimson rosehip and haw, then edged the arrangement with alder leaves turned translucent by the hand of frost. She tied it all together with a strip of bark, then, satisfied with her work, looked up at him.

'I've nae rightly said good-bye to Jem, Duncan. Will ye tak' me to her grave?'

He nodded, his mouth dry, and helped her up.

As they passed the knot of well-wishers around James and Mhari, James signalled to him with his eyes. He nodded back. He must find a way to warn her of the exciseman.

CHAPTER TWENTY-SIX

HE'D BURIED JEM where she liked to lie—at the side of the byre in a sandy spot warmed by the midday sun. Wrapping her limp body, he'd wept uncontrollably, and with each spadeful of earth he showered over her, had cursed Hugh McBeath to hell. He didn't know if dogs went to heaven, but he'd fashioned a wooden cross to mark the place, hoping it might make her entry more likely. If any animal deserved a place in heaven 'twas surely Jem.

'Oh, Duncan.' Rowena dropped to her knees before the mound of earth. 'I can hardly believe she's gone. I keep expecting to hear her bark and come running to lick my face.' She laid her posy with trembling fingers. 'I'm sorry I didna share yer last few moments, Jem, but I'm glad Duncan was wi' ye. No one could've loved ye more.'

He made a strangled sound as he choked down his grief.

She got to her feet, her tears flowing unchecked. 'Poor Jem. I'm sorry, Duncan.' Wrapping her arms around him, she pressed a wet cheek to his chest.

He brought his arms up and tentatively stroked the length of her back. Encompassed in her herb-rich scent, so many wistful longings surfaced, he near swooned.

'What happened?' She released him, swiping at her cheeks. 'Can ye tell me?'

He nodded, wondering how he'd do so, scuffing the ground with his boots. ''Twas the Black Gauger's dog. Thon vicious, bow-legged brute. It attacked her, biting the back o' her neck. She was only trying to protect me.'

'From the dog?'

'From the gauger.'

'Hugh? But why?'

'I punched him, and he tried to throttle me.'

She stared at him. 'Why would ye do that? I dinna understand.'

'We had sore words. It doesna matter what about, but he's nae the man ye think. He had Morna arrested. She's dead because o' him.'

She paled, blinking at him. 'Ye're wrong. Hugh's helped us. Why would ye say such a thing?'

'Because it's true, and I believe he had a hand in thieving James' cattle. He kens too much about it nae to be involved.' He waited, his heart in his mouth, fearing she'd defend the man—knowing what it would mean if she did.

She frowned. 'Ye're wrong. Hugh's a decent man trying to do a difficult job. Ye're prejudiced against him.' She pressed her fingers into the flesh between her brows. 'I dinna blame ye, niver think that, but nae all government men are the same. Hugh's different. He's helped us and at great risk to himself.'

'Please, Rowena, ye must listen to me. I'm telling ye this to warn ye. Ye're precious to me. I think ye know that.'

She regarded him for long moments; he sensed she was carefully wording her reply.

'I ken ye mean well, but I dinna need yer help. I'm in no danger.'

He squeezed his eyes shut—she was lost to him.

'I couldna bear it if he hurt ye.'

'He'll not. Why would he?' She gave him a puzzled look, pity shining in her eyes. He shrank from it.

She sighed. 'Perhaps James is right. We should all put smuggling ahind us and try and survive wi'out it. 'Tis a desperate and dangerous business. Ye ken it more than most. Fer smuggler and gauger alike.'

A fine sentiment. But what had fine sentiments done for James? Only, he didn't say it; what would be the use? She cared for the gauger. There was no denying it now. He'd little hope of convincing her to beware the man. She was plainly smitten with him.

Looking down at the sad little mound of earth, he thought of what lay beneath it, wondering how his heart, battered and crushed, still managed to beat. But eventually, he nodded.

* * *

The crowd of glenfolk waiting to wish James and Mhari well had begun gathering since dawn. They waited by the edge of the track they'd take, lining it, more folk gathering all the time. Returning from the byre, Rowena heard the strange keening they made and squinted into the risen sun. At the sight, the tears she'd been holding in for days welled hotly. She choked them back. She must be strong. Tears only made partings harder. Her tears would come, but she prayed they'd wait until she could be alone with them. Tightening her jaw, she stumbled back to the cot-house.

'Ye canna pull the cart yerself,' her da was saying. ''Tis fifty miles ower hill and moor. Ye'll rupture yerself. You tell him, Mhari.'

'We dinna wish to be taking what's nae ours.' Mhari wrapped the infant in her shawl. 'From now on, we must make our own way.'

'God in heaven! Can I nae give my own son a miserable garron? A son I might niver see again. My grandson,' he choked.

'What use would we have fer it, Da? We'll be in a rented room; I'd have to pay stabling. Ye'll be needing all yer garrons fer the whisky. You and Duncan. We've little enough to carry.'

James had piled all their possessions in his handcart. His farm implements he'd sold, knowing he'd have no use for them. He'd even left the rooftree in place at Druimbeag—something unthinkable. Timber was precious. Folk commonly took the ridgepole with them if they moved, but James couldn't even do that. All there was to show for his twenty-three years on this earth were a few sticks of furniture, a meal kist and some blankets and bowls. Mhari's parents had given them a wickerwork cupboard as a wedding gift. It took pride of place on the cart beside Duncan's cradle.

Looking at the miserable collection, Lachlan had to turn away. He seemed to have aged these last few days. Grim-faced, he glanced at Grace, who was wrapping bannocks and salt-beef for their journey.

'I've some news might cheer ye, Da.' She attempted a smile. 'Malcolm MacRae has asked me to wed him. I was waiting fer the right moment to tell ye.'

He gaped at her. 'And ye imagined this was it?'

'I thought the news might gladden ye.'

'Christ!'

'Oh, Grace.' Rowena went to her at once. 'I'm that pleased fer ye.'

'Your time will come,' Grace whispered. 'Ye'll see.'

She smiled back feebly, knowing her time would never come.

Duncan was quick to wish Grace well. Watching him kiss her tenderly, a pang of longing pierced Rowena's heart. One day another lass would know Duncan's love; his heart would belong to another. A sweet lass, she hoped, for he deserved a loving wife. As each day passed, guarding her heart against him seemed harder and harder.

James embraced them all in turn but had few words. Tight-faced, he nodded to his father, his eyes dry and raw-looking. Mhari wept enough for them both, keening and swaying with the infant in her arms. When Rowena kissed little Jamie, Mhari clung to her, afraid to whisper words of farewell for fear 'twould make their parting permanent.

Finally, James turned to her, clasping her so hard he squeezed her breath away. Before she could tell him how much she'd miss him, he'd taken up the handles of his cart and was hauling it away. Duncan rushed to help.

The wheels creaked into motion, then rumbled over the infield toward the waiting folk. Reaching them, sombre glensmen pressed James on the shoulder, bonnets clutched in hands, wanting him to know they wished things had gone differently. He trudged on, folk scrambling to find a place at the rear of the cart until there was not an inch left on which to gain a handhold. The cart rattled on to the wailing of women who thrust wee keepsakes for the baby in among the pile of goods—gifts that one day might tell him something of the glen where he'd been born.

Mhari clung to her mother until Ismay had to thrust her away. She walked after the cart with her head held high. Grace hurried after her, but Rowena remained rooted among the infield stubble.

Alone now, she turned toward Carn Mèilich. The hill's forested slopes would give her comfort, the trees like family around her. From the top, she'd be able to watch her kin until the last when their blurry images would merge with the land.

The climb was arduous. When she reached the treeless summit, her breath steamed in the cold air. The river, the lifeblood of the glen, snaked away below her, lost in mist. Trees rose ghostly from this smirr, thick with alder, her mother's tree, and hauntingly beautiful, but the mist obscured the winding track by the river and all trace of her kinfolk who trudged along it. More stricken by that than she could endure, tears came in a choking spate, and she fell to her knees in the heather. There, upon all fours with the fierceness of a she-wolf, she vented her grief to the heavens, her despair echoing through the hills.

* * *

As they neared the Bridge of Avon, built by the redcoats three years earlier to move troops swiftly into the Highlands, folk fell away, returning to their holdings. Fear of the soldiers was deep-seated, and when the stone bridge finally came in sight, only Lachlan and Grace remained with Duncan to help James pull his cart. A thick mist rose from the river. Duncan blinked the dew from his lashes, straining to see ahead. Sitting on the parapet of the bridge, a shadowy figure watched their approach.

When the figure rose, clad in a long black cassock, he exhaled in relief.

'James.' Father Ranald wore a strained expression. 'I hoped I'd meet ye here. A sad day. A day I prayed never to see.'

'And I, Father.' James let go of the cart to knead his back. 'But I'm nae the first to be put from this glen. I doubt I'll be the last.'

'Eviction.' Lachlan spat the word. ''Tis happening all ower the Highlands.'

'A tide of misery,' the priest agreed. He delved in the folds of his robe, bringing out a slip of paper and handed it to James. 'The name and whereabouts of a priest in Inverness. Father Tobias Murray, hiding among the faithful of the town. A good man. Only get in contact with him through the measures detailed here and be wary. Attending Catholic Mass is outlawed, as ye know, having your child baptised in the Catholic faith could see ye banished from these shores, your child taken from ye. I'd not wish that upon ye, but I imagine you want the boy baptised.'

James folded the paper into a pocket. ''Tis our wish, Father, aye.'

'Then remember the perils for Father Tobias are grave. Try nae to put him in danger.'

'We'll be mindful.'

The child began to grizzle; Mhari rocked him in her arms.

'I'd have baptised the boy myself had I been here. As ye perhaps know, I've been away on Jacobite business. I've not yet forsaken all hope in that direction.'

'Nor I,' Duncan assured him.

The priest smiled approvingly.

'I'm surprised to see ye wearing yer robes, Father.'

'Aye,' said Lachlan. 'Are ye nae feart the redcoats might catch ye?'

'I wish to bless James and Mhari before their journey. On this sombre occasion, frayed breeks hardly seem fitting.' He nodded at the path leading down the side of the bridge to the river's edge. 'Perhaps we might do so down there.'

Under the bridge, James and Mhari knelt in the shingle to receive his blessing, wraithlike in the mist. The father made the sign of the cross over their heads to the plaintive cry of oyster-catcher and snipe, raising his voice over the surging water.

'Almighty Father, we entrust those who must leave us into your hands.
We pray you will keep them safe and guide them on their path,
for you are the beginning and end of every road we take.
We call upon you, Lord, to walk by their side, to watch over their every step,
and to one day bring James, Mhari and young Jamie home safe to us.
We ask this through thine own son, Jesus Christ, our Lord.

May the Lord bless you and keep you.
May He make His face shine upon you
and be gracious to you.
May the Lord lift up His face to you,
and grant you both peace.'

Tight-faced, he urged them to rise, clutching their hands.

'May the road rise up to meet ye.
May the wind be always at yer back.
May the sun shine warm upon yer face;
The rains fall soft upon yer fields
And until we meet again,
May the Lord hold ye in the palm o' His hand.
Amen.'

Clearing a gruffness from his throat, he murmured, 'Be of good courage, both. And no matter how far ye must travel, I pray one day your road will bring ye home.'

He turned away, averting his gaze from tearful faces while he removed his cassock and bundled it with his things. Even clad in humble home-spuns, to Duncan, he looked every inch the warrior priest.

Finally, the excruciating moment came when James and Mhari must go on alone.

Neither could voice their sorrow. They clutched hands, kissed cheeks, then, holding the now sleeping infant, crossed the Avon into the Hills of Cromdale with heavy heads and hearts. Duncan watched the trundling cart until it vanished in the mist.

'Will ye walk back wi' me, Father?' he choked. 'I would speak with ye, if ye've no objection.'

The priest raised a brow. 'About naught dire, I hope.'

'James tells me there's work in Inverness. I'm minded to join him or go elsewhere if there's naught to be found Inverness-way.'

The father slowed his steps. 'But why?' He glanced back at Lachlan, beginning to trudge after them. 'Wouldn't that finish Lachlan?'

Glancing back, Duncan watched Grace slip her arm around her father, appearing to hold him up. 'I'd send back coin. I dinna intend to abandon the man who took me in. Never would I do that.'

'I didn't imagine you would. So why leave him?' As they walked on, the priest nodded slowly. 'But it's not Lachlan you're leaving.' He peered through the mist at the surrounding hills. 'Nor is it this ravaged land. It's Rowena. It's always been her. But why leave the woman ye love?'

'She doesna approve o' the smuggling. She wishes I put it aside.'

'I've long wished for that, too, although I've always understood your reasons. You wish to strike back. Your hatred's a potent force, and you need to channel it. But that's not the reason you're leaving.'

Duncan sighed; he'd never been able to fool the father. 'I canna bear to stay. To witness how he'll treat her, his cruelty. I love her too much.'

The father stopped in his tracks with a baffled sound. 'You must start at the beginning, lad.'

He nodded, glad of the opportunity. 'At first, I only wished to protect her. She healed me. 'Tis what she does. She healed my spirit; she gave me joy again, something I'd forgotten existed. From the start, she drew me under her spell. At five years old, she had more grace in her than I'll ever have. She gave me a reason to live, Father. She *is* my reason to live. But as I grew to love her, to ...' he swallowed, 'to desire her, I selfishly wanted more. I hoped she might feel as I do, might even wed me.' Frowning, he kept his gaze on his feet. 'I ken what ye're thinking.'

'What am I thinking?'

'That I was ower-bold. That I'd no right even to imagine such a thing.'

'Why would I think that?'

'On account o' I'm a craven creature.'

'Whatever do ye mean?'

'I'm spineless. Ye ken it as well as I. All those years ago, I did naught. I let soldiers burn my home and family. My mother, who was always kind, my wee sister, who never harmed a soul, my granny, too sick to rise from her bed. I hid while they burned. Trembling, pissing my breeks instead o' coming to their aid.'

'Och, lad.'

He wrung his hands. 'I heard the roar as the roof went up, the soldiers shouting. I felt the heat o' it, Father, like the flames o' hell. I still hear their screams. I waken wi' them ringing in my ears. I've never found the courage to tell Rowena that. She's innocent, while I'm contemptible. Ye've always known what happened, that I'm a coward, so ye must know I could never hope to make her mine.'

'You were a child. What could you've done?'

'Mebbe naught, but I didna even try.'

'No, lad, because they'd have cut ye down. They had no compassion, those men.'

He shrugged, the memory still sharp, shame and bitterness twisting his guts. 'Perhaps I was meant to die there wi' them.'

The father drew to a halt, his expression fierce. 'And deprive me of your companionship? Nay, lad. You've given me joy. I like to think 'twas something of the joy a father feels. You've been a blessing to Lachlan, a brother to James and those lasses. You're the best smuggler this glen has ever seen. So I'm told. Hardly a coward. You're the most faithful of men. If you see naught else, you must at least see that?'

He shrugged, aware of Grace and Lachlan close behind now, Lachlan breathing heavily, dragging his feet. He walked on.

The priest glanced sidelong at him. 'Forgive me, but I cannot believe you were meant to die that day. Nor do I think you're a coward. You mustn't think it either. You did what any child would do—you lived. I, for one, am mighty glad of it. Why do you suppose I'm still living? A fugitive ministering to the followers of an outlawed faith. A wanted Jacobite. 'Tis because I'm mighty good at hiding. I've cowered under many a riverbank, too, and in places far worse. I've done what I must to survive. There's no shame in that. The shame belongs to those who make us do so. I see no difference between you and me.' He exhaled. 'If you're a coward, then I'm one, too.'

He frowned; the father was no coward. 'Anyhow,' he muttered, 'Rowena doesna feel the same. Why would she? I've accepted it. 'Tis the hardest thing I've ever done. She doesna want me, no matter how I might wish it otherwise.' He faltered, a quiver in his voice. 'She'll always have my heart; she's more precious to me than life. Wi'out her, my life hardly matters. But I must let her go.'

The father shot him a look. 'More precious to you than God?'

He hung his head. ''Tis Rowena I wish to walk aside through life. 'Tis why, in spite o' everything I once said, I can never be a priest. I love her, but more than that, I desire her as a man can only desire a woman—wi' every fibre o' my being.'

The father reddened, disguising his embarrassment by kissing the crucifix around his neck. 'Then, knowing how much you once wished to join the priesthood, I believe I understand something of your devotion.'

''Tis generous o' ye, Father. But since the day she turned me down, I've known she'll one day find a better man. One wi' a braver heart, and he'll be the one to love her. 'Tis how it must be, fer I'm nae worthy. I knew I'd be envious, would likely resent the man.' He swallowed. 'But if he truly loved her, I told myself I'd be glad fer them. I'd ask the Lord to help me be so. I'd still watch ower her as a brother should. I'll always protect her.' He thrust his hands into his pockets. 'But the man she's chosen, Father.' He kicked viciously at a clump of bracken.

'Who has she chosen?'

'The divil himself. He'll have her. I ken he will.'

'Who do you mean?'

'The Black Gauger. *McBeath.*' He spat the name. 'He wants her fer his wife. Lusts after her. A cruel, vulgar man who thinks only of his pleasure. I canna bear to think of her wi' him, how he'll treat her. It makes me sick thinking of it. Forgive me, but I canna stay and watch him ill-treat her.'

'Rowena has chosen this man?'

'I believe so.'

'Surely not. I mean, she was always a strange child, preferring the company of that heathen creature to decent Christian folk, but she's tender-hearted. I find it hard to believe she'd wish to wed that brute.'

'She cares fer him; I've seen the signs, though I'd no wish to see them. He wields power here. Something I believe women find attractive. He can give her things. Wed to him, she could better herself. I've no wish to hinder that. Only,' he clenched his fists, 'I love her too much to stand idly by while he misuses her. I've not the courage.'

The priest sighed. 'It takes a special kind of courage to walk away from what you love most in the world.'

'To run away, ye mean?'

'No, that's not what I meant.' The father frowned. 'But I feel something here doesn't bear scrutiny. Even if what you say is true and Rowena cares for this man enough to wed him, I urge you to think long and hard. Your home's here, Duncan. Lachlan needs you. You'd not forsake him, would you? When he needs you most?'

He groaned, pressing his eyes shut as he walked blindly on, consumed by his thoughts and the images they created.

'Lachlan's never found it easy to show he cares.' The priest snorted.

'He hardly knows how. Yet, he does care. He lives for his family, whether they sprang from his loins or not. He depends on you, Duncan. I expect, now James is gone, he'll do so even more. No matter how sore your heart, I urge you not to leave him. Would James not have given all he had to remain here on land his ancestors doubtless bled for? I believe so.'

As the priest's words struck home, he fell silent. The father was right; James would trade with him in a heartbeat. His sorrow at leaving had been palpable, so real they'd all felt it. After all James' troubles, his noble ideals of living within the law and showing others it could be done, it seemed shameful to deliberately turn his back on the glen and its folk. Especially Lachlan, who'd treated him like a son. What kind o' man did that?

'Aye,' he conceded. 'I must stay. I see that now. I owe it to Lachlan. To James.' He nodded grimly. ''Twill be my penance, then, to watch the Black Gauger make Rowena his. To forever dream o' what mighta been. Wondering if she's happy. Or even if she's safe.'

CHAPTER TWENTY-SEVEN

TO ROWENA, IT seemed no sooner had James gone than Grace was also preparing to leave. She spoke of little but her marriage. Once wed, Grace would move to Delnabreck. Only days ago, at Martinmas, Malcolm MacRae had put his mark on a lease agreement for the holding. He would still smuggle whisky, James' experience had taught him he must, but together they would build a farm and, God willing, a family.

'Will ye miss me?'

They were sitting on the trunk of the ruined birch tree, looking out across the glen. Cold air nipped their ears and nostrils, but for November, the day was rare, the heather wearing its winter colours.

'Will ye, Rowena?'

'D'ye need to ask? I canna imagine nae sharing this closeness.'

'I'll only be a couple o' miles away.'

'I know, but I canna remember a time wi'out ye.'

They both knew things would never be the same. Once wed, Malcolm would be Grace's priority. As her husband, he would claim that right. Rowena would play second fiddle. Or third or fourth. Ultimately, she would fade from Grace's life, living somewhere on the fringe.

'I worry about ye, Rowena. You and Duncan. Ye're so distant wi' him. Why d'ye keep him at arm's length when any fool can see he loves ye? 'Tis tearing ye both apart. You dinna fool me; I ken ye care fer him.'

Her heart fluttered. 'Love's dangerous.'

'Who told ye that?'

'Morna, but I've aye known it. All love dies or is taken from ye.'

'I think ye're feart to risk yer heart fer fear he'll break it.'

Her cheeks flamed. 'I couldna bear to lose him, to feel how I did when Mam died—all empty and despairing. And Duncan's been hurt more than anyone. 'Tis better fer us both.'

'To let him think ye dinna care fer him?'

She nodded, avoiding Grace's eyes.

'But if ye canna bear to lose him, why push him away? Does it nae come to the same thing? The same pain?'

'If I dinna allow myself to love,' she reasoned, 'to let it root in me, or him, then we canna be hurt by the loss o' it.'

Grace shook her head, baffled by this. 'D'ye nae think 'tis a bit late fer that? Duncan's already devoted to ye. Has been since the day he came, and his ardour's only grown. 'Tis as plain as the wart on Jock Findlay's nose.' She sighed. 'And I've seen how ye look at him—all wistful longings. I'd say yer love's already well rooted and budding. Or are ye going to say I'm mistaken?' She snorted.

Such talk made Rowena uncomfortable. 'I'm married to the earth,' she muttered. 'Nature's love never dies. It always endures.'

'So ye'll nae be caring if he leaves, then? If he canna bear to stay, since ye'll still have yer precious hills and forests to keep ye company?'

'Leave?' She shot Grace a look.

Grace sighed, looking down at her hands, grimy from endless toil. When she looked up, her eyes had softened with pity. 'I overheard him talking wi' Father Ranald. Nae all he said, but enough to know he doesna wish to stay. He believes ye care fer another. He canna bear to watch that man make ye his.'

'Another?' She blinked. 'What other?'

'God forbid, he believes the Black Gauger means to mak' ye his wife. Please tell me that's nae true.'

The blood fled her face, then surged back in a guilty red tide. How did he know of that? And worse, how could he believe she'd want another? But then, what hope had she ever allowed him? When had she given him cause to believe she cared for him, still less desired him? Yet her ravaged heart told her she did.

''Tis true Hugh's asked me to be his wife.' She frowned into her lap. 'I healed him; he was grateful. Likely, 'tis all it is.' She looked up tightly. 'He calls me a witchling. He says I've cast a spell upon him to make him desire me, that he's the kind o' man who aye gets what he wants.' She looked away. 'If only I were a witch; I'd make him leave me be. But he's a decent man in his way. He walks a difficult path. I believe he wishes to help us if he can.' She hesitated. 'He's a hard man to refuse. I confess, I'm a little afraid o' him.'

'But ye have refused him?'

'More than once, though I doubt he's given up.'

'What'll ye do?'

She shook her head. 'Pray he loses interest. But I canna lose Duncan.'

'Ye must convince him to stay, then.'

'Aye, but ....'

'Ye're afraid to risk yer heart?'

She nodded, and Grace looked tenderly at her. 'If ye want him to stay, ye must tell him. Give him some hope.'

She swallowed. 'I dinna ken if I can. If I'm ready. If I'll ever be ready.'

Grace sat back, her exasperation beginning to show. 'I'll tell ye what I think. Ye've shaped yerself in Morna's image—strong and self-contained, hoping 'twill shield ye from hurt. Ye've feelings fer Duncan, but ye imagine that means ye're weak. But loving doesna mean ye're weak. I believe it makes ye strong in heart and spirit. 'Tis what the Lord put us here to do—to love each other. Denying it only hurts ye in the end. Turns ye bitter.' She frowned. ''Tis what I think, but you mebbe know different.'

Rowena blinked, turning this over in her mind while her heart, a crippled thing, beat woodenly. She saw what lay ahead—her soul without its mate. Was she strong enough to endure that?

'Thank ye,' she managed and got to her feet.

Grace caught her by the hand. 'Ye must risk yer heart, Rowena. We all must to find love. Aye, it can be taken from ye, but at least ye'll have had it. Ye loved Mam, and she was taken, but at least ye had her fer a time. Ye'd nae change that fer the world, I'm thinking.'

'Never.'

Grace smoothed her thumb over the back of her hand. ''Twill be all right. Duncan will stay if ye want him to. I expect he'd go to the ends o' the earth if ye asked him.' She flashed a smile. 'But he's only gone to the A'an to guddle trout. To be alone wi' his thoughts. Ye'll find him by the Pool o' Ballagan ... should ye wish to.'

She nodded and turned away, but the sound of hooves thudding at pace over the infield made her turn back. A man was galloping toward them, bent low on a garron's back, another garron tethered to it and galloping behind. As the rider neared, she recognised Willie Gow—Isobel's father.

He reined the pony in and slid from its back, the animal lathered and snorting.

'Mister Gow.' Grace gawped at him. 'Is something the matter?'

He snatched his bonnet from his head, wringing it in his hands as he nodded to Rowena. 'Beggin' yer pardon, but 'tis Isobel. She's bleeding—great glops o' dark blood.' Catching his breath, he glanced warily at Grace. ''Tis unclean blood. The divil's wickedness. It spills from her, and she writhes in pain.' He glanced at Rowena, then nodded at the other pony, saddled and ready. 'She said you'd ken what to do. Will ye help her?'

'I'll get my things.'

She sprinted to the cot-house. Cramp bark was oft-times helpful for women's troubles, but this sounded serious. She searched among her herbs for raspberry leaf, yarrow, lady's mantle and comfrey, and packed them into her creel along with her pestle and mortar. Strapping the creel to her back, she mounted the spare pony.

'Dinna be long,' Grace cried. 'Remember what I said. And stay away from the gauger.'

Mister Gow again urged his garron into a gallop; her pony lurched after it. As they made away, she glanced back over her shoulder, but Grace was already a blur.

Willie Gow made no attempt at conversation during their ride to Drumin. It was left to her imagination to supply answers to her many questions. Chiefly, would Hugh be waiting there for her? Her stomach churned at the prospect. Glancing at the man's stiff back, she thought better of asking.

Isobel's father was a staunch kirkman, likely well versed in the many routes the Kirk's intolerance of meddling women could take. Healers and midwives were considered cunning witches. Letting her tend his daughter would be a breach of Kirk law, yet he'd come to fetch her. What he thought of her ways, she could well imagine, yet he'd judged her assistance necessary.

At Drumin, there was thankfully no sign of Hugh. Isobel lay on the floor, shivering and weeping. She'd wrapped herself in a linen sheet, bunching it between her legs. It was stained with blood. On seeing Rowena, she tried to rise, revealing a further puddle of blood on the floor beneath her.

She knelt at her side. 'Dinna get up, Isobel. What happened? When did this bleeding start?'

Isobel glanced at the doorway where her father stood.

Grim-faced, he muttered, 'I'll be seeing to the garrons. 'Tisna decent to be hearing aboot the workings o' a woman's body.' He shifted his gaze to Rowena. 'Ye'll help her?'

She nodded, and he left them to it.

'Oh, Rowena.' Isobel clutched at her with bloody hands. 'Look at me. I've lost it; I ken I have.' She slumped back on the floor, sobbing.

A quick examination of the sheet and its contents confirmed Rowena's suspicions. 'Ye were carrying a child, Isobel. Ye knew that?'

'Aye, God forgive me.'

'The infant had barely formed and has come away wi' a deal o' blood, but the worst's ower now. The pain will fade, the bleeding, too. I've herbs will help, but first I'll clean ye and help ye to bed. Ye must rest.'

She hung a pot of water over the fire to boil and rummaged in her creel for herbs.

Isobel sobbed brokenly. ''Tis punishment fer my wickedness. God's angry. I've sinned. Lord, in so many ways. Forgive me, Rowena, I've even sinned against you.'

She looked curiously at her. 'Dinna upset yerself. 'Tis a common thing to happen. Likely something was amiss wi' the infant. 'Tis nature's way. It seems cruel, but nature's wise. She kens what's best. Ye're young; ye'll have other bairns.' She faltered. ''Twas mebbe a blessing. After all, ye're nae wed.'

The sobbing increased, and Rowena wondered how much Isobel's father knew. He'd claimed this was the devil's work. Did he suspect anything other than women's troubles? She thought not. He'd be angry, would likely condemn Isobel, even disown her. The Kirk would judge her a whore. The whole community would. And what of her employer? Hugh had claimed his father was a Kirk minister. She could imagine his reaction. At best, he'd dismiss the girl.

She cleaned away all trace of blood and helped Isobel to bed, a straw-stuffed mattress in the corner. The bleeding was only a little now. Moss would catch it. Isobel was white-faced and trembling, quieter now, tears sliding over her cheeks.

'Try to rest.' She squeezed her hand. 'I'll make ye some healing tea.'

She poured hot water over dried raspberry leaves, leaving them to infuse while she bundled up the tell-tale sheet and dealt with the bloody floor. When the brew was ready, she handed Isobel a steaming cup. 'Sip slowly but be sure and drink it all. 'Twill lessen the bleeding, ensure everything comes away, for it must.'

The girl took the fragrant brew between trembling fingers. Her face was flushed and mottled, yet she shivered, her chest still spasming from the shock of sudden miscarriage. She needed tenderness. Smiling encouragingly, Rowena pushed a lock of damp hair from Isobel's brow, gently drying her tears.

Between sips, Isobel tried to smile back, but her face twisted, and she turned away. 'Ye're kind, Rowena, but I dinna deserve yer kindness. I'm that ashamed I can barely look at ye.'

She made a dismissive sound. 'Ye're nae the first to fall fer a young lad's wiles; I doubt ye'll be the last. Dinna judge yerself too harshly. Ye've suffered enough.'

'Ye must think me a jezebel,' Isobel choked. 'A trollop fer trying to trap him. I confess I hoped he'd wed me when he found I was carrying his bairn, but I love him, I swear.'

'Och, now; I ken ye've a good heart. I saw how ye cared fer Mister McBeath when he was hurt. Nae many would do that. Nae fer a gauger.' She swallowed, glancing at the bloody sheet. 'Only, I worry what he'll do when he learns o' this. He'll likely dismiss ye.' She squeezed Isobel's hand. 'While there's still time, I could take the sheet away. Bury it. He need never know.'

'Ye'd do that fer me?'

''Tis a small thing, but it might save yer place here.'

In answer, Isobel began to sob in earnest again. 'I dinna deserve yer kindness. I'm a wicked sinner.'

'Hush now, dinna weep, 'twill be alright.' Yet her chest tightened, the thought of Hugh catching her with evidence of Isobel's transgression churning her stomach. Time was wasting, though. She needed to see Duncan. Albeit, what she'd say to him, she'd little notion.

'Ye're hardly a sinner,' she muttered. 'All ye did was love.'

She gathered up the bloody sheet, stuffing it into the base of her creel, then covered it with her pestle and mortar and piled her herbs on top. Returning to Isobel's side, she squeezed her hand. 'I'll find a peaceful place to bury it, lay a posy o' rowan or holly, whatever I can find. Something to mark the resting place o' the wee soul that never was.'

'Oh, God. I've nae right to such kindness.'

'Hush, now.'

'I was that full o' the want o' him, I could think o' naught else. 'Tis no excuse, I know, nae fer what I've done.'

'What've ye done?'

Isobel gripped the steaming cup until her knuckles shone white. 'I could find no work other than to sell myself. I needed to pay our debts. He saved me from that wicked place and brought me here. He gave me decent work, paid Da's debts, and I was grateful. He's that handsome and bold. Ye've seen it, I think, felt the draw he has ower women. God help me, there's naught I've nae done fer him.' She swallowed, looking wretched.

'What, though? What've ye done?'

Isobel's face twisted, and she glanced away. 'I've let him do such things, Rowena, committed acts the Kirk calls sins, though I wanted to as much as him. We've coupled in every imaginable way. Whatever he desired, fer I wished to please him. I love him. I crave his touch.' She shivered. 'I've done far worse, too, treacherous things to win his favour. God help me, I've sinned against everyone I know. Even you, who's only been kind. Lord, Rowena, I think I've sinned against you more than anyone, fer I was jealous.' She hung her head. 'I've long known 'tis really you he wants.'

Rowena gasped. 'Then who is the father of yer child?' But there was only one man it could be. 'The gauger? He preyed upon ye?'

'No. I love him.'

'So, how have ye sinned against me?'

Sobbing, Isobel hid her face in her hands. 'I spied fer him upon the smugglers o' the glen. I coaxed and flattered and wheedled fer word o' convoys, befriending any who'd clype to me. Anything to please him, for whenever I returned wi' word o' a bothy or a convoy, he was that pleased, he'd carry me to his bed. Love me like I was precious.' Her face crumpled. 'Forgive me, but I betrayed yer kinsmen. I told him o' their trip to Banff. I tattled o' James' cattle, how he'd bought a herd to drive to Crieff, and I ken something ill befell those beasts.'

Rowena's legs gave way, and she sank to the floor.

'I ken ye can never forgive me, but I'm mair sorry than I can say.'

Isobel was crying again, but she barely heard. Her mind reeled. She'd thought Hugh decent, even found him attractive, though he'd made her uneasy, too. But she'd imagined him fair, had understood he wished to repay her for saving his life. He claimed he wanted to help her kinsmen, would risk his life to do so, and believing that and wishing to keep him safe, she'd told no one.

The blood fled her face. While he'd talked of making her his wife, of the advantages such a match would bring, he'd been ruthlessly exploiting Isobel, using her in all manner of degrading ways. What kind o' man did that? She drew a quivering breath. The kind who knew how to get what he wanted. The kind who gave nae a tinker's curse who he hurt in the getting o' it.

Her mind staggered. What else might a man like that do? Remove her kinsmen to make her vulnerable? Was James gone because o' him? She'd told him of James' plans; did he steal his cattle? Pay reivers to? 'Twas hard to believe, yet Duncan had said as much. Her stomach churned. He'd claimed he wanted to protect her in this villainous place. *Yet he was the villain here.*

Getting to her feet, she stumbled across the room. What had Duncan said? Hugh wasn't the man she thought. *Morna was dead because of him.* Morna, who'd spoken with nature's voice, who'd been earth-wise. And she'd lose Duncan now, too. Her Duncan. Only, he wasn't hers. He'd confessed his love to her in the shingle, hoping she'd open her fortressed heart, but she'd been too afraid. Since then, she'd squandered every opportunity to tell him she felt the same. Grace was right; she'd pushed him away.

Quivering, she picked up her creel, looping it over her shoulders, and crossed to the door. 'I must go.'

'God, Rowena.'

She drew a ragged breath. 'I wish ye to know I dinna blame ye, Isobel. The divil beguiled me, too. But ye must do no more spying.'

There seemed naught else to say. She pushed the door open and fled into the cold November air. The Pool of Ballagan lay two miles away. Let Duncan still be there.

CHAPTER TWENTY-EIGHT

HUGH MCBEATH swayed in the saddle, negotiating the rough track by the Avon on his way to Drumin. His visit to Inchfindy Hall had been doubly profitable. Not only had he relieved McGillivray of considerable coin, for he'd been gambling with cards since his school days and had long since mastered the art of sleight of hand, but the factor had brought him welcome news. James Innes didn't even wait to be evicted. He'd left the glen of his own accord.

He chuckled, a glow of satisfaction warming his innards, recalling the upstart's mocking bow as he'd allowed him and his kinsmen free passage to Banff. Relieving him of his cattle had been a fitting penalty for his insolence. But, of course, James was not the brother of concern. That dubious honour remained with the Young Jacobite. Or Young Pretender as he'd now dubbed him. The Pretender would receive his undoing soon enough. But James had been singularly impudent in his defence of his sister, while Rowena was all the more vulnerable without him.

Thinking of the witchling, the glow in his innards spread to his loins, and he groaned, shifting in the saddle, imagining how he'd have Isobel employed the moment he reached home. Grunting, he urged his horse into a canter.

From what he'd learned from McGillivray, Rowena's sister was to marry now, too. The plain one of the family—he'd forgotten her name— would also be leaving Tomachcraggen. He'd not spoken with Rowena in a while, generously allowing her time to consider her options, but he'd seen her often enough. He'd recently discovered her secret washing place:

the pool at the foot of the Lochy Falls where she washed her clothes. That dripping place had become his favourite haunt for observing her. But 'twas time he once more stumbled upon her alone in some isolated spot and pressed her for an answer. She'd accept him now, surely.

She was not in love with him. He'd never fooled himself that she was. Love was hardly required for the kind of union he had in mind. His offer of marriage was a pragmatic one. He simply wanted her. Without her brother and sister, and particularly without the crone he'd removed from Sithean Wood, she was more vulnerable and in need of his protection. She'd see that now.

Rounding a bend in the track, his horse whinnied and shied to the side. A young woman was hurrying toward him, carrying something on her back. He inhaled sharply. *The witchling.* And alone. 'Twas almost as if he'd conjured her with his thoughts. His stomach swooped with excitement.

'Rowena! Good God. What a welcome surprise.'

She didn't slacken her pace but eyed him warily, setting her gaze back on the track ahead. She appeared agitated. Her chest heaved quite magnificently, her colour heightened as if she were fever-ridden. Presumably, since she was a healer, not to mention a witch, she was not fevered, but there was something different about her.

When she made to pass by him without so much as a sideways glance, he exclaimed, 'Are you no' even going to acknowledge me? After everything I've done for you and your kind.'

She halted and lifted her chin, fixing him with a hard stare. 'My kind? Is that how ye see us? A kind. A lower breed set apart from decent southern folk.' Her jaw tightened, her eyes bright with tears.

What had he said? Naught that wasnae established fact, surely? But he'd never seen her like this. She trembled with a strange fire. 'Twas in the flare of her nostrils, the set of her jaw and darting flash of her eyes. By God, she was the devil's temptress.

Looking at her, ablaze with some strange passion, he couldn't help imagining how she'd respond when he lay with her. Perhaps with a hunger to rival his own. The heat in his loins intensified, reddening his face, the urge to violate her coming powerfully upon him. He fought to master it. She must give herself to him willingly. Forcing her would tarnish the act to the ordinary.

He took a quivering breath. 'You're no' yourself, Rowena. I hardly know what ye mean.'

She flashed him a scornful look. 'Likely not. 'Tis the pity of it.' She seemed to consider him briefly and find him wanting, then glanced away. 'I've someone I must see. As have you. Ye'll excuse me.' She hurried on.

'What? Who must I see?'

She turned back. 'Isobel. She needs you. You must go to her.'

'Isobel? Whatever for? She's my servant. She's no business *needing* me.'

'She's more than your servant. We both know that.' Her eyes flashed. 'You've taken her to your bed. Used her shamelessly. The lass loves you, but ye've preyed upon her, fashioning her into yer spy.'

His mouth fell open, and a gust of wind blew out. 'God's blood! What's the strumpet been saying? By God, I'll skin the bitch alive.' His eyelid spasmed. 'I can assure you—'

'I've no wish to hear it.' She turned her back and walked away.

He was out of the saddle in a trice and caught her by the arm, yanking her back. But her expression threw him awry. 'You're ill, Rowena. Fevered.' He released her arm, staring into the dark-eyed perfection of her face. Tears shimmered there. They left him at sea.

'I've no idea what lies Isobel's been spreading, but I swear, I've never touched the girl. Nor would I.' He shuddered, the thought now repugnant. ''Tis you I want.'

She dismissed him with a shrug. 'It hardly matters what ye want. Isobel told the truth, hard though it was to tell. And there was evidence aplenty.'

'Evidence?' His innards tightened.

'You've lain with her as it pleased ye. Put a bairn in her belly, though the infant's been lost. She'll recover, though she's grieving sorely. She needs you. If you've any feeling in that black heart, you'll go to her and make this right.'

He gaped. A bairn? Why hadn't the trollop told him? Damn her blabbering tongue. Damn her for a half-wit. He clenched his teeth, smothering his rage. He must limit the damage. Only how?

'Very well, I'll admit I took what was offered. The strumpet threw herself at me. I'm only a man, Rowena; a red-blooded one. The comforts of the flesh are no' so easy to resist when they're offered so brazenly, but it meant naught. 'Tis you I want.' He swallowed, softening his tone. 'And you've kept me waiting so long. 'Tis no excuse, I know, but I've needs like any man. I suppose I used her. There, I've said it. But the strumpet used me, too.'

Her eyes narrowed. 'She's nae a strumpet. You used her to spy for you. Even upon my kinfolk. Maybe, especially upon them.' Her expression hardened. 'Did you steal my brother's cattle? Tell me the truth.'

'Of course, no'. What d'you take me for? You're overwrought. Here, let me get you a drink.' He moved to the rear of his horse, where he kept a small keg of seized whisky, something useful for loosening tongues. A drop o' whisky never failed to lubricate the jaws. 'Twould calm her, and she'd see reason. Drawing a cup from his saddlebag, he slackened the tap on the keg, letting some whisky run into the cup.

'Where did ye get that?'

He looked blankly at her.

'The keg. One that size?'

Grimacing, he tried to remember, then paled as the circumstance of its procurement came back to him. 'I hardly recall. I was given it, likely. Smugglers often imagine they can buy my favour.'

'They can. Only I believe you call it "passage."'

Frowning, he offered her the cup.

She ignored it, reaching out to rotate the keg in its cradle, then fell back, staring at a small mark in the wood. Her hand flew to her mouth.

He squinted at it. It depicted a leaf, beautifully carved, something he'd not even noticed. He groaned inwardly. Evidently, it signified something.

''Tis true! Everything Duncan said. And Morna. The danger born of ignorance, intolerance.' She backed away. 'That was Morna's keg. Did ye take it from her? Were ye there when the soldiers took her?'

He squirmed at her questions, at her accusing tone, a tell-tale flush scorching his neck. She was afraid of him now. For the love of God, would she never accept him? Yet, her fear was perversely arousing. He remembered in vivid detail the many dreams of her he'd had, each essentially the same. His breathing quickened.

In his dreams, she teased him, darting through the trees. He chased her, snapping branches as he went, closing in, goaded by her girlish shrieks, overpowering her almost at once. She tumbled to the forest floor. In a frenzy of excitement, he held her down in the leaf mould, fumbling with her skirts, pressing himself into virgin flesh. Yet, in those dreams, although she'd teased him, she'd trusted him not to hurt her. He ruthlessly broke that trust, exchanging her giggles for whimpers and his brutish grunts.

'Does it matter?' he rasped. ''Tis a keg of whisky, for God's sake. I'm an exciseman. I come by illicit whisky near daily. 'Tis hardly unusual. But aye, since ye ask, I confiscated that keg from the witch I've seen you consort with. I was present when they arrested her. Indeed, she was seized at my insistence. The creature was doing her best to make you a witch.' He exhaled; he mustn't lose control. 'I did it for you. To save your soul, no' to mention your reputation.'

She stared at him, her face twisting. '*How could ye*? Morna was my friend. The wisest woman I've ever known. The most selfless. She glimpsed other realms, was at one with a world most folk barely notice. 'Tis because of her ye healed from your injuries. She was a *draoidh*. Maybe the last of her kind.'

He rolled his eyes. The creature had been vile, naught but a hag. Clenching his teeth, he strove for tolerance. 'I did your community a service. In time you'll see that. Once you're my wife, you'll thank me. I know ye will.'

'I'll never be your wife. You must wed Isobel.'

'Isobel! How ridiculous. You're overwrought. Allow me to comfort you.' He moved purposefully toward her.

'You killed her.'

'I did no such thing! I understand the creature died, but 'twas no' at my hand.'

'You took her from her home. The hills and forests were Morna's church. You imprisoned her far from them. She died shut away in a loathsome place that strangled her spirit.'

'You make too much of it. I merely had her removed from a place she had no business being. The evidence we found there was unmistakable. It pointed unquestionably to the craft she was engaged in.'

She moved with a swiftness he'd not credited her with and slapped him hard across the face.

The blow stung his pride as much as his cheek. 'Good God!' He jerked back, staring at her. 'By Christ, you're the devil's temptress.' He hurled the cup into the bushes. 'So, you like to play rough, do you?' His nostrils flared. 'By God, I do, too.'

She froze, the blood draining from her face. Pulling the woven basket from her back, she hurled it at him, then bolted into the trees.

He dodged the object and was after her.

The thrill of the chase sent blood pumping around his body. It pounded in his ears, and his heart hammered. 'Twas just like his dreams; his buttocks tightened. He knew how it would end. Despite his good intentions, there'd be no waiting for her to give herself to him now. He'd violate her the moment he caught her. He'd no' be able to help himself. Once defiled, she'd have little choice but wed him.

Only, her fleetness confounded him. While he crashed and thundered through the trees, he caught barely a glimpse of her. A flash of limb, a wisp of raven-winged hair, and she was gone. Soundless as the faeryfolk. The trees seemed to absorb her.

He was not so favoured. The forest plotted against him, the birds giving him away with their shrill alarm calls, the undergrowth with its rustling and snapping and confounded roots that snaked around his boots, tripping him at every turn. Even the light played tricks upon him. Cursing, he drew his sword, slashing at the bushes, blundering through the trees until he began to suspect his wrathful floundering had taken him in circles. Panting, he drew to a halt. Could she have doubled back to the track where he'd left his horse? It seemed implausible, but she could plainly slip sprite-like through the trees.

Stifling his breath, he listened for her, his heart racing, sweat trickling down his back. A curious wind arose, rustling the leaves, teasing them into the air. The trees creaked, the same unearthly sound he remembered from his night in the haunted wood, and the hair rose on the back of his neck. He shivered; someone had stepped upon his grave. He recalled the face of the crone.

* * *

Never was Rowena more thankful for a life spent in forest and glade. To the trees, she was perhaps one of their own. They were a network of living spirits. Her flight took her through moss and leaf litter, cushioning her feet, propelling her over tussock and log as agile as a hind with a huntsman on her scent. A breeze rose, the leaves whispering, swirling from the ground as the trees embraced her and the crashing of her pursuer faded away.

She slowed, catching her breath, her heart pounding. The aroma of rotting pine needles filled her nostrils, a beloved scent, and her mind began to clear. She must find the track but not travel it. The devil would ride her down. If he caught her, she knew what he'd do. His lust had been ugly, twisting his face, but the shadows at the edge of the track would be her friend. Concealed by bramble and broom, she could follow the route south. Find Duncan. She longed to make things right between them.

Her heart slowed to a steady drum, and as she stole through the woodland separating the track from the river, she sobbed. How could she have been so foolish? Duncan tried to warn her, but of course, she'd known better. Not once had she told him the truth: her heart was his. Afraid to admit her feelings, she'd been cruel.

Finding the track, she crept into its fringing bushes. Her flight had taken her farther than she realised, but she must keep out of sight. The devil would be searching for her. Hidden in the whins, her heartbeat slowed again, and in silent prayer, she thanked the forest for her escape. Yet no sooner had she given thanks than the drum of hooves sounded, and she flattened herself against the tussocky bank.

'Twas not the exciseman; he rode an iron-shod mount, a swift, slender-limbed animal. This was a solid workhorse, unshod. Holding her breath, she peered through the bushes, then whimpered with joy. *Duncan,* riding her da's sturdiest garron, his gaze fixed grimly ahead. Sobbing in relief, she burst from the bushes.

He jerked toward her, his face registering surprise, then reined in the garron and leapt from its back. She faltered, dread tightening her chest as his gaze strayed over her shoulder, and his face stiffened. When she turned, the exciseman was stalking up the track, his sword drawn and expression ominous.

'Keep behind me.' Duncan caught her by the wrist and pushed her behind his back. 'Grace was worried. I see she was right to be. I'll nae let him harm ye.'

At the courage in his voice, her stomach knotted. 'Forgive me; I've angered him. I couldna give him what he wanted. I struck him. Beware, I believe there's little he's nae capable of.'

Duncan exclaimed at her boldness, then hissed, 'I ken well the man's black heart. He'll nae harm ye, nae whilst I still breathe.'

The gauger was panting with rage, twigs snagged in his hair, his coat-tails torn, the imprint of her fingers still visible on his cheek. Drawing to a halt, he fixed Duncan with a cold stare.

'Well, well, if it's no' the Young Pretender. Move away from my bride.'

Duncan stood firm.

'Do it now.' The gauger raised his sword.

When Duncan stood his ground, McBeath dismissed him with a sneer. 'Come out from behind this upstart, Rowena. I'm prepared to overlook your behaviour.' He fingered his cheek. 'I admire your spirit. I relish the challenge of breaking it. I like a woman with metal in her veins. 'Twill make for a thrilling union. Come here. I mean you no harm.'

'I'm not your bride,' she retorted. 'I told you I'd never marry, I'm wed to the earth, but I didn't know my own heart. 'Twas already given, only I wasn't ready to admit it.' She groped for Duncan's hand. 'I know my heart now.'

'Glad to hear it,' he muttered. 'Come here, then, before I run this stripling through.'

'You heard her,' Duncan growled. He squeezed her fingers. 'She'll never be yer bride. Ye mun leave her be.'

'Be warned,' McBeath levelled his sword at Duncan's chest. 'My patience wears thin. Mount that flea-bitten cuddy and be gone.'

'I'll nae leave my sister.'

'I suppose no' since you want her yourself.'

'I love her, aye, but I'd nae leave so much as a dog in your care. I've seen how ye treat such creatures. Ye've had yer answer. Be on yer way, and there'll be no need fer trouble.'

An eyelid spasmed. 'It seems there'll be every need. Step aside, or by God, I'll run ye through.'

Heart thumping, Rowena moved into the open, then slipped in front of Duncan. Hugh's sword now hovered a scant inch from her throat. Duncan sucked his breath in, trying to drag her back, but she squeezed his hand. Bringing it to her lips, she kissed his cold fingers.

'Good God!' McBeath lowered his sword. 'I could've cut your throat.' He stared at her. 'He's your brother. Let go of his hand. 'Tis incestuous. Once you're my wife—'

'Aye.' She laced her fingers through Duncan's. 'He's my brother. I've always considered him so, but there's no blood between us. Naught incestuous. Duncan's my love.' The admission brought a rush of tenderness; she shivered, letting it ripple through her. She'd guarded her heart for so long, unmasking it was daunting, like standing naked before the world. Yet, naught had ever given her more joy. She locked eyes with the gauger. 'He's my soul's companion. The only man I could ever wed.'

McBeath exhaled, his lips curling back to reveal sharp teeth. How had she ever imagined him handsome?

'You cannae mean that. Good God, I'll no' have it!'

Duncan gasped in astonishment, drawing her back to search her face, perhaps fearing he'd misunderstood. She smiled at his wonderstruck expression, pressing his fingers to her cheek. His answering caress came butterfly-soft.

'Filthy muck-the-byre. Take yer hands off her!' The gauger pulled Duncan's hand away, viciously yanking him aside. Roaring with rage, he swung his sword high.

She reacted instinctively, grasping the blade near its hilt. Blood welled and trickled to the guard; Hugh stared at it in horror. For a moment they remained frozen, face to face, the blade held motionless between them, Hugh gawping, aghast, at her.

Duncan shrieked, dropping to his knees at the gauger's feet. 'Dinna hurt her! Please. 'Tis me ye wish to hurt.' He lowered his head for the blow.

The pressure on the blade eased, and she snatched her hand away. The pain was sharp, but she gritted her teeth, throwing herself at Duncan, shielding him with her body, her arms wound tightly around him. A wild joy tore through her when he gripped her fiercely, burrowing his face into her neck.

'*Mo gràdh,*' he groaned. My love.

When she dared look up, Hugh was gaping at them. Duncan cradled her bleeding hand and helped her to her feet, and she locked eyes with the exciseman. His thunderstruck expression stirred a stab of satisfaction.

''Tis likely I've left it too late to make things right.' She swallowed, the pity of that wringing her heart. 'I've been cruel. I let Duncan believe I cared little for him when in truth, I've always loved him. In my foolishness, I hurt him, and he means to leave. Yet, no matter where he goes, my heart will always be his.'

'If I thought ye'd let me love ye,' Duncan choked.

'Always. I canna bear to lose ye.'

The breath quivered from him.

She turned back to the gauger. 'So, I'll never be your wife, Hugh, no matter your scheming. You must wed Isobel. Right the wrongs you've done.'

He made a strangled sound, letting his sword drop. Duncan kicked it away.

'Ye see that, Hugh?'

When he gave no answer, she took the garron's reins and turned the pony toward home. Duncan slipped an arm around her, gingerly holding up her dripping hand, and they walked away.

'Rowena! Come back here. Ye're no' thinking straight. Let me protect you from that villain.'

She walked on until his protests faded, and all she could hear was the distant murmur of the river. At a bend in the track, Duncan pulled a handful of moss from the bank and pressed it into her palm. Helping her onto the garron, he climbed up behind. As they made away, she looked back over her shoulder. Hugh was still standing in the centre of the track, staring after them.

* * *

They stopped by the pool in the river where Duncan had left his catch. At the water's edge, he held her hand under the cold water, letting the current whisk all trace of blood away. The wound was superficial, a stitch or two would bring it together, although she'd need to show him how. For now, moss would protect it. He pressed more in place.

With trembling fingers, she brushed aside his hair and kissed the back of his neck. 'Can ye ever forgive me?'

He shivered, looking up at her. 'There's naught to forgive.' His face tightened. 'If ye meant what ye said, ye've filled me fuller than any man has a right to be. My heart's that swollen, there's scarce room fer it in my chest. Only, did ye mean it? I need to know.'

She smiled. 'I've loved ye since we were bairns, though, I suppose that was a childish love. But I didna know I loved ye as a man, that I desired ye, till I saw ye all bruised and bleeding efter the soldiers had finished wi' ye.'

'Ye desired me then?' He quirked a brow. 'Looking like butchered meat?'

She blushed. 'I'm thinking the yearning wasna so much ower how ye looked, but fer what ye are, in here.' She pressed her good hand to his chest. 'Yer courage and decency, and what ye suffered fer it.' She blushed. 'Though even afore, my heart would leap whenever I saw yer handsome face.'

'My courage?' He exhaled bitterly.

'Ye're the bravest man I know.'

'Ye dinna understand.' He got to his feet, his face tightening. 'I let my kinfolk die.' He lifted her injured hand. 'I didna even protect you.'

'That wasna yer doing.'

'I'm a coward.'

'Hush. I love you. Can that nae be enough?'

He blinked, his eyes shining. ''Tis more than I deserve.'

'Can ye forgive my foolishness?'

'Can you forgive mine?'

She nodded, tears coming.

He exhaled, a cautious smile lighting his face. 'So, if I were to go down upon one knee again.' He lowered a knee to the shingle. 'Even being I'm landless, penniless, have naught to give ye but myself, are ye saying ye'd nae turn me down again?'

The corners of her mouth twitched. 'I'm thinking ye must do it, so I can better decide.'

His eyes widened, searching for signs she jested. Swallowing, he tried to compose himself, wiping his hands down the side of his breeks. He took a deep breath. His face now suitably grave, he retook her hand and lowered one knee.

'I will.'

'I've nae asked ye yet.'

'I thought I'd save ye the trouble since ye've asked me afore.' She shook her head. 'I feel that alive ... bursting wi' love, though I doubt Father Ranald will allow me in his chapel.'

'Oh, he will. Supposing I've to sell my soul to convince him.'

She laughed. 'They call him a heather-priest. D'ye suppose he might wed us in the heather?'

He nodded, eyes shining, hardly able to countenance his change in fortune. His gaze moved to her mouth then, and as he drew her close, she knew he would kiss her. Her heart quickened.

It began as a tentative exploration, a discovery of sensations, his hands cradling her head. Shivering, she breathed his earthy scent, overwhelmed with new feelings. Pushing her fingers into his hair, she drew him close as she returned his kiss.

He groaned, and she sensed his hunger for her. A fire seemed to ignite between them. A melting sensation spread through her innards, dissolving flesh and bone until she floated bodiless, all her awareness focussed upon this one man and her love for him. A little yearning sound slipped from her lips.

He broke away, kissing her neck, her eyes and the tip of her nose, then rolled onto his back in her lap, gazing up at her.

'Lord,' he laughed, breathless. 'I've never wanted anything as badly as I want ye right now. We'll need the banns read mighty quick. I fear ye're in danger.'

'Danger?'

He smiled wickedly. 'I might take advantage o' ye.'

Laughing, she wriggled down beside him.

'God would think that bad, I suppose.' But she didn't hear his reply, only his scandalised gasp as she pressed her mouth over his.

After a moment, he stirred and took her injured hand, gently lifting away the protective covering. 'This needs attention.'

'Stitching, aye. I can show ye how.'

He swallowed. 'I might hurt ye.'

'Ye will, but it must be done.'

Nodding, he rose and helped her up, lifting her onto the garron, then leapt up behind. With a shiver, she settled back against his reassuring warmth, tingling as he held her tightly against him. A fluttering in her belly reminded her they had the rest of their lives to explore these strange new feelings. As they rode away, anticipation tingled through her body.

At the track leading to Achdellmore, Duncan nudged her and pointed. A figure was walking toward them down the track, one they both recognised. He tightened his hold on her, kissing the back of her neck as they waited for the man to reach them.

As he neared, Father Ranald blinked in confusion, taking in their shyly smiling faces, Duncan's arms around her and their bodies nestled closer than was entirely decent. He halted, gaping at them.

'Duncan ... this is ...' he exhaled, shaking his head.

'A surprise?'

'Aye, though a welcome one.'

'We've something we wish to ask ye, Father,' she said shyly. She turned to Duncan.

'If it's what I think it is,' the Father gave a breathless laugh, 'then the answer's yes. Oh, dear Lord, yes.'

Duncan slid to the ground, twisting his bonnet. 'I ken yer chapel's the right place fer a wedding, Father. 'Tis only proper, but we wond—'

'Anywhere, lad. I'll wed ye wherever Rowena feels most comfortable.'

'Mebbe in the heather?' she ventured, sensing Sìthean Wood or inside the stone circle atop Seely's Hillock would be a step too far.

'If it's what ye wish.' He looked at her with shining eyes. 'Though ye're welcome in chapel any time ye please.' He glanced skyward, clasping his hands together, and nodded jubilantly. 'Oh, my dear, ye hardly know how this gladdens my heart.'

She smiled back, remembering him saying something similar before, long ago, when she was still a bairn. That had also been about Duncan. 'Perhaps,' she ventured, clearing her throat, 'perhaps, then, our faiths are nae as different as ye imagine?' Morna had once dared to suggest such a thing.

He grunted in amusement, clearly remembering.

'I've long wondered,' she persisted, 'if *your* God, the one of churches and altars, is the same creator whose hand I see in every leaf and flower. The same spirit that fills me to bursting whenever I walk through a forest.' She faltered. 'Though 'tis perhaps blasphemy to even think such a thing.'

He looked strangely at her, and she feared she'd offended him, that her words amounted to a grievous sin, but eventually, he nodded. 'Your healing's a gift from God, Rowena.' He sighed. 'I believe you're filled with Holy Spirit. Call it Mother Earth or nature-magic, but I sense 'tis the same power I've served all my days. We'll nae argue ower the name. I'll wed ye, my dear. Of course, I will. Ye hardly need to ask.'

Duncan's face twisted, and he pressed his fist to his mouth, hardly able to contain his joy. 'Thank ye, Father,' he croaked. He looked up at her, and she laughed at his euphoric expression.

'Oh, my love,' she whispered.

Such a swell of emotion rose in her chest, she feared her heart must burst. He was healed. Finally, she had cured Duncan's brokenness.

AN AFTERWORD

Thank you for reading *Under A Gravid Sky*. If you enjoyed it, I would be particularly grateful if you'd take a moment to leave a review on the book's Amazon page. Reviews are important to me and only need to be a few words, but let other readers know my work is worth reading.

The Blood And The Barley was my first novel, introducing Strathavon and its community of smuggler-farmers rooted in their Gaelic culture's traditions and superstitions. Of course, having done that, I should then have written a sequel, as most writers would have done. But I've never been good at doing what's expected, and I wanted to write about what came before. In the aftermath of Culloden, Strathavon was occupied by Hanoverian troops. I wanted to explore how the tenant farmers and smugglers of the glen might have endured this. Many were Catholic and so were naturally loyal to the Stuart cause. A number from the area joined the Jacobite army.

Then there was Hugh McBeath. I wanted to get under his skin and understand what made him the man he is. To a degree, he is a product of his background and upbringing, as are we all. I felt unable to move on with Morven and Jamie's tale until I had done that. For readers of *The Blood And The Barley*, I hope you can forgive my deviation into the deeper past. As promised, I will continue Morven and Jamie's story in my next book.

If you would like to know when the next book is available and receive a sneak preview of the first few chapters before its release, please sign up at https://www.subscribepage.com/underagravidsky.
You can learn more about Strathavon and see some images of the area at www.angelamacraeshanks.com.
Or on Facebook, at www.facebook.com/angelamacraeshanksauthor.
You can email me at angela@angelamacraeshanks.com.

THE SCOTS TONGUE

The Scots language is wonderfully expressive, and I have used it freely to add both authenticity and a sense of time and place. I hope the meaning can generally be inferred, but for the more challenging words, a glossary is provided below.

anker – a liquid measure of spirit and the barrel containing it; approx. 10 gallons.

arisaid – a long draped garment worn as part of female Highland dress.

bairn – a child, male or female.

bide – to dwell or reside.

blatherskite – a silly, foolish person; a babbler.

breeks – breeches, trousers.

but-and-ben – a two-roomed house of one storey.

bothy – a primitive dwelling or shelter.

clabber – soured milk with a thick, yoghurt-like consistency.

ceilidh – a social gathering, usually with music and dancing.

clype – to tell tales or inform against someone.

coorie – to nestle or snuggle.

crottle – dye-producing lichens.

corbie – a crow or raven.

cuddy – a donkey or obstinate horse.

dram – a small drink of liquor, especially whisky.

far – where.

flit – to remove or shift a person or thing from one place to another.

garron – a sturdy Highland horse or pony.

gauger – an exciseman.

golach – an insect, especially an earwig.

gowk – a fool, simpleton or dolt.

greet – weep, cry.

guddle – to grope for fish with the hands in water.

kertch – a triangular piece of white linen worn on the head by married women.

kirk – a church, generally a Presbyterian or non-Episcopalian place of worship.

Kirk – when capitalised, refers specifically to the Presbyterian Church of Scotland.

lowp – to bound or walk with long, springing steps as if through heather.

mind – to remember or call to mind.

muckle – large.

neep – a turnip.

oxter – the arm-pit.

philabeg – the little kilt.

pibroch – classical Scottish bagpipe music consisting of a theme and series of variations.

puckle – a few.

quaich – a shallow two-handled drinking bowl or cup, usually wooden.

reiver – an armed robber or plunderer.

runrig – a portion or strip of arable land.

Samhain – a Gaelic festival marking the end of harvest time and the beginning of winter.

sark – a shift or shirt worn near the skin.

shieling – upland pasture where cattle were driven for the summer and where their attendants lived in temporary bothies.

scudgie – a drudge or person who does menial work.

skelp – to strike, especially with the palm, specifically to smack the bottom.

skirl – a shrill, piercing sound, particularly produced with the bagpipes.

smirr – a fine drizzle.

smoor – to dampen down a fire at night but not extinguish it.

unchancy – ill-omened or threatening.

thegither – together.

whigmaleerie – a contraption.

whin – common gorse.

wynd – a narrow winding lane leading off a main thoroughfare in a town.

Made in the USA
Las Vegas, NV
19 September 2021